A Death for a Dancer

...

A Death for a Docter

Robert Forsythe 3 and 4

DUET

A Death for a Dancer

...

A Death for a Docter

E. X. Giroux

FELONY & MAYHEM PRESS • NEW YORK

All the characters and events portrayed in this work are fictitious.

A DEATH FOR ADONIS/A DEATH FOR A DARLING

Robert Forsythe 3 and 4

PRINTING HISTORY
A Death for Dancer
First edition (St. Martin's): 1985
A Death for a Doctor
First edition (St. Martin's): 1986

Felony & Mayhem Duet edition: 2024

ISBN: 978-1-63194-308-9 (paperback)
978-1-63194-309-6 (ebook)

Manufactured in the United States of America

Cataloging-in-Publication information for this book
is available from the Library of Congress.

The icon above says you're holding a book in the Felony & Mayhem "British" category. These books are set in or around the UK, and feature the highly literate, often witty prose that fans of British mystery demand. If you enjoy this book, you may well like other "British" titles from Felony & Mayhem Press.

For information about British titles or to learn more about Felony & Mayhem Press, please visit us online at:

www.FelonyAndMayhem.com

Other "British" titles from

FELONY&MAYHEM

Who is the killer?

SIR AMYAS DANCER — The head of the family, whose bizarre plans to build a Roman amphitheater led him straight to Katherine's body?

CARLETON DANCER — Amyas's son and a former rock star, who now collects buttons such as those on the dead girl's blouse?

MRS. LARKIN — The loyal family retainer who loathes being called a servant—and who saw right through Miss Katherine St. Croix?

DAVID PROCTOR — The young poet whose regard for the Dancers may not be as pure as it seems?

CASSANDRA DANCER — Amyas's daughter, determined to marry David Proctor—whatever the cost?

This book is for Maureen and Dimitrios Nikas

A Death for a Dancer

Chapter One

Willis Seton possessed a number of favorable attributes—a professional competence, a portly, reassuring appearance, and a resonant voice. He had one drawback—a loquacity that could be alarming, at times irritating, and once in a while, amusing.

Generally Robert Forsythe found the solicitor amusing and for the first twenty minutes of the monologue had exercised patience. For a time Seton conversed about his new office, pointing to each improvement and enlarging upon it. Forsythe had murmured compliments about the amount of space, the dazzling expanse of glass, the thick wall-to-wall carpeting, and the well-fitted bar cunningly concealed in paneling. Forsythe was relieved that his secretary, Miss Sanderson, couldn't see Seton's office. She was becoming increasingly insistent about moving from their own cramped chambers in a centuries-old structure into something like this in one of the new buildings springing up all over London.

When Seton abandoned this subject, Forsythe leaned forward hopefully only to find himself listening to details on the Seton family, particularly the birth of a new grandson. Weather followed the Seton saga, unseasonal as always for the month of July.

2 *E. X. Giroux*

He started to squirm and Seton promptly returned to his first topic. "Can't see, my boy, why you don't chuck those chambers of yours. Know they were your father's, and his, but time to move on. Shouldn't think they're even healthy."

"I like them."

Seton gave a chuckle that appeared to work its way up from his sizable paunch. "What do you like—mildewed walls, smoky hearths, steps leading up and down for no apparent reason?"

"I like the feel of it."

Hard to explain, Forsythe mused, what that feeling was exactly. The old building did have noticeable defects but the atmosphere seemed eminently suitable for the practice of law. The narrow corridors and poky rooms had an odor of ancient parchment, leather, and smoke from long-perished pipes. The smell in Seton's building was positively antiseptic. The solicitor was settling back comfortably and before he could release another barrage of words, Forsythe said, "You *did* ask to see me, Willis."

Seton chuckled again. "In other words, get to the point. You young chaps aren't long on patience. I thought Miss Sanderson might have filled you in. You're a lucky man, Robert. Wish I could lay my hands on a legal secretary like her. Remember when she first came to work for your father—"

Hastily, Forsythe broke in. "Sandy didn't seem to have a clear idea about the problem."

"Can't see why not. This Dancer case, as the newspapers are calling it, has been on front pages for a fortnight."

"I'm just back from abroad and Sandy has been on vacation. All I know is that the murdered body of a girl was found on the Dancer property. And, of course, that Sir Amyas wishes to retain my services."

"Wrong on one point. The St. Croix female was a woman, not a girl. The Dancers, and the police at first, thought she was in her early twenties. Turned out she would never have seen thirty again. St. Croix wasn't her name either. She passed herself off as Katherine St. Croix but she was born Katerina

Padrinski." Pushing himself up, he opened a filing cabinet and started flipping through folders. Fine looking man, Forsythe thought, overweight but not gross, a mane of snowy hair, a wide florid face. "Ah, here we are." The solicitor plumped a fat manila envelope down in front of Forsythe.

Forsythe hefted it. "Seems a lot of material."

"Copies of police reports and a bunch of background material. Thought it might help you understand the Dancers."

"I suppose Sir Amyas has been charged." For a man of many words Seton's answer was incredibly brief, simply a negative jerk of the leonine head. "One of his family?"

"No charge been laid as yet. Young fellow was called in to help with the investigation—minor villain and a known associate of the St. Croix or Padrinski woman, who was something of a villain herself. Understand he's cleared himself with an alibi for the time of the woman's murder."

Forsythe' s hand fell away from the heavy envelope and he raised his brows. "Then what in the devil did you call me in for? Until a charge is laid, a barrister is about as much use as a pen without ink."

The solicitor's eyes avoided the younger man's. "Sir Amyas is most determined. You would have to know the man to understand that he doesn't request, he orders; have to know the relationship between the Dancers and Setons to understand why I jump when he yells. My family acted as stewards for the Dancer family as far back as their history goes. It was Grandfather who finally tried to break loose from them. Got a legacy from a cousin who emigrated to Australia and did rather well and had my father educated as a solicitor."

Forsythe smiled. "It would appear your grandfather wasn't successful."

"Shamed to admit it, Robert, but no. Father inherited Sir Crawford Dancer and when my turn came I got his son Amyas. Only difference is that instead of counting livestock and collecting rents for the Dancers, the Setons now handle their legal affairs, and fish them out of the most astounding messes."

He fingered his thick hair. "Still pulling the old forelock and saying 'yes sir,' 'no sir.'"

"That doesn't explain why Sir Amyas has his heart set on a barrister when—"

"Doesn't want a barrister. Wants a private investigator." Forsythe's mouth snapped open and the solicitor raised a hand and continued. "Don't get your back up. It's your own fault, young Robert. Getting your picture in the papers and accounts of the cases you've solved. Know what the news lads are calling you? 'Mission Impossible' Forsythe!"

Forsythe's normally pale face was now as ruddy as Seton's. "Bunch of asses! Certainly I've been pulled into a few cases, but not of my own volition. Either I've been on the scene or someone I know has been involved. I practice law and *that* is quite enough to keep me occupied. Surely you've put Sir Amyas onto a good private inquiry agent?"

"Tried to. Chap who was formerly an inspector with the C.I.D. has undertaken confidential investigations and he's reliable. Sir Amyas wouldn't hear of it. Wants you. Says he always gets the best. Compliment, young Robert."

"Not to me it isn't." Forsythe stood up. "Give him my regrets and tell him I'm not available. Tell him if he doesn't want an investigator, to put his trust in the police. They'll get to the bottom of it."

"Doubt with this one they will. It's distinctly weird. Much like the people involved. Didn't want to do this but it looks like I must. In the past I've done some good turns for you, haven't I?"

Sinking slowly back into the armchair, Forsythe stared at his friend. Willis Seton had indeed done some good turns. At one point in his career when he desperately needed friends, Seton had come to his assistance and stood staunchly by. "That goes without saying. Are you about to present the fee?"

The solicitor had the grace to look abashed. "Said I didn't want to do this. Not asking you to take the case. Only asking you to see Sir Amyas, listen to him, and tell *him* you won't do it."

"More or less get you off the hook, eh?"

"Exactly. Case of the messenger who brings the bad news. You won't have to see him again. Me…I'm stuck with the Dancers for life."

"Very well. Sandy and I will drive up, hear him out, and politely suggest your retired inspector." Forsythe was on his feet again. He picked up the envelope. "I'm curious, Willis. Are you afraid of this man?"

"Afraid?" The leonine head shook. "Feel a sense of responsibility. Suppose it's habitual." His eyes seemed to see a procession of shadowy Seton ancestors serving shadowy Dancers. "And this family…done the most outrageous, ridiculous, godawful things. To put it mildly, they're terribly eccentric people. Yet…" His eyes returned to his colleague. "When you know more about them you'll think I'm gaga myself but, Robert, the Dancers are innocents."

Chapter Two

"*Innocents*," Miss Sanderson said scathingly. She was curled up on the Rover's leather seat beside Forsythe, a black briefcase resting in her lap. "Willis Seton must be fast approaching senility if he hasn't already reached it."

Forsythe took his eyes off the road long enough to cast an approving look at his secretary. She looked quite fetching in a dark green linen suit and a lighter green silk shirt. To protect her freshly styled gray hair she'd bound green chiffon around it. "Willis did mention the Dancers are eccentric."

She snorted and thumped the briefcase. "More like bizarre."

"Past or present?"

"Didn't you read any of the material he gave us?"

"Only the police reports of the murder. Hardly seemed worth it to wade through that lot when all we're going to do is say 'no,' kindly but firmly."

"That at least is a blessing. Anyone who gets mixed up with this bunch seems to end up just as weird." She zipped open the case and extracted a thick sheaf of typewritten pages. "Care to have a history lesson?"

"Sounds dull but it will help while away the time."

Her face was as austere as usual but her eyes glinted with wicked amusement. "The Dancer house is called the Priory. Seems an ancestor, early on, booted out an order of monks and took the building for his own. Named the lake behind it Priory Lake. Original chap. A century or so later his descendant decided the Priory was tumbling around his ears and built the present house. The name was retained."

Forsythe yawned. "Maybe I'll skip the history."

"I'll give you a few highlights. Sir Harold Dancer followed his king on the Crusades. When Harold got home he found his lady dallying with a man-at-arms. He drugged the lady, beat the unfortunate lover to death, quartered him, and slipped him into bed with the sleeping girl." Miss Sanderson shook her head. "What an awakening that must have been."

"What was the lady's reaction?"

"Doesn't say here but she lived to a ripe old age and gave Sir Harold a number of children. How's that for innocents?"

"The punishment for adultery in those days was swift and barbaric." He pointed to a road sign. "Ah, the county of Cheshire. Nice, isn't it?"

"Idyllic. Either Constable or Turner or a little of each." She looked with delight at the verdant countryside, the gentle slopes and thick hedges guarding the roadside. "One of these days I'm going to invest in a cottage in a place like this. I've always longed to live in the country."

"I thought you were raised in a village."

Miss Sanderson shrugged a green linen shoulder. "Born not raised. Father was a country parson with more children than income. I was farmed out to a childless aunt and uncle and raised in London. Yes, I long for a cottage, a garden, flowers. I could get away from the maddening crowds—"

"I believe that's madding, Sandy."

"—and grow vegetables and—"

" 'And a small cabin build there, of clay and wattles made: Nine bean rows—' "

"Robby!"

"Sorry. It's only that my imagination is strained by picturing you in a rural setting."

"Perhaps right now. Later on, after I retire…"

Forsythe vainly tried to picture life without Miss Sanderson. He couldn't remember his mother but from his earliest days there had always been Sandy. To him she'd been all, a mother, an older sister, at times a conscience. "There's always the old manse in Sussex."

"That's yours. I want some little corner of my own." Sharp blue eyes veered toward him. "And I know what you're up to. Trying to avoid your history lesson. Won't work. Where was I?"

"Sir Harold the Crusader."

Paper rattled. "We move on in time. Shortly after the American Civil War, Sir Charles Dancer, who greatly admired the Confederacy, had the entire front of his Elizabethan home covered with a façade. Reproduced an antebellum home from the deep South complete with pillars and balconies and a gallant effort at wisteria. He was more successful with that than with his retainers who balked at calling him the ole massah. While Sir Charles was on his deathbed his son, who had sympathized with the North, had carpenters in to rip down the façade. Sir Charles died to the sound of saws and hammers."

Forsythe drew the car up beside a signpost and eyed it doubtfully. Impatiently, Miss Sanderson pointed left and Forsythe steered the car onto a narrower road. The Rover rattled over a humpbacked bridge and Miss Sanderson selected another sheet of paper. "You're going to love this one. Turn of this century and Sir Godfrey Dancer. Never went to the mysterious East in his life but acquired a passion for the Orient. Built on the shore of Priory Lake a miniature Chinese temple and promptly renamed the lake the China Sea. Called the temple Mandalay. To give it atmosphere he came up with a gentleman who claimed to be a spiritual descendant of Confucius and was called Confucius Again. Robby, will you stop that?"

Forsythe, who had been softly humming, now broke into riotous song. "'On the road to Mandalay, where the flying fishes play, and—'"

"Will you shut up! Robby, this temple played a part in the murder of Katherine St. Croix."

"I told you I read the police reports."

"Confucius Again," his secretary continued doggedly, "moved in with Sir Godfrey and his family, donned exotic robes, and converted his patron to an odd blend of Eastern mysticism and religion. The locals were rather used to the Dancer family and raised no objections until the baronet, spurred by Confucius Again, decided to convert *them*. There were screams of idolatry and paganism and the populace led by—"

"Beginning to sound like the closing scene from the old Frankenstein movie. Remember the torchlight parade to the evil castle?"

"Wasn't far short of it. The locals were led by clergy and Sir Godfrey's son Cuthbert who happened to be a devout Lutheran. Sir Godfrey prepared to repel them and armed all his manservants. Seems his second passion was collecting antique weapons and seeing they were all he had in hand he surrounded his temple with guards brandishing cutlasses, blunderbusses, and battle-axes."

"Good Lord!"

"For his own weapon Sir Godfrey chose a crossbow. The avenging mob arrived to find Confucius Again waiting on the steps of the temple hoping to overcome their bloody-mindedness with words of peace. He was immediately recognized by a cabinet maker from Chester. Seems the sage was none other than Jimmy Chang, formerly an employee of a Chinese laundry. Incensed by this duplicity Sir Godfrey turned his ire and his crossbow not on the mob but on Confucius Again."

"I rather hope Sir Godfrey's aim was true, Sandy."

"He missed his target but the whole affair ended tragically. Sir Godfrey had a stroke of apoplexy and fell dead on the spot.

His son, now Sir Cuthbert, overcome by remorse reacted as a true Dancer."

"Let me guess. Cuthbert renounced his own religion and converted to Buddhism or whatever."

"As a detective you have the makings of a barrister. No, but he insisted his father should be buried as befitting an Oriental gentleman. He had the body laid out in a Chinese robe and had workmen in to turn Mandalay into a crypt. Two cement box affairs were installed to receive the coffins of Sir Godfrey and Lady Dancer, who at that time was very much alive. Cuthbert also bought, at great expense, four jade statuettes, one white, one green, and two pink. After his father's body was installed in the crypt, Cuthbert had some runes put over the door. They were carved in Chinese characters but were more Egyptian in content. A curse on any who defiled the tomb. Cuthbert's mother seems to have been strong-minded and refused to be interred with her husband; she was buried instead in the Harper graveyard with the other Dancers. A huge padlock with only one key was put on Mandalay's door and until recently the crypt was never entered."

"Until Katherine St. Croix was found there."

"Exactly." Neatly aligning the edges of the papers, Miss Sanderson tucked them back into the case. "I've only touched on a few anecdotes from the history of the family. It makes lively reading."

The Rover had reached another crossroads. Without glancing at the signpost, the barrister asked, "Which way, Sandy?"

"Left."

"You're amazing. Did you memorize that map?"

"Merely glanced at it," she said airily. "But when we get to Harper you're on your own. There's such a maze of lanes around it, I can't figure where the Priory is. Robby, I'm starving. Do you suppose the Dancers will feed us?"

"We can hardly expect bed and breakfast from people we're going to turn down cold."

"To say nothing of firmly and gently. Want more history to while away the time?"

"Do you have any more recent?"

"Loads. What do you know about Sir Amyas and his household?"

"Very little. At the Priory are his two children and his father-in-law, and two sisters live on the estate too."

"Let me fill you in. Sir Amyas married twice. His first wife—"

He glanced at the briefcase. "Aren't you going to rustle more paper?"

"Don't need to. To get back to Sir Amyas. I suppose I should start at the beginning."

"Do try to condense it, Sandy."

"The baronet inherited a large chunk of money but it appears Sir Amyas allows money to slip through his fingers. Always has some project going that's not only time-consuming but money-consuming. But at the time of his first marriage he still had enough assets to marry for love. His first wife was a Lady Amanda Gore-Carleton, strong on blue blood and short on cash. She promptly gave her husband a son and a couple of years later choked to death on a wishbone—"

"Surely you mean fishbone."

"Uh-uh. She was delicately nibbling meat from a wishbone, sucked it back into her windpipe, and expired. By this time Sir Amyas was feeling the financial pinch. A year later he took to his bosom a seventeen-year-old girl, Viola Gillimede, daughter of a wealthy industrialist. Horace Gillimede gave his new son-in-law a handsome marriage settlement that not only solved his current money crisis but promised more of the same in the future."

"It sounds as though this Dancer lands on his feet."

"Sir Amyas does but in the strangest ways. His plans for living off his father-in-law came to disaster shortly before Viola presented him with a daughter. Horace Gillimede was a hard-headed businessman, far more interested in his firm than his family. One day he came home unexpectedly and caught his wife having fun and games with a young Welsh boxer. Horace drove the erring pair from his door and they made their getaway in the boxer's car. Outside of Liverpool their car was hit broadside by a lorry and Mrs. Gillimede and her lover died.

"Horace was not only filled with remorse but something else that wasn't recognized at the time. He had a complete mental collapse. Seems he blamed himself for his wife's fall from grace, thought he'd neglected her for his business. To atone he liquefied all his holdings and gave his money away—"

"Did you say *gave*, Sandy?"

"Every last pound. To religious organizations and charities. When he was suitably broke he returned to Sir Amyas and Lady Dancer in sackcloth and ashes to pay penitence for his sins for the rest of his life. So, Sir Amyas was not only stuck with a mad father-in-law but with a wife he apparently couldn't stand."

"Did Viola Dancer also conveniently choke on a wishbone?"

"She drowned in Priory Lake or, as it's now called, the China Sea. But that was only a year ago, so Sir Amyas endured her company for about a quarter of a century."

Despite himself, Forsythe was becoming interested in the Dancers. "I understand Sir Amyas is a fabulously wealthy man."

"He has the oddest luck. Before his second marriage Sir Amyas decided to run an experiment. He bought a ranch in western Canada and proceeded to try to cross Highland cattle with bison. Apparently he figured not only deer and antelope still roam the range but also buffalo. It didn't work and he rented the ranch to a man who was content to raise Herefords. Sir Amyas returned to England and promptly forgot about it. Shortly after Horace Gillimede gave away his money the tenant rancher decided to sink a new well. What came spouting up was black."

Forsythe chuckled. "He'd struck oil."

"He had indeed and the proceeds flowed into the Dancer coffers. This enabled Sir Amyas to continue happily with his harebrained schemes. Some of them have been dandies. Robby, turn right at this next crossroads."

The barrister obeyed, swinging the wheel and piloting the Rover to the right. "From that grin you're wearing, Sandy, I take it you have a favorite."

Miss Sanderson's smile broadened. "I've taken a fancy to the Great Fox Hunt Saga."

"Fox hunt? I'm not terribly taken with the sport but it sounds harmless."

"Not Sir Amyas's version. This happened five years ago and at that time his passion had turned to nudity—in a wholesome way, sun and health and bodybuilding and that sort of thing. He'd joined a nudist association in London and was trying to get permission to turn the Priory into a nudist colony. The residents of Harper and the surrounding district fought him tooth and nail. They won and Sir Amyas was out of luck. He didn't take his defeat tamely. He organized a fox hunt, complete with outriders, hounds, and horns."

"Tallyho and shades of John Peel, eh?"

"Except for one detail. The hunt pelted all over the district, ending with a triumphant ride up the high street in Harper with Sir Amyas in the lead."

Miss Sanderson dissolved into helpless laughter and Forsythe said with a smile, "I can guess the rest. The hunters were from his nudist club."

Miss Sanderson sputtered and reached into her outsize handbag for a tissue. She wiped at streaming eyes. "All any of them, including Sir Amyas, was wearing were riding boots and derby hats. Harper is a staid little place with staid inhabitants, and their relations with the Dancers since that hunt have been distinctly cool. Robby, I can *see* that ride up the high street."

"Our baronet must have broken innumerable laws with the hunt."

"He did but one of his dearest friends happens to be the chief constable. As usual the Dancers came out unscathed."

"Are the rest of the family as colorful?"

"Not all of them. Sir Amyas's sisters, both older than he, appear to be quiet ladies. Miss Sybil and Miss Arabella are still personae gratae in Harper. His daughter Cassandra, now twenty-one, was educated in Switzerland, though she went to a convent school in Italy for a time. She did spend some months on a commune in the States but that's not unusual. Horace Gillimede only ventures off the estate to attend protest rallies. He turns up waving placards and ranting about salvation. Sounds fairly harmless."

"Horace also sounds like that bearded prophet at the funeral in Bury-Sutton."

All signs of amusement left his secretary's face, leaving it closed and cold. Miss Sanderson still hadn't recovered from their experiences in that town. "Similar," she said tersely and continued. "Sir Amyas's son and heir, Gore-Carleton, mercifully known as Carleton or Carl, seems to have inherited his father's tendencies. Carleton has traveled a great deal, done a number of crazy things, but the highlight of his life thus far has been the rock group he organized and led. It was called Carl and His Cannibals and they had rather a ghastly gimmick. During their performances they threw dismembered parts of bodies into the ranks of fans. Arms and legs and heads. Made of plastic and papier-mâché but Carleton insisted on the look of authenticity and they cost a bundle to make up. The expense eventually broke up their act."

"Thanks to the merciful God. How old is this chap?"

"Twenty-eight."

"What's he up to now?"

"After his group broke up he returned to the Priory and for the last year has devoted his life to collecting buttons."

"*Buttons?*"

"According to Willis Seton, buttons. Incidentally, Robby, I think Willis deserves a hero's medal for trying to handle this bunch of maniacs." She patted her flat stomach. "I'm *starved*."

"You're the navigator. How much farther to Harper?"

"Down this twisty lane and we should arrive at the high street. Ah, there it is. My! Talk about stepping into the past, shades of Merry Olde England."

As the car rumbled over cobblestones Forsythe silently agreed. The village looked like an old print. A narrow street was flanked by half-timbered buildings housing small shops. The chemist shop bore red and green globes in its window and the signs, flapping in the breeze, were almost illegible. "All that's needed, Sandy, is a coach drawn by spanking horses. Ah, there's the Harper Arms. Care to stop?"

"You'd better; my stomach is complaining audibly." Getting out of the car onto a narrow walk, she peered up at the faded sign. "Prop. M. Bantam. Tom Jones land." She swung around toward her companion. "Let me tell you what we'll find inside. Genuine beams, dark old furniture, sloping floors—"

"Don't get your hopes up, Sandy. Could be tarted up with chrome and imitation leather and tankards from Japan."

"—and hunting prints and a fireplace large enough to roast an ox. Want to bet?"

"I no longer bet with you. Good way to lose money. Let's have a look."

It took a few moments for their eyes to adjust from sunlight to the dim interior. Forsythe blinked and was heartily glad he hadn't bet. Not only was it as Sandy had described but the barmaid, polishing glass behind the counter, *was* straight out of Tom Jones. She had a mass of dark curls, a jovial expression, and a buxom figure. Leaning majestically on an elbow watching a checker game was the proprietor. M. Bantam fit the decor perfectly. He too was stout, running greatly to stomach, which was covered by a checkered waistcoat. The only other people in the room were the two elderly checker players.

Four pairs of eyes swiveled to inspect the arrivals and M. Bantam moved with stately grace to a position behind shining taps. He made them welcome in a deep baritone, allowed it was a fine day, and asked what their pleasure was.

"Nut brown ale," Miss Sanderson breathed.

"Two pints of bitter," Forsythe said hastily.

The pints were duly drawn. The landlord apologized for the brew, mentioned he thought the last lot of bitter might have had a bit too much air, watched them sample it, and beamed when both declared it good. Queried about food he admitted, after some thought, the missus could come up with a mixed grill. Lowering his voice he confided, "My suggestion is bread and cheese. Missus is a dab hand with bread and it's straight out of the oven. Got a nice chunk of aged Cheshire." Leaning over the counter, he tapped the older checker player lightly on a bald head. "Stop your ogling, Bob," he roared. Both Forsythe and his secretary started and Mr. Bantam said in a lower tone, "Old Bob coming up ninety-five and stone deaf but still got an eye for a likely lass."

Miss Sanderson, who could scarcely be considered a lass, pinkened with pleasure, and without consulting her companion ordered bread and cheese. They carried their drinks to a seat resembling a church pew and deposited the glasses on a table.

"Bread and cheese doesn't sound like much of a meal, Sandy."

"When in Tom Jones land one must have nut brown ale and bread and cheese. Wish you'd bet with me."

"I'm not Horace Gillimede and I don't give my money away. Ah, here comes lunch."

The plump barmaid deposited a platter before them bearing a crusty loaf of warm bread, sweet country butter, and a huge chunk of cheese. More bitters arrived and they proceeded to stuff themselves. It was tasty and more than substantial. When the plates were removed their host stepped over to ask how they'd fared. Behind his broad back old Bob winked a rheumy eye at Miss Sanderson and gave her a lecherous toothless grin. Miss Sanderson smiled back.

"Could you tell us," Forsythe asked, "where the Priory is located?"

Bantam's shrewd eyes gave them a closer scrutiny and then he allowed he could do that. He gave lengthy and detailed instructions. Forsythe paid no attention. His human computer,

Miss Sanderson, was storing the information away in her memory bank. Bantam had the necessary quota of human curiosity. He stuck out a big hand and announced, "Matthew Bantam, at your service."

Forced into a declaration, Forsythe shook the hand and said, "Miss Abigail Sanderson and Robert Forsythe."

"Not my place to ask, Mr. Forsythe, but will you be staying at those Dancers' house?"

"I'm inclined to doubt it."

"Long drive back to London."

While Forsythe was agreeing, he wondered how the devil Bantam had figured that out. Bantam rubbed his lowest chin. "Got a couple of nice rooms here. Clean and comfortable. Missus is a fair to middling cook. No choice, have to take what she has a mind to put together. Got a snuggery back there you could use for meals. Get you away from the crowds." He waved a hand at the checker players as though there were standing room only.

"We'll probably be here only one night," Forsythe told him.

"Might's well be comfortable. Place up the street takes in boarders but rooms are cupboard size." He lowered his voice. "W.C. outside in the yard, too. Willing to give you special rates." He named an amount that hardly sounded Tom Jonesish.

The barrister glanced at his secretary but she was dreamily eyeing a dim hunting print. "Sounds fine."

"See to them rooms." Turing away he caught the older checker player in the act. "Get them eyes off the lass!" he roared at old Bob.

Forsythe grinned and turned to Miss Sanderson. "You're playing hell with Bob's concentration."

"And mine host is playing hell with your wallet," she retorted.

"At least you won't have to run out in the night air to locate the W.C. Mr. Bantam's ancestors were probably pirates but one night won't break me."

She stood up and picked up her large handbag. The clasp was large too, a shiny brass grill-like ornament. She touched the clasp. "Want me to use the snooper when we get to the Priory?"

"I doubt it. Use your own judgment."

"Thank God for electronics. No more writer's cramp taking notes."

At the door Miss Sanderson turned to wave a hand at her admirer. Old Bob enthusiastically waved back.

Chapter Three

Settling behind the wheel, Forsythe asked, "Where away, navigator?"

"Further up the high street until we reach the church. There it is. What a beauty! Wonder how old it is."

"Possibly fourteenth century." Forsythe slowed to admire the structure. The gentle slope around it was covered with moss-encrusted tombstones, tilting and tottering, bearing witness to other, perhaps gentler, days.

Miss Sanderson touched his arm. "That white Victorian house dead ahead. Turn there."

They turned onto a lane. The cobblestones trailed off and the Rover's tires hit gravel first and then a dirt surface. A few widely spaced houses lounged to their right in the July sun. To their left was a row of high-shouldered, narrow, attached houses. Miss Sanderson pointed at the end one. "That's the home of the Widow Hawkins who takes in boarders. Turn there."

"How do you garner all these details so quickly?"

"I have to. You never listen to directions. Mine host told me there was a stone lion on the lawn. Observe the noble beast.

The reason I know it's his competition is because of the sign in one of the front windows. Hey, look at that."

He followed her pointing finger. "The widow has a neat garden and what looks like a tool shed. What's so startling?"

"What's missing. Nary a sign of the outside W.C. that Bantam warned us about."

The barrister laughed. "Propaganda, my dear Sandy. A neat way of steering people away from the competition. Any more turns?"

"None. There are the gate posts of the estate. It's practically on the doorstep of Harper. Half a mile from these posts to the house." Miss Sanderson cast a disgusted look from her window. "Blimey, but this is a mess."

"Unkempt, but then it would take an army of gardeners to keep a place this size under cultivation. Probably it will be better around the house."

It wasn't. The Elizabethan house looked forlornly across a sea of tangled grass and wild bushes. The drive slashed through it like a riverbed through a ravine. Drawing the car up before the front entrance Forsythe got out, circled the car, and opened the door for his secretary. A stiff breeze rippled through the tall grass, bending their heads. It playfully tugged at the chiffon over Miss Sanderson's gray hair and she reknotted the scarf under her chin. For a time they stared up at the house. It seemed as neglected as the grounds. Touching his companion's arm, Forsythe led the way up the shallow steps. The knocker, green with verdigris, had hardly thumped the oaken panel before the door jerked open and a young woman bolted out. "David, you're late!" She skidded to a stop and stared accusingly at them. "You're not David."

Forsythe admitted this and gave her their names. They didn't appear to interest her and she stared over his shoulder. Miss Sanderson was running glacial eyes up and down the girl. From the neck up she wasn't eye-catching at all. Her face was round with a pug nose and eyes set too close together. Straw-colored pigtails stuck out stiffly from her head. From the neck down was a different matter. She wore a flesh-colored body stocking under what looked like a pink bikini. The figure revealed was not spectacular but more than adequate.

The barrister cleared his throat and without removing her eyes from the drive the girl told him, "You're wasting your time. We never buy at the door."

"We're not peddlers," Forsythe told her amiably. "Willis Seton sent us."

"Willy? Oh, Amy will know all about that. There David is now!" She ran past Forsythe and down the steps. "Where have you been? You can't put inspiration on hold, David."

The man drew the bike to a wobbling stop, dismounted, and bent to remove the clip from a gray flannel trouser leg. This should have been a simple operation but the girl had cast herself upon him and was clinging like a limpet. Firmly he detached her, snapped off the clip, and straightened. "You can't fight fate or this broken-down bike. Ruddy thing blew a tire and I had to push it back into Harper to have it mended. Who are your guests?"

"They aren't guests. They've come to see Amy."

"Manners," the young man chided. "And introductions, Cass."

She waved a hand. "Mrs. Sanders and Mr. Foster."

"Forsythe," Miss Sanderson bit off the word. "*Miss* Abigail Sanderson."

"Proctor." The young man gave the secretary a pleasant smile and extended a hand to Forsythe. "David Proctor. And this hasty young lady is Cassandra Dancer."

Forsythe noticed that Sandy had melted and was returning Proctor's smile. The man possessed a sort of dreamy handsomeness. Lush dark hair curled down over his collar and flopped forward over a rounded brow. His brown eyes were soft and warm. Forsythe also noticed the flannel suit was shabby and the collar frayed. Cassandra Dancer wasn't wasting any time on them. She shoved Proctor through the doorway and appeared about to close the door in their faces. "Miss Dancer," he said quickly. "Will you tell Sir Amyas we're here?"

"You tell him. Go around to the rear—"

"Are you sending us to the tradesmen's entrance?" Miss Sanderson asked. Battle flags of color rode high on her cheekbones.

"Of course not. Amy and Carl are mooching around Mandalay. You can't miss it. Just follow the fall of the land." The door closed.

"Well!" Miss Sanderson snapped. "How positively uncouth. We should have rung up Sir Amyas and told him 'no' from London."

"I'm inclined to agree but since we're here we'll tell him in person. On to Mandalay."

His secretary picked her way through the long grass along the side of the house. "Thank God I wore walking shoes. That spoiled brat wouldn't care if we were barefoot. What do you suppose she does that calls for that outlandish getup and David?"

"To say nothing of inspiration. I've no idea but you rhymed David off very quickly. He made an instant hit with you, didn't he?"

"He looks so much like young Lord Byron—that hair, those eyes, that expression."

Smothering a grin, Forsythe gazed around. They were passing the back of the house and could see a good-sized kitchen garden. Farther on a copse straggled down the hill. "You didn't mention servants, Sandy."

"I can see why you mention them. Looks as though there aren't any. There happen to be two. A Mrs. Larkin who is housekeeper and her brother George. Incidentally Willis put a note beside their names. Warned us under no circumstances to refer to them as servants. He didn't say why. They've been imported because the locals refuse to work for the Dancers." She muttered, "And I damn well can see why."

They entered the wood and beneath the shelter of oak and hemlock branches found a welcome coolness. Forsythe found he was enjoying the exercise and the pure air. Quite a change from the exhaust-laden fumes of London. After a time the trees thinned out and sunlight again beamed down on them. Miss

Sanderson paused long enough to slip off her linen jacket and gaze down at the view. "Heavenly," she breathed.

Silently, her companion agreed. The land sloped down to the shores of an ample lake. Willows and alder grew along the banks and directly below them they could see a wooden dock on which could be discerned two men bending over a pile of lumber. Beside the dock a white painted rowboat rode the peaceful water. Directly behind the dock was a structure completely alien to the country scene. If Sir Godfrey Dancer had wanted to reproduce a temple in miniature he had succeeded.

"I adore it," Miss Sanderson said. "It's perfectly enchanting. Look at that red-tile roof, the way it curls up at the edges."

"A charming setting for a murder," Forsythe said laconically and led the way down toward the dock. "What do you think our reception will be?"

"Judging by the daughter of the house I'd say they'll probably toss us off that dock."

This time Miss Sanderson erred in judgment. The older man spotted them first. Throwing down a hammer he strode to meet them. He was short, almost as wide as he was high but it looked like muscle, not fat. Like his daughter's, his face was round but his hair was thinning. A long lock that looked as though it was ordinarily brushed across a bald spot stood out at right angles from his head. His attire was simple and made Forsythe think irrepressibly of Dancer's career as a nudist. All he wore were stout boots and a pair of knee-length khaki shorts that looked like those worn by tropic-zone policemen. The skin over his nose, his arms, and chest was pinkened with what by nightfall would be a bad burn. By the time he reached them his hand was outstretched and he was talking. "Mr. Forsythe and Miss Sanderson, delighted to meet you. Willis said you'd be down today. So good of you to take the trouble. Carleton, come and meet these people."

Carleton came at a lope. He was a head taller than his father and had a reedy build. He had a dark tan and most of it showed. All he wore were slashed-off jeans and desert boots. He was a great deal more hirsute than his sire. A mane of light brown hair fell to his shoulders and his lower face was partially masked by a beard. The beard wasn't a success. It was thin and scraggly.

"Hi," Carleton said, bobbed his head at Miss Sanderson, and gave Forsythe a sweaty hand.

"Doing a little repair work?" Forsythe asked.

Sir Amyas's face became even pinker. "Be doing more than this if it wasn't for those stupid police. Have a look at this." He led them around to the front of the temple and pointed at the brass-covered door. Above an antique padlock was a large red seal. "Damn fools have done everything there is to be done in there. Practically pulled the place to pieces. Even wanted to open Sir Godfrey's tomb. Put my foot down. Told them they'd desecrate my dead over *my* dead body. Phoned Roland—Lord Wabbersley, the chief constable—and he backed me up."

"The body was discovered about two weeks ago, wasn't it?" Forsythe asked. Out of the corner of his eye he noticed Sandy was fishing in her handbag. Turning on the tape machine, he guessed, force of habit.

"About that," the baronet told him wrathfully. "Rang up Roland this morning and he promised a lad would be out to take that ruddy great seal off."

"There's not that much hurry, Father," his son told him. His voice matched his frame, light, high, reedy.

"Of course there's a hurry. When I get an idea I like to carry it through." Sir Amyas looked around. "Where can we talk? There's a bench over there under that willow. Come along."

Miss Sanderson and Forsythe trailed along after the Dancers. In the shade of the willow was a splintery wooden bench. Dragging a grimy handkerchief from his pocket Sir Amyas spread it on the bench and gallantly seated Miss Sanderson. Forsythe sank down beside her and father and son promptly dropped onto the grass at their feet.

"Suppose you'll want to ask questions," Sir Amyas said. "Fire away."

"Well, my secretary and I do know the details but..."

"Bare bones, eh? Want some flesh put on them." The baronet prodded his son's angular shoulder. "You better begin. You're the one responsible for this whole mess."

"I am *not*. I merely brought the girl home. You're the one who offered her a job."

"And I wouldn't have offered her a job if you hadn't sneaked her into the house. What's more—"

"I think," Forsythe said hastily, "it would be simpler if Mr. Dancer—"

"Carleton. Might's well call me that. Everyone does."

"—if Carleton told his story first."

"Not much to tell." The boy's scanty beard bobbed up and down and came to rest on his narrow chest. Both hands were busily engaged in uprooting grass and he looked down at them as he spoke. "I picked her up on the other side of Harper one night about four months ago. Brought her home and the next morning Father—"

"Details," Forsythe said patiently.

With much prompting the story was dragged from him. It seemed the younger Dancer had been attending an auction in Chester and was driving back to the Priory when he first saw Katherine St. Croix. "Buttons," he explained. "First Thursday in every month they have a dandy auction in Chester. Pick up some marvelous buttons there. You must see my collection. I hate to brag but it's the finest—"

"Will you forget those stupid buttons?" his father roared. "Get on with it."

"Mr. Forsythe did say he wants full details, Father."

"You were driving home," Forsythe prompted.

"It was a bad night. One of those early April nights, cold and slashing rain. Visibility was poor and I was driving slowly and I suppose I might not have noticed her. She was standing by the side of the road, not thumbing, just standing there. I could see her hair blowing in the wind and she had a shoulder bag and this carryall at her feet. It was late, after midnight, and I couldn't figure what a kid like that was doing—"

"She wasn't a kid," his father grunted. "Turned out she was a helluva lot older than you."

"She didn't look it. You figured she was a kid too. In the light from the headlights she looked about eighteen. I stopped the car and asked if she wanted a lift. Told her I could take her into Harper. She said she might as well walk because she had no money to take a room anyway. She was kind of weaving around and I asked whether she was sick. She told me no, she was just lightheaded because she hadn't eaten in a couple of days. I jumped out and persuaded her to get into the car. When I turned on the interior light I could see how wet and forlorn she looked—like a drowned kitten."

"Pretty too," his father said in a milder voice. "A pretty little piece. Fantastic figure but she didn't seem to realize it. Face was so innocent and she had this modest, timid manner. Must admit she took me in too."

"Took us all in," his son admitted gloomily. "Where was I?"

"You put her in the car," Miss Sanderson prompted.

"Asked her some questions and she told me she was an orphan, no one to look to for help. Katherine said she'd lost her job at the library in Chester and run out of money to pay her rent. Landlady had slung her out and she was trying to get to London to find work. I couldn't boot her out in that rain so I brought her home. Everyone was bedded down so we went to the kitchen and I got some food into her. She argued all the time, about not wanting to bother me, and what would my family think. Ended up she agreed to spend the night so I made up one of the guest rooms for her and she bedded down. The next morning—" Breaking off, he glared at his father. "You can take it from there."

"Not yet. You left out the buttons."

"So I did. In the kitchen Katherine took off her anorak and under it she had a blouse with five buttons on it. I must admit they riveted my eyes. They were pieces of bone carved into little skulls. I asked her about them and she told me her father had been in Germany at the end of the Second World War and had picked them up. Katherine said he told her they were carved by a guard in a concentration camp and were made from human bone. I…I coveted them. I offered to buy them on the spot but she said no, they were all she had left to remember her dad. She had tears in her eyes when she said it. If you want to see them, Mr. Forsythe, I've added them to my collection. As it turned out she lied about them too. Had them checked and they're carved from the bones of a sheep, interesting though."

Forsythe nodded. "You bought these buttons from Miss St. Croix."

"The morning of the day she left…at least the day we thought she'd left."

Forsythe's eyes and Miss Sanderson's handbag turned towards the older Dancer. Sir Amyas was vainly trying to pat the long lock across the bald spot. "While I was breakfasting she came down. The rain had stopped and sunlight was beaming into the morning room. She looked as fresh and lovely as a daisy. Katherine told me how kind my son had been and that she wasn't going to infringe on our generosity. She was ready to leave. Had her shoulder bag and her carryall with her. I insisted she have breakfast and she ate ravenously. We talked and she told me the same story she'd told Carleton. I must admit it touched my heartstrings. I'd been thinking of having the family history written and privately printed and when I heard she'd worked in a library—"

"Crap!" His son said inelegantly. "You'd never even considered it."

Sir Amyas rubbed his round chin. "I'll be truthful. It hadn't occurred to me. But I did want her to stay on. She was too proud to accept money without working and she was so young and such a stunner, I figured some cad would take advantage of—"

Carleton glared at his father. "You figured you might as well keep her here and take advantage of her yourself."

His glare was returned and Forsythe looked from one man to the other. Neither had much claim to good looks but shared wonderfully shaped, high-bridged noses. Too bad, he thought,

Cassandra hadn't inherited a nose like theirs instead of her small snout. He asked the men, "Could you stick to the facts?"

Sir Amyas took a deep and apparently calming breath. "Correct. Katherine made asses of us all. With the exception of Mrs. Larkin and my daughter. They saw through her immediately." He broke off a long blade of grass and nibbled at the end. "After much persuading Katherine agreed to stay on and research and write the book. I set up the library for her and she went to work. She seemed so...so sincere and serious about it. I provided her with all the old records, the diaries, and every time I saw the girl she had a sheaf of notes or a book. With my permission she interviewed the rest of the family, my father-in-law and my sisters. She even went to Harper to see young Proctor—"

"Is David Proctor a relative?" Forsythe inquired.

"No, but we regard the lad as family. David was a protégé of my late wife. He's a poet and completely unworldly. Viola insisted Proctor leave London and come down here and I feel rather responsible for him. His only sources of income are from music lessons and an occasional poem he has published. Right now he's playing for my daughter while she—" He turned to his son. "Exactly *what* is Cassandra doing?"

Carleton shrugged a leather-brown shoulder. "Haven't the foggiest."

"Anyway, whatever Cassandra is doing, young Proctor is helping her."

"How long was Miss St. Croix with you?" Forsythe asked.

Sir Amyas looked baffled. "Never keep track of time. Eight...maybe nine days."

"Ten," Miss Sanderson said crisply. "Carleton picked her up in the early hours of Friday morning and she disappeared a week from the following Sunday."

"That's right. Funny, it seems much longer. Must admit I took a fancy to the girl and spent a lot of time with her. Told her all about the family and she seemed interested. Wonderful listener, Katherine was."

Forsythe regarded the Dancer father and son. The baronet was nibbling on a fresh spear of grass and Carleton still seemed intent on uprooting the rest. "Neither of you had any hint she was thinking of leaving?"

Sir Amyas removed the strand of grass and gazed down at it. "Only time I saw her Sunday was at breakfast time. She seemed the same as usual, quiet and demure. Of course, Cassandra never let on to anyone about what she'd found out and she didn't speak to Katherine until midmorning."

"You didn't see Miss St. Croix for the rest of the day?"

"At lunchtime she sent George down with a message. Said she wasn't feeling well and was going to rest."

Carleton looked up. "I saw her. Three times. At the breakfast table and later in the morning. Not sure of the time. It was before lunch. Maybe about eleven-thirty. She came to my room and asked whether I was still interested in buying her buttons. Told her yes and we haggled on price a bit. Finally settled on ten pounds per, so I went down to Father and he got fifty pounds out of the safe. All small bills so I stuck an elastic band around them. I took them up to her room and she opened the door, handed me the buttons, and took the money. Said she had a headache and was going to rest. That was the last I saw of her."

Miss Sanderson said, "I understand you never keep money anywhere but in the safe."

"Not now," Sir Amyas told her. "Used to have it lying around in drawers but last year our London house was burgled and we lost money, a few bits of jewelry, and some silver. Since then Cassandra insists we keep the valuables in our bank and only a small amount of cash in the safe. Sensible girl, Cassandra." He rubbed the sunburned tip of his shapely nose. "Terrible shock the next morning when Mrs. Larkin told us Katherine was gone and her baggage, such as it was, with her. Couldn't believe she'd leave like that."

"Your daughter didn't let on to you about the reason for Miss St. Croix's hasty departure?"

"Didn't even peep about it until her body was found and then Cassandra had to tell the police. Couldn't believe that, either. A common crook!"

Rather an uncommon one, Forsythe thought, able to inveigle her way into the Dancer house and enthrall not only Carleton but his father. Sir Amyas was still rambling on about the shock and his son was staring into space. Better check the time span, the barrister thought, and turned not to the two men but to Miss Sanderson. His secretary told him crisply, "Sir Amyas discovered the body three months and ten days from the time she arrived here."

Sir Amyas gave her a beaming smile. "Wish you worked for me, Miss Sanderson. Got a good mind."

"Fifteen days ago," Forsythe mused. "How did you happen to enter the temple, Sir Amyas?"

Miss Sanderson leaned forward. "And weren't you afraid to?"

"Afraid?" Sir Amyas rolled the word around on his tongue, as though tasting it.

"The runes. The curse."

"Oh, that. No, that's only for defiling the place. And I shouldn't think it would apply to Dancers."

His son gave him a sidelong glance. "Should think uprooting Sir Godfrey's ancient bones would be defiling it."

"Only to move them to our burial plot at St. Jude, son. Nothing wrong with that. Planning to give Godfrey a little service too." Sir Amyas swung his head back toward Forsythe. "First time I'd ever been inside Mandalay. Maybe the first time anyone has been since Cuthbert locked it up. Except for Katherine, of course."

"I understand that there's only one key for the padlock?"

"Whacking great thing. Always been kept in the drawer of a table in the entrance hall. Had to root through a mess of junk to find it. Wondered afterwards how Katherine laid her hands on it."

"You told her," his son muttered. "I heard you, when you were raving on about Mandalay and Sir Godfrey."

"Don't recall that. Anyone could have told her. No secret where the key was kept."

Forsythe shifted on the bench. "Your reason for entering the temple?"

"Wanted to look around and see whether there were materials there I could use in the Roman amphitheater."

Forsythe and his secretary spoke like a Greek chorus. "Amphitheater?"

In the midst of the scraggly heard Carleton's full lips turned up into a broad grin. "Father's going to pull down Mandalay and put up a Roman amphitheater."

"Not the full oval," Sir Amyas confided. "Just a chunk of one like this." His hands formed a slice shaped like a piece of pie.

Carleton was convulsed with laughter. "Better change the name of the lake, Father. How about the Adriatic Sea?"

Sir Amyas's round face, which had been getting steadily redder, now was purple. "You perfect ass! Making fun of a fine idea! You've got a lot to talk about. Not long ago you were on stage swinging your hips and tossing out legs and arms to a bunch of young twits!"

His son sobered and said sulkily, "It was a gimmick, Father. Rock bands have to have gimmicks."

"Ghoulish one. Didn't like it at all. Didn't like it when you pelted the audience with severed heads for a finale either. Glad you had to give it up."

Having squelched his son, Sir Amyas turned his attention back to Forsythe and his secretary. Hastily, Miss Sanderson asked, "What will you *use* it for?"

"Use?" The baronet paused apparently to savor this word too. "Aesthetic value. There's an amphitheater at Chester. People come in droves to see it."

Carleton entered the fray again. "Wouldn't put it past Father to throw it open to the public and charge admission."

"Day trippers on my property? No, son, this is for the family's use."

Miss Sanderson was fascinated. "But what *use*, Sir Amyas?"

He pondered and then said, "Musical evenings. We could make up our own group. Carleton plays an electric guitar and Proctor's good on the piano. I play the drums or did at one time. Cassandra—what instrument did she take lessons on, Carleton?"

"Think it was the harp. Hey, this isn't a bad idea, Father. Mrs. Larkin sings rather well and so does George. Have to find a gimmick."

"No gimmicks, son. No legs or arms or heads."

While the Dancers argued about gimmicks Forsythe shook a baffled head. Vainly he tried to picture an electric guitar, drums, and a harp pumping music from a Roman amphitheater out over the placid lake. Miss Sanderson muttered in his ear, "Think we'd better get out of here. Whatever they have is contagious. This whole business is starting to sound logical, Robby."

Forsythe broke into the argument. "I think we'd better get back to the discovery of Miss St. Croix's body."

"Righto," Sir Amyas said. "When I got the temple unlocked I found a couple of candles standing in their own wax on top of Sir Godfrey's tomb. Turned out Katherine had taken them from the dining room. There's no electricity laid on in the temple so I'd brought a torch. Shone it around and caught sight of the glass cabinet where the jade statuettes were kept. They'd been sealed in and now the glass had been smashed and the two pink ones were missing. I lit the candles and started looking around. Figured at first some vandals had managed to get in. Then my foot touched something on the floor and I looked down and saw Katherine's carryall with the top gaping open. Looked further and found her shoulder bag against the wall."

"You recognized both of them?"

"Not the carryall—plastic affair with a zipper and a couple of carrying straps. Cheap. Could have been anyone's. But the bag was distinctive—big and kind of homespun material with a pattern of red and yellow and orange, not stripes, kind of zigzags. Primitive. Could be Mayan—"

"Aztec," Carleton corrected.

"Took a closer look and found brown splotches all over the floor around the carryall. I finally decided they looked like blood and I got alarmed. Then I saw the metal bar. Flat end of it had stuff encrusted on it. Caught hell from the police afterward for using it—"

"Was this bar kept in the temple?"

"Must have been. The police had it examined and it's old. It might have been left after Sir Godfrey was stuck in the tomb." Sir Amyas paused and looked down at his hands. He looked suddenly older and sick. "I picked up the bar and slid it under the top of the empty tomb. It took a little doing but I got it open and the smell was awful. She'd been crammed down into it and..." His mouth worked. "Don't care if Katherine was a crook; that's a hideous way for a woman to die. Back of her head battered in." He covered his face with his hands. "God!"

His son awkwardly patted the bowed shoulders. "Father was shattered and so was I. We'd just been getting used to the idea she'd left without a word, and then that."

Forsythe addressed himself to the younger man. "The police found some interesting things in her carryall, didn't they?"

"The two statuettes were wrapped up in her clothes and there was money. The money was near the top and had been splattered by blood and...other things. From her head, you know. There were two lots of notes. One was the fifty pounds I'd given her for the buttons. I had no trouble identifying them. The elastic band I put around them came from ones I use for boxes of buttons. Wide pink affairs. The other bundle of notes had an ordinary thin band around it. There was a hundred pounds in that one."

"Miss St. Croix couldn't have stolen that hundred pounds from any of you?"

Carleton's shaggy head shook. "Our money is in Father's safe and none was missing. The aunts never have much cash around their house and Grandfather Gillimede doesn't have money. Hates it. No, Katherine didn't steal it from us."

Miss Sanderson was thoughtfully nibbling her lower lip. "The police think the victim was on her knees beside the carryall, perhaps putting the second piece of jade into it, when she was struck on the back of the head. The murderer didn't leave a trace. Just smudges on the top of the tombs. They think the killer was wearing gloves. They also say the jade is incredibly valuable. Why on earth was it left in the temple?"

"It has always been there," Carleton said earnestly. "We never thought of it in terms of value. It was simply part of Sir Godfrey's mausoleum."

Forsythe bent forward. "Have either of you any idea of the identity of the murderer?"

Sir Amyas's hands fell away from his face. "Some villain must have killed her. When the police brought in that young fellow who'd helped her dispose of some of the things she stole…what was his name?"

"Fred Small," Miss Sanderson said. "Alias Scoppy Smaile. He has a record of petty crime and did work with the murdered woman on occasion. But he has an alibi. At the time of her death Scoppy was in jail for drunken driving."

Carleton straightened and said, "I think it's someone from Katherine's past. She ripped off a lot of people, you know. Got herself into their homes and took everything that wasn't nailed down. Like Aunt Pru Pyne in Harper. Katherine did her a few months before she had a go at us."

Forsythe cocked his head. "You feel one of the people she victimized followed her here and killed her?"

"Well, if she'd had a falling out with a confederate I think he'd have taken the money and the jade. Looks to me as though it was revenge."

Carleton Dancer might be a bit odd, Forsythe thought, but there was nothing wrong with his reasoning. When his father spoke it was apparent a certain amount of clear thinking did run through the family. "Wrong, son. I'd like to think that but there are a couple of things wrong with that solution. How did this avenger know Katherine would be in the temple? And how on earth did a stranger know where to put the key back? It was returned to the table in the hall, you know. Has to be someone connected with the family, someone who knew where the key was kept."

"If you hadn't gotten that idea about pulling Mandalay down, Father, this mess would never have happened. The body could have been in there for a hundred years and no one would have been the wiser."

"And if you hadn't dragged the girl here in the first place, son, she'd still he alive." Sir Amyas added, "That's all we know, Mr. Forsythe. The police are stymied and I'm banking on you to clear this up."

Time, Forsythe thought. He stood up and nodded at Miss Sanderson. Her hand crept into her handbag to turn off the tape recorder. Their two companions pulled themselves up, the younger man lithely, Sir Amyas with more effort. The baronet, even half-naked, sunburned, and with the lock of hair sticking waggishly out from his head, had a kind of dignity. Before the barrister could speak, he held up a silencing hand. "I know what you're going to say, Mr. Forsythe. You're going to tell us you won't take the case. You're going to tell us the police have much better facilities than you have to get to the bottom of it."

"Yes. And I was about to suggest a professional private investigator. Sir Amyas, I'm truly sorry."

"I'm sorry too. Sorry you don't understand our position. I thought you would. That was one reason I asked Willis Seton to talk with you. You must realize, Mr. Forsythe, that the police have no evidence to charge any of us. You must also realize they have no evidence to *clear* any of us." The baronet held Forsythe's eyes. "I happen to know a good deal about your own past. Not from Willis, from other sources. Some years ago you were under a cloud yourself. You cleared your professional reputation but you must know how we feel. Friends turning away from you, papers printing personal details that are almost, but not quite, libelous. If the person who murdered Katherine St. Croix isn't exposed this will get worse with time. The public will forget she was a petty crook. They'll think of her as an innocent young girl who was lured to this estate and foully murdered by a mad Dancer."

Sir Amyas paused for breath and then asked quietly, "How did *you* feel when a veil of suspicion hung over your life?"

"Like a pariah," Forsythe said bluntly.

"And that's how we feel but in our case there's little chance of reprieve. Mr. Forsythe, I'm imploring you to at least try."

"If I agree I must warn you that the murderer I uncover may be a member of your family. Perhaps it will be you."

Carleton leaped forward. "Father *found* the body. He's the one who insisted on calling *you* in. Would he do that if he'd killed Katherine?"

"What better way to avert suspicion from himself?" Forsythe asked evenly.

Sir Amyas put a restraining hand on his son's arm. "I'll take that chance. If one of my household is guilty I want him or her punished. It's terrible to even contemplate, but the innocent shouldn't suffer for the rest of their lives. Find the person who killed Katherine, no matter who it is."

The barrister took a deep breath. "Very well. I'll take the case."

Wiping a hand down his khaki shorts, Sir Amyas extended it and Forsythe solemnly shook it. The bargain was sealed.

Chapter Four

In the woods above the China Sea Forsythe leaned against the bole of an oak and watched Miss Sanderson deftly inserting a fresh tape into her little machine. As she closed the flap of her handbag he said, "Let the other shoe drop, Sandy. I can't stand the suspense." She lifted a brow and he added, "Make some remark about turning Sir Amyas down kindly but firmly."

"No comment."

"Why not?"

"When he dragged up our past, there was no other answer you could give him. That Dancer may be bizarre but he's bright enough."

"Perhaps bright enough to get away with murder."

She tucked her bag under an arm and linked her other arm with his. "Where away?"

"To interview another member of the household. Anyone we can get our hands on."

When they reached the kitchen garden they found a man stooping over the long rows of vegetables. He straightened and stared but said nothing. He looked about forty and wore dark trousers and an immaculate white jacket. His most outstanding feature was his neck—long, thin, serpentine. The bulge of an Adam's apple in that stringy throat reminded Forsythe unpleasantly of a mouse being slowly digested by a snake.

"That has to be George," Miss Sanderson muttered.

"Strong silent type."

"Silent, anyway." They rounded the house and Miss Sanderson pointed. "Looks like we're in luck. Cassandra is waving goodbye to David Proctor."

They glanced from the figure hunched over the handlebars of the ancient bike to the girl standing on the top step, shielding her eyes against the sun. Cassandra was still wearing her scanty costume but had added a sweatband over her hair. As she turned toward the door she caught sight of them. "Hello, again."

They mounted the steps and Forsythe asked, "Could you spare a few moments?"

"I suppose so. David tells me I was madly rude to you earlier."

"You were," Miss Sanderson told her.

"Sorry. I get so worked up when the inspiration arrives and David doesn't. Do come in and grill me all you wish."

Forsythe raised his brows. "You know why we're here then?"

"Amy told all of us and warned we'd better cooperate. I'll give you a guided tour before I tell all." She pointed at a long table standing against the wall in the entrance hall. "The fatal key is, or rather was, kept in that drawer. Right now the police have it and Amy, poor darling, is raising hell about it."

The table was cluttered. Among other objects Forsythe noticed an unstrung tennis racket, a number nine iron, a motorcycle helmet, a pair of driving gloves, and a half-eaten candy bar. The drawer the girl pulled out was filled with odds and ends, balls of twine, envelopes, a broken cigarette case. Cassandra ran a fingertip along the surface of the table and left a mark. "This house is a mess," she said.

From what Forsythe could see he was inclined to agree. The tiled floor was grubby and the noble staircase undusted.

A picture hung crookedly over the table. Cassandra, talking steadily, led the way up that noble dusty staircase. "When Mother was alive it was different. Of course the aunts were still with us and Aunt Sybil is one person who can get some work out of the Lark. And Aunt Bella is worth about six housemaids."

"You do have a couple of servants," Miss Sanderson pointed out.

"For heaven's sake, don't let the Lark hear you say that." Casandra reached the landing, took a sharp right turn, and continued to lead the way steadily upward "According to her, George and she are distant connections of the Dancers and they're 'helping out.' The Lark also prides herself on 'standing by us in our time of need.' The truth is that you couldn't pry her loose. Has her heart set on being the next Lady Dancer."

"How long has she been with you?" Forsythe asked.

"Five…no, about six years."

Miss Sanderson was starting to pant. The third set of stairs was even steeper and Cassandra set a rapid pace. The secretary had been clinging to the banister and she examined the coating of dust she'd picked up on her palm. "Don't you have cleaners?"

"We did until the news leaked out about Katherine jammed in that crypt. I offered the cleaners double salary but they ran for cover, fearing for their lives. That ruddy woman is more trouble dead than she was alive and that's saying something."

"How much farther?" Forsythe gasped.

"One flight. At the end of this hall." Cassandra looked back. "You're out of shape. Should do some exercises." She led the way down a long corridor floored with faded carpet and lithely started climbing a structure much like a ladder.

"Do you live on the roof?" Miss Sanderson groaned.

"In the attic. Artists should always live in garrets, don't you think?"

Miss Sanderson hauled herself up through a trapdoor and sank onto the first chair she reached, a straight-backed wooden affair. Thankfully, Forsythe lowered himself on the only other chair and looked around. The room was huge, bare, and spotlessly clean. On uneven planking an exercise mat was stretched, and the far wall was covered with a mirror, a bar running its length. Against the other wall was an upright piano with yellowing keys. Cassandra took up a position in front of the mirror and put a hand on the brass bar. She wasn't breathing heavily. "Pretty nice, isn't it? I had it fixed up when I came home from the States. Bedroom and bath through there. Think I'll have a sauna installed. Dancing is such sweaty work."

"Ballet?" Miss Sanderson asked.

"Started out that way. I studied ballet for a time and then found it wasn't...I suppose you'd say expressive enough for me. David and I are working on dancing that is complete self-expression. A terrible grind and takes so much time but he says sacrifice is essential for a true artist. Mind if I do a few exercises while we talk?"

"Not at all." Forsythe leaned back in his chair, watching one trim leg lever itself up over the bar. Cassandra definitely had a good build.

"You'll want to hear all about the wicked witch of the west."

"In time. Perhaps you could fill in your background first."

"Where would you like me to start? The Crusades or the Magna Carta?"

"With your mother, I think."

Cassandra executed a pirouette and raised the other leg. "She's dead. Died almost a year ago—on her birthday. I think I'd better be totally honest with you. Most of my earlier life was spent at boarding schools and I didn't know Mother all that well. What I did know about her I didn't like. Her death was a shock, but I'm not a hypocrite and I won't pretend a grief I don't feel."

Miss Sanderson looked faintly taken aback. "What didn't you like about her?"

"She had a terrible strength—the strength of the weak. I'm not very good with words but she was like a...vine. Wrapped herself around one and choked out the life."

"An ivy and an oak?" Forsythe murmured.

"Similar. Mother was fragile and kind of droopy and very decorative. She didn't have any luck with me and Amy is not the kind to be choked but she did one hell of a job on Carl. He was only about three when Amy and Mother were married and she devoured him. Carl deludes himself about adoring her but deep down I think he disliked her as much as I did." Deserting the bar, Cassandra fell gracefully on the mat and proceeded to do pushups. Her skin was glossy with sweat and she spoke in jerks. "From as far back as I can remember Amy was angling for divorce. He gave Mother every excuse to get one. Amy's a great man for the ladies, particularly young ones, and he's had a succession of totties he's kept in Chester and London. He really was quite blatant about his girls but Mother didn't turn a hair. In turn she had a succession of protégés. All young and male and good-looking. Her way of fighting back, I guess."

"Physical affairs?" Forsythe asked.

"If you mean did she sleep with them—no. Not her way. These were unions of the mind and spirit—soulful…sonnets and such, looking deep into eyes and sighing. I remember a few of them. The curate of St. Jude was an early one. Dabbled in painting and did rather horrible little watercolors." The girl rolled over on her back and looked up at the rafters. Her breasts, Forsythe noticed with some satisfaction, were heaving. She giggled. "Must tell you about Alec. Mother had become interested in rehabilitation. Took young, always artistic, and nice-looking men from places like clinics and mental institutions and brought them here for weekends. None of them gave us any trouble until she came up with Alec. Alec was definitely a horse of another color. Mother never provided any details on their pasts and I don't think she really knew much about them herself. Went strictly by soulful eyes and nice features. Alec was a handsome brute, dark and swarthy and madly sexy. He also, as we found out, had tried to poison his entire family. The weekend he came the Lark served fresh strawberries for dessert and we were all spooning sugar on them like crazy. They tasted a little gritty but we licked the bowls clean and then Alec looked soulfully up and told us he'd mixed arsenic with the sugar."

"Blimey," Miss Sanderson whispered.

Cassandra groaned and pulled herself into a sitting position. She massaged one calf. "Cramp. That hurts. How one must suffer for art! Ah, better. Where was I? Oh, Alec and arsenic. We bolted from the table and every W.C. in the house was filled with people forcing their fingers down their throats and upchucking. Amy couldn't find an unoccupied one and bent over the sink in the scullery. That was the end not only of Alec but of Mother's charity work; Amy and Uncle Roly put down their feet."

"Arsenic," Miss Sanderson said faintly.

"Uncle Roly?" Forsythe asked.

Cassandra's close-set eyes turned to him. "It wasn't poison. Alec couldn't come up with any on the spot, thank God, so he settled for fruit salts. Uncle Roly is not an uncle. He's my godfather. He's chief constable and comes in handy." She settled gracefully and effortlessly into a full lotus.

In that position, Forsythe thought, with her body gleaming with sweat, she looks like a metal statue. Except for the round plain face, of course. Pity that face didn't live up to the body's promise. "David Proctor was Lady Dancer's last protégé?"

"The last and the best. Mother met him at some do in London and persuaded him to give up his little job, come to Harper, and devote all his time to writing. He's a wonderful writer, sensitive and talented. But he's working in the wrong area. Poetry isn't really for him. He'd do much better writing novels." Her expression was dreamy and she looked into space. "This is my time to meditate. The sacrifices I make for Amy."

"As well as for art," Miss Sanderson said tartly. Lowering her voice she muttered, "Three guesses about the handsome genius she meditates about."

"Your father," Forsythe prompted, "How did he feel about his wife's protégés?"

"Ecstatic. Always hoping his Viola would fall madly in love and run off and leave him. When David hove into view

Amy was delighted. Practically chucked the old girl into David's arms. Offered Mother a handsome settlement if she would up and divorce him."

"Why didn't *he* divorce her?"

A gleaming shoulder moved in a shrug. "A number of reasons. His Viola was clever enough not to give him grounds. And Dancers never divorce. The aunts are dead set against divorce. I really think Aunt Sybil would rather that a relative knock off an unwanted spouse than divorce. And to give Amy his due, he's a gentleman. Let his name be sullied, not his wife's. As for Mother…she seemed so easily swayed but I noticed she never did anything she didn't want to. Prattled on about duty. How she *loved* using that word. Duty to stay with her children even if her husband was a beast, duty to her dear old dad, who is even loonier about divorce than the aunts. Duty! She stayed because she *liked* being Lady Dancer, *liked* being considered a martyr. But she really fell for David and it looked as though she was going to forget duty and devote her life to him. Then her birthday arrived and she drowned."

"Do you mind telling us about her death?" Forsythe asked.

"No, but I fail to see what bearing this has on Katherine the crook."

"One never knows. Anyway, it does help fill in the family relationships."

"I suppose so." Cassandra looked dubious but continued, "On the first day of August we had a bit of a birthday bash for Mother. Even Gramps came and he seldom sets foot in this house. Considers it a mixture of Sodom, Gomorrah, and a sporting house. He was invited for dinner but he didn't eat. Among other things he's sort of a vegetarian. Lives off the land, he boasts. What Gramps does is sneak into our kitchen garden and the aunts' in the dark of night and swipes vegetables. He could have all he wants any old time but he prefers snitching them. Gramps is a bit loony, you know."

"As well as everyone else in the family," Miss Sanderson muttered.

If Cassandra heard that remark she didn't let on. "Let's see, there were Mother and Amy and Carl and me. The aunts weren't there. They decamped after Aunt Sybil had a blazing row with Amy about a fortnight before. Took up residence in the Dower House. Anyway, Gramps arrived all tarted up in a new toga and had made a crown of oak leaves for his hair. He—"

"Neither your aunts nor grandfather live in the house?"

"As I said the aunts are living in the Dower House. I miss them. They're old pussies and Aunt Bella is a wonderful cook. The Lark handles that now and she dishes up some unbelievable messes for meals. If she's trying to become Lady Dancer she's wasting her time. No one can get to Amy through his stomach anyway. Luckily he could eat boiled shoe leather and not notice it. No, the Lark will have to use sex. She's not a bad-looking woman for her age."

"How old is Mrs. Larkin?"

"About thirty-five. Too old for Amy. You'll loathe her. She's so *genteel*. You've got me confused. What did you want to know?"

"Your Grandfather Gillimede—his quarters."

"He's lived for years in the ruins of the Priory, a rubble of stones on the other side of the woods. Incidentally, when you interview him don't let him tempt you into his lair. Both Gramps and his quarters smell like old goat. I told him that cleanliness is next to godliness but he countered that he's mortifying the flesh and feeding the soil. But he's quite harmless and rather a dear. To get back to the birthday bash, Gramps arrived in his weird costume but this time Mother had done him one better. Usually she lounged around in filmy romantic dresses but when she came down for dinner she was dressed as a sailor—"

"You're joking." Miss Sanderson massaged her temples.

"Not at all. She'd had the outfit made up on the sly and sprang it on us that night. All white and red and blue, middy blouse, bell-bottomed pants, even a little sailor hat. Amy seldom notices anything but he noticed *that*." Cassandra smiled but there was a touch of sadness in the smile. "David was the unwitting reason for the outfit and I suppose, in a way, for her death. They both, Mother and David, had this terrible fear of water. Between the sonnets and the soul-searching glances they'd decided they should overcome this weakness. So, Mother put on her sailor suit and later that night without telling a soul went down to the China Sea and got into the boat there. It overturned and..." Cassandra's voice trailed off. "Sorry, but it was rather a beastly way for a person terrified of water to die. Mother wasn't missed until the following morning. I rang up David and he came out from Harper and we all searched. We went through the woods and around the Dower House and the Priory ruins and— Gramps was the only one who went to the lake—we didn't think she'd be near water. He shouted and when we got down there we found the rowboat overturned and adrift and her little white hat floating on the water. Carl was the one who pulled her out..."

"Don't continue," Forsythe told the girl gently. "I'm sorry to distress you."

Cassandra unfolded and came to her feet. She began touching her toes. "The most distressing part of it is that except for Gramps and David, none of us really cared that much. Oh, we were stunned for a time, but we didn't love her. They did. Carl seemed shattered but, as I said, I think he was subconsciously relieved. Mother really was a trial."

"Now we will move on to Katherine St. Croix," the barrister said. "Your father said you and Mrs. Larkin distrusted her from the time she arrived."

"I think the Lark distrusted Katherine more as competition than anything else."

Miss Sanderson shifted on the hard seat. "What was Miss St. Croix like?"

"A stunner—fantastic figure." The girl straightened and her hands described airy lush curves over her more modest ones. "She had a face like a Madonna, oval, with huge brown eyes and long dark lashes. She had a mass of light hair, bleached, but it was a splendid job, no dark roots. But it wasn't her looks that were dangerous; it was the way she used them. Had a habit of casting her eyes down, so modestly, and shoving out her—like this." Cassandra lowered her chin slightly and looked down so her straw-colored lashes hid her eyes. At the same time she arched her back, bringing her breasts jutting against the pink bikini top. "Touch me, touch me not, if you know what I mean. Such a modest, innocent stick of dynamite. I took one look at her and thought, you'll bear watching, my girl."

"What was her manner to you?" Forsythe asked.

"Same act she used on the others, smarmy and ingratiating. Kept telling us she was too much trouble, she didn't want to impose. In the meantime she was raising hell. She had Amy and Carl at each other's throats and even George was trailing along after her with his tongue lolling out. When she went to the ruins to interview Gramps I was hoping he'd give her short shrift. Thought he'd take one look and decide she was a sinner from hell. Odd thing is that's exactly the line she took with him. Had him convinced she was repentant and he could save her soul. Katherine must have thoroughly researched the family before she wormed her way into the house." Cassandra chuckled. "She had no luck with the aunts. Aunt Sybil saw through her immediately and told her to get out and stay out."

"And you distrusted her and took steps to stop her?"

"I had to. There was no one else." The girl leaned back against the exercise bar. "I watched the havoc she was wreaking. There was no sense in trying to talk to Amy or Carl. Both of them were infatuated with the woman. I could see she had her sights on Amy and was using Carl to push the poor old dear into a proposal. Imagine having Katherine St. Croix as a stepmother! But the bitter end was when she went after David. While she was here David was in and out but she didn't pay much attention to him. Then she went into Harper to see him. David and I had a row over that and he took *her* part. Said I had a filthy mind and the poor kid only wanted advice on how to start her book. *Kid.* Katherine was years older than David."

"That's when you hired a private investigator?" Forsythe asked.

"Katherine went to see David the Monday after she arrived. On Tuesday I hotfooted up to London and picked a name from the telephone directory. Turned out I got a little chap who specialized in divorces. Private investigators are such slimy creatures, aren't they?" She glanced at Miss Sanderson's outraged face and said hastily, "Present company excepted, of course. Anyway, Mr. Forsythe, this work is only your hobby, isn't it?"

"You could call it that," Forsythe said wryly. "What happened then?"

"Nothing much for a couple of days. Katherine strolled around clutching notebooks and rubbing herself against Amy and Carl. George's eyes were swiveling and the Lark was looking pure murder at the woman. Then...then the bitch had the audacity to go to Harper and visit David again. That was a Thursday and I felt much like the Lark did. I could have slit the woman's throat!"

"Are you and David engaged?" Miss Sanderson asked.

"As far as I'm concerned we are. David is being difficult. He says it's too soon after Mother's death. But he'll come around. All David needs is a firm hand." Cassandra's mouth set in a firm line. "He doesn't realize what a narrow squeak he had. If Mother had lived and divorced Amy, David would have married her and she'd have ruined him. Kept him writing those silly poems and dancing attendance on her. Then there was the age difference."

"How old was your mother?" Miss Sanderson asked.

"Forty-two. Not much younger than you. Positively ancient!"

Forsythe cast an apprehensive look at his secretary. Cassandra Dancer had put her foot in her mouth this time. Sandy's weak point was her age. It was her secret and she disliked any reference to it. And if looks could kill Cassandra was now being annihilated. Oblivious to the faux pas, the girl rushed on. "On Friday I rang up my slimy little man and asked whether he had any information on Katherine. He said he had a batch and could mail it to me. I told him I would come up on

Saturday and pick it up. The next day I found out David was going to London to see a publisher or agent or something and I thought we could get our business done and make a day of it. But David had too much to do so I drove back by myself. David stayed the night and he had the most incredible hard luck. A hotel thief ripped off his room and got all the little presents Mother had given him—a gold cigarette case and pencil set and an expensive watch."

Forsythe raised a brow. "Did your mother, ah, support Mr. Proctor?"

"Not exactly. Mother wasn't all that generous. When she tempted David down to Harper I believe she paid his expenses for a few months but then insisted he give music lessons to take care of his room and board. Oh, she gave him silly useless presents and perhaps a little check now and then but you've seen him. His clothes are a disgrace and he won't take a penny from me. So proud."

Forsythe was wondering why David Proctor had been willing to take everything he could get from the mother and was too proud to take a penny from the daughter. Cassandra was smiling, a tender, wistful smile. "When we're married it will be different. David will have everything he deserves. Carl and I have our own money. Grandfather Dancer didn't quite trust Amy with money so he provided for his grandchildren and his daughters." The smile expanded and became a laugh. "I chatter so much, I get right away from what I'm trying to tell you. Back to Katherine and the denouement. I came back from London clutching my ammunition and I must say I was delighted. Katerina Padrinski alias Katherine St. Croix alias Katie Parr had a past that was a beaut.

"Her specialty was much the same as the scam she'd pulled on us. Look over a prosperous family, eel her way into the house, and then steal anything that wasn't nailed down. Sometimes she worked with a male confederate, sometimes she worked alone. When she was stealing she ordinarily handed down the loot to her male friend from her bedroom window. Most of the time she posed as a domestic and with the servant problem had little difficulty getting into houses. Like Aunt Pru's for instance."

"Prudence Pyne," Miss Sanderson told Forsythe tersely. "Harper."

"That's correct," Cassandra said. "Courtesy aunt. She's creaking with age, much older than either of my aunts, but she's close friends with them. Aunt Pru was good with Mother too. Let her rave on about her tough life and being pulled two ways, duty versus love. That sort of thing. Everyone talks to Aunt Pru. I do. She has a lovely shoulder to cry on. Anyway, Katherine turned out to be a disgusting crook. There was one thing the investigator dug up that really disturbed me. Katherine took a position as a companion to a very old woman, partially invalided. The woman didn't have much, her cottage was rented and all she had were a few sticks of furniture, a little jewelry, and a small insurance policy. But she willed all of it to Katherine and then she fell downstairs and broke her neck. Her son was convinced Katherine had pushed his mother and he raised a stink, but there was no evidence and no charges were laid."

Forsythe asked, "Did you face Miss St. Croix with this evidence when you returned from London?"

"No. I suppose I took time to gloat. But the next day— Sunday—I asked her to come up here after breakfast, and then handed her the report. She started to read it and went positively livid. Quite honestly, with her mask off the woman was terrifying. She cursed and raved on about everyone in the family. Called Amy a dirty old man and Carl an idiot and...on and on. Not in those words. Katherine was a guttersnipe and talked like one."

"Were you afraid of a physical attack?"

"Hardly." Raising an arm, Cassandra flexed a sizable muscle. "It was worse than that. After a time she calmed down and she was even more frightening. Promised if I exposed her she'd swear Carl had held her down and Amy had raped her. Told me she would smear the whole family. Tell the police Gramps had attacked her and he would be put in a looney bin.

With her record I knew the police wouldn't take it seriously, but it would be spread all over the yellow sheets and people would believe that filth. They always do, you know.

"That was when I realized I had to use her own tactics on her." Cassandra raised her chin with hauteur and Forsythe could see the centuries of breeding that had produced this girl. Plain or not, she was an aristocrat.

"What did you do?" he asked.

"She knew Uncle Roly—Lord Wabbersley—is my godfather. I told her I'd swear I saw her stealing my pearl necklace and she would go to jail. Katherine was clever and she knew whose word would be taken on something like that. I watched her face change and she went right back to meek, smarmy old Katherine. She started to cry like someone turning on a tap and told me I had no idea what it was like for a girl to have to make her own way. Sobbed about being an orphan and falling in with bad companions. Threw herself on my mercy and told me if I let her stay on she would be able to reform. Katherine was a wonderful actress. For a few moments she had me wavering and then I remembered the old woman who fell to her death. So I made a bargain with her. She agreed to get out of the house and out of our lives. I told her if she was still here on Monday morning I'd go to the chief constable."

Regarding the girl with curiosity, Miss Sanderson asked, "Once you had Miss St. Croix's record why didn't you take it to your father and brother?"

"You'd have to know them better to understand, Miss Sanderson. Amy and Carl have to be...they have to be protected. They're mere babes; have their own little worlds and seldom touch reality. I couldn't have them faced with this dirty business."

"So," the barrister drawled. "On Monday morning when you found Miss St. Croix was gone you thought she had fulfilled her end of your bargain."

"Yes and I was delighted. I thought that was the end of her. Carl and Amy wandered around like lost souls but I knew they would get over it. They're both resilient. I comforted them by saying Katherine was probably a rover and had just gotten bored and left. Time passed and they both bounced back. Then—" The girl's body sagged with dejection. "Amy had to get that idea about turning Mandalay into an amphitheater and discovered the bloody body. The police swarmed in, just about drove us mad, and didn't come up with a solid lead. The papers are raving on about those decadent Dancers and—oh hell!"

"Yes," Forsythe agreed, "an uncomfortable position for you and your family. Could you tell us about the Sunday night that Miss St. Croix was murdered?"

The girl sank down on the exercise mat. "I'm tired of the whole business. But you are trying to help and Amy says you're our only hope of clearing this up. I didn't see Katherine for the rest of that day. She was holed up in her room. We had dinner and then did much the same things that we usually do. Dancers don't stay in a pack. We all have our own interests. I hung around downstairs for a bit and then came up here about ten. Did some exercises, had a shower, tumbled into bed. I had a pile of novels I'd been looking over. I'm not much of a reader but I thought I'd better get some ideas about construction to help David with his when I persuade him to write it. Afraid they didn't hold my interest and I went sound asleep and stayed that way until morning."

"Your father?"

"After dinner he closed himself up in his study. I looked in on him before I came up and he wanted to tell me all about the paper he was writing—some project about the Masai. He said he worked until after eleven and then went to his quarters and to bed. Carl was up in his suite brooding over his buttons and the Lark told the police she was in her sitting room on the main floor. She said she watched—"

"Yes." Forsythe got to his feet. "We can get these details from Mrs. Larkin and her brother. Would it have been difficult for any of you to leave the house unobserved?"

"Nothing easier. Katherine came down, took the key for Mandalay from the table in the hall, and left with nobody the wiser. Dozens of ways to get in and out of here. Long windows you can step out of on the main floor. Two staircases. This is a big place, Mr. Forsythe, and so few people in it."

"Have you a theory on the murder?"

She pulled herself up and faced him. "When they picked up that Fred Small I thought it must have been he. But he had an unbreakable alibi. Then I remembered the old woman that Katherine had killed. I thought of her son. But the police checked him out and he was in Germany. Now, I don't know what to think. The key was returned to its exact location...I simply don't know." The close-set eyes blazed up at Forsythe. "Whoever killed Katherine should get a medal! That woman was a menace. The world is the better without her."

"I can't argue about her character or her worth." Forsythe's face was cold and so was his voice. "But Katherine St. Croix was brutally murdered and that murderer is at large. The first killing is always the easiest."

"You think that one of us did it, don't you?" Cassandra drew herself to her full height. "Dancers have *killed*. Relatives of mine were in Africa and India. In many wars they died defending their country. But Dancers don't *murder*." She turned her back. "Show yourselves out!"

Chapter Five

Miss Sanderson sprawled on the leather sofa contentedly sipping a large whiskey and soda. Forsythe had settled on a matching chair and was working on his own drink. The curtains hadn't been pulled across the narrow windows and darkness crowded up against their panes like an unwelcome visitor. "How do you like your room, Sandy? Still Tom Jones?"

"Decidedly so. I had a few qualms when I saw the bed. Huge thing you can picture Henry the Eighth bedding down in. Luckily the mattress is new. Rather wish Mr. Bantam hadn't stuck to tradition with the bathroom, tub large enough for three and a pathetic trickle of hot water. But I can't quarrel with this room. Snuggery is a good name for it. All we need is rain lashing against the window and a crackling fire on the hearth."

"Sounds more like Christmastime than July. Hungry?"

"Famished. Do you realize Cassandra Dancer didn't even offer tea?"

"From the description of Mrs. Larkin's cooking that may have been a mercy. Mr. Bantam tells me supper will be served in good time. No choice, of course."

Miss Sanderson rubbed her stomach. "Right now I could eat that boiled shoe leather Cassandra was mentioning." She sat up and slid her feet to the floor. "Ah, food!"

A chubby maid bearing a laden tray pushed open the door. Behind her Mr. Bantam balanced a smaller tray on his swelling paunch. The maid wore a wide smile and a velvet bow bobbed in frizzy fair hair directly above one eye. It looked like a blue butterfly poised for flight. Setting down the tray on a side table she laid the cloth and proceeded to arrange the dishes. Her employer contributed a coffee pot, two balloon glasses, and a squat bottle. Mr. Bantam told them jovially, "Thought you might care for a nip of brandy with your coffee, folks. How did you find the Dancers?"

"Appeared to be fine," Forsythe said.

"Townspeople are glad you're here, Mr. Forsythe. All of us are hoping you'll clear this dirty business up. Makes us look bad, you know."

Miss Sanderson's eyes widened. "How do you know why we're here?"

He chuckled, the sound rippling up from his paunch, reminding Forsythe of Willis Seton. "News travels fast in a place this size, miss. George Clark out to the Priory told our Nell all about you being invited to come out to the place. Didn't he, girl?"

Nell blushed to the roots of her frizzy hair. "George said you folks were going to find the maniac who did that girl in, sir."

"The reporters have given you a bad time?" Forsythe asked.

"Reporters and police and curiosity seekers." Mr. Bantam rubbed a hand over his gleaming skull. "Full of questions. Didn't get much from us. May not care overly for Dancers but we don't gossip to outsiders. Don't wash dirty linen in public." He nudged the maid toward the door and followed her. "Need anything else, ring. Nell will look after you. Bar keeps me hopping. Folks flooding in."

He closed the door softly and Miss Sanderson shook her head. "It's a good thing we're not working undercover Robby.

About as much privacy as a fish tank." Losing interest in the innkeeper, she inspected the contents of the covered dishes. "Roast beef and Yorkshire pudding. Dig in."

They applied themselves to generous helpings and conversation languished. Scraping up the last morsel of apple crisp, Miss Sanderson reached for the cheese board. "The missus is better than a fair to middling cook, Robby. I can see where our host gets his girth." She accepted coffee and brandy and leaned back. "I suppose tomorrow we go back to the Priory and interview the rest of the household."

Forsythe was packing his pipe bowl. "We'll have a change of pace, Sandy. Concentrate on Harper. Ring up Miss Prudence Pyne and David Proctor and don't let them put you off. If necessary be pressing."

Holding up the balloon glass, Miss Sanderson wistfully looked into its amber depths. "David Proctor is one man I really wouldn't mind pressing, Robby."

As they passed the stone lion reclining on the grass, Miss Sanderson patted its noble head. Catching her employer's eye, she jerked her head at a window. Peeking out between lace curtains a sign announced that bed and breakfast was available within. Before they reached the steps the door opened and a stout woman bounced out. "The Widow Hawkins," Miss Sanderson muttered. "Cupboard-size rooms and an outdoor W.C."

The widow wore a girlish ruffled dress, had girlish curls clustered on a round head, and had applied lavish amounts of pink lip rouge. Her voice matched her appearance, shrill and gushing and girlish. "David is waiting for you. Naughty boy, should be in his bed. Delicate chest, you see, and coming down with a cold. Nursed him through bad bouts all last winter. Come in, do come in."

They went into a tiny dark hall and the widow threw open a door to the left. "David," she cooed, "your company is here."

David didn't look ill. He sat in a spill of sunshine at a table in the curve of a bay window. The strong light was kind to his classic features and thick hair. He wore a shabby smoking jacket with a scarf at his throat. Before him was spread as lavish a breakfast as the one they had consumed at the Harper Arms. "Miss Sanderson," Proctor said and bent over Miss Sanderson's hand. "And Mr. Forsythe. Do make yourselves comfortable. Would you care..." He wafted a slender hand over the table.

"Thank you, no," Miss Sanderson simpered. Definitely simpered, Forsythe thought, and darted a look at her. Her thin face, usually so austere, was glowing.

"Rest," the widow said and pressed the young man firmly back in his chair. "I'll bring coffee for your guests. So delicate," she told Miss Sanderson as she passed her chair.

Miss Sanderson was regarding Proctor with concern. "If you're not feeling well this could have waited."

He touched his chest. "Always have bouts of bronchitis and rotten colds but Mrs. Hawkins makes rather too much of it. If I even cough she has me swaddled in flannel and mustard. Good woman though, and she's been marvelous to me."

Silently the barrister agreed. The room was large and well furnished. It smelled of furniture polish and all surfaces gleamed. Proctor followed Forsythe's eyes complacently. "That door leads to the bath and the one next to it to the bedroom. The police were most interested in the third. Leads directly to the garden. Mrs. Hawkins had this suite made up for her father and he was an independent old chap. Insisted on going and coming without tracking through the rest of the house. Police made a big thing about me being able to slip in and out unobserved."

Mrs. Hawkins, bustling back with a coffee pot and extra cups, caught the last few words. "Terrible people," she said indignantly. "Told that inspector that David is a perfect lamb. Wouldn't sneak around bashing girls' heads in. Not my David."

Proctor gave his landlady a bewitching smile and her fat face pinkened with pleasure. "You defended me nobly. For a time I thought you might bean the inspector with your skillet." He added firmly, "That's lovely, Mrs. Hawkins."

She took the hint and left them. Proctor gave a rueful laugh. "So, I'll start by telling you I have no alibi for the night of Miss St. Croix's death. I was here working. Also, when I don't wish to be disturbed I put a pink card on the door. When that card is there Mrs. Hawkins leaves me strictly alone. That night the card was on the door. However, as I told the inspector, I worked until after midnight and then went to bed."

"You remember the night clearly," Forsythe said, "yet it was over two months ago."

The young man spread marmalade lavishly on a muffin. "You must realize the following day when I went to the Priory the family was in an uproar. During the night Katherine had taken off. Rather sets the circumstances in one's mind."

"Like John Kennedy's assassination," Miss Sanderson murmured.

"Exactly. On a much smaller scale, of course."

Forsythe again darted a look at his secretary's bemused expression. Proctor appeared to have a profound effect on women. "Were you surprised that Miss St. Croix had left so unexpectedly?"

"Astounded. I knew little about the woman but she seemed to be settling in nicely with the Dancers and there had been no hint of her leaving. After her body was discovered in Mandalay and Cassandra had to tell the police about her investigation of the woman's past, the reason for her hasty departure was quite clear."

"Miss Dancer didn't let on to you what she'd discovered?"

"Didn't say a word. Cass can be closemouthed and we'd had a heated argument about Katherine a few days before. You'll want to know about my relations with the dead woman. I had a devil of a time recalling the dates when I saw her. Oh, we'd passed a number of times when I went out to play for Cass but Katherine did come in to Harper see me twice." He poured coffee and handed the cups around. "The first time was on a

Monday. The second on the following Thursday. Cass exploded when she found out about the Monday visit and that's when we quarreled. Quite frankly I thought it was *my* business and Katherine seemed to be a harmless person."

"She wanted advice on her book?"

"Katherine hadn't a clue on how to get the actual writing started. She said she was a great reader and fairly good at research, but she did need help getting her notes in order. She knew that I am a published writer—"

"Really," Miss Sanderson exclaimed, "how exciting."

"Far from exciting, dear lady. A few poems in little publications and this." He reached for a bookshelf and took down a slim volume bound in violet-colored leather. "Privately printed. Viola Dancer made the arrangements. Perhaps you'd care to borrow it and look it over."

Miss Sanderson tenderly deposited the book on her lap along with her copious handbag. Forsythe wondered if she'd had sense enough to turn on her tape or snooper as she called it. He tried to catch her eyes but she was staring at Proctor as though he were the Holy Grail. Women, Forsythe thought wrathfully. "Are you and Miss Dancer engaged?" Forsythe asked.

"Not formally. Cass would have been willing to marry a few weeks after her mother's death but I couldn't see it. Wouldn't have looked well, you know."

"But you are in love?" Miss Sanderson gushed.

"Cass is. I've been quite frank with the girl. I don't love her. She has a fine nature but she's not terribly attractive. Viola not only had a beautiful nature, but she was lovely. Considerably older than I but she had heavenly looks. Misty dark hair, great dark eyes, and a skin like...Tall and slim and elegant. I loved Viola and if she had lived..."

"Lady Dancer acted as your patron?" Forsythe asked.

"She did. We met at a poetry reading in London, not mine—I was in the audience. Viola sat down beside me and we got into a bit of a discussion about the poems. One thing led to another and afterward we went for a drink. Viola found I wrote a little poetry and asked me all about myself. Quite flattering for a young chap to have a beautiful older woman interested in him. Elegantly dressed too. Clothes that quietly shrieked money. I confessed I had a silly job selling insurance and lived in a dingy room. After that..." Proctor leaned back and crossed his legs. "She came up to see me in London several times and suggested I chuck my job and devote myself to writing full time. Viola insisted I come to her country home."

"To the Priory?"

"At the time I assumed she meant the Priory. It wasn't until I got down here that I found she'd made arrangements with Mrs. Hawkins for this place. I'll admit I was far from pleased." At the memory David Proctor looked far from pleased. His mouth, Forsythe noticed, was definitely petulant. "I also assumed Viola would be taking care of my expenses. But she paid my rent for only two months and then insisted I start giving music lessons to the country brats. She told me it would be much better for my self-esteem if I earned my own way." Sighing heavily, Proctor said, "As I have written,

> O woman! in our hours of ease,
> Uncertain, coy, and hard to please,
> And variable as the shade
> By the light quivering aspen made;..."

"That," Miss Sanderson said sharply "is not David Proctor. It's Sir Walter Scott."

Proctor looked faintly surprised. "How discerning of you."

She gave him a wicked grin. "Try this. 'I'm not denyin' women are foolish: God Almighty made 'em to match the men.'"

"I'm afraid, Miss Sanderson, I can't quite place that quote."

"George Eliot," she said smugly and moved the leather-covered book from her lap to the table at her elbow.

Ah, Forsythe thought, Sandy getting her wits about her again. He turned his attention back to the poet. "Did Lady Dancer not assist you at all?"

"Once in a while she'd give me a small gift of money. And on my birthday and at Christmas she gave me expensive presents—a wonderful watch, Patek, a gold cigarette case and trifles like that. I had them stolen from me in a hotel in London. Cass and I had driven up and I stayed over to see a publisher about a couple of poems he showed interest in. Served me right. That hotel was a sleazy hole. Mistake to stay there."

"Miss Dancer mentioned that," Forsythe told him. "That was the day she picked up the background information on Miss St. Croix."

"Cass is madly practical. Right now she insists I work on a novel. She may be right too. No money in poetry."

Miss Sanderson lifted her brows. "Money is important to you?"

"Major importance. I know all the myths about true artists preferring to starve but that's pure fiction. I've never seen any reason why art can't be produced when one is in comfortable circumstances. My marriage to Cass will take care of that. She has her own money and we'll take a nice house and..."

Miss Sanderson was looking like a thundercloud so Forsythe said hastily, "Lady Dancer was contemplating divorce at the time of her death?"

"If she'd lived she would have divorced Sir Amyas. Viola admitted she despised him. I rather like the man and he's been decent to me but they should never have married. Viola was a mere child at the time and her father bartered her off like a horse for a title. Horace Gillimede has lived to regret that. Yes, Viola and I were in love and we would have had a meaningful life. She was so sensitive, so attuned to art. There's a little poem I wrote to her in that book, Miss Sanderson. You'll enjoy it. It's called 'Violet, My Violet.' I always thought of her as a violet—shy and sweet and hiding her beauty from the eyes of the world." He rubbed his brow, pushing back the lock of hair that fell there. When he removed his hand, it promptly fell back into place. "When Carl carried his mother out of the lake my heart broke. She lay there at our feet, her hair plastered down like seaweed against her face. Horace was howling like a wolf. He was literally tearing at her sailor suit."

Bending forward, the young man buried his face in his hands. "She must have had that suit made for me. I've always been afraid of water. Had a bad experience when I was a child. Viola was just as afraid. We talked about it and decided we must overcome our weakness. Viola must have wanted to show me her courage and she knew nothing about boats…not the first thing."

Forsythe frowned. "Why was Horace Gillimede tearing at the sailor suit?"

"God knows. The old fellow is bonkers, you know." Proctor uncovered his face. "He was ranting on about it being the instrument of the devil. He kept it up and none of us knew what to do. Then the aunts arrived and Miss Sybil calmed the poor devil down. She sent Mrs. Larkin to get a dressing gown and blankets and then Miss Sybil and Miss Bella stripped off the sailor outfit and gave it to Horace. He even took the little white cap. Then he went bolting into the woods crying that he must destroy the devil's work. It was simply horrible."

"Could Lady Dancer have committed suicide?" the barrister asked.

"No! Viola adored life! It was an accident."

"You think she was planning to divorce her husband?"

" I *know* she was. On her birthday morning she phoned me. I naturally thought I would be invited for dinner but Viola said I wasn't to come. She said she wanted to dine with her family that evening. Viola assured me the next day she would have news for me. I knew she'd finally come around and decided to chuck Sir Amyas."

"Did she say so?"

"Not in so many words. But she hinted about it and she sounded so happy and relieved."

"How would her family have accepted the divorce?"

"Amyas would have been as happy as I was. He cared no more for Viola than she for him. The rest of them were dead set against it."

Miss Sanderson leaned forward. "But divorce is so common."

"Not for Dancers. For them it's a deadly sin. No Dancer has ever divorced."

"Surely Cassandra doesn't feel that way."

He smiled at Miss Sanderson. "Cass was only worried about her mother being free to marry me. She tells me she had her sights set on me from the moment we met. Kept warning me Viola would destroy my writing ability."

Making a sound suspiciously like a snort, Miss Sanderson settled back.

The barrister said, "Can you think of anything, Mr. Proctor, any small thing about Miss St. Croix that might help us?"

Bracing an elbow on the table, Proctor lowered his chin onto the back of his hand and appeared to be deep in thought. It was a graceful posture and showed off the lines of his head and face to good advantage. After a time he said slowly, "I believe I've told you all I know about her. Little things...she was easy on the eyes and had a reserved, ladylike manner. At the time I would have described her as prim, even prudish. Now that I know Katherine's past I can only say she was crafty and one hell of a good actress." He raised his head. "Sorry, that's all I can tell you."

"Have you any idea who could have killed her?"

"I'm torn two ways. On one hand I'd like to think it was that criminal element she was mixed up with. But the evidence doesn't point that way. I'm completely baffled."

Forsythe got to his feet and as he did he noticed that Miss Sanderson's hand was fumbling in her handbag. She had remembered to turn on her snooper. "Thank you, Mr. Proctor. If you should think of anything else we can be reached at the Harper Arms."

Proctor offered the barrister a hand and his secretary a bewitching smile. Forsythe accepted the hand but Miss Sanderson ignored the smile. This time as they passed the sprawling lion she didn't pat it. They walked along slowly. As they neared the corner and the ancient church Forsythe noticed that Miss Sanderson didn't even glance in its direction. Her head was bent and she appeared to be eyeing her sensible brogues as they marched over the cobblestones.

"You forgot the book of poems," he pointed out.

"So I did," she said indifferently.

"Do I detect an aura of disillusionment?"

"Disgust. A young Lord Byron!" She snorted, this time loudly.

"Because the man tried to pretend Scott's work was his own?"

"Because the man is nothing but a pretty face balanced on a monstrous ego. Robby, when he lost Viola and her marriage settlement he immediately fastened onto Cassandra and her grandfather's legacy."

"I'm inclined to think Cassandra fastened onto *him*."

"The girl must be a fool."

"I doubt that. What time will we be seeing Miss Pyne?"

"She invited us for tea. We just passed her house." Miss Sanderson turned and pointed. "That white Victorian opposite the church. Nice house and she has a nice voice." She added gloomily, "With our luck her voice will be the only nice thing about her."

Chapter Six

Not only the exterior of the house was nice but so was the parlor in which Forsythe and Miss Sanderson were comfortably seated. It was a good-sized room, filled with furniture of the Victorian era, and it was well cared for but not stiff. Over the fireplace hung a poster by Toulouse-Lautrec. It looked rather exotic among velvet swags, antimacassars and whatnots. Miss Prudence Pyne, dispensing tea and conversation from behind the tea table, was, as David Proctor would have said, pleasing to the eyes.

"Yes," she was saying, "I consider myself a newcomer to Harper. Most of the villagers' families have been here almost as long as the Dancer family. The Pyne ancestry in this village dates only back to my grandparents."

Forsythe regarded her with pleasure. Her fine skin was cobwebbed with wrinkles and the delicate hands hovering over the tea table were marred with rusty marks of age but there was something incredibly youthful about her. She wore a gray tweed skirt, a rose twin set, and sturdy shoes, but her legs were excellent and her bright blue eyes were unfaded by time. In her younger days Prudence Pyne must have been a beauty.

Miss Sanderson accepted her cup and selected a fairy cake from the tiered cake plate. "You have known the Dancer family for a long time?"

"All my life. I clearly remember Amyas's father, Sir Crawford and his wife, Dora. Sir Crawford was much like his son but Dora, although regrettably plain, had a fine mind and was an excellent businesswoman. Dora was the one who urged her husband before his death to set aside funds for his daughters and his grandchildren. I believe Dora was fond of Amyas but she knew he was hopeless when it came to money management. Amyas allows money to trickle through his fingers. I do hope his oil money is as inexhaustible as he acts."

Miss Sanderson nodded. "You've heard about the amphitheater?"

"Oh, yes. I suppose one should be glad he hasn't set his heart on a replica of the Taj Mahal."

"Or the Leaning Tower of Pisa."

Miss Pyne's eyes sparkled with mischief. "To say nothing of the Hanging Gardens of Babylon."

Forsythe gazed from one woman to the other. They were regarding each other with delight. Kindred spirits, he thought. Miss Pyne leaned toward the younger woman and asked, "Have you heard about the famous fox hunt?"

"A few details. How I wish I could have seen it!"

"I did."

"Really?"

"A balcony seat for the hunt. Literally. I was chairing a meeting of the Women's Institute and we have rooms in that large building as you enter Harper, at the foot of the high street. The windows were open and suddenly there was this perfect din. Voices holloing and horns blowing. All the ladies crowded out on the balcony in time to see Amyas leading the group of thundering nudes. Oh, my dear!" Cupping a hand over her mouth, Miss Pyne quivered with mirth.

"Do tell us," Miss Sanderson implored.

"It was the high point of my life. I didn't dare let on, of course. The other ladies were scandalized; one fainted, and I had to pretend to be shocked. But when I looked down and saw the hounds bounding along and the riders shouting tallyho…you should have seen the buttocks and breasts bouncing. And there was Amyas with a wide smile and a derby tilted over one eye, having the time of his life. It was simply marvelous!"

Miss Sanderson had collapsed into helpless laughter and Forsythe asked with a smile, "And from that moment on the Dancers were not welcome in Harper?"

"There have always been strained relationships between the village and the Priory. Dancers have scandalized the locals for centuries. At the same time I believe the people here have a perverse kind of pride in the Dancers. You may deplore them but you must admit they can't be ignored."

"How do you regard them?"

"With a great deal of affection. I discovered their secret long ago. They're simply a group of people who reach adolescence and then stay there. Their actions and reactions are those of children. I find them rather endearing people. Admittedly they try one's patience but they're never boring. I'm speaking of true Dancers, of course. Once in a while one comes along who eventually grows up. Cassandra is very young but she has her grandmother Dora's common sense and I should imagine business sense. However, Cassandra's attachment to young Mr. Proctor certainly doesn't prove my point. I'm so hoping she will change her mind about that man."

Miss Sanderson regarded her hostess approvingly. "I take it you don't like David?"

"How can one? He has quite enough liking for himself. Completely self-centered and I've always thought he would have made an excellent mate for Viola Dancer. She was his female counterpart."

"Cassandra told us her mother often came to talk with you, Miss Pyne."

"Indeed she did. All Dancers come to me—even Carleton. But Viola didn't talk *with* one, she talked *at* one. Completely absorbed and delighted with her own feelings, her own problems.

Amyas and she should never have married. In fact it would have been better if Amyas had remained a bachelor. There's simply no place in his life for either wives or children. I'm being very candid, Mr. Forsythe, but I should imagine that is what you wish."

Forsythe nodded. "It's the only thing that can help us. We know nothing about the Dancers and to get to the bottom of this tragedy we must look to the past. We must understand the people who were involved with Miss St. Croix."

Touching the short silver hair that clung to the lines of her finely shaped head, she said softly, "I understand that. The past never really dies, does it? Now, how to make you understand Viola? She was very lovely and dressed to complement her romantic beauty. But underneath she was quite different. Viola had a great thirst for power. For a time she tried to dominate her family. With Carleton she succeeded. Viola was the only mother the boy ever remembered and their relationship was far from healthy. Viola was the embodiment of Carleton's ideal woman. The boy worshiped her. But when she contemplated divorce, in his eyes, Viola fell from her pedestal."

"This seems incredible," Miss Sanderson said. "Carleton had a rock band and yet you speak of him as though he has the values of the eighteenth century."

"Strip the modern veneer from him, my dear, and you will find a man from an earlier, more romantic age. Carleton was outraged that this perfect woman could even consider leaving his father and entering into an association with a man of his own age." Miss Pyne sighed. "Viola appeared to require victims."

"Her protégés?" Forsythe asked.

"Exactly. Viola's first power play was with a young curate who was at St. Jude. His name was Hopkins and he was a nervous, moody man. Hopkins painted as a hobby, and poorly I fear, but Viola took him up and persuaded him he was on a par with Rembrandt or Van Gogh. Then, without warning, she dropped him cold. Hopkins gave up his post and went to Liverpool. I heard he fell into drink and bad company and eventually committed suicide. After that Viola had a succession of protégés. She treated them the same way. Lavished attention on them, let them fall in love with her, and then discarded them and went on to another."

"She did treat David Proctor rather shabbily," Miss Sanderson admitted.

"Yes. Viola enticed the young man down here on false pretenses. Mr. Proctor thought his future was assured and he soon found he was only a toy. Viola was rapidly losing interest in him when she discovered Cassandra was much attracted to Mr. Proctor; that revitalized her mother's interest."

"Dog in the manger?" Forsythe asked.

"Similar."

"Do you think Proctor really did love Lady Dancer?"

Miss Pyne touched her chin with a slender finger. "As much as his nature allows, I suppose he did. She was lovely, as I said, and doubtless physically appealing to the opposite sex. Cassandra, poor child, is as plain as Dora was. As soon as Viola sensed her daughter's interest in Mr. Proctor she took him up again. She talked to me at great length on her love for him, how torn she was between her duty and that love."

"Had she made up her mind to marry Proctor?"

"I'm inclined to think so. Viola was here the day before her birthday and she seemed much different. In fact she said she was through soul-searching, she was going to live her life as she wished. Yes, Mr. Forsythe, I'm positive she was going to divorce Amyas." The bright eyes caught the barrister's. "Would you like my opinion of the other members of the family?"

"Please."

"I've touched on both children. Cassandra hungers to marry Mr. Proctor and manage his career. Carleton contents himself with his button collection. In time that will pass. No doubt he will decide to row across the Atlantic or something of the sort. The Dancer sisters will continue their lives—"

"I understand they are quiet women," Miss Sanderson said.

"They live quiet lives but they are Dancers. Sybil is the elder and she completely dominates Bella. Sybil is highly intel-

ligent and Bella on the dull side. Bella's whole mental processes
revolve around cooking, cleaning, and gardening. Sybil's...well,
you'll soon discover hers." Miss Pyne darted an impish smile at
Miss Sanderson. "They were both pretty girls but Sybil had an
unfortunate love affair and never married. So, of course, neither
did Bella. Too bad. Bella would have made a wonderful wife
for a man not interested in sparkling conversation. Sybil has a
horror of modern devices. She refuses to keep a car and only had
a telephone installed at the Dower House under protest."

"They do come in to see you," Forsythe said.

"Bella comes frequently. She's tremendously athletic and
walks in to do the shopping. Generally she stops for a chat and
to deliver some of her baked goods. She's really an inspired
cook. Sybil comes once a month, on a Sunday for tea."

"Does Sybil walk in too?" Miss Sanderson asked.

"Heavens, no! An old chap who used to garden at the
Priory hitches up an equally old mare to a cart and brings Sybil
in style. I must admit I don't really look forward to these visits.
Sybil can be a trial but it has been much more pleasant since she
got rid of that dog she was convinced was her mother—"

"Now I believe you're joking," Miss Sanderson told the
older woman.

Throwing back her head, Miss Pyne laughed. "I've let the
cat out of the bag. I should have allowed you to meet Sybil and
discover this for yourself, but Sybil is obsessed with a bewil-
dering belief in reincarnation. She picked up this pup, a small
nasty mongrel with bulging eyes, and became convinced her
mother's spirit inhabited its rather smelly body. Every time Sybil
came to visit me, the dog came too. She sat it on the chair, Miss
Sanderson, that you're sitting on now and fed it cakes and tarts
and so on. Madness can be contagious. After a time I found
myself addressing the little beast as Dora."

"Sybil really *is* a Dancer," Miss Sanderson muttered.

"There's only one other person at the Priory, Horace
Gillimede. Not a Dancer by birth but he fits in marvelously
well with the family. A pathetic old fellow, driven mad by guilt

because of his wife's fall from grace and the manner of her death." Miss Pyne eyed Forsythe, his long narrow head, and his slender body in impeccable tweeds. "I think *you* will see past Horace's wild appearance and wild words, Mr. Forsythe. Most people tend to write him off as a religious fanatic but some part of his mind operates on a sane level still." She folded her hands in her lap. "I could talk for hours about the Dancer family but—"

"That's fine, Miss Pyne," Forsythe assured her. "Could you tell us what you know about Miss St. Croix?"

"She had many names, I understand. I still think of her as Katie Parr. Do you mind if I use that name?"

"Of course not."

"This part of your interview I've been dreading. I hate to even think about the woman and to talk about her…" For a moment the rose-clad shoulders sagged, but then the old woman straightened them. "There is no excuse for me having admitted that woman to my house. I've handled servants all my life and, as my mother taught me, have been most cautious about references. I'd better find a place to begin. During my parents' lifetime we had a large staff. Through the years it dwindled down to Susan, the parlor maid, and the cook, Mary. To properly look after the place this was an inadequate number of servants but with taxes and inflation my income became pitifully small.

"We made out fairly well though and lived quite happily. Then, a year ago June, Mary died suddenly in her sleep. Neither Susan nor I had ever done much cooking. Oh, we can make a salad and scramble eggs but that is about all. And a capable cook in a small place like Harper is hard to find."

Forsythe said, "I understand from the police reports that Susan was the one who brought Miss St. Croix to the house."

"She was. On her free day Susan goes to Chester for her weekly treat. She takes the four o'clock bus into the city, has supper at a café, goes to the cinema for the evening, and returns to Harper on the bus at eleven. Susan is a friend of the proprietor of the café and knows the waitresses well. They chat to her about her job and me and so on. Susan is a great talker. After Mary's death they asked her frequently whether we'd found another cook and no doubt teased Susan about her lack of culinary skills."

"And that café is where Miss St. Croix heard about you and this house?"

"It must have been. Susan can't remember seeing the woman there but Katie must have been sitting in a corner—it's a busy place—and overheard. Anyway, about the middle of July Susan went in for her treat as usual and that night she did notice a pretty girl in a corner, having coffee and reading a book. Susan chattered on about her mistress not getting a decent meal without a cook and so on. After the film Susan caught the bus back and the same girl got on it. She sat down in front of Susan and when the bus stopped in front of the Harper Arms Susan was surprised to see the girl get off. Except for locals, few travelers stop at that time of night in the village.

"The girl stood looking around as though she were lost, and Susah, who's a kindhearted soul, asked whether she needed directions. Katie Parr inquired whether there was a youth hostel in the village and Susan said no, there was only the Harper Arms and the Widow Hawkins's, but she probably could get a room in one of them. The girl told her the only reason she'd gotten off the bus was that she had no money to continue and couldn't pay for a room. Susan was distressed at the girl's plight and even more so when Katie started swaying around and clutched at her arm for support."

"Because she hadn't eaten in several days," Miss Sanderson said caustically.

"Exactly. Susan felt she couldn't leave the girl there and so she brought her home to me. I always wait up for Susan and when they arrived the girl did look sick so I sent Susan to warm up some tinned soup." Miss Pyne's lips set in a bitter line. "That was where I made my first mistake. I should have given her a little money and sent her on her way. But Katie Parr played the part of a timid, sweet orphan magnificently. I couldn't turn her out. Susan took her up to a room and I thought after breakfast the next day I'd send her on her way."

"It didn't work out that way?" Forsythe said.

"My second mistake was in letting my gluttony get in the way of common sense. I have never been a large eater, but I do relish well-cooked, attractively served food. For over a month I'd been existing on tinned food and scrambled eggs. The next morning when I arose I smelt the most heavenly odors. Katie had got up early and to earn her night's keep had cooked breakfast. You should have seen that breakfast! Waffles and bacon and sausage. Grilled tomatoes and an omelet made with apricot preserve."

"A clever woman," Miss Sanderson muttered.

"And a marvelous cook. I questioned Katie about her past. She told me she'd been a cook for a family in Birmingham until they had left the country. She said she was on her way to London to get another job but her savings were exhausted. So, without asking about references, I literally begged her to stay with us for a time. I assured her she could save her wages and then go her way. She agreed. As Horace Gillimede would say, I had opened my door to a devil.

"For a week all went well. Susan and Katie got along well and I was so happy with the meals. If I hadn't been such an idiot I would have noticed something rather odd. Katie never set foot out of this house. Part of her duties was the food shopping and she didn't refuse to do it, she merely made excuses so Susan would have to."

Forsythe jerked his head up. "Sounds as though she didn't want anyone to be able to recognize her."

"Quite. Katie must have already been planning to move in on the Dancers. She knew by that time that I seldom go to the Priory so she wasn't worried about Susan or me. But she didn't want the villagers to remember her. Strange…"

"What are you thinking?"

"Time. Katie left us in early August. In fact it was August the third. The reason I remember the date is because Viola had died two days before and then that dreadful scene with Katie Parr. Rather sticks in the mind. But, Mr. Forsythe, it wasn't until last April that Katie managed to get into the Priory. Why the delay?"

"A puzzling question, Miss Pyne. Why did the woman wait eight months before approaching the Dancer family? Was it because of Lady Dancer's death? Did Miss St. Croix not wish to disturb the family while they were in mourning?"

Miss Pyne said dryly, "I hardly credit Katie Parr with that kind of sensitivity."

"Would it be possible to ask your maid a few questions?"

The old woman hesitated and then said, "I'd really rather you didn't. Susan is such a nervous woman and she's relived the whole business since the woman's body was discovered."

"Miss Sanderson and I don't practice third degree, Miss Pyne."

"Of course you don't. How silly of me." Reaching for a silver hand bell, she tinkled it.

In moments the door of the parlor creaked open and a trimly uniformed maid took a step into the room. Susan looked sixtyish and her most outstanding features were kindly eyes behind thick glasses and a sharp pink-tipped nose. Her mouth was quivering as she said, "You want me, Miss Pru?"

"This is Miss Sanderson and Mr. Forsythe, Susan. Mr. Forsythe would like to ask you some questions about Katie."

The maid's mouth continued quivering and the pink nostrils flared like a frightened mare's. "It's all my fault!" she wailed. "I wished that awful creature on Miss Pru and the Dancer family!"

"Come now, Susan." With a light, youthful movement Prudence Pyne rose and drew the maid to a chair facing the barrister. "We've discussed that many times and it's certainly not your fault. Do sit down, silly girl, and relax."

Susan perched on the edge of the chair and regarded Forsythe with the fascination a cornered rabbit might show for a vicious dog. Forsythe gave her a reassuring smile and said gently, "I should imagine you miss Mary, Susan."

"I do. Like sisters we were." The kind eyes behind the heavy lenses misted and her mistress pressed a lace-trimmed hankie into her hand. "When our work was done Mary and me would sit in the kitchen and talk. We watched my telly every night and…"

"You must have been lonely after Mary's death. Did you find Katie Parr good company?"

The maid flinched when he said the name and Miss Pyne put a comforting hand on her shoulder. "She…she liked to hear me talk. Guess maybe I was kind of proud such a pretty girl would hang on every word I said. She didn't talk much, but I did."

"What did you talk about?"

"She wanted to hear about people in the village. Where they lived and what they did. First off she said she thought when she saw this house that the mistress must have lots of money. And I told her no, Miss Pru doesn't have much. Then we got chatting about people who still have bags of money."

"And that's when the Dancers' name came up?"

"Kind of. She never went out but we were looking out the window and I saw young Mr. Proctor who stays with the widow down the road a piece and I says, 'that's a poet and isn't he good looking.' Katie she says, 'he sure is and does he have money?' And I says, 'no, but Lady Dancer looks after him.' And Katie says…that's when I told her all about the Dancers."

"Did Katie Parr see any of the Dancer family?"

"They was always in and out. Katie never set foot out of the kitchen when folks came in but she was always peeking through the door when they was in the dining room. She seen Lady Dancer and Miss Cassandra and—" Susan peered up at her mistress. "Mr. Carleton was here too, wasn't he, Miss Pru?"

"He was. He dined with me the night that Cassandra was here. I believe Amyas was also in for tea one afternoon."

"That's right. Clean forgot about Sir Amyas. Kind of puffing myself up in front of Katie 'bout how much I knew about them."

Forsythe nodded. "You told Katie Parr about Carleton's button collection?"

"Right off. 'Bout that and his rock group. Told her about Mr. Carleton going regular to Chester for that auction. Told her everything I knew!"

The rabbit nose and mouth were quivering convulsively and the maid was twisting her apron in both hands. Miss Pyne sent the barrister an imploring look and he said mildly, "That's fine, Susan. You've answered my questions marvelously. Thank you."

The maid lurched to her feet. "All my fault, sir! Brought this down on Miss Pru and the Dancer family."

Taking her arm, Forsythe piloted her to the door. "It isn't your fault, Susan. Katie Parr was a bad person. If you hadn't told her she would have found out elsewhere. Put this whole business out of your mind."

He returned to his chair and waited until Miss Pyne had seated herself behind the tea table. She smiled at him. "I'm grateful, Mr. Forsythe. You were very good with Susan. Now you understand how the woman knew so much about the Dancers."

"Yes. The reason she provided herself with those bone buttons shaped like skulls, her knowledge about the members of the family. It's quite clear. She used your house as a listening post to see whether there were people in Harper worth her peculiar talents." His long fingers tapped the arm of his chair. "You said for a week everything went smoothly. What happened then?"

"On the Monday I heard that Viola had drowned in the China Sea. Tuesday is only a blur in my memory. Elderly people feel so helpless, when faced with a close friend's death—almost guilty, as though it should be they who died and not a younger, more vital person. I didn't intrude on the family's grief but I did write a letter of condolence and I sent flowers. All the silly useless things one does at a time like that. Katie's meals that day were as good as ever but I could hardly swallow. Wednesday I remember clearly. I wish I could forget!"

Leaning her head back, Miss Pyne closed her eyes. The color had drained from her face, leaving the wrinkled skin chalky. This is what she will look like when she is dead, Forsythe thought sadly. Without the vividly expressive eyes her face was skull-like, beautiful bones tautly covered with parchment. The bone structure was remarkably lovely and strong. He didn't prompt her and finally she said, "I will tell you everything. I didn't…I couldn't force myself to tell Inspector Fitzgerald some of this but…" Her eyelids lifted and she looked directly into the barrister's eyes. "In the morning I went out to work in the garden. I can't afford a gardener and the neglect bothers me. I was puttering around, doing some weeding, when my neighbor leaned across the fence.

"Mrs. Froud is a nice young person with three tiny children, and very busy with the wee ones. She is not a gossip and I've grown fond of her. I could see she was perturbed and uncertain but finally she said that the week before her youngest child had been ill, a stomach upset, and she'd been up and down all night with the tot. She'd glanced out the nursery window, which faces on the side of this house, and had seen Katie Parr climb out of her window, down to an attached shed, and then drop to the ground like a cat. Mrs. Froud wasn't sure of the time but my house was dark and she knew Susan and I were in bed. She also said this hadn't been the first time Katie had left that way. Mr. Froud had been working late another night and had also seen her. Mr. Froud had advised his wife to tell me about it but she had hesitated, thinking I might consider her a meddler."

Forsythe's brow wrinkled in thought. "Had you forbidden Katie to leave the house in the evenings?"

"Of course not! I'm not a jailer, Mr. Forsythe. I had told the girl to come and go as she liked, but I did ask her to let me know when she left the house after nine. One has to know where the servants are."

"What did you think?"

"I found Katie's conduct quite inexplicable. I thought perhaps she might be sneaking out to see a boy but—" Miss Pyne smiled wryly. "I returned to the house to ask for an explanation but I'm afraid I did procrastinate. The meals, you know, I hated to lose her. So instead of going to her I went to my desk, over there." Miss Pyne pointed at a highly polished rosewood desk. "On Wednesdays I always bring my household accounts up-to-date. I am meticulous, as my mother trained me; I keep account of everything spent. When the accounts were tallied I balanced the figure against the money in the cash box. This is a small wooden box used long ago for stationery. No, I can see the question trembling on your lips. It had no lock. There had never been any reason to lock up the household money. Both Mary and Susan were absolutely honest. But that day twenty pounds was missing. I checked my figures and I knew there was no possibility of a mistake."

"And that is when you questioned Katie Parr?"

"I rang for her and she came in here. Looking at the girl, so meek and mild and respectful, I simply couldn't believe she was a sneak and a thief. But I told her what Mrs. Froud had said and asked for an explanation. Her mask, I suppose you would call it that, fell away and I truly saw the woman for the first time. She was simply dreadful.

"Katie flew into a rage and I'll admit I was afraid she might attack me. She told me Susan and I were old and should be dead and that it was no fun to live in a house with a couple of corpses. She said it was her business how she left the house. Her language...I've read the words, Mr. Forsythe, and hearing them didn't shock me as much as the way she said them. As though she *thought* in that dreadful way."

Miss Pyne paused and Miss Sanderson gave an involuntary sound of sympathy. "It must have been *awful* for you."

"It was, Miss Sanderson." Miss Pyne's chin lifted. "But I am not without courage and so I told her she was also a thief and I would have to call on the police to deal with her. I told her there was money missing from my desk. Then her anger appeared to vanish. Katie said if I called in the police she would tell them she saw *Susan* taking the money. I told her Susan had been with me for almost forty years and in that time she hadn't taken a shilling. Then..."

"Yes?" Forsythe gently prompted.

"This is what I didn't tell Inspector Fitzgerald. Katie smiled and I still remember that smile. She leaned across the desk and I could feel her breath touching my face. She whispered. She said she would tell the police that Susan and I…that there was an unnatural relationship between us. That I went to Susan's room and—"

"I understand." Forsythe leaned across the table and patted a fragile, age-spotted hand.

"I felt as though this room, this house, had been covered with slime. As though Katie Parr had encased me with *filth*. I couldn't fight her. As soon as I could speak I told her to leave, to get out. To go and never let me see her face again. She went and with her she took the only pieces of my mother's jewelry I had left. A cameo brooch ringed with pearls and a garnet ring. Not valuable in terms of money but of inestimable value to me." Miss Pyne's head dropped like a silvery flower on a slender stem. "I didn't dare call the police to recover them!"

Leaning over, Miss Sanderson dug a sharp finger into the barrister's ribs but he didn't take the hint. "You've been candid with us, Miss Pyne, and I hate to bother you further but I must ask you a question. Who—"

"I know what your question is." The silvery head lifted. "The identity of the woman's murderer. Many of the villagers think it was someone from the woman's past and I would like to think that myself. But it's impossible. Whoever killed Katie Parr was no stranger to this area. The murderer was someone who knew the village and the Dancer estate, knew the Priory and the grounds, knew about Mandalay, knew the key to the temple was kept in the table in the entrance hall. That narrows it down to a member of the Dancer family or someone who visited the house frequently. The Dancers don't have many locals in the house. There are delivery people, of course, but they go to the tradesmen's door and don't enter the house. Doctor Beam and the vicar are there once in a while. Doctor Beam plays chess with Amyas and the vicar loves to argue with Horace Gillimede. Says it keeps him on his toes. But the night that Katie Parr was killed

Doctor Beam was in Scotland visiting relatives. As for the vicar I can hardly picture a man of nearly ninety being that active and, of course, his nature goes against it."

"You've narrowed the suspects down, Miss Pyne."

"Yes. At the Priory are Amyas, the two children, Horace Gillimede, Sybil and Bella, and the servants. In Harper there are Mr. Proctor and myself. You will want to know my movements that Sunday evening. I attended the service at St. Jude, returned here at nine, and spent the rest of the evening reading. I have trouble sleeping and frequently go for long walks, hoping my sleep will be sounder. Susan, as soon as dinner was over and the kitchen straightened, went directly to her room to watch her television as she does every night."

"Did you walk that evening, Miss Pyne?"

"That night, Mr. Forsythe, I slept soundly. A better sleep than I'd had in months."

Miss Sanderson was prodding him again and this time Forsythe got to his feet. Miss Pyne rose with her light grace. "Two more questions and then we'll leave, Miss Pyne. When did you discover that Katie Parr and Katherine St. Croix were the same woman?"

"After the discovery of her body in the crypt a police constable came to my door. He had a picture of Katherine St. Croix. I told him she had worked for me as a cook for not quite a fortnight last year. Then Inspector Fitzgerald, who seemed a pleasant man, came and I told him most of what I've told you."

"And you had never connected Katie Parr and the woman Amyas had employed to write the family book?"

"I had only heard about Katherine St. Croix. Carleton and Cassandra and Amyas had mentioned a girl had worked at a library and was at the Priory. All any of them said was that she was quite nice looking and seemed intelligent. There was certainly no reason to suspect it was my former cook."

Forsythe looked down at the elderly woman searchingly. "Why did you tell us the detail you had concealed from the police?"

"That's the third question, Mr. Forsythe. But I will answer it." She circled the table and stood at his side. One hand touched his sleeve. "I would urge you and Miss Sanderson to leave Harper and go back to your own lives. Let it go, Mr. Forsythe, let it go."

"The woman was murdered, Miss Pyne. Brutally murdered."

"Executed. There is a difference. Think of her past, Mr. Forsythe. Think of her victims. Think of the people like myself who welcomed her into their homes. Consider the way Katie Parr used decency and kindness against them. She used good instincts as weapons. I am *glad* she's dead. I am *happy* Katie Parr will never find another victim. She came into my house and she violated it. Katie Parr *violated* me."

Once outside Miss Pyne's house Miss Sanderson set off at a rapid pace. Even with the advantage of longer legs Forsythe had difficulty overtaking her. He managed to catch up with her as she passed the stone lion in front of the Widow Hawkins's. "Sandy," he panted, "you're going the wrong way."

Her low-heeled shoes hit the dirt road and tiny spurts of dust puffed up. "No, I'm not." She stopped abruptly and pointed. "Robby, there are the gates of the Priory. Not far from Miss Pyne's house."

"Not far."

"She said she walked at night. She said she didn't sleep well. When you asked Miss Pyne if she'd walked the night of Katherine St. Croix's murder she was evasive."

"She was indeed. She merely said she slept soundly."

His secretary's slender shoulders sagged. "Robby, could she have walked that night? Could she have walked to the Priory grounds? Could she have seen Katherine heading toward Mandalay and followed her? Could she have seen that woman *violating* the crypt?"

"To all your questions there is only one answer. Yes, she could have." He put an arm around the sagging shoulders and Miss Sanderson turned and buried her face against his shoulder. "Sandy, tell me what you're thinking."

"Let's drop this." Her voice was muffled. "Let's go back to London."

"I'll put you on a bus this evening. You go back."

"Not you?"

"I *have* to stay."

"Then we both do." Pulling away, Miss Sanderson kicked a rock and sent it careening into a hedge. "I like her, Robby. Miss Pyne is the kind of woman you'd like to have as a mother. She reminds me of an aunt I loved dearly. At times like this I *hate* what we do. Poking and prying!"

"I know." Forsythe's expression was somber. "Perhaps, Sandy, this is our destiny. If it is, we're quite powerless."

"Oh, hell!" Miss Sanderson wheeled and strode toward the high street.

Chapter Seven

"Since I have been very young I have believed in the force of destiny," Miss Sybil Dancer said firmly. "No matter how an individual strives, one is condemned to complete a certain pattern. We have no control over our fate."

"All roads lead to Samaria," Robert Forsythe murmured.

"*Precisely.* I seldom take to strangers but the moment I glimpsed you on my doorstep I said, yes, Sybil, here is a Seeing Soul. I had a fantastic flash of precognition. You and I, Mr. Forsythe, in another life achieved a oneness. Do you feel this way, too?"

While Forsythe groped for words his secretary eyed the woman who was claiming a oneness with him. An unlikely pair, Miss Sanderson thought. Amyas Dancer's older sister was tall and possibly possessed a wiry build. Her figure could only be guessed at. From neck to heels the woman was swathed in a black satin garment resembling a tent. Her small head was covered by a black and yellow striped turban and one claw-like hand made great play with a silk fan. Against its black background the signs of the Zodiac were brilliantly detailed in yellow. She had a long scrawny neck and black beady eyes. Any beauty she had possessed as a girl had long since fled.

Instead of answering Sybil's question Forsythe countered with one of his own. "You feel we are not accountable for our own actions, Miss Sybil?"

"Of course we aren't! We merely play out our roles and then go on to another in yet another life. Wearying, but that is destiny. Ah, here is my sister. Bella, we're scarcely up from the lunch table and you are pressing food upon us."

Bella pushed the tea wagon into the prim little parlor of the Dower House and proceeded to unload it. Compared with her exotic sister, Bella looked prosaic. She had a build much like her brother—short and wide and muscular. She wore faded jeans, a cotton shirt, and Adidas sneakers. Graying hair fell in a single plait down her broad back. Both sisters had the handsome high-bridged Dancer nose. "I thought our visitors would welcome a snack after the walk from Harper, Sis."

Sybil waved the fan. "Only an excuse for you to stuff yourself. I'd swear if you didn't work as hard as you do you would be so heavy you would have to be trundled in a wheelbarrow." Turning back to Forsythe, she declared, "I eat like a bird, Mr. Forsythe. Do we share appetites, too?"

Forsythe was helping himself to hot cheese puffs and merely shook his head. His secretary, who had lunched on toast and coffee, helped herself liberally. Bella beamed at her and pushed a plate of butter tarts closer.

"Our mother was a smelly bitch," Sybil said flatly.

Miss Sanderson nearly dropped her cup and Forsythe gulped. "Sis means," Bella explained, "she thinks Mother's spirit came back in a dog."

"It did. You remarked on the resemblance yourself."

"I did not! It was a bad-tempered thing and snapped at me and made messes on the carpet. Mother never bit me or made messes—"

"Don't be obtuse. A dog is a dog even if a former soul does inhabit it."

Miss Sanderson carefully set her cup down. "Do you still have the dog?"

"No," Sybil told her. "She got old and quite smelly and I had her put down. Now, Mr. Forsythe, I was explaining my theories—"

"Dangerous ones. If what you think is true none of us are responsible for our own actions. Does that include murder?"

"It would have to. Let's consider it this way. Some are born to be victims, others born to be aggressors. The aggressors prey upon the victims."

"In that case, where do you place Katherine St. Croix?"

"Aha!" Cocking her head, Sybil winked a bright eye. "There *is* a oneness! You and I were once owls. I was your mate, of course. The wisdom carries over. Now, your shrewd question. Katherine was both. For a time she was an aggressor; then another stronger aggressor came along and made her the victim. It was nice to hear she was dead but we're not rid of her. Katherine is now a serpent and crawls upon her belly." Snapping her fan closed, Sybil aimed it at her sister. "If you see a snake in the woods or the garden, Bella, you must kill it."

"I couldn't, Sis."

"Then you may find Katherine in your bed. Silly girl!"

Forsythe darted a look of sheer frustration at his secretary, who grinned back. "How well did you know Miss St. Croix?"

"Hardly at all. Bella picked up pieces of gossip about the woman from Mrs. Larkin. I never set foot in my brother's house but Bella sneaks into the kitchen to take them casseroles and pies and cakes. I've told you over and over not to go to the Priory and not to waste our food on that brother of ours."

Bella flushed. "Not just Amyas I'm thinking of, Sis. There's Cassie and Carl. Mrs. Larkin is not a good cook, you know."

"Mrs. Larkin is a *terrible* cook. And an awful housekeeper. Just what Amyas deserves. He's such a fool. Keeping a servant around who spends all her time painting her nails."

"The house looks awful, Sis—floors not washed and dust all over the place."

"Good! A pigsty for a pig. Yes, Bella, in his next incarnation Amyas will be either a pig or a jackass. I can't decide which."

"Miss Sybil," Forsythe said. "Cassandra tells us you moved out of the Priory shortly before the death of your sister-in-law."

"Indeed we did. Divorce, Mr. Forsythe. Amyas had been trying to persuade my sister-in-law to divorce him for years. He said they weren't happy, but I assure you neither Amyas nor Viola would have been happy with anyone else. As I told him, why not stay together and not ruin two houses. I've never liked Amyas and I couldn't bear Viola but—"

"I liked Viola," Bella said timidly. "She was so pretty."

"Your taste is strictly in your mouth. Mr. Forsythe, if Jack the Ripper came to the door my sister would not only serve him tea and biscuits but offer to sharpen his knife."

"The quarrel with your brother," Forsythe reminded.

"The last straw was when I heard my brother bribing Viola to set him free. He offered her any amount she wanted if she would divorce him. I was outraged. Never, in any incarnation, have Dancers divorced. I beseeched him to change his mind and he told me to mind my own business. I told him I could no longer stay under his roof, so Bella and I came here. Since that moment I have not spoken a word to him. Viola dropped in once in a while and I could tell Amyas and that Proctor man were swaying her. I urged her to remember her vows and her duty but she refused to listen and that is why she died."

"Why did she die?" asked a bewildered Miss Sanderson.

"Destiny. Viola was destined to remain my brother's wife. When she tried to forsake her sacred vows, fate struck her down. The night of her birthday dinner I knew she was to die. Bella and I had been invited but—"

"I *wanted* to go, Sis."

"Hold your tongue. You jabber incessantly. After dinner, Mr. Forsythe, Viola came to this house attired in a ridiculous costume. A sailor suit! I took one look and told her she resembled Popeye the Sailor and she got quite haughty. I asked her whether she had decided to divorce and she told me she intended to do what *she* wished. I warned her. I said, 'Viola, that way lies destruction.' She laughed at me. I told her she was a foolish vain creature and would come back to this world as a peacock—"

"Peahen, Sis. A female is always called—"

"Peacock, Bella. Spreading her tail and looking for admiration. David Proctor will be a peacock also. Egotistical chap."

Forsythe was rubbing his brow. "And fate struck Lady Dancer down."

"The moment that Carl came running over to tell us his mother's bed hadn't been slept in and they couldn't find her I knew she was dead. Bella insisted on joining the searchers and I like a nice stroll so I went along. We were looking in the woods when we heard Horace shouting from the direction of the China Sea. We got down there just in time to see Carl dragging Viola's body out of the water. The boy had stripped right down to his undershorts and was shivering. I told him to get some clothes on and then I had to look after Horace. The poor man was going berserk and no one could understand what he wanted. It was that sailor outfit. Horace didn't want his daughter to meet her Maker in that garb. I had Mrs. Larkin hold blankets and Bella and I disrobed Viola and put her into a dressing gown. When Horace got the sailor clothes he was content and ran into the woods to hide them." Sybil paused to catch her breath and then said graciously, "In a matter of days, Mr. Forsythe, it will be a year since Viola's death. You must come to the celebration Horace is planning—"

"Celebration," Forsythe echoed weakly.

"Call it a memorial service. It sounds like fun. Horace is planning on having all of us throw flowers into the lake— he can't buy them because he has no money, but I believe Cassandra is providing them—and there'll be music and that sort of thing. He's holding it rather late unfortunately. Viola was over here shortly after ten and we assume she must have drowned soon after she left, so Horace has set the time at midnight. Do come!" She added offhandedly, "You may bring your secretary if you wish."

"Thanks a heap," Miss Sanderson mumbled.

"You're quite welcome," Sybil told her politely and then proceeded to ignore her again. "I suppose, Mr. Forsythe, you would like to hear about Katherine St. Croix."

Forsythe breathed an audible sigh of relief. "That is why Miss Sanderson and I are here."

"I think in your next incarnation you will be a...yes, a bloodhound. I shall be a hummingbird, darting around from flower to flower. We may meet."

"We may. Miss Sybil, Katherine St. Croix."

"An unpleasant creature. As I said Mrs. Larkin gossiped on and on to Bella about the woman. Told her Katherine was making a dead set for Amyas. I rather wish he *had* married the woman. Serve him right. But then Katherine had the audacity to come here. Pretended she wanted to know if I had mementos from the family that she could look at. As a matter of fact I have a trunk in the attic simply stuffed with letters and photographs, but I wouldn't let her see them. I took one look at her and saw she had a bad aura—her head was ringed with black—and I thought, if you were in my house, my girl, I'd lock up the silver."

"What day was she here?" Forsythe asked.

"I've no idea. Bella?"

"It was Wednesday, Sis. I always walk into Harper on Wednesdays to pick up the meat and groceries and when I got back—"

"That's correct. You got home just as I was admitting Katherine. I sent you to the kitchen to put the food away and brought the woman in here. I didn't waste any time with her. I told her if my brother was mad enough to let a person of her type into his house that was his business, but I wouldn't have her in mine. Then I showed her the door. She didn't come back."

Bella, who had been stuffing cheese puffs into her mouth, sputtered and her sister said sharply, "Don't talk with your mouth full and do wipe the crumbs off your chin. Now, what are you trying to say?"

Bella swallowed, wiped off her chin, and blurted, "That wasn't all, Sis. Katherine asked you a lot of questions. She wanted to know when Cassie had gotten back from the States and where her commune was located. She asked when David Proctor had come to Harper and where he'd lived before that. Then she asked about Horace's wife, when she died and how. She asked you why Carl hadn't continued with his rock group and—"

"That's right," her sister interrupted. "I'll admit I forgot that."

Forsythe was frowning. "Did you answer these questions?"

The turban shook violently. "I told the woman if she wanted questions answered she could go elsewhere. I assured her my brother might be hoodwinked into thinking that butter wouldn't melt in her mouth, but I could see her for what she was. By the time she left she was so angry her aura had turned to deep red and—" Stopping abruptly, Sybil wheeled on her sister, snapped the fan shut, and struck Bella's wrist sharply. "How do you know what we said? You were in the kitchen all the time she was here."

"I was listening at the door, Sis. That's the only way I find anything out."

"Sneaky, nasty, and sly. Full of too much curiosity. Arabella Dancer, in your next life you will be an alley cat. You'll be cold and bony and find your food in rubbish bins!"

Bella cowered back and tugged abstractedly at her braid. "Don't say that, Sis. Please!"

Miss Sanderson took pity. She patted the older woman's broad shoulder. "I'm sure you'll be a house cat, Miss Bella. Much loved and you'll sleep on a pillow and drink cream."

"An alley cat!" Sybil divided a hostile glance between her sister and Miss Sanderson. The beady eyes shifted to Forsythe and she gave him a sweet smile. "Any further questions, Mr. Forsythe?"

Thankfully he got to his feet. "That about covers it. Thank you. Oh, could you direct us to the ruins? We'd like to meet Horace Gillimede."

In a rustle of satin, Sybil came to her feet. "You could circle the woods, but that's a long walk. There's a shortcut through the woods. Better take that."

"Sis, the woods are full of bogs and sinkholes." Bella gave Miss Sanderson a shy smile. "I'm taking some goodies over to Horace. I'll show you the way."

Sybil sighed heavily. "More food for Horace. Oh well, I don't mind. He's not a bad old chap. Bella not only cooks things for him but plants a kitchen garden twice the size we need so Horace can steal from it. I won't have him in the house though. He smells even worse than Mother did."

"She means the dog," Bella confided.

"They know whom I mean. Run along, Bella, and get your basket and don't go near the Priory. Be sure to take good care of Mr. Forsythe. I shouldn't want him to meet his end in a bog." Putting a possessive hand on Forsythe's arm, she led him to the door. Miss Sanderson trailed along behind. "Drop in any time, Mr. Forsythe. It's so pleasant to meet another Seeing Soul. If we don't meet again in this life we certainly will in another."

They stopped to wait for their guide and Miss Sanderson glanced back at the stone cottage. "Seems you're at the top of the Seeing Souls' hit parade, Robby."

"Rather looks that way."

"Miss Sybil wouldn't give a hoot whether *I* fell into a bog."

"Your aura must not be right."

"Did you notice she left me out of her predictions? I wonder what I will be in my next life?"

He stroked his chin. "Lets see…"

"Perhaps a butterfly?"

"Doesn't seem to fit. You have a remarkable memory. Sandy, how would you like to be an elephant?"

"How would you like a smack across the mouth?"

"Temper! Your aura is turning red."

"And yours—Here's Bella."

Bella had donned a wide-brimmed straw hat and carried baskets over both arms. "Keep right behind me," she ordered, and plunged into the woods.

Abigail Sanderson and Robert Forsythe plunged in behind her.

Chapter Eight

Bella Dancer was the first to trot out of the shadows of the trees into the sunlit glade. She pulled to a stop and her companions slowly came into view behind her. Miss Sanderson paused to catch her breath. "Robby, it would seem all Dancers either race through tangled underbrush or clamber up flights of stairs." She detached several dried leaves from her hair and pulled a burr from her linen skirt.

He mopped at a hot brow. "They do seem to move like locomotives. Pleasant spot."

The glade where the ruin of the Priory was located was sylvan. Parts of the building still stood and around them gray stones were scattered as if a giant child had petulantly knocked over a stack of blocks. Vines coiled around the stones and wild flowers grew profusely up through the turf. Bella strolled back toward them and held out a wicker basket to Forsythe. It was covered with a linen cloth. "Give this to Horace. He'll be around somewhere. I must take this other one over to Mrs. Larkin."

Smoothing back her rumpled gray hair, Miss Sanderson said, "Your sister said you weren't to go to the Priory."

"What Sis doesn't know won't hurt her." Bella straightened the straw hat and tugged at her braid. "Miss Sanderson..."

"Yes."

Bella's wide mouth moved convulsively and then she blurted, "Cats *eat* birds!"

Clutching the basket destined for Mrs. Larkin, Bella fled back into the woods. Looking after her, Miss Sanderson said solemnly, "Indeed they do."

"Let's beard the goat in his lair."

"I hardly think goats live in lairs, Robby."

They walked slowly toward the ruins. As they drew closer they could see that one block, overgrown with vines, had an iron stovepipe sticking rakishly from a tin roof. The only opening, a low doorway, was covered with what looked like burlap sacking. As they approached the sack was thrust aside and a tall man emerged, bending his head to clear the lintel. Miss Sanderson stopped abruptly and gripped her companion's arm. "Robby." She moaned.

"He's not the man we saw in Bury-Sutton. Take a closer look, Sandy."

She took a closer look and then gave a deep sigh of relief. "No, he isn't. He's taller and his shoulders are wider. But at first glance he..." She gave a shaky laugh. "I'm acting like a fool. I had a nightmare, you know. We were sitting in that church and staring at that coffin covered with orchids and that bearded man was howling like a wolf outside and..."

"It's over, Sandy. Come."

They walked to meet Horace Gillimede. As they drew closer Forsythe realized what a size the man was. He towered over both of them; his shoulders were immensely wide, his chest the size and shape of a barrel. He wore a single garment, obviously made of burlap sacks, reaching to his knees. A chunk of rope girded it and he was shod in leather sandals with thongs laced to his calves. Long matted hair fell to his shoulders and an equally matted beard touched the rope at his waist. His voice was deep, rich, and clear. "You come looking for a killer and you have found one."

"We come looking for Horace Gillimede," Forsythe told him.

"And a killer. My son-in-law told me of you. I know who you are and whence you came." He darted a look at the wicker basket.

Forsythe proffered it. "Miss Bella sent this for you."

"A good woman. Come into my humble abode and I will give you refreshment."

Miss Sanderson shook her head violently and Forsythe, who had also caught the stench wafting from the old man, said hastily, "Too nice a day to be inside. And we had rather a lot of refreshment at the Misses Dancer, Mr. Gillimede."

"You must call me Horace. I do not use titles. What are your given names?"

Forsythe told him and the man bobbed his unkempt head. "Abigail and Robert. We will sit over here. There is some shade."

The spot he indicated was not only in the shade cast by a tall crumbling wall but also had three widely spaced flat stones. Miss Sanderson selected the stone farthest from their host and perched on it. Looking from one to the other, Horace repeated, "You have found a *killer*."

"I don't think you're confessing to the murder of Katherine St. Croix."

"No. I speak of my wife who was wayward and fell into mortal sin. Her sins I shouldered, as I should have had thought more of her, but instead spent my days grubbing for the Devil's tool—money. I drove my erring wife and her lover from my house and they perished. Even this—" He waved a huge hand. "This is too good for me. I am the lowest of the low. But the good Lord is merciful and He allows me to atone."

Piercing gray eyes moved from Forsythe to his secretary. "I came, after I had rid myself of the Devil's tool, to watch over my daughter. Viola was a lamb washed by God, and for a time she was sinless. Then she fell into the sins of the flesh and was tempted by another man. She sought to forsake her vows and commit adultery. But, as I said, the good Lord is merciful and He reached down and plucked her up to His bosom while still her soul was pure."

"Lady Dancer drowned," Miss Sanderson murmured.

"The waves rolled over her. When we searched for Viola I went immediately to the lake. I knew it was there I would find my child." Horace stared down at his knotted fists and his voice changed. "She was always afraid of water. When she was a tiny child I tried to rid her of that fear. I'd take her into the pool and tell her, 'darling, there is nothing to be afraid of.' Viola would cling to me and scream. She was such a pretty little thing and she grew into a beautiful woman. How terrified she must have been when she died. Daddy wasn't there to save her. I feel…I feel she must have called out to me. I dived into the lake to find her but it was Carleton who touched her arm and drew her out on the bank. She wore the same blasphemous clothes she had worn the evening before. Trousers! In all her life Viola had never worn trousers. I never cared for them and when Viola was small and begged for the overalls her playmates wore, I wouldn't allow them. I'd tell my wife, dress my daughter as a *girl*."

"The sailor outfit upset you?" Forsythe asked.

"I couldn't bear to see her in it, Robert. Of all the people gathered around my daughter's body only Sybil understood. She clothed my child in a robe and gave those Devil's garments to me."

"What did you do with them?"

"Cut them into pieces and burned them. There." He jerked his head toward the stone hut. "I've made a petrol drum into a rude stove and I consigned them to its flames. Then I spoke of them no more. But I tell you now, as the Lord may direct your search. You look for the hand that slew Katherine St. Croix."

"We do. Can you help us?"

"The woman sought me out. First she spoke of the Dancer history, but I could tell her little. She asked about the family, but I had no answers. Time and tide make little difference to me. I have forsaken the world. My granddaughter came to me and warned me against the woman, but I told Cassandra the woman had asked me to wrestle the devil in her soul. I could not turn her away."

Miss Sanderson was looking rather helplessly at her employer and finally he said, "Do you remember the questions Miss St. Croix asked?"

Under the tangled hair the broad and rather noble brow furrowed. "I cannot. They were questions of a temporal nature and as such held no interest. I would answer if I could. I can tell you little about the woman. She was fair to look upon, but we mustn't let beauty blind us. Jezebel and Delilah were also fair."

The old man fell silent, perhaps considering the danger of feminine beauty. "There was evil in the woman but some good. She confessed she was a sinner but said she had taken to sin because she was an orphan and had been raised in poverty. The woman said she might find her salvation here." He lifted his head and a gleam of shrewdness crossed his massive features. "I have not quite lost all connection with the world and I knew what she was hinting at. She had hoped to become my son-in-law's wife. I warned Katherine that Amyas is a man without sensitivity or consideration. I told her I had given Viola in her tender youth into this man's hands and he had cast her aside for scarlet women. I recounted my own sins and she commiserated with me. There were tears in her eyes as we spoke of my poor dead wife and she told me she understood why the shock had been so great when my daughter went to her judgment clad in men's attire. She begged me to intercede on her behalf with my granddaughter as she felt Cassandra was against her." The huge shoulders moved. "I can tell you no more."

Forsythe shifted on the rock. "Do you remember the night of Miss St. Croix's death?"

"As I have told you time is not important to me. I live, I forage in the woods for my sustenance. The Lord provides mushrooms and berries and roots. I eat neither the flesh of animal nor fowl nor fish. I cut dead trees to provide fuel for my stove and I walk the land and look upon the miracles the Lord has created for man."

"Could you have been walking the night that she died?"

"I walk every night, Robert, upon the fields and through the woods. I roam along the banks of the lake and sometimes when the night is windy I hear my daughter calling to me. 'Daddy,' Viola calls, 'Daddy, save me!' " A hand wrenched violently at his hair as though he would pull it from his scalp. Miss Sanderson made an involuntary sound and his hand fell away. He gave her a reassuring smile of great sweetness. "Be calm, my child. I have frightened you. It's only that memory tears at my heart. The evening of Viola's birthday I was severe with her. I did not speak of her costume while we were at the table. I ate nothing as I have sworn never to let food from my son-in-law's table pass my lips. But I watched my daughter, flaunting her body, and I thought, my wayward lamb, you go the way your mother trod before you. After the dinner, when I walked with her over to the Dower House, I reasoned with her and Viola laughed and called me foolish. She reminded me I had put her into Amyas's hands and I could not refute this. She reminded me she had been only seventeen at that time but now she was old enough to make her own decisions. Always when we parted she kissed my cheek. This night she did not. Viola was hot with anger and flew from my side and entered the house where I could not follow. So I walked the land and prayed for her soul."

Forsythe looked at his bowed head and got slowly to his feet. Miss Sanderson shut off her snooper and followed his example. "Thank you, Horace," the barrister said gently. "Can you direct us back to the road?"

"Please, not through the woods," Miss Sanderson said.

"I will take you." Horace pulled himself to his feet. "You must watch your footing. The land is rough."

Horace not only smelled remarkably like a goat but he moved like one, fairly bounding over the turf. At a slower pace, the other two followed. "The poor old fellow," Miss Sanderson muttered. "But a complete waste of our time."

"Looks that way. But one never knows. Tired?"

"Exhausted. I wish now I'd let you bring the car." She looked up at him. "We're not doing any more interviews today I hope."

"Nary a one. Too late. The sun is going down."

"I'll be heartily glad to get back to the snuggery and a cold glass of brew."

They walked on. The land dipped and they lost sight of their guide's prancing figure. As they climbed the other sloping side Miss Sanderson stumbled and swore heartily. Forsythe grabbed her arm. "Careful, Sandy. Holes all over the place."

"And I just stepped into one and twisted my ankle. Thank God, there's the road."

"And the gateposts. Ah, Horace is bidding us goodbye."

He stopped, turned back toward them, and raised a bare arm. Sunset cast a golden glow over his beard and face. "Your road lies that way. God go with you!"

"He'll have to." Miss Sanderson stooped to rub her ankle. "Robby, I don't think I can walk any farther. My ankle hurts like hell!"

He sank to a knee and touched her leg gently. "You've done a job on it. Swelling up like a balloon. Lean on me."

She hobbled along, leaning heavily on his arm. When they reached the ditch she sank down with a groan. "Sorry, Robby, guess this is as far as I go."

He looked around. "I don't like to leave you here, Sandy."

"You'll have to. Go and get the car. I'll be fine."

He didn't argue and simply strode off down the road. She shivered and buttoned up her jacket. The air was becoming fresh and the breeze was cool. Long shadows fell over her from the hedgerow. Exercise! she thought wrathfully. Not only did her ankle ache but so did her head. Wearily she pillowed her face on her arms. Then she started and jerked her head up. A shadow not from the hedgerow darkened her face.

"What in hell are you doing down there?"

She recognized the voice and said sharply, "Why did you sneak up like that, Mr. Proctor?"

"Sorry. Didn't mean to give you a start. I saw this huddled thing by the hedge and thought it might be an animal."

"A wounded animal. Twisted my ruddy ankle and Robby's gone for the car. Where's your bike?"

"Old Faithful blew another tire and I had to walk out here today. Flaming nuisance, that bike. I'll be glad when I have a car."

"Perhaps Cassandra will give you one for a wedding present," Miss Sanderson said tartly.

"You must be psychic. That's what she promised." Proctor added smugly, "A Jaguar, to be exact."

"Quite suitable."

"Yes. Like me to hang around until Mr. Forsythe gets back?"

No time for false pride, she thought. She didn't like the man but any company was better than sitting helplessly in the dark. She gestured hospitably, "Draw up a chair."

He sank lithely down at her side and touched her swollen ankle. "Hurt?"

She winced. "You could say so."

"Detecting can be dangerous work. How is the investigation coming?"

"No idea. Robby's the brain; I'm only the hired help."

He flipped back the lock of hair from his brow. "You forgot the book of poems yesterday."

"Completely."

"I have it here. Was going to drop it off at the inn tonight." He tugged the thin book out of a gray flannel pocket and gave it to her with a charming smile. "Tell me what you think of my work."

She nodded and tucked it into her handbag. "Our charger arrives. Care for a lift?"

"Delighted. I'll return the compliment when I get my Jaguar."

"Will that be soon?"

"Hopefully. Cass proposed again today and I accepted."
He added righteously, "In a few days Viola will have been dead
for a year."

The headlights from the Rover glared in their faces,
blinding them. With the young man's assistance Forsythe lifted
his secretary into the car. With Proctor in the back seat they
headed back toward Harper.

Chapter Nine

Forsythe pulled the Rover up in front of the Widow Hawkins's narrow brick house and deposited David Proctor. Proctor stuck his head in the window. "If you need any help with Miss Sanderson..."

"Everything in hand," Forsythe told him.

"I'll bet," Miss Sanderson said glumly as they rolled past Miss Pyne's house and made the turn beside the church. "I'll never be able to get up those steep stairs."

"Wait and see."

At the Harper Arms she found a cluster of people waiting. Matthew Bantam, flanked by two husky barmaids, came to meet them, followed by old Bob hobbling along on a stout cane. Mr. Bantam gave orders like a top sergeant. "Annie, you get back to the bar. Nell, come along with us. Bob, get out of the way. Now, Mr. Forsythe, we'll make a seat with our hands. That's the way. Up we go, Miss Sanderson. Bob, let go of the lass's leg!"

Perching comfortably astride Bantam's balloon of a stomach, Miss Sanderson was borne up to the first floor and deposited on her bed. Disregarding the landlord's orders old

Bob peered in from the doorway. "Out you go, Bob! You come along too, Mr. Forsythe. Nell can get Miss Sanderson ready for the doctor, can't you, girl?"

"That I can, sir. Stripped down my mum many the time when she was blind drunk."

"I," Miss Sanderson announced with what dignity she could muster, "am not blind drunk."

Shooing the barrister and old Bob before him, Bantam made a stately departure. As soon as Miss Sanderson had been completely stripped and clad in pajamas, pillows piled behind her shoulders and under her injured leg, the doctor came into the room. He was a young man with bristling red hair and an ill-tempered expression. "Let's have a look," he grunted, and proceeded to pull and tug at the injured leg. Miss Sanderson bit down hard on her lower lip and tears of pain sprang to her eyes. Dropping the leg back on the pillow, he straightened, fished in his bag, and slapped down a vial of white capsules. "You're lucky. No bones broken. Nell, get some towels and ice and apply cold compresses. When the swelling goes down I'll put an elastic bandage on it. Get two of these pills into Miss..."

"Sanderson," Forsythe supplied. He'd returned and was leaning against the door frame.

"Two pills every four hours." He glared down at the patient. "Stay off that leg for at least forty-eight hours—"

"I can't," Miss Sanderson wailed. "I've work to do."

"Forty-eight hours now or a couple of weeks later if you put weight on that sprain. Suit yourself. Makes no difference to me." Snapping the bag shut, he shoved past Forsythe.

"Well!" Color flared in the secretary's face. "Fine bedside manner!"

Forsythe grinned. "Doctor Beam knows his business and that's the main thing. Follow doctor's orders and I'll bring supper up and we'll dine together."

The pills and the cold compresses helped and by the time Forsythe reappeared with a loaded tray Miss Sanderson was in a better mood. The barrister noticed the mishap hadn't dimin-

ished her appetite. Only after she had finished did she comment
on the daisies stuck into a jar on the tray. "Your contribution?"

"Old Bob's. Probably a thank you for the neat feeling up
he gave your leg."

She laughed. "He's an opportunist, right enough. But,
Robby, stuck here for two days while you race around interviewing? How will you get along without the snooper? You can't
carry the handbag and thrust it at people."

"It would look a trifle odd. I'll have to play it by ear, Sandy,
and trust to memory,"

She snorted. "Lots of luck! But there's only Mrs. Larkin
and George left."

"I'm not looking forward to either of them. I've a hunch
they won't prove to be my favorite people." Forsythe sighed.
"Tomorrow afternoon I'll tackle them."

"Cheer up," she told him. "They can't possibly be worse
than the Dancers."

The next day proved to be the hottest and the sultriest thus
far that season. Forsythe settled for casual slacks and an open-
necked shirt. When he pulled the Rover to a stop before the
Priory he took a moment to roll his shirt sleeves above the
elbows. As he stepped out into the heat he spotted one of the
people he wanted to interview close at hand. George was lazily
and ineffectually scything tall grass near the drive. Mouse-
colored hair fell forward over a low brow and his face glistened
with sweat. He stopped his desultory motion, wiped a shirt
sleeve across his face, and stared. In the snake-like throat the
lump of Adam's apple bobbed unpleasantly.

"I want to talk with you," Forsythe said curtly and waded
through the grass toward him.

"And I know why. Sir Amyas told me to tell you what I told
the police a dozen times. Here goes." He leaned on the scythe and
spoke rapidly. "Didn't see the St. Croix woman arrive and didn't

see her leave. Got no alibi the night she was done in. Was driving around in my sister's car and didn't stop no place. No use checking for a police record. Only black mark against me is car theft and I was just a kid at the time. Sister's clean. Not even a parking ticket. Clarks may not be gentry but they're honest. Anything else?"

Forsythe stopped and looked the man over. George Clark still wore black trousers, now covered with grass seeds, but had exchanged his white jacket for a cotton shirt. He was lanky and had shifty eyes. Hardly prepossessing, the barrister thought. "Like to enlarge on that a bit?" Forsythe asked.

"Told you everything."

"Hardly. How long have you been in service here?"

" 'Bout five and a half years."

"How do you like it?"

"Pretty dull place but Maggie and me been in worse. Lotta work but the old man don't bother us none."

"Are you speaking about Sir Amyas?"

"Sure am. Not a bad bloke. Always in cloud cuckoo land but he pays good."

"Before you came here—were you in service?"

"Maggie and me been in service since I was—guess I was about eighteen. This is the best job we've had." George became more expansive. "Can hit some rough places. 'Fore we came here we worked for a family in Leeds. Slavedrivers! That's where Maggie—sister wants me to call her Margaret now but she's still Maggie to me—anyway, where Maggie met her Ned. Hear her talk about Ned Larkin you'd think he was the second coming but he was no good. Smooth talker but hit the bottle something fierce. One night old Ned wrapped himself around a bottle of gin and tried to drive a Bentley through a stone wall. Maggie was glad to get rid of him. Maggie gives herself airs. Our old mum used to tell her, 'Girl, better remember your station in life. Don't go breaking your heart for what you can't have.' Think Maggie listened? Not on your life. Pored over those fashion magazines learning to dress proper and took a course in how to talk. Has her heart set on getting Sir Amyas."

Forsythe cocked his head. "I shouldn't imagine you'd object to being Sir Amyas's brother-in-law."

The shifty eyes turned dreamily to the Elizabethan house. "Bet your bottom on that. Sit in a big chair smoking cigars and drinking brandy and watch someone else work. But Mum was right and Maggie's just pipe dreaming. Got as much chance of pinning the old man as I have in walking a tightrope. After Lady Dancer died Maggie got pretty hopeful. Swarmed all over the old man like a hen with one chick. Didn't do her no good. Sir Amyas couldn't see her for dust and if he was gonna get married he would have taken that St. Croix bird."

"Do you think Katherine St. Croix had a chance of becoming Lady Dancer?"

"She was a shoo-in before Miss Cassandra got the dirt on her and turfed her out. Had the old man breathing fire. Could give you my opinion of the woman in one word not usually heard in mixed company." George Clark eyed the barrister and apparently decided against the word. "She was the kind of bird got a bloke all steamy wriggling her tail at him and then cooled him off in one hell of a hurry. Tell you the truth don't think she *liked* men."

Forsythe was uncomfortable. He could feel sweat gathering in the small of his back and trickling down. Taking out a handkerchief he wiped at his face. "The Sunday that Miss St. Croix disappeared—did you see her that day?"

"Had me running my legs off all day. My bunion was giving me trouble and I was up and down those stairs taking her trays any number of times. Started at lunch time. Took up her lunch and later coffee and then her dinner tray."

"What was she doing?"

"Sprawling on a lounge thing, taking her ease. Said she was sick but she sure didn't look it. Cleaned up every scrap on her trays, too."

"Did she talk to you?"

"Gimme orders is all. Do this, draw the shades, put the tray down over there. Sure high and mighty for a sneak thief!"

"Of course, at the time you had no idea about her past."

"Didn't know nothing about it 'til Sir Amyas found her rotting down at Mandalay. Didn't break my heart when he found her body, but she *was* a good-looking bird."

Sliding the handkerchief down his shirt, Forsythe dabbed at his wet chest. "This alibi you mentioned. You say you drove around that Sunday evening."

"Left the house as soon as dinner was done. Maggie cooks dinner and then charges in to eat with the family and play lady of the manor while I serve. After they eat Maggie leaves it to me to clean up. That night I stuck the dishes in the washing-up machine and dabbed at the kitchen a bit. Then I went into our sitting room and asked Maggie for the keys to her car. She's got an old Morris Minor. Left the house around ten and drove around. Fine night it was. Warm and balmy."

"Any particular direction?"

George waved a hand. "Over toward Chester. Took a bunch of back roads just to put in time. This place is dull enough at the best of times but on Sunday it dies. Came back here after one—"

"That was rather a long time to drive aimlessly around."

"That's my story," George said pugnaciously.

I'd better get out of this sun before I melt, Forsythe thought. He took a couple of steps toward the house and then spun around. "To your knowledge did Miss St. Croix leave her room that day?"

"Nah. Just lay there like a cat full of cream ordering me around. Mr. Carleton said she went down to his suite—he's on the second floor—and picked up the money for them buttons, but I didn't see her go." The man wiped both hands down his pant legs and then blurted, "Hey, clean forgot! She *did* go outta that room. I had to take some towels up to the bathrooms—"

"What time?"

"Let's see…must've been a little before two. Yeah, that's right. Always have a cuppa with Maggie at two and I was thinking of that when I went up with the towels. The woman's door was open and I looked in and she wasn't there. Wondered where she'd gotten to. Figured she might be in the bathroom but she wasn't. Then I noticed the door of this little room they call a writing room was closed. Never seen anyone writing in there and the door's always open. So I open it and walk in. The St. Croix woman was sitting at the desk using the telephone. She looks up and brings the receiver down and gives me hell. Tells me I'm an eavesdropper and I tell her if I was I wouldn't have opened the door; I would have my ear glued to it. She walks past me, goes into her room, and slams the door."

"Did you hear any of the conversation?"

"No. Like I said she banged the receiver down when she seen me."

"Could she have been speaking with someone in the house?"

"Sure could have. They put phones in where all you got to do is press the right button to get the library and study and kitchen. Phones up in Miss Cassandra's attic and in Mr. Carleton's rooms too. But she could have been using an outside line too."

"I see." Forsythe looked searchingly at the older man. "That drive you took…did you pick up a passenger at the Harper Arms?"

George swore lustily. "I suppose that bird has been talking a blue streak! Yeah, I took Nell for a ride. Trust a bird to talk!"

Forsythe grinned. "As a matter of fact Nell hasn't said a word."

"How'd you know then?"

"Mr. Bantam mentioned you'd told Nell about Miss Sanderson and me. And you don't seem the type to drive around alone."

"You caught me out. Nell and me plan to get married. She's not a bad sort of girl."

Too good for you, Forsythe decided silently. Aloud he said, "Why didn't you tell the police?"

"Maggie. If my sister finds out I'm courting a maid the fur is going to fly." The lump in his throat moved convulsively. "You gonna tell Maggie?"

112 E. X. Giroux

"I see no reason to. It will be our secret. Where can I find your sister?"

George peered at his watch. "Maggie will be in our sitting room. Walk right in and down the hall toward the kitchen. Take a right turn where the hall branches." He glanced up. "Take it easy on the old girl. Maggie's as much in cloud cuckoo land as Sir Amyas is." He added glumly, "She'll be coming down to earth soon enough anyway."

Despite the domestic shortage, Forsythe thought, the Dancers had scraped the bottom of the barrel with George Clark. His sister proved to have acquired a smoother veneer. She welcomed the barrister to her sitting room with all the panache of a seasoned hostess, seated him, and pressed a tall, frosty, and welcome glass of iced tea into his hand. Forsythe scrutinized the room and Margaret Larkin. The room was comfortable and, unlike the rest of the house, immaculately clean. A large color television and a stereo dominated it. Mrs. Larkin was a Junoesque woman, her ample curves expertly and probably expensively corseted into an hourglass shape. Her legs were a touch heavy but shapely and her Italian sandals had four-inch heels. This housekeeper didn't stoop to a uniform but wore a white silk dress ornamented with thin gold chains. She waved a well-kept hand with long painted nails. "This suite belonged to Sybil and Bella but when they moved Sir Amyas suggested George and I might be more comfortable down here. I do miss the dear aunts. Bella did all the cooking and a great deal of the cleaning. She's very good at both."

She spoke of the Misses Dancer as though they were servants for whom she might be giving a recommendation. "They seem quite comfortable in the Dower House," he told her.

"Sybil may be but Bella hungers to be back here. She has boundless *energy*. Bella tells me you met Horace yesterday. Dear old chap but a little…well, peculiar. When his daughter died he seemed to go quite strange. Carried a Bible around and made us swear on it never to reveal about the clothes dear Lady Dancer was wearing when she drowned. I couldn't quite understand it. Horace seemed more disturbed by that than by his daughter's death."

Forsythe took another cool delicious sip from the frosted glass. "Your brother tells me you've been here for a number of years."

"So long it seems like home to us. Oddly enough neither of us really welcomed the idea of burying ourselves in the country. But we had to come. Lady Dancer simply couldn't find anyone willing to help out and, as I always say, blood is thicker than water."

"You're related to the family?"

She bent her head and treated him to the sight of a straight white part in the midst of glossy black hair. "Distantly connected—on our mother's side."

The old mum, Forsythe mused, who had warned this woman not to aspire above her station. "Miss St. Croix's death must have been a shock to you."

"I was stunned. Many people in our position would have left the Priory immediately. The scandal, you know. But George and I feel we must stand by the family in their hour of need."

"Most commendable, Mrs. Larkin. Miss Dancer mentioned you distrusted Miss St. Croix."

"At sight. A perfectly horrible woman! Set Sir Amyas and his son at each other's throats. Deplorable."

"You were here the night of her death?"

"Yes. I seldom leave the estate except for an occasional visit to Chester." Polished nails touched the black hair. "Mainly to have my hair done. One must look after one's appearance."

Definitely genteel, Forsythe thought. Speaking with careful and slow diction. "Could you tell me how you spent the evening?"

"Right here. As soon as dinner was finished I came in to watch a couple of programs on television. Educational, of course. I do so deplore most of the trashy shows the public is forced to watch. I retired about eleven and read for about an hour. The police asked whether I had heard Miss St. Croix leave the house and I told them no. The Dancers are amazing people, so talented and exciting, but I fear they're a wee bit lax when it comes to locking up. As I tell George we could all be murdered in our sleep and none the wiser."

They're a wee bit lax when it comes to servants too, Forsythe decided as he put down his glass and rose. "One last question, Mrs. Larkin. A hundred pounds were found in Miss St. Croix's carryall. Could she have stolen the money from you?"

"Heavens no, Mr. Forsythe. Dear Sir Amyas insists we keep our funds in his safe. Such a considerate, thoughtful man he is."

That's not what I've heard, Forsythe thought as he thanked her and took his departure. He retraced his steps to the hall in time to see Cassandra, her arm linked with David Proctor's, skipping down the stairs. She wore a pastel pink jogging suit and the material between her breasts was darkened with a sweat stain. She dragged her close-set eyes from Proctor's handsome face and said with no evidence of delight, "Oh, it's you again. David tells me your friend had an accident."

"Twisted her ankle. I've just come from Mrs. Larkin. Can you give me one good reason why you keep that pair on here?"

Proctor looked at a dust smudge on his hand and echoed the words. "One good reason, Cass."

She giggled. "Inertia. They're fixtures now. And they weren't always so slack. When Mother was alive and the aunts were here the Lark and George boy earned their salaries. Now they act as though work was a four-letter word. But Amy hates change and Carl wouldn't notice if he was wading through garbage." She beamed up at Proctor. "Good news, Mr. Forsythe. David has finally decided to let me make an honest man of him. We're going to be married very soon."

"Congratulations." Forsythe shook the younger man's hand. As he did he noticed a slender gold band on the poet's wrist. "Patek. Did the police locate your stolen watch?"

"Hardly. Didn't bother reporting the theft. No use. They never find anything anyway. This is a wedding present."

"When will you be married?"

Cassandra twirled away from them, coming lightly to her toes. For a moment Forsythe thought she was going to do knee bends but she ended up possessively grasping her fiancé's arm—a bare arm with dark hair curling down to the wrist, Forsythe noted. Proctor had forsaken his shabby flannels and wore designer jeans and a scarlet polo shirt. Perhaps more wedding presents. The girl squeezed the bare arm and smiled dazzlingly. "Soon. On Saturday Mother will have been dead for a year. David says any time after that. We'll have a quiet service and then take off for a tour of the Continent. When we return we'll select a house."

"You don't plan to stay on here?" Forsythe asked.

Proctor shook his head. "Cass and I have had enough of the Priory and Harper. We're thinking of Belgravia. I think I could work well there."

"Inspiration," Cassandra confided. "It's most important for an artist to have the proper surroundings. I rather hate to leave Amy and Carl to the mercy of the Lark but perhaps they'll spend more time at the London house and maybe sack her and that revolting brother of hers." The girl's eyes widened. "Oh, I nearly forgot. Gramps was tossing rocks at my window last night at some ungodly hour. He wants me to issue an invitation to you and your secretary, if she's able, to come to the little do for Mother on Saturday night."

"I hardly think Miss Sanderson and I should attend. After all, it's a family affair."

"The more the merrier. According to Gramps it's a joyful affair. Probably with Mother sitting on a pink cloud and strumming a harp."

"Cass!" Proctor jerked his arm away from her grasp. "That's hardly in good taste."

The straw-colored head drooped and Forsythe asked, "I wonder whether I could see Sir Amyas?"

"He's not here," Proctor told him. "Where did he go, Cass?"

"Amy hustled in to Doctor Beam's to have his burn looked after. I urged him to put a hat and shirt on when he was repairing the dock but he wouldn't listen. He's covered with blisters." She looked up at Forsythe. "I don't know when he'll be back. Amy was muttering something about the amphitheater in Chester so he may have gone over there too."

Forsythe opened his mouth but the front door swung open and Carleton Dancer loped in. He was still wearing cutoffs and desert boots but had yanked his mane of hair back and secured it with what looked like a shoelace. His tanned torso was dripping moisture. "Hi, Carl," his sister said and tugged Proctor toward the door. "I'll drive you into Harper, darling; it's too hot to walk. Tata, Mr. Forsythe."

Carleton fingered his sparse beard. "Can't for the life of me see what Cassie sees in that chap. Wishy-washy. Thought when Mother died we'd seen the last of him."

"How do you like the idea of their marriage?"

"Hadn't heard of it. Are they really going to be married?"

"That's what your sister told me."

He shrugged a bony tanned shoulder. "It's Cassie's funeral. Anything I can do for you?"

"I was wondering whether the seal had been taken off the temple's door?"

"Uncle Roland was as good as his word. Inspector Fitzgerald came out yesterday and took it off. Brought back the key too. Like to have a look?"

"If it's not too much trouble."

"No trouble at all." Carleton fished in the drawer of the long table and pulled out a huge ornate iron key. He also extracted a crumpled envelope. "This is for you. When Father told the inspector you and Miss Sanderson were down here looking into the murder Fitzgerald scribbled a note and asked us to give it to you. Going to be a hot walk down to the lake. Better wear this." He swept up a straw hat from the litter on top of the table and plunked it on the barrister's head. "Wouldn't want to get sunstroke. Let's go."

They waded through tall grass where George was still waving the scythe around in lazy arcs and apparently not hitting anything. The sun glared down and Carleton slowed his rapid pace to accommodate his companion. "Father was pretty sick last night. Too much sun."

"It doesn't seem to bother you."

"I work outside a lot. All year round."

"Are you still working on the dock?"

"Finished that this morning. Went a great deal faster without Father getting in the way. Now I'm working on some lighting for Grandfather Gillimede's ceremony. Hooked up a generator and put up a string of light bulbs the length of the dock. Going to take time to get it working right but it'll keep the old gentleman happy."

The sun glared down and there was not a hint of breeze. Forsythe's shirt was sticking clammily to his back. "You like to work with your hands?"

"Always have. From the time I was a kid. If I'd been born into a poor family I would have had a better life. Probably been a carpenter or electrician and lived in a council house with a cute wife and a batch of children." Carleton looked dreamily into the distance. "Plant a garden and go to the pub to have a pint and play darts. Take the kids on walks and picnics. Hell of a thing to be wealthy."

"Money can be a curse," Forsythe said dryly.

"And a bore. Traveled all over the world trying to find my niche. Haven't found it yet. Tried the VSO for a time. Labored to teach the poor the miracle of birth control and planting crops. Gave it up when I decided they were happier than I am."

"You could take a job."

"And wrench some poor devil's pay away?" Carleton pointed. "See, that's the lighting I put up for Grandfather. Neat, eh?"

The future Sir Carleton Dancer had indeed done a neat job. Two strings of bulbs were stretched from a post at the end of the dock to one in front of the temple. A couple of sawhorses and a pile of lumber were directly in front of the door. Carleton wormed his way around them and patted a plank. "Making up a couple of benches for Aunt Pru and the aunts. Can't expect them to stand. Hope the weather holds."

Looking up at the cloudless brass-colored sky, Forsythe said, "I can't see why Saturday shouldn't be a fine night."

Carleton's fine nose quivered like an animal's scenting the air. "Get muggy weather like this and it's usually followed by a hell of a storm." He bent and stuck the key in the rusted padlock. The door groaned open. "Wait a sec. Need flashlights." He fished around in a canvas sack that was leaning against a sawhorse. "Ah, here we are. Should put some lights in the temple but what's the use? Father's going to tear it down soon."

They stepped into darkness and swung their flashlights around the interior of the small building. Forsythe's nostrils quivered much the same as his companion's had. The air was clammy and bore a sickening odor. His light settled on a long cement box and he walked over to it. On the top two red candles had guttered in their own wax. A small brass plaque told him that here rested the remains of Sir Godfrey Franklin Dancer, R.I.P. On the far side another cement box stood with its top turned sideways. He flashed the light into the cavernous hole and took a deep breath. This was the source of the sickish sweet odor.

"She was a mess," Carleton said in his ear. "Over three months in there. Body positively squirming with maggots."

Forsythe withdrew his light and his nose from the tomb. He shone the light toward the rear of the temple. On a dais he could see the remains of an oblong glass case. Within the case were two exquisite figurines. Stepping up on the dais he examined them. The green one was a Buddha, the white a delicate figure of a girl. Both pieces were marvelously detailed and the jade was translucent. "The pink ones were even prettier," Carleton told him casually. "Inspector Fitzgerald says they're being held as evidence. He wasn't too pleased that these pieces are still here."

"I hardly blame him. Surely they should be removed."

"They will be when Father tears the place down. Katherine's shoulder bag was against the wall. Right there. Her carryall was sitting here." Carleton pointed his torch at the floor. A mass of rusty marks disfigured the white marble and a trail of spots led down off the dais toward the empty tomb. "The police figure she was battered to death right here and the body dragged down to the tomb."

Forsythe stepped down and put a hand under the tilted top of the empty tomb. "How heavy is this thing?"

"Fairly weighty but with the pry bar not hard to move. Leverage, you know. I'd show you but the police still have the bar. More evidence, I suppose." He snapped his fingers. "Hey, I've got a heavy screwdriver out with my tools. Want to try that?"

Forsythe shook his head. "I'll take your word for it. Wouldn't take much strength, you say?"

"Be a snap. Anyone could do it."

"Cassandra?"

"She's stronger than I am. All that exercising she does. Aunt Bella's strong as an ox and so is Mrs. Larkin." He swung on Forsythe. "Jesus. I see what you're getting at and I don't like it!"

"I don't expect you to but every possibility must be explored. That's my job."

"Thank God I don't have one. Lousy way to make a living."

"This is *not* the way I make my living," the barrister said sharply.

"Sorry, forgot for a moment Father and I practically got down on our knees to beg you to do this. Tell you what, Mr. Forsythe, we'll go back to the house and have a drink. I could use one."

"So could I."

They didn't speak on the return trip to the Priory. Both men were engrossed in their thoughts. Forsythe's weren't pleasant. In that dark oriental crypt Katherine St. Croix had assumed a reality to him. Before she had simply been a name and a description. Now she was flesh and blood. Flesh that had been tossed like a piece of garbage into a tomb to rot, blood that had dripped from her body to mark the path that body had taken. Forsythe wondered whose hands had dragged Katherine's body over the marble floor.

Chapter Ten

Carleton Dancer's quarters were on the second floor rear and consisted of a room that had obviously once been a lady's sitting room, a bedroom, and a bath. The former sitting room had an ornate ceiling of tinted cupids and flower garlands and the only furniture were a table and two straight chairs in the center of a rug. Three walls were lined with glass cases displaying a multitude of buttons. The air was stifling and Carleton threw up a window before pouring generous portions of Glenlivet. Forsythe noticed that the place was as clean as Cassandra's garret. Not a grain of dust marred the long sheets of glass. "It looks like Mrs. Larkin does do some work here," the barrister said.

"The only area Mrs. Larkin does any work in is Father's room and his study. She takes good care of those. Other than that and opening tins for meals, any cleaning is left to George. Cassie looks after her rooms and I wouldn't have servants mucking around in here even if they did offer." Pouring down half of his Glenlivet, he tapped a glass top. "Have a look. I've divided my collection into categories. This is my royalty case."

Royal purple velvet covered the bottom of the case and on it were clusters and single buttons all with white cards neatly lettered. While Forsythe looked suitably interested, his host expounded. "These jet buttons came from a dinner gown belonging to Catherine the Great. This doeskin-covered button came from a boot belonging to Queen Victoria." He pointed a tanned finger at a tiny gold button with a diamond center. "Wonderful find, this one—a button from one of Henry the Eighth's jerkins."

"Are these authentic?"

"They wouldn't be here if they weren't. And some of them cost a great deal. I've traveled to Paris and Rome and Vienna for them. This silver button once belonged to Marie Antoinette. A very old lady who was a descendant of one of the queen's ladies-in-waiting discovered it in a jar of buttons she had in her attic. The bidding on it was fierce." He moved to the next case. "This is the military segment. Buttons representing every major war and some minor ones. These are the American Civil War, both North and South. This one was from the tunic of Lord Kitchener; and this is the gem of the collection—a button from the waistcoat of Napoleon Bonaparte."

"Extremely interesting," Forsythe said truthfully. "Where do you keep the bone buttons you bought from Miss St. Croix?"

"Over here. I call this my Crime Collection."

The Crime Collection was displayed quite suitably on a black velvet background. These buttons were more contemporary and contained few valuable metals or stones. Enthusiastically Carleton explained. "That pink button came from the cardigan of the fourteen-year-old raped and killed in Manchester last year. This leather one was on the mackintosh worn by that man who went door to door selling magazines and knifing housewives. This—"

"How did you get these?"

"Simple. I watch the papers and get in touch with the families of either the victim or the killer. You'd be surprised what people will sell for a few pounds. Of course there are setbacks. One father of a murdered girl blackened my eye."

Good for him, Forsythe thought. Aloud he said, "And this lot came from Katherine St. Croix. Could you take them out?"

Digging out a ring of keys from the pocket of his cutoffs, Carleton unlocked the case, lifted the top, and picked up the buttons. He poured them into the palm of the barrister's hand. Forsythe prodded at the tiny objects, turning them this way and that. All of the buttons still had pink thread attached and one of them still retained a strap of a pink cotton material. "Looks like she ripped these off in a hurry."

"Must have cut them right off the blouse without caring whether she ruined it."

Selecting the button with the dangling scrap of material Forsythe held it up for closer inspection. The tiny skull leered with empty eye sockets. "Good detail and carving."

"The best." Carleton's face glowed with fervor. "If she had lived they wouldn't have had much value except as a curiosity but with her death...Well, I've already received an offer of five hundred pounds for them. Of course, I wouldn't part with them." He held out a possessive hand and the barrister dropped the buttons into it.

While the younger man carefully arranged the buttons Forsythe read the card below them. In tiny printing it announced that these buttons once belonged to Katherine St. Croix and were cut off her blouse a few hours before she was murdered. Despite the heat he felt suddenly chilled. He said slowly, "Do you realize you are attracted toward death?"

"I beg your pardon?"

"Death and possessions of the dead. Particularly the violently dead. Skulls and those replicas of parts of dead bodies you used with your rock group."

"It never occurred to me before." Carleton locked the case and returned the keys to his pocket. "You could be right." He raised candid eyes to Forsythe. "I do find death and the process of becoming dead much more interesting than the living. At least it doesn't bore me."

When Forsythe returned to the Harper Arms he didn't immediately go to his secretary's room. He had a leisurely soak in the enormous claw-footed tub and donned fresh clothes before he sought her out. Miss Sanderson had been made extremely comfortable. She lay against a pile of pillows and was attired rather nattily in blue silk pajamas a shade darker than her eyes. She was working on a crossword puzzle and the table beside her was heaped with books, an open box of chocolates, and a bowl of fruit. Beside the humble jar of daisies a mass of varicolored roses glowed. In one corner a revolving fan sent ripples of rose-scented air through the room.

Sinking into a chair Forsythe crossed his long legs at the ankle. "You look remarkably cool and well looked after. How's the leg?"

She tugged up a pajama leg and displayed an elastic bandage. "The Sunbeam was around this afternoon practicing his bedside manner again. Rude as ever but he did say the swelling was down and it was coming along as well as could be expected."

"Where did all the goodies come from?"

"Prudence Pyne sent the roses; the missus contributed the fruit; Nell brought up the fan; and our host gave me the chocolates. Probably Mr. Bantam will put them on your bill but it was a nice gesture."

"The books?"

"Nell scurried over to the lending library. Mainly sticky romances so I sent her back for this crossword puzzle magazine. Neighborly people in Harper, Robby."

"So it would seem."

"But I've been so bored—"

"Please. Not that word!"

She put down her pencil. "You've had a boring day?"

"Far from it, but that word was used too often by a young man with the most gruesome tastes. Carleton's managed to turn a button collection into something quite grisly."

"It doesn't surprise me. That rock group is a tipoff to the lad's interests. Think he could have bashed Katherine's head in to add more interest to his collection?"

"Stranger things have happened."

"Rather a weak motive but I'll keep it in mind. Tell me about your interviews."

Forsythe reported in detail. When he'd finished she tapped her thumbnail against her front teeth as she always did when she was thinking, an irritating habit but one that appeared to stimulate her thought processes. Finally she lowered the hand and ticked points off on her fingers. "George Clark is courting Nell and was with her the night of the murder. Margaret Larkin is still in pursuit of a title. Carleton is engrossed in a combination of manual labor and death. That's about it."

"Wrong, Sandy, there's something else." His brow furrowed. "Can't for the life of me pin it down. A remark…one of those niggling things you don't notice at the time but strike a chord afterward."

She leaned forward and the crossword magazine slid off her lap. "What remark?"

He shook a baffled head. "That's what I can't pin down."

"Don't worry about it. It will some back if you leave it alone. By the way, what's in the envelope peeking out of your pocket?"

Pulling out the wrinkled envelope he tossed it to her. "A note from the inspector in charge of the case. Gives us a pressing invitation to drop into the station at Chester and confer with him."

She ran her eyes over the sprawling writing. "Inspector Fitzgerald says we received a glowing recommendation from none other than Chief Inspector Kepesake of the Central Bureau. I didn't think Adam Kepesake thought that highly of us."

"When we were working on those moor murders he certainly didn't but he may feel more kindly since we worked together on the Farquson affair. Adam feels we were the ones who solved the case."

Miss Sanderson bit her lip. "Little does he know he still hasn't the correct solution. Are you going to take Fitzgerald up on his offer?"

"I might as well. We don't seem to be getting far here. I'll drive up tomorrow and—Ah, here is our supper."

The door swung open and Nell entered bearing a bed tray for Miss Sanderson. Mr. Bantam, puffing mightily, carried another tray for the barrister. The maid bent over the bed, snapped down the short legs on the tray, and positioned it. As she moved, the bow in her frizzy fair hair, today a bright red, bobbed frantically. The innkeeper deposited the other tray on the table at Forsythe's elbow. "Eat hearty, folks. Cold food tonight. With the heat and all, the missus don't feel up to cooking a hot supper." He tapped a frosty pitcher. "Iced tea. May hit the spot."

"It will. What's this envelope?"

Picking up the envelope from the tray Mr. Bantam scrutinized it as though he'd never seen it before. "Found it this morning. Meant to catch you 'fore you went out but it clean slipped my mind."

Forsythe looked at the envelope. All it bore was his name in block printing. "Found it where?"

"Slipped under the door. Must have been put there late. Wasn't on the floor when I locked up." He watched Forsythe as he sliced open the envelope and pulled out a single sheet of writing paper. "Something important?"

Refolding the sheet the barrister slipped it back into the envelope. He glanced up. "You haven't any idea who could have left it?"

"None." Mr. Bantam scratched at the shining dome of his head and uattered, "Queer way to deliver mail."

Forsythe's gaze fastened on his secretary. She was examining a plate of cold chicken and salad with approval. "Mr. Bantam, I'll be driving to Chester in the morning. I don't like leaving Miss Sanderson by herself so much. Could you have a maid stay with her until I return?"

"No problem, Nell's been looking after her. Care to stay with the lady tomorrow, lass?"

The red bow bobbed as Nell nodded. "I'll stay right with her."

Forsythe knew Miss Sanderson was staring at him and avoided her eyes. "If she has any visitors, Nell, don't leave the room. Understand?"

The maid told him she understood and Mr. Bantam caught Forsythe's eyes. He nodded as though something had passed between them and said jovially, "Keep an eye on her myself, Mr. Forsythe. She won't get lonesome, I promise. Now, Nell, come along. Let these folks have their meal."

After the door closed Miss Sanderson said sharply, "Give me that letter."

"I don't—"

"Now!"

He nudged the envelope onto her tray and watched as she opened it. It contained five words in block printing. *Get out or get dead.*

Chapter Eleven

Detective Inspector Fitzgerald of the Chester police wore half-moon reading glasses that rode precariously on his fleshy nose. The half-moons and the eyes behind them examined the sheet of paper on the blotter. "I'll have this checked for fingerprints but I doubt we'll get any but yours, your secretary's, and Matt Bantam's. Anyone smart enough to use stationery that can be picked up anywhere and write in block printing isn't going to give himself away by putting his prints all over the note." Snapping the glasses off, he tapped his chin with their frames. "Looks like you stirred something up in Harper, Mr. Forsythe."

"I've been wondering whether this could be a local's idea of a joke."

"Could be but I'm inclined to doubt it. I think our murderer just stuck his head up a bit. Going to take his advice?"

"No."

"Might be a good idea to send Miss Sanderson back to London."

"Sandy can't be *sent* anywhere. And I doubt she'll go. She doesn't like being threatened anymore than I do."

Fitzgerald scrutinized his visitor. Robert Randolph Forsythe, Q.C. A much younger man than he'd expected. Looked hardly into his thirties. Soft-spoken and mild-mannered. Tall and slender and dressed with subdued elegance. The inspector mentally draped that slim form in a black silk robe, surmounted the long face with a high gray wig. Forsythe's brilliant reputation as a barrister had preceded him. No, Fitzgerald decided, I really wouldn't want to face this man from the witness box. I also wouldn't be foolish enough to threaten him.

Forsythe was as busy assessing the inspector. Much brighter than Chief Inspector Kepesake, he thought. Carrying too much weight on his big-boned frame. Ginger-colored hair, darker mustache, placid face, sleepy eyes. Good at his job and he knew it.

Fitzgerald tapped the note with the frame of his glasses. "What do you know that warrants this?"

"Quite frankly I'm baffled. As I explained, I didn't get any more information than you already have."

"With the exception of George Clark and that business about him taking his girl joyriding that night."

The barrister shifted on the hard wooden seat. "Have you come up with any prior association of the St. Croix woman with any of the suspects?'

"Looked into all their backgrounds and can't find a trace. The only connection Katherine St. Croix or Katerina Padrinski had with anyone in Harper was the few weeks she spent in Miss Pyne's house. Those people and Katerina moved in different circles."

"The Dancers have done a fair amount of traveling. Could they have met the woman in another country?"

"Katerina never made application for a passport. As far as we can find she never left the British Isles. I'm inclined to think the first time she saw any of them was from Miss Pyne's kitchen door and her windows."

"Does that include David Proctor?"

"Proctor was born, raised, and lived his life in London. Katerina was in the city, of course, mainly to have stolen objects fenced. But she seemed to prefer smaller places, towns and villages."

"What about Proctor's background?"

"He was raised by a widowed mother and she doted on him. Only child and his mother used most of her income to give him a musical education. Must have figured her boy was a genius. Appears he was barely adequate. When his mother died he was forced to go to work. Had a number of jobs. Played piano in the lounges of a couple of hotels, sold furniture in an uncle's store, modeled men's clothes for a time, and ended up selling insurance. Not a flaming success at any of them."

"Any romantic interests?"

The inspector fingered his mustache and smiled. "Odd word to use for young people today. Proctor had a number of casual affairs but only one serious one. He and a female model lived together for over a year. Her name was Vanessa Linquist and she was fairly successful. Appeared in television commercials for cosmetics and perfumes and so on. According to their friends Vanessa was the one who broke off the affair. Left Proctor without warning and married a wealthy man who'd been one of her sponsors. It would seem Proctor was crushed."

"Or had a badly battered ego."

"Quite. If he did know Katerina they must have kept it quiet. Neither her associates nor Proctor's knew anything about it."

Fishing in his pocket Forsythe extracted his pipe and a leather tobacco pouch. "What about Katherine or Katerina's background?"

"Makes grim reading." The inspector touched a file folder with a blunt forefinger. "If you like I can give you the gist of it."

"Please."

"One thing the woman always told the truth about was the fact she was an orphan. Her parents were killed in a car crash when she was a little girl and she was put in the custody of an aunt, her mother's sister. The aunt had been a prostitute but as she got older she must have decided there was more money in handling a string of girls than doing the work herself."

"She must have made a wonderful guardian," Forsythe said dryly.

"The aunt put Katerina to work immediately. Quite profitably. An amazing number of men have a taste for very young girls and—"

"How old was the girl?"

"Eight."

"Good Lord!"

"It must have been hell on wheels for the child. Anyway, when Katerina was twelve she ran away from the aunt and ended up in a series of institutions, and turned quite naturally to crime. Petty theft, at first. She had a list of juvenile offenses as long as your arm. By the time she reached twenty-one Katerina branched out into extortion. She served two short prison terms and then apparently smartened up. From then on she was up to everything you can think of but she was never again charged. It seemed she had a way of stealing from people and finding some way to keep their mouths shut. Similar to what she tried to use on Cassandra Dancer—threatening to smear them or a relative all over the yellow sheets."

"Yes." Forsythe continued tamping tobacco down in the pipe bowl. He thought of Prudence Pyne and the tactics Katherine St. Croix had used on her. "It certainly didn't work with Miss Dancer."

"She's one in a million. A spunky young woman." The inspector's sleepy eyes glinted with admiration. "We called in our consulting psychologist for a profile on Katerina Padrinski and he tells us it's conceivable, because of the horrendous childhood she had, that Katerina was a woman who hated society and was out to get her revenge. She not only stole for gain but to strike back at people. He says she probably had no sexual drive but achieved satisfaction from tormenting and degrading decent people."

Again Forsythe thought of Prudence Pyne. "What happened to that monster of an aunt?"

"Poetic justice. The aunt was dragged into an alley and several thugs, never identified, beat her to death—slowly. By the time the woman was killed Katerina had a good many connections in the underworld. Doesn't take much to put two and two together."

"For that I can't find fault with Katherine. Seems a fitting end for a woman who'd corrupted her own niece. Any theories about Katherine's death?"

"Ten, Mr. Forsythe. Eight people at the Priory and two people in Harper had the opportunity and sufficient reason to bash her head in. Only problem is to cut the guilty one out of the herd." He laced his hands over his swelling waistcoat. "The way I reason it is this. Katerina, calling herself Katie Parr, weaseled her way into Miss Pyne's house in Harper. She looked over the area and settled on the Dancer family for a future target. She knew they were wealthy and probably thought there would be jewelry and money lying around their house. When she got there she found nothing of value to steal. So she changed tactics and fastened onto Sir Amyas. I should imagine she was going to let him rush her into marriage and then confess her past to him. Sir Amyas would have to pay heavily to get rid of his crooked wife. Cassandra put a stop to that and frightened Katerina into leaving. She left but she stopped off at the temple to pick up some jade for her troubles and one of my ten suspects caught her in the act and bashed her head in."

After two tries, Forsythe got his pipe drawing nicely. He puffed out a tiny cloud of fragrant smoke. "Her body wasn't discovered for over three months. Are you positive she *did* die that Sunday night?"

"You mean could she have sneaked onto the estate at a later date and tried to rob the temple? Everything points against that. In the first place the pathologist managed to locate the remains of broccoli spears in her stomach. Broccoli was served for dinner that Sunday night and—"

"Hardly conclusive. Katherine might have had broccoli at any number of dinners later on."

"True. But—" Breaking off, Fitzgerald consulted his pocket watch, a turnip-shaped affair on a heavy chain. "Thought I was getting a mite peckish. Care to continue this over lunch?"

They lunched at a restaurant near the station house. Inspector Fitzgerald was greeted as a valued patron and they were escorted to a table in a quiet corner. They ordered pints of beer and the inspector finished half of his off at one gulp. "I'm going for something hearty. My wife has me on a diet and all I get for supper is cottage cheese and grated carrots. They do a lovely borscht and cabbage rolls here."

Forsythe settled for salad and a Scotch egg. His companion dug into his food and seemed able to eat and talk with no problem. "Where was I, Mr. Forsythe?"

"About to explain the other evidence that points to the date of the murder."

"Right." Breaking off a chunk of bread, Fitzgerald dipped it into the borscht. "The candles sitting on Sir Godfrey's tomb—not ordinary candles and you couldn't pick them up at a store. Lady Dancer had them made up specially for her. Wine red with a gold thread woven into a pattern on them. Those two candles were on the dining room table that Sunday night when the family dined. The next morning Katerina was gone and so were the candles. Mrs. Larkin is positive about that." He waved a hand at a waiter. "Eric, more beer over here."

Forsythe pushed the Scotch egg around. "It does strain the imagination to picture Katherine carrying those candles around and bringing them back at a later date to burgle the temple."

"There's more." Inspector Fitzgerald spread hot mustard liberally on a cabbage roll and cut into it. "After that night Katerina dropped out of sight. Her confederates in London, who disposed of her loot, never saw her again. The daily she had in her flat and the janitor of the building—ditto."

Losing any interest he'd had in lunch, the barrister put down his fork. "London?"

"Chester." Fitzgerald dabbed mustard off his chin. "She kept a flat here for the last couple of years under the name of Kay Parnell. Posed as a well-to-do lady who traveled a lot. The lads went over it with a fine-tooth comb but didn't turn up much except that crime seems to pay. Talk about luxury! Rugs you can sink up to your ankles in and expensive furniture. Two wardrobes in the bedroom. One with cheap clothes, skirts and blouses and anoraks—probably the ones she used when she acted the role of a girl down on her luck. The other one chockfull of clothes that cost a mint. Among other things a fine mink coat and a sable jacket. Some of the gowns had the black and gold label of Madame Helena's."

"Didn't we pass a shop with that name on it in discreet gold letters? The window display featuring only a handbag, gloves, and a scarf?"

"Don't miss much, do you?" Fitzgerald waved for more beer. He sat back and rubbed his bulging waistcoat. "Ah, that hit the spot! Now let the wife bring on her rabbit food. Yes, Mr. Forsythe, that is Madame Helena's. She caters only to the carriage trade, and I've heard it costs a pound just to step in and breathe the air. Calls herself—some French word."

"*Couturiere?*"

"That's it. Rather a nice woman."

"You have asked her about Katherine?"

Fitzgerald chuckled. "Operating on the same idea you're mulling over. Women tend to talk to their hairdressers and dressmakers. But Kay Parnell, as Madame Helena calls her, didn't do any talking. If you'd like to have a go at the dressmaker I'll give you my card."

"I think I will." Forsythe waited until the inspector dug out a card and scribbled a few words on it. "There was nothing else of interest in the woman's flat?"

"All there was in the desk was stationery and stamps, receipts for her rent and a few things she'd bought. No letters or

136   *E. X. Giroux*

checkbooks or even a postcard. She paid cash for everything she bought and for her rent. Suppose she had money squirreled away somewhere, but not there. Besides the clothes and cosmetics there was a jewelry case in her dressing table. Quite expensive stuff in it. Gold chains and a diamond pendant and a couple of dinner rings."

"And that was all?"

"All except what we found in a hidey-hole behind the bed."

"You do enjoy cliff-hangers, don't you?"

The wide mouth below the heavy mustache curved up. "That I do, Mr. Forsythe. But don't get your hopes up. All that was in it was a bundle of clippings from the papers and magazines and a little box containing two pieces of jewelry—antique jewelry."

"By any chance was one of them a garnet ring and the other a cameo brooch circled with pearls?"

"Seed pearls to be exact. No real value there. How did you know?"

It was the barrister's turn to smile. "I should leave *you* hanging but I won't. Those pieces are the property of Prudence Pyne. They were her mother's and Katherine stole them from her."

Rubbing a hand over his thick hair, the inspector frowned. "Miss Pyne didn't mention that to me. Had a feeling she was holding something back. She tell you any other tidbits she withheld from me?"

Forsythe debated and then said slowly, "If Miss Pyne told me anything in confidence that proves to have a bearing on the case, I will put it at your disposal."

"At the proper time, of course," the other man mocked. "I'll hold you to that. Miss Pyne happens to be way up on my list of suspects. Didn't like the way she tried to keep me from questioning that maid of hers. Hung right over the woman while I was talking to her. And Miss Pyne does have a good motive for wanting Katie Parr, as she knew her, dead. That was a pretty filthy trick that was played on her."

"Susan seems to be a highly strung person and she feels guilty about introducing Katie Parr into her mistress's house. As for Miss Pyne being our murderer, quite frankly I can't see it. I'll concede that she could very well have killed the woman with that pry bar but I doubt she could have dragged a body across the floor and hoisted it into the tomb. Miss Pyne is far from young and she has a slight build."

"She also has a hefty maid who could have helped. I could tell Susan was devoted to her mistress."

"Prudence Pyne is not the type of woman who would involve her maid in murder."

"My, you are defensive of this lady, Mr. Forsythe." Fitzgerald's large head bobbed. "First rule in this business is not to get emotionally involved with suspects. Clouds your judgment."

"Tell me more, Inspector," Forsythe said a bit coldly.

"Teach my grandmother to suck eggs, eh? You'll be happy to hear I also have my eyes on the Dancer sisters. Any objections?"

"None. But I can hardly see Miss Sybil being able to do the manual work any more than Miss Pyne could. I suppose you think Miss Bella was her accomplice?"

"She could easily have been. Clear enough Miss Bella is right under her sister's thumb."

"Cats eat birds," Forsythe muttered.

"I beg your pardon?"

"A passing thought. Now, what about the clippings in the murdered woman's flat?"

"All of them concern the Dancer family, dating back to the accounts of Lady Dancer's drowning and her funeral. Katerina had a full collection of data on them, clipped from gossip columns and the society pages. The last one was dated the day before Carleton Dancer picked her up and took her home."

"I'd like to see them."

"Thought you might. I've had copies made and you can pick them up before you leave Chester. Now, Mr. Forsythe, you've drained me dry. Anything you'd like to contribute?"

"I've covered everything I know."

Sighing, the other man wiped a napkin over his mustache and pulled himself to his feet. "When Chief Inspector Kepesake rang me up I had high hopes. He tells me you have an uncanny habit of picking up on tiny things, items no one seems to notice, and building a case out of them. Can't think of some tiny thing, can you?"

"The larder's bare but if anything comes up I'll be in touch."

"Is that a promise?"

Forsythe hesitated. "If you're willing to take my advice on the use of the information, it is."

"Strings attached, but I'll accept them. I'm at a dead end with this case. You off to see Madame Helena now?"

"Yes. Then I'll pick up the clippings and get back to Harper."

"You're worried about your secretary?"

"I made arrangements for her to be looked after but, yes, I'm a bit concerned."

"Matt Bantam seeing to her?"

"And one of the maids who seems a reliable girl."

"Matt's reliable too. Overcharges scandalously but he's a good sort. Brighter than he looks."

In front of the restaurant they parted. The inspector headed back toward the station house and Forsythe walked to the building that housed the shop of Madame Helena, Couturiere.

The reception area was white and gold and chill. On white shag carpeting tiny white and gilt tables and spindly chairs perched. The cool air was faintly perfumed and behind a Lous XIV desk a receptionist, an attractive blonde, raised glacial, appraising eyes. Those eyes took a thorough inventory of the barrister, from his collar to his highly polished shoes, before traveling back up to his face. They noted the cut of the clothes, possibly came to a quick estimate of the cost, and thawed a fraction. "May I assist you, sir?"

He placed his own card and Inspector Fitzgerald's on the desk top. "I'd like to speak with Madame Helena."

She read the cards, picked them delicately up between her thumb and forefinger, gestured at one of the spindly chairs, and disappeared behind white and gold hangings. Forsythe looked the area over. The hangings swayed, and the blonde beckoned him into another room, this one larger but as cool and white and gold although empty of merchandise. Here Louis XIV gave way to deeply cushioned sofas and chairs upholstered in white leather. He followed his comely guide, watching the tantalizing sway of her neat behind, the flash of long silken legs. If this was the receptionist, Madame Helena would probably be intimidating. Behind more white hangings was a stout door and this led to an area that appeared to be the nerve center of the establishment. White shag gave way to worn plank flooring, white paneling to rather grubby green paint. From an open doorway came the whir of machines and behind ranks of sewing machines a number of women wearing blue smocks labored. At the end of the hall the blonde swung open a door and announced him.

The room was small and cluttered. A rolltop desk loomed against one wall; in front of the window a drawing board stood and a long deal table was piled with swaths of cloth and measuring tapes. Madame Helena matched the room. She was short and plump with untidy hair and laughter wrinkles deeply graven around her eyes and mouth. A cigarette was clenched between her teeth and one eye was closed against its smoke. She wore jeans and a plaid shirt and held a scrap of claret-colored velvet.

"A barrister, Mr. Forsythe," she said. "And Inspector Fitzgerald asking me to give you all possible assistance?"

"Retained by Sir Amyas Dancer. To look into the death of Katherine St. Croix, Madame Helena."

"Helena. The madame is strictly for clientele. Any assistance I can give is yours. Not only was Lady Dancer a valued client but she brought me many prestigious ladies including

Lady Wabbersley. Do sit down. Take that armchair. You'll find it more comfortable than that horrible furniture in the salons. Perhaps a drink?"

Forsythe glanced apprehensively at the array of cut glass decanters filled with a rainbow of colors and she laughed, bringing the wrinkles into play. "I wasn't thinking of a liqueur. The ladies love or pretend to love sticky chocolate and cherry and mint but I happen to prefer double malt."

The double malt was produced from a desk drawer, poured, and Forsythe took a reverent sip. "Where on earth did you come up with this?"

"An aged uncle brews it quite illegally in the Scottish Highlands. Inspector Fitzgerald rather fancied it too." Helena perched on a stool and butted her cigarette in an overflowing ashtray. "You'll want to hear about Katherine St. Croix, or Kay Parnell, as I knew her."

"Please."

"Generally I require references to take on a new client but in her case I made an exception. She spoke and acted like a lady and the fact that she didn't wince at prices helped. In all I made four ensembles for her. Two afternoon dresses, an evening gown, and a heavenly heather tweed suit. It was a pleasure to work on her. For once I could display curves rather than try to conceal bulges. Kay was a fine-looking woman, a brown-eyed blonde, and she had a fabulous figure." Helena spread a hand with short blunt fingers. "And that is all I can tell you."

The double malt sliding silkily down Forsythe's throat was sending pleasant warmth through his body. He leaned back and crossed his long legs. "Surely you must have had some conversation."

"Of course. Mainly about styles and materials." Spreading the scrap of velvet on a knee, Helena stroked the soft nap. "She had excellent taste. I rather wish I had something to confide, some important fact she let slip. But all she said about herself was that she had a flat in Chester and was away a great deal traveling. I gathered she had inherited money and had always had a good life. Education and ease and that sort of thing." Helena raised shrewd eyes from the material. "To fool me she had to be good. I've dealt with women for years and usually I can spot a phoney immediately. Katherine's death was a loss to the theater. She'd have made a wonderful actress."

"She paid in cash?"

"Every time and she also picked up the garments rather than having them delivered. When I found my Miss Parnell was actually the Dancers' Miss St. Croix I was amazed. Also dismayed. If my ladies find I made clothes for a con woman who had the bad taste to have her head bashed in, it may hurt business."

"I see no reason to bring your name into it, Helena. I'm certain Inspector Fitzgerald feels the same way."

Her eyes crinkled with laughter. "And I hope you're right. As I said, Lady Dancer was a valued client and I'm hoping to capture her daughter. Do her wedding gown and trousseau, you know."

Forsythe put his empty glass down and the squat bottle immediately tilted over it. "You've heard about Miss Dancer's engagement so soon?"

"Ah, it is official then. This is a small place, Mr. Forsythe, and I've heard rumors about the impending nuptials for months. Then there have been tidbits about Cassandra Dancer and David Proctor in the gossip columns."

"You've met Mr. Proctor?"

"David escorted Lady Dancer when she came for fittings a couple of times. Handsome young devil. Not my type—I prefer rugged men—but Lady Dancer certainly seemed to dote on him." Helena refreshed her own glass and turned the velvet one way and then the other. "I'd met him before."

"In Chester?"

"London. I did alterations on one of his girlfriend's dresses. For a perfume commercial. Lovely gown, silk and chiffon. She was a model. Can't recall her name."

"Vanessa Linquist?"

"That's it. You're well informed, Mr. Forsythe. Yes, David came and hovered over his Vanessa. He was mad for the girl. I think that's why he was attracted to Lady Dancer. Same basic type. Their features were quite different but both were tall and willowy and graceful, with marvelous dark hair. Vanessa was much the younger, of course." Helena sighed. "Lady Dancer was such a loss. Lovely looking woman and she knew exactly how to dress to display her looks. We used chiffon and velvet and silk for her gowns and kept them simple and flowing. Elegant!"

Forsythe set his glass down again and this time shook his head when the bottle was extended. Uncle's Highland brew was not only delicious but potent. He could feel it down to his toes. "Did you by any chance make the sailor suit for Lady Dancer?"

Her eyes widened. "That was a deep dark secret! But yes, Mr. Forsythe, to my undying shame I was the one who created that monstrosity. I had no desire to do it but Lady Dancer was too good a customer to refuse. Not only did she swear me to secrecy but she insisted I do all the work on it myself." The laughter wrinkles appeared again. "It's been a number of years since I have done any sewing. All I do now is designing and fittings. Would you like to see the sketch for the infamous suit?"

"I think I would."

She slid open a file drawer and burrowed in it. "Here we are. As you see it was a modified suit of an actual sailor. I nipped in the blouse a bit and used blue velvet for the collar and silk for the red bow. The rest of it was fine white cotton. I used heavier cotton for the cap and put a little blue and red anchor on it. Ghastly thing!"

Forsythe examined the tinted sketch. "Did Lady Dancer tell you why she wanted it?"

"No, she was most secretive about the whole affair. I'll admit I was curious. Her taste was excellent and she *never* wore trousers. It would have been a pity to cover those marvelous long legs. All she said was that it was a surprise and all I asked was whether it would be a pleasant one. Lady Dancer merely smiled."

"Have you told anyone about it? One of your other ladies?"

"Heavens no! In the first place you never discuss one lady's clothes with another. In the second place I'm not exactly proud of creating a tawdry item like this."

"No one could have seen this sketch? Say when it was lying around here?"

She shook her head. "Designs don't 'lie around.' They're kept in that file cabinet. When I leave the room it's locked. And except for staff and police and barristers no one enters this room. The ladies are kept strictly in the salons."

Standing up he handed back the sketch. "I was wondering. I'd like a small gift for a lady. Could you make a suggestion?"

"You're under no obligation to buy, Mr. Forsythe. I was only too happy to try and help."

"I appreciate that but this lady happens to be my secretary who's laid up with a twisted ankle. I thought it might cheer her up."

"In that case..." A stubby finger touched her chin. "Lingerie is out. Perhaps a handbag or gloves. I have some marvelous scarves that have just arrived from Paris."

"A scarf sounds fine."

"Then on to the accessory salon. I'll show them myself. Colette, that's the iceberg who mans the desk, is wonderful with the carriage trade; she quite overawes them but is an awful snob."

In her working clothes Madame Helena looked out of place in the white and gold salon. She seated Forsythe on a leather sofa, spread a velvet cloth on the table before him, and turned to a paneled wall. "Where on earth do you keep the merchandise?" Forsythe asked.

"Right here." She pressed a gilt button and the panel slid silently back, revealing rows of narrow drawers. "Trick of the trade, Mr. Forsythe. Keep all the goodies concealed and the ladies feel they're worth the obscene price tags. Now, what is your secretary's favorite color?"

Forsythe mulled this over. "Sandy wears a great deal of green."

"Presto!" Helena opened a drawer. "The perfect scarf."

She draped it expertly on the velvet. "Gossamer silk, hand-painted, observe the artist's signature chastely worked in with the pattern."

The barrister fingered the apple-green silk, admired a spray of pink flowers looking somewhat like cherry blossoms, and nodded. "Sandy will love it."

She grinned wickedly down at him. "And you'll pay three times as much as you would in a department store. Serves you right for coming to a woman who calls herself madame."

Forsythe found he greatly liked this earthy woman. "How did you come to have a place like this in Chester?"

"The hard way. Long years of being a seamstress and then I met a very generous old gentleman who took a fancy to me. We were extremely close. He insisted on backing this store and lo and behold, Helen became Madame Helena. Lady Dancer was the one who got this shop off the ground. She went to Paris a couple of times a year for her clothes but she dropped in here on impulse and found I could design what she wanted without having to make a trip so she brought more carriage trade and Madame Helena became a minor celebrity."

While Helena had been chatting she had whipped out a black and gold box, nestled the scarf in white tissue, tucked in a sachet, and handed the box to Forsythe. "Brace yourself, Mr. Forsythe. I will now tell you the price."

He winced at the figure and she laughed and accepted the wad of five and ten pound notes. Then she escorted him through various hangings back to the lair of the blonde ice maiden. At the sight of the box in the barrister's hand the woman rose gracefully and opened the door for him. Helena stuck out a hand. "I'm sorry I couldn't have been of help."

"Oddly enough, I think you have been."

She raised her brows. "Give me a hint?"

"Not yet. It's...nebulous."

"In that case come back when you crack the case and we'll have more of Uncle's double malt. You can tell me all and when you're quite tiddly I'll sell you a gown for your secretary."

He smiled down at her. "Helena, even Uncle's brew won't get me *that* tiddly."

Chapter Twelve

The public saloon of the Harper Arms was doing a roaring business. Matthew Bantam was drawing pints at top speed and Annie, the buxom dark barmaid, was whipping around with plates of salad and cold cuts. As Forsythe made his way to the bar he caught snatches of conversation. Close to the door two young men clad in identical violet pants and matching shirts were in intimate but shrill conversation. The blond one was telling his dark companion, "I grant you Evelyn has a wonderful *body* but, my dear, he can be so *madly* beastly. Why just yesterday he said to me..."

Passing a table surrounded by husky young women in shorts, hiking boots, and knapsacks Forsythe caught a storm of words. All the women wore skin-tight T-shirts and none of them favored bras. Forsythe squeezed in beside the checker table and nodded at old Bob. Bob didn't nod back. His ancient but lecherous eyes were busily assessing the unfettered breasts of the hikers. Mr. Bantam busily worked the taps and told the barrister, "He's at it again. Always after the lasses! How was Chester, Mr. Forsythe?"

Forsythe told him all seemed to be in order in that city and asked whether there had been any visitors for Miss Sanderson.

Mr. Bantam opened his mouth but Forsythe caught a whiff of exotic perfume as an arm wearing a gold bangle thrust two glasses past him. "Two more gin and tonics, dear. And just slip a couple of cherries in. Toddy and I are *wild* for cherries."

The innkeeper served the gin and tonics with genial tolerance and told the barrister, "Three people, Mr. Forsythe. Miss Bella Dancer and Miss Pyne both wanted to see Miss Sanderson but I told them the lass was resting. Miss Bella left a box of cookies for her and Miss Pyne a jar of plum preserves. Mr. Proctor dropped in to inquire about her health but didn't ask to see her."

The perfume and gold bangle withdrew and a mild odor of perspiration and a plump freckled arm took its place. Forsythe was aware of something warm and soft and pneumatic pressing against his elbow. The girl was nearly as tall as he and much broader. She had red hair cropped short and rather nice eyes. As the innkeeper drew the bitter those eyes examined Forsythe, the breast continued to nudge him, and she gave him a wide smile. The smile was a disappointment. Her teeth were poor. On the barrister's other side Bob was craning his neck to have a closer look. Mr. Bantam gave the girl the pints and old Bob a crack over the bald head. "Down and stay down or out you go!" he roared. He lowered his voice. "Can hardly blame the old devil though. Talk about big bazooms! Now, Mr. Forsythe, I think you'd do better to tell me what was in that letter. Something is worrying you."

Remembering the inspector's words about the innkeeper, Forsythe came to a decision. Keeping his voice low enough so the hum of conversation covered it he told Mr. Bantam what had been in the note. Mr. Bantam shook his large head. "Figured it was something bad. Might be best to get the lass out of here. Hate to lose her but that don't sound good."

"Sandy won't go. Mr. Bantam, could this be a local's idea of a joke?"

"Was going to deny that right off but you never can tell about people. Even people you've known all your life. Remember a butcher we had here at one time. Nice little chap. Came in every night regular for his pint. Quiet and polite. Took his meat cleaver to the boy who done deliveries 'cause he got the idea the boy was making eyes at his missus. Never can tell what goes on in another chap's head." The innkeeper mulled over the mysteries of other people's heads while he filled glasses and handed them out. The robust hiker was back, this time on Forsythe's other side. Her tankards dropped on the counter with a clatter and she shrieked. Mr. Bantam left his taps and bent over the counter. "What's up then?"

"He's got his hand on my—" She pointed at the aged hand clutching the bulging rear of her shorts. "The dirty old bastard!"

Bantam drew himself up and his face reddened. Apparently it was all right for him to criticize old Bob but he wasn't taking it from anyone passing through. "No dirty talk, lass, and he don't mean no harm. Can you lend a hand, Mr. Forsythe?"

Forsythe lent a hand. He pried the aged fingers loose from the girl's fat behind, took the reluctant oldster to a safer seat beside the fireplace, and returned to buy him a pint. Mr. Bantam refused the money. "On the house." As Forsythe deposited the bitter in the surprisingly strong hand of old Bob, Bantam bellowed, "One more time and out you go, Bob! Sit there and don't touch no one." As Bob ducked his head and sampled his pint, the innkeeper said slowly, "No need to trouble about the lass, Mr. Forsythe, long as she's in the Harper Arms. No harm come to her here. You going up now?"

"Yes. I want to see Sandy before I bathe and change."

"Won't find her upstairs. She's down in the snuggery with Nell seeing to—"

"She came *down*?"

" 'Bout an hour ago. Old Bob lent her his spare cane and down she come. Nell and me helped her on the stairs. Tried to tell her—"

Forsythe was away, down the hall, and slamming open the snuggery door. Miss Sanderson, comfortably ensconced on the leather sofa, glanced up from a magazine. "Just what do you think you're doing?" he demanded.

"Calm down, Robby. I—"

"I worry about you all day and here you are walking down the stairs. The doctor told you—"

"She done nothing wrong, sir." Nell leaped to her feet. "Doctor says she can come down if she's careful like. I heard him." The maid giggled. "Miss Sanderson talks to him so funny, sir. Called Doctor her little sunbeam and he *smiled*. Then she says he better watch out, he keep doing that and word'll get around he's lost his bedside manner and Doctor burst out laughing. Never saw Doctor laugh before!"

Forsythe dropped a manila envelope on the table. "All right, ladies, it appears I'm in the wrong. But I've a hunch, Sandy, you wheedled your way down here." He took the deep chair the maid had vacated. "Be a good girl, Nell, and have Mr. Bantam pour a very large neat Scotch for me."

"And an even larger one for me, Nell," Miss Sanderson said. She sniffed. "You smell like a distillery, Robby."

"Courtesy of a Highland uncle." Robby tossed the black and gold box into his secretary's lap. "You don't deserve this."

"Madame Helena! How thoughtful of you." Miss Sanderson ripped the cover off like a child opening a Christmas present. "Simply stunning! A signature scarf." She draped apple-green silk over the lapels of her dressing gown. "What ever possessed you, Robby?"

"An impulse. I was interviewing Madame Helena and thought of you tucked up in your bed."

"Just what did she have to do with Katherine St. Croix?"

"She designed some clothes for her and—"

Miss Sanderson leaned forward. "As the Red Queen said, begin at the beginning and go on to the end."

"Did the Red Queen actually say that?"

"If she didn't she should have." Miss Sanderson accepted a tall glass from Nell and took a deep swallow.

Nell handed another glass to the barrister. "Would you like a little snack with this, sir?"

Miss Sanderson shook her gray head. "Better not, Robby. I understand the missus is preparing steak and kidney pudding for supper."

"I'll wait for supper, Nell." Forsythe didn't speak until the door closed and then he turned to Miss Sanderson. "I spoke to Inspector Fitzgerald and showed him the note."

"What was his opinion about that?"

"Similar to ours. Someone feels us breathing down his or her neck and would like very much for us to vanish. Now, Sandy, kindly let me tell you this my own way."

Forsythe was still detailing the conversation to his secretary when supper was served. As they ate he finished reporting his interview with the dressmaker. Miss Sanderson shoved away her empty plate and tapped a thumbnail against her front teeth. "You told Madame Helena she had helped, and for the life of me I can't see how. She told us nothing we hadn't already heard."

Refilling his coffee cup, Forsythe added sugar and cream. "Bounce some ideas around, Sandy."

"Very well. Fitzgerald is correct. There are ten people who had motives and opportunity. None of the ten can account for their movements the night of the St. Croix woman's death."

"The opportunity we don't have to go into. Tell me the various motives."

"What about physical abilities?"

He rubbed his chin. "We'll take it for granted that the two women who don't have the necessary strength—Prudence Pyne and Sybil Dancer—worked with the maid Susan or Bella Dancer. Start with the suspects with the weaker motives."

"David Proctor. I can't stand the man and I'd love it to be him but I can't see the reason in his case. Maybe he simply was walking, saw Katherine sneaking into the temple, found she was stealing, and bopped her over the head. We know Prudence's motive and I won't go into that. Sybil…she may be eccentric but she has a strong sense of family. Sybil could have been outraged to find Katherine desecrating her ancestor's crypt."

"Good reasoning so far, Sandy. Carry on."

"The housekeeper, Mrs. Larkin. She obviously felt Katherine was a threat to her and wouldn't have wanted her to marry Sir Amyas. She could have killed Katherine to get rid of a rival."

"And brother George?"

The clicking sound increased in volume. "Have to be tied up with his sister's welfare, Robby. Plus the fact that Katherine obviously appealed to him." Her thumb dropped away from her mouth. "Maybe George Clark found Katherine in the crypt, made advances, and when she laughed at him picked up the bar and let her have it."

Forsythe chuckled. "Nothing wrong with your imagination. Next suspect—Sir Amyas."

"Well, Katherine did lead him down the garden path. Had the old chap mad for her and when he found her burgling the crypt, reacted violently. Only trouble is *he* was the one who rooted her body out and called us in. His son was right when he said the body wouldn't have turned up for years if his father hadn't gotten that idea about an amphitheater." She made a helpless gesture. "I simply can't work Sir Amyas in."

"How about Carleton Dancer?"

"I rather like him as the murderer. The boy may have decided it was time to have a taste of death at first hand. Perhaps it was because Katherine had led him on too. Yes, Carleton is one of my favorite suspects."

"And the other is Cassandra."

"Definitely." Miss Sanderson glowed with enthusiasm. "Strong motive. She'd gotten the goods on Katherine, forced her to leave. Suppose she found the crook lifting the family jade? I can *see* Cassandra bashing Katherine's head in."

"Only one left. Horace Gillimede."

Miss Sanderson slumped back against the pile of pillows. "Damned if I can work him in. Oh, I suppose I could rave on about him struggling with the devil in Katherine's soul and then finding her sinning in the temple but it won't wash. Robby, if Horace didn't lay a finger on either his wife or her lover when he caught them in the act I can't believe he'd hurt Katherine St. Croix. There's no violence in that poor old man."

"You know better than that, Sandy. There's potential violence in all of us."

Miss Sanderson was looking morosely into the cold hearth. "So there is. But we only go round and round. Any of them could be guilty as hell but how to figure which one. We're back where we started, Robby."

"No, we're not, Sandy. Consider this. Is it possible we're working from the wrong end of the whole business?"

"The wrong end?" She ran long fingers through her neat hair. "Do you mean the wrong motive?"

"Exactly."

Miss Sanderson continued to ruffle her hair up until it was no longer neat. "I give up. If you're trying to tie Katherine in with one of these people before she came to Harper I think Inspector Fitzgerald rather cut the ground out from under you."

"Katherine came to Harper not once but twice, Sandy."

"So she did. But...those clippings! Have you gone through them?"

He picked up the large envelope he'd thrown on the table and opened it. Taking out a sheaf of papers of uneven sizes he divided them into two lots. "I haven't had time. We'd better look them over now. You take the early bunch, I'll take the later ones."

For half an hour all that could be heard in the small room was the ticking of the clock and the rustling of stiff paper. They were interrupted once, by Nell, who gathered up the supper dishes and tiptoed out, closing the door softly behind her. Finally Miss Sanderson tossed the copies of the clippings down. "Waste of time. Bloody hell!"

"Your aura's turning red again." Forsythe grinned, leaned back, and started packing his pipe.

"According to Miss Sybil you were a wise old owl in your last life. Act like one."

"What conclusions have you drawn from Katherine's secret cache?"

"Only that she researched the Dancer family thoroughly before she arranged for Carleton to pick her up and take her to the Priory. Katherine started this collection in August of last year. Every reference to the Dancer family in the Chester and London papers was clipped. She had five accounts of Lady Dancer's death, more of her funeral, scads of junk about the entire family from society pages and gossip columns, any number of newspaper and magazine pictures of them." Miss Sanderson selected a paper and tossed it to Forsythe. "Sir Amyas, his son and daughter, and David Proctor at a bash in London. All I can say is the Dancers look great in evening clothes and Proctor wears his well too. Looks even more handsome in tails. Cassandra is almost pretty with her hair done and swathed in fur and tulle and diamonds. As usual she's holding on to Proctor with both hands."

"Anything else?"

"Oodles. The papers really love the Dancers. Here's Bella becoming president of a meals-on-wheels organization. Seems right in character. Her sister Sybil giving an address to one of those weird societies delving into the supernatural. The address is printed in full and contains a mass of the same terms Sybil used with us. Seeing Souls and auras and whatever. But all that this proves is that Katherine was interested in the Dancers and we already know that."

Reaching for her papers, Forsythe aligned the edges, and started going through them. Miss Sanderson watched him for a few moments and then said impatiently, "I told you everything that's in there."

"Not everything. You omitted one important fact."

"I am *not* playing guessing games," she said wrathfully. "You're on to something."

"Now why would you think that?"

"Because I know you and I know that expression. Your lips crinkled up at the corners like a large cat about to pounce on a mouse."

"Do cats' mouths crinkle at the corners?"

"*Robby.*"

"Calm down. Your aura's verging on bright purple now."

She threw a pillow at him. He caught it, laughed, and tossed it on the floor. "See, even Abigail Sanderson has violent impulses."

"Abigail Sanderson is fast becoming homicidal. You know who murdered Katherine St. Croix, don't you?"

"I believe I do." He sobered. "But there's not a shred of evidence that will stand up in court. Unless we do something extremely sneaky and underhanded this murderer is going to get away clean."

"You're saying we must lay a trap."

"Exactly."

"Give me a hint."

"In a moment I'll tell all. But for now I'll tell you this. Tomorrow is the first day of August. Tomorrow night I'm attending Horace Gillimede's little service—"

"And so am I."

"You can't, Sandy. The memorial service is to be held down at the lake. It's a long rough walk. Your ankle won't—"

"I'll be there if I have to crawl."

He sighed. "No sense in arguing. Knowing you it's useless. Now, you keep off that foot and I'll do the legwork. Tomorrow I'll have to see all of our suspects either in the morning or the afternoon. It won't take much of their time. I'll ask only one question. If the answers bear my theory out I'll have to enlist an ally."

Miss Sanderson's face had brightened. "Now you can tell all."

"I'll begin at the end. Sandy, how mad is mad?"

Chapter Thirteen

The first day of August dawned with a brassy cloudless sky and heat pressing down like a stifling blanket. Nonetheless the villagers eyed that sky and shook their heads. Old Bob wasn't at his usual place at the checkerboard and when Forsythe questioned the innkeeper he shook his head. "Storm brewing up and old Bob's scairt out of what wits he's got left by a summer storm. Says they're worse than the ones in the winter."

"There's not a cloud in the sky, Mr. Bantam."

"Wait and see. Can smell it in the air. Shame, Mr. Forsythe. Spoil your visit."

Forsythe smiled expansively. "On the contrary, it may make it."

Leaving a puzzled innkeeper he went on his rounds. In Harper he saw Miss Pyne and David Proctor for only moments a visit. His trip out to the Priory took the rest of the afternoon. When he left the last person he saw there, Horace Gillimede, and pointed the hood of the Rover back toward the village, he could discern a haze moving in from the west. By sunset a stiff wind was blowing in from Wales, herding ominous dark clouds before it. Neither the barrister nor Miss Sanderson had much appetite for supper. Leaving the table Miss Sanderson hobbled on Bob's extra cane to a window. "Going to be a dirty night, Robby. Do you think Horace's service will be canceled?"

"Not a chance. But I would urge you to reconsider going out there."

She echoed his words. "Not a chance. What time does the shindig start?"

"On the dot of midnight. We should be out there around eleven. Better wrap up well."

"It's a good thing we stuck our macs in. We're going to need them."

And they did. By the time they stepped out of the car the wind gusted around them, driving their raincoats against their bodies. They were admitted to the house by Cassandra, clad in jeans and a heavy sweater. Closing the door against the blast, she told them, "Awful night. I tried to talk Gramps into postponing this deal but he couldn't be budged. Come hell or high water Mother is to be honored. Come into the drawing room."

The drawing room was of magnificent proportions with a high vaulted ceiling, but it was as unkempt as the hall. The baronet was sitting, looking morosely into the dusty fronds of a palm on the hearth. His long lock of hair had been plastered down over his bald spot and he wore a checkered jacket and plaid trousers. The only other person there was David Proctor. He was modishly garbed in a fawn-colored raincoat with large tortoiseshell buttons marching up the front. It looked new and Forsythe decided it must be another item from his trousseau.

Seating Miss Sanderson, Forsythe asked, "Where are the others? Are they going to be here?"

"There'll be a full house," Sir Amyas told him. "Horace is down at the lake and Carl and Mrs. Larkin and George are with him. Prudence is spending the night with my sisters and they'll walk from the Dower House to the lake."

"Shouldn't we start down?"

Cassandra shook her head and the pigtails bobbed. "Carl will let us know when all is ready. I don't want David out in that wind too long." She perched on the arm of her fiancé's chair and captured his hand. "Darling, I do wish you would skip this. You'll catch your death."

"For God's sakes, Cass! Will you stop fussing? I'm not made of glass."

"Your chest. You know—"

He turned away from her and yanked his hand free. "You're worse than the Widow Hawkins."

She draped an arm around his shoulders. "Don't snap so. I only want you in fine fettle for our wedding."

"Wedding?" Sir Amyas jerked his head up. "Oh, that's right. You did tell me. I do hope you're not planning one of those huge affairs with ushers and—"

"Dear Amy." His daughter looked indulgently at him. "You never listen, do you? I told you David and I are going to sneak away and you won't be troubled with having to put on tails and marching me down the aisle."

Proctor managed to look both reproachful and petulant. "You *did* give us your blessings, sir."

"Of course I did, my boy. Glad to see Cassie so happy. As they say, it is better to marry than to burn." He paused and looked at his future son-in-law. "My head's stuffed with sayings like that and I never know where they come from. Who did *say* that?"

Proctor shook a baffled head and Forsythe hazarded, "The Bard?"

"*First Corinthians*," Miss Sanderson said crisply.

Forsythe laughed. "I'll bet you could give chapter and verse, Sandy."

"Amazing mind," Sir Amyas said heartily. "Tell you what, Miss Sanderson; you ever give up on Mr. Forsythe, you come and work for me. With your memory and my imagination we'd be unbeatable."

The door crashed open and Carleton bounded into the room. His hair had been blown into an untidy mass and he brushed a witch's lock out of his eyes. "All ready to go. The aunts and Aunt Pru have arrived. Flashlights on the hall table. Grab one. Black as the ace of spades."

In the hall they milled around, picking up lights, buttoning their coats. Cassandra produced a woolly scarf in a violent pink color and was wrapping it around Proctor's throat. "I am *not* wearing that thing, Cass."

"Don't be silly, darling. Here, I'll tuck it under your coat and no one will know it's there. It will keep you comfy." She told Miss Sanderson, "He has such a delicate chest, you know."

"We've heard about Mr. Proctor's chest," Miss Sanderson said dryly. "You better go on ahead. Robby and I will be slow."

"Watch your step," Carleton warned and loped off after Cassandra and her fiancé.

Sir Amyas walked beside Miss Sanderson, directing his light on the ground. She hobbled along supported by her cane and Forsythe's arm. "Decent of you to come tonight," the baronet said. "Ruddy foolishness, you know, but we're humoring Horace." As he spoke a jagged streak of lightning rent the blackness, making the hillside momentarily as bright as day. Right behind it a boom of thunder sounded like a barrage of artillery. "On top of everything else there's going to be a downpour. So, my little girl is getting married. Hate to lose her. Cassie handles everything. Nice girl. Not like her mother at all, thank God!"

"Horace seems the only one to truly mourn your late wife," Forsythe said.

"I was glad to be rid of her. Awful thing to say and I wish she hadn't died like that but the woman was like an albatross around one's neck. Dreadful person. Viola had a streak of cruelty, you know. Awful hard on those young chaps she took up. Ah, you can see the lights on the dock. Be careful, Miss Sanderson, bit steep from here on."

Panting, Miss Sanderson clutched Forsythe's arm. He pulled her to a stop and they looked down at the lake. Dozens of light bulbs illuminated the dock area and the people on it. Light reflected on the swells moving against the pilings. The white rowboat bobbed beside the dock like a cork.

"Ruddy insane," Sir Amyas muttered and helped Forsythe guide Miss Sanderson down the hillside.

They finally arrived at the dock and Miss Sanderson sank gratefully on one of the rude benches beside Miss Pyne. On the older woman's other side was Sybil Dancer and then her sister. Forsythe took a place beside his secretary and looked around.

Careful preparations had been made. Directly behind his bench was another with Cassandra, David Proctor, and Sir Amyas seated on it. Behind them the temple loomed, its façade looking rather ghastly in the light. At the far end of the dock Horace Gillimede stood behind a wooden structure that looked a little like a lectern. Behind him and to one side were Mrs. Larkin and her brother. George was muffled to the ears in a sheepskin coat and Mrs. Larkin wore a full-length evening cloak that billowed around her like the wings of a gigantic bat. Near them Carleton was setting up an electric guitar. A blaze of color was at his feet—a wicker basket, looking like a laundry hamper, spilled over with flowers. Cassandra Dancer had done her grandfather proud.

"Look at Horace," Miss Sanderson breathed In the barrister's ear. "I can hardly believe it's the same man. He looks so *clean*."

Horace was not only clean but looked as if he'd stepped right out of the Old Testament. He wore an immaculate white toga that swept to his sandals, his hair and beard blew like silver silk, and his face was alive with an expression of exaltation. A circlet of leaves was bound across his high noble brow. The wind was howling but Horace's rich voice soared over it. "Friends, relatives, you know why we stand here tonight in the storm raised by our Lord and Master. We come to honor Viola Gillimede Dancer who now is handmaiden for our God." He raised his face toward the storm-racked sky and right on cue lightning zigzagged and thunder rumbled. "Dear child, I know you hear Daddy's voice. I know you look down and see into our hearts. Look deep, my child, and see our love."

Horace lowered his eyes and swept them across the people seated on the benches. "The ceremony begins; those who are able will embark upon the waves and cast their floral offerings into the waters that took my child's life. Those who aren't may cast their flowers from the dock. While the flowers are being strewn we will offer up a prayer and appropriate music will be provided. Prudence Pyne, will you step forward and choose the flowers you deem suitable for your beloved friend."

Prudence Pyne rose and made her graceful and dignified way to the old man's side. Dancing light turned her hair into a cap as silvery as Horace's. They briefly conferred and as she bent over the basket of blooms Carleton strummed his guitar and Mrs. Larkin and her brother broke into song. They did have good voices—Mrs. Larkin's soaring soprano, George's a sweet and true tenor. "You'll take the high road and I'll take the low road," they sang.

"Dear Lord," Miss Sanderson whispered, "*Appropriate* music."

"In a way it is," Forsythe whispered back.

Miss Pyne selected a bouquet of sweet peas, stepped to the edge of the dock, and threw them into the waves. She bent her head briefly and then turned and took her place beside Miss Sybil. "Sweet peas are *not* suitable for a peacock," Miss Sybil hissed.

"Hush," Miss Pyne said.

The song ended and Horace beckoned to the singers. "Margaret Larkin and George Clark, step forward and make your choice." Mrs. Larkin's choice proved to be a spray of green orchids and her brother settled for a handful of daisies. Horace pointed down at the rowboat but both brother and sister shook their heads. They stepped to the edge of the dock while Horace Gillimede, in a magnificent baritone, worked on "Rock of Ages." After they returned to their places, Sybil and Bella were invited to honor the dead. Sybil picked up a bunch of blood-red poppies and her sister mauve gladioli garnished with a gilt bow. Deserting his post, Carleton stepped forward to assist his aunts into the boat while Horace extended a hand to help them down the ladder. Neither of the women needed help. They climbed down into the bobbing craft as agilely as primates.

"Ought they to do that?" David Proctor said hoarsely. "It's awfully choppy."

"Dancers are all like seals around water," Sir Amyas assured him. "Strong swimmers and good at handling boats. Besides, Horace has the boat secured to the dock with a stout rope. See?"

"I still don't like it. It makes me queasy even to watch."

While the boat bobbed the younger sister competently rowed it out to the length of the rope and Sybil tossed her poppies and the gladioli into the water. In the meantime George, with Carleton's guitar accompaniment, did a wonderfully moving job on "Danny Boy." "Quite a spectacle," Miss Pyne whispered and both Forsythe and Miss Sanderson agreed.

After the Dancer sisters had safely returned Horace raised his arms and voice. "Cassandra and Carleton, come forward." Carleton and his sister complied, selected flowers, and climbed down into the boat even more agilely than their aunts had. This time Mrs. Larkin undertook a solo of "Greensleeves." Afterward Sir Amyas performed his part in the pitching boat and as he returned to his seat clapped his future son-in-law jovially on the shoulder. "Pitch your flowers in, my boy, and let's get back to the house. It's starting to rain."

After the first tentative drops the heavens opened and the mourners were lashed with gusting wind and rain. Miss Sanderson turned up the collar of her coat and shivered. Forsythe didn't seem to even notice the downpour. He was watching David Proctor's slender back as he strode down the dock. Before he got to Horace's side the old man bent and picked up a tiny nosegay. "For David Proctor who called my child his violet. Violets for my daughter." He appeared to be urging the young man toward the ladder leading to the boat but Proctor was hanging back.

"Amy," Cassandra demanded, "what does Gramps think he's up to? David can't possibly get into that boat!"

"David is young and a man and Horace probably thinks he should. Let them work it out."

"Like hell I will!"

Cassandra started toward her fiancé but before she could reach him her brother and grandfather lifted Proctor bodily and dropped him into the boat. Proctor was shouting and Cassandra screaming and Mrs. Larkin decided to sing a chorus of 'Oh, Promise Me." The spectators left their benches and gathered along the edge of the dock. Proctor was hanging on to the gunnel with one hand and reaching desperately for the ladder with the other. All he managed to do was push the boat farther away from the dock. Horace lifted a mighty arm and tossed the violets into the bottom of the boat. "Pick them up! Give your violets to my daughter. She's waiting for them."

The young man was frantic with terror. He scrabbled for the flowers and couldn't reach them. He lifted an imploring arm to the people peering down at him. "He's mad!" he shrieked. "He's going to drown me. Help!"

"Yes," Horace roared. "I am mad. Mad with grief. You *killed* my daughter!" He brandished his arm again and this time his huge hand clutched a knife. The blade glinted in the swaying lights. "Confess or I will cut the rope and you will perish and vanish beneath the waves!"

Cassandra threw herself upon the old man but her brother hauled her away. "Amy," she screamed. "Help me! Gramps and Carl are crazy. They're going to drown David!"

Her father paid no attention. He bent over the edge of the dock, his eyes intent on David Proctor. Horace lifted the knife over the stanchion where the rope was fastened. "Your last chance, murderer! Confess or die."

Proctor's mouth was moving and his eyes were rolling frantically. They couldn't hear a word he was saying. "Shout!" Horace cried. "Lift your voice so all may hear."

Proctor's mouth writhed and then he threw back his head and bellowed, "I killed Viola! I killed Katherine! For the love of God, save me!"

Horace dropped the knife and turned to Forsythe. "It is over."

"Yes. Get him out of that boat."

In the circle of her brother's arms Cassandra was now standing quietly. Carleton pushed her gently toward their father and Sir Amyas cradled the girl, his cheek pressed against her wet hair. Horace pulled mightily on the rope until the boat nudged the pilings. Carleton swarmed down the ladder, lifted Proctor's limp figure, and started pushing him up the ladder. Bending, his grandfather seized Proctor under the armpits and lifted him as though the other man were a child. He tossed Proctor onto the planking and stood back, his chest heaving.

Everyone but Forsythe was staring down at the wet, bedraggled figure. Forsythe had turned away and was looking up at the shadowed walls of the temple. Three figures were trotting down toward the dock. The one in the lead halted by the barrister's side. "Could you hear?" Forsythe asked.

"Clear as a bell," Inspector Fitzgerald told him. He gestured at his sergeant and constable. "Get him up to the house, lads. The rest of you people get up there too."

Miss Sybil, straightening her turban, raised a haughty chin. "I have sworn never to enter my brother's house again."

"Tonight you will," Fitzgerald told her grimly.

"Well, perhaps I can make an exception in this case. Bella, in Mr. Proctor's next incarnation he will be a weacock."

"What's a weacock, Sis?"

"A cross between a peacock and a weasel. Do you agree, Mr. Forsythe?"

The barrister put a comforting arm around his secretary's shoulders. "I couldn't agree more, Miss Sybil."

They watched while the policemen lifted the weacock and, half carrying him, bore him up the hill in the direction of the Priory.

Chapter Fourteen

By the time Forsythe and a wet, bedraggled, and thoroughly exhausted Miss Sanderson had climbed back up the hill and entered the drawing room of the Priory, Cassandra had recovered from shock. She was standing, arms akimbo, wrathfully facing Inspector Fitzgerald.

"Was this atrocious charade your doing, Inspector?"

"No, Miss. Mr. Forsythe rang up this morning and told me to be down at the temple tonight before midnight. He said I might hear something of interest in the St. Croix case."

The girl swung on Forsythe. "So it was *you.* And you had Amy and Carl all primed to help Gramps."

Seating his secretary he helped her remove her sodden raincoat. "Not primed. I merely asked them not to interfere."

Carleton gave his sister a satisfied smile. "I enjoyed helping Grandfather, Cassie. Never did like Proctor."

Paying no attention to him Cassandra spun around. "And you, Gramps. How could you do this?"

Horace straightened the wilted leaves over his brow. "Robert came to me this afternoon as an emissary of our Lord and pleaded for my assistance. He told me he knew David was a murderer and had killed my child but he couldn't prove it. Robert said the only way justice could be done was to force a confession from the sinner."

"*Force.*" The girl returned to her attack on the policeman. "David would have said *anything* to get out of that boat. This is confession under duress. It will never stand up in court."

Fitzgerald's sleepy eyes looked benignly at her enraged face. "I realize that and so does Mr. Forsythe. But Mr. Proctor does have some explaining to do."

"David will *not* say a word. I'm going to ring up Willis Seton and we'll blow this whole smelly affair to smithereens."

"Sit down and shut up, Cass." Proctor slumped in a chair, moisture beading on his raincoat, his dark hair plastered to his head. "For the past year I've lived in hell. I'm glad it's over. I'm prepared to make a statement. But first I'd like to ask Mr. Forsythe a question."

"Ask away," the inspector told him.

"I thought I'd covered my tracks. How did you get on to me?"

"With difficulty," Forsythe told him. "We had ten suspects and it seemed impossible to single out the guilty one. For a time I struggled with Katherine's murder, trying to find the person with the strongest motive for it. But in each case the motive was too weak. After all, if one of you had discovered Katherine looting the temple it wasn't necessary to kill her. The natural reaction would have been to call the police and have her charged. Both the inspector and I tried to establish some previous link with the dead woman and one of you but there was no link."

The barrister templed his fingers. "Three rather odd things kept reoccurring. The costume Lady Dancer was wearing the night of her death, a hundred pounds in Katherine's carryall we couldn't account for, and the resemblance between Vanessa Linquist, a model once loved by David Proctor, and Lady Dancer."

Cassandra had sat down but she didn't shut up. "Bunk! Mother's sailor suit was simply a foolish whim. Katherine could very well have brought that money with her. As for the resemblance between this model and my mother…men do tend to fall for the same type of woman, you know."

"No, Miss Dancer, Katherine wouldn't have brought a hundred pounds to a house in which she was posing as a penniless orphan. In a way the woman was an artist. She kept a special wardrobe of cheap clothes for her roles and she was too shrewd to bring money into a house when it could have been discovered by a servant. Katherine St. Croix acquired that hundred pounds while she was in this house and the person who gave it to her wasn't about to admit it. Miss St. Croix was an old hand at extortion. Ergo, she was blackmailing one of you."

Forsythe looked at Cassandra and she stared back with hostile eyes. "I asked you a question this afternoon."

"You asked me whether I had ever talked about Mother's sailor suit with anyone but a relative or David or Aunt Pru. I said no. Gramps made us swear on the Bible we wouldn't tell about it and the only other people I discussed it with were you and Miss Sanderson. And I did that because Amy asked me to speak freely with you."

"That is exactly what all the rest said too. Yet—" Forsythe turned to his secretary. "Sandy, will you read that excerpt from the interview with Horace Gillimede?"

Twisting sideways Miss Sanderson pulled a notebook from her pocket and leafed through it. " 'I recounted my own sins and she commiserated with me. There were tears in her eyes as we spoke of my poor dead wife and she told me she understood why the shock had been so great when my daughter went to judgment clad in men's attire.' "

Forsythe nodded. "The 'she' Horace was speaking of was Miss St. Croix. If none of you talked, how did Katherine know about Lady Dancer's outfit?"

"Simple." Cassandra spat the one word. "Gramps told her all about it when he was raving on about his sins."

Her grandfather's silvery head shook. "No, my child, I didn't mention it to the woman. At the time I was so upset

I didn't notice what she said. Katherine didn't learn about it from me."

"That is what Horace told me this afternoon," Forsythe said.

Cassandra was frowning. "There're other ways."

"Name one."

"The dressmaker who made up the suit…she might have babbled."

"That occurred to me and when I found the woman had made clothes for Miss St. Croix also, I thought the dressmaker might have told her. Or that Katherine, who was an accomplished criminal, had gone through the records at the establishment. But it was demonstrated to my satisfaction that Katherine hadn't found out there."

Miss Pyne bent forward. "Katie found out while she was at my house. I can see that now."

Forsythe nodded. "When you combine the interest Katherine had in the Dancer family and her nocturnal absences from your house, Miss Pyne, you can understand that she wasn't *told* about the sailor suit, she *saw* it. Last year, at this time, Katherine St. Croix must have been roaming these grounds and she must have seen Lady Dancer die. She also saw who was with Lady Dancer when she died. I came this far in my reasoning and then I hit another snag."

"What was that?" Sir Amyas demanded.

"Katherine waited for eight months to return to Harper and worm her way into your home. Why didn't she start blackmailing immediately? The only answer to that was that the person involved in Viola Dancer's death didn't have enough funds to make it worth Katherine's while. That neatly disposed of half the suspects at one time. Sir Amyas, his son and daughter, his sisters—all are wealthy. I had to look at one of the other five, the ones without funds."

The lump in George Clark's throat jumped convulsively. "Maggie and me."

"That would also include me," Miss Pyne said.

Forsythe nodded. "And Horace Gillimede and David Proctor. While Katherine St. Croix waited she collected every reference she could find to this group of people and made a collection of newspaper clippings." He leaned back and closed his eyes. "You can picture the woman like a pretty blonde spider sitting in a web waiting for her fly to fatten." His eyes snapped open. "The moment I examined those clippings I realized the identity of the murderer. Horace, Miss Pyne, George and Mrs. Larkin, were not mentioned. But David Proctor—he was photographed with the Dancer family, gossip columnists were linking his name with Cassandra, rumors were drifting about their impending marriage. At the time of Lady Dancer's death Mr. Proctor wasn't worth black-mailing. But now he was to marry a girl not only wealthy in her own right but with expectations of an inheritance from her father."

Miss Sybil's turbaned head bobbed. "And the snake Katherine came to the Garden of Eden."

"She came with two ideas. To prepare her blackmail victim to be sucked dry and to pick up any item of value she could find. Katherine discovered there was nothing in the house to loot so she turned her attention to Sir Amyas. She would have been delighted to marry him and milk him dry too. But Cassandra took steps against the woman and forced her to leave. Katherine St. Croix then decided to pick up what money she could from David Procter and also to steal the jade from Mandalay. What she got, as we know, is death."

Forsythe leaned back wearily and Inspector Fitzgerald cleared his throat. "Now, Mr. Proctor, are you ready to make a statement?"

"Don't," Cassandra implored. "Please, David, let me call Willis Seton."

"I told you to shut up." Proctor's hair had dried and he shoved it back from his temples. A lock fell forward over his rounded brow. He looked from the inspector to the sergeant who held a pencil poised over a notebook. "I want all of you to hear this confession. I want you to know that I was with Viola when she died."

"David," Sir Amyas said softly. "Viola was going to divorce me and marry you. Why?"

Proctor's mouth snapped open and for a moment it looked as if he was going to order the baronet to shut up. Instead he said, "The morning of Viola's birthday she rang me up. Viola asked me not to come to the dinner but to meet her near the temple at eleven that night. I was delirious with joy. I *loved* her. She'd given me to understand that soon we would be together for the rest of our lives. I was there early, sitting in the moonlight, so happy. She came, dressed in her sailor suit, and pirouetted in front of me. She told me she'd had it made especially for me. I took her in my arms but she broke away and danced down to the dock. Viola said she wanted to talk to me on the water, that we had one last thing to do. We must break through our morbid fear of water."

The young man paused and looked into space. "I didn't want to get into the boat but the water was calm and I couldn't let Viola believe me a coward. So I took the oars and she sat opposite me in the bow of the boat. She took off her little white cap and threw it in the bottom of the boat. Then she ran her fingers through that marvelous silky hair and she smiled at me. She told me she'd come to a decision and she had a sacrifice to make. Viola said her father would be shattered by a divorce and there were Cass and Carl to consider as well as the aunts. She said it was her *duty* to stay with her family." Proctor gave a bitter laugh. "Duty! I knew what she meant. Viola preferred to be Lady Dancer, not Mrs. David Proctor. I saw her as she was—cruel, capricious, shallow. But I loved her and I argued, trying to change her mind. She was adamant."

Proctor looked not at Cassandra or the inspector but at Forsythe. "You mentioned Viola's resemblance to Vanessa. Yes, they looked alike. Vanessa said she loved me and married a wealthy man. Viola said she loved me and was going to stay with a wealthy man. I couldn't stand it."

"So you chucked the other peacock out of the boat," Miss Sybil said jovially.

"I did *not*. I said I would stay on in Harper and hoped she would change her mind. Viola flew into a fury. She jumped up as though she'd forgotten where she was. She screamed that she wanted me out of her life and out of Harper. She said she would go to the parents of my music pupils and tell them to discharge me. She said she would have Mrs. Hawkins throw me out of her house. She was rocking the boat and I was terrified she might upset it. I stretched out an arm to her and she must have thought I was going to strike her. Viola backed away and her legs caught on something and she fell into the water." He buried his face in his hands. "She went down like a stone."

"And you rowed back to shore and then overturned the boat and set her cap adrift," Inspector Fitzgerald said.

"I was afraid her body wouldn't be found. I left them as…as markers."

Cassandra's close-set eyes were distressed. "David, when I rang you up the next morning you pretended to search for Mother; you acted so worried. How could you?"

"I couldn't tell the truth. It was too late for that. Cass, I've gone through hell!"

"Then, Mr. Proctor, you were approached by Miss St. Croix," Fitzgerald said.

"Shortly after Viola's death, Cass told me she loved me. Up to that point I'd been so involved with her mother I hadn't even noticed Cass. I wouldn't marry…I couldn't. I was too heartbroken. But time passed and I started to heal. I thought perhaps Cass and I could have a life together." He took a deep breath. "When Katherine arrived at the Priory I hardly even noticed her either. But she came to see me and told me she had been on the grounds that night and she had seen and heard all. Katherine said at that time I wasn't worth bothering with but now I was in a position to pay her large sums. I told her it had been an accident but she laughed and said she'd tell the police and Dancer family I'd deliberately drowned Viola. Katherine was horrible; she gloated, I told her I didn't have a pound and she said—"

"She said you'd better raise some money on your watch and cigarette case," Forsythe said.

Cassandra snapped forward. "David," she wailed. "Those things weren't stolen."

"They were pawned and the old devil would only give me a hundred pounds for all of them. On Sunday Katherine rang me up and told me—"

"Ah," George Clark said triumphantly, "that's who the bird was phoning from the writing room."

"Katherine told me that Cass had found out about her past and she must leave the Priory. She told me to meet her at Mandalay that night at eleven-thirty. When I got there the candles were burning and she was breaking the glass in the jade case with the bar. I gave her the money and she tossed it on top of her carryall. There was another bundle of notes already in it. Katherine took out the pink jade and wrapped them up in her underwear. She knelt beside the carryall and pushed the jade in under the money. All the time she was talking. She ordered me to marry Cass and to do it fast. She said Cass had lots of money for both of us. She said I would never be free of her. Katherine's head was bent and her hair fell away from the nape of her neck. It looked so…fragile."

Proctor rested his head back against brocade. His face was drained and exhausted. "A red haze seemed to come down over me. When it cleared I was standing over her, the bar in my hand, and her head was…Oh God! I'd killed her. I'd gone mad and battered her head in!"

"The best way to kill a snake," Miss Sybil said approvingly.

Inspector Fitzgerald shot a bemused look at the elder Dancer sister and then asked Proctor, "Why did you put the body in the tomb and leave the shoulder bag and carryall exposed?"

"I didn't think the temple would ever be entered and I couldn't just leave her there, sprawled on the floor. I was temporarily insane. I think...I must have been trying to give her a burial." Proctor put a dramatic hand over his eyes. "That is all."

"Not quite," Forsythe said crisply. "I had just about given up on this case when I got your threatening note. It was foolish of you to do that."

The hand dropped limply. "What note?"

Miss Pyne touched the barrister's sleeve. "Mr. Proctor didn't put that note under the door of the Harper Arms. I did."

"Why?"

"I wanted you and Miss Sanderson to leave. I can see now I did the wrong thing. But Katie Parr was a demon and I didn't want you to find Mr. Proctor had killed her."

David Proctor's fine warm eyes were wide. "You knew it was me?"

"I guessed. The night that Katie Parr disappeared from the Priory I took a walk. I had just turned in at my gate when I saw you walking down the road from the direction of the estate. It was a moonlit night and I saw you clearly. At the time I thought you had been visiting Cassandra. Then when Katie's body was discovered I realized it had to be you who had killed her. You'd sworn you hadn't left your rooms that night. So I tried to frighten Mr. Forsythe and Miss Sanderson away from Harper."

"And that's where you made a mistake," Inspector Fitzgerald told her. He got ponderously to his feet. "Mr. Proctor, you will please come with us."

"Gladly," the young man said and went with the three officers.

Cassandra collapsed on the sofa, weeping. Helplessly her father patted her shoulder. "Better ring up Sarah and Roland," he told his son. "Cassie needs a woman to look after her."

In record time Lord Wabbersley and his stout wife arrived and scooped up their weeping goddaughter. Soon after, Miss Sybil, without glancing in her brother's direction, took a stately departure with her sister and Prudence Pyne. Mrs. Larkin was fussing around Sir Amyas and he curtly ordered her and George to their quarters. Then the baronet said to his father-in-law, "Better spend the rest of the night with us."

"No." The old man was on his feet. He adjusted a fold of his toga. "I will walk this night beside the lake."

"Grandfather," Carleton said. "You can't go out in that storm."

"Your ears are not keen, my boy. The Lord has calmed the wind and stopped the rain. He raised the storm to unmask a sinner and that work is done." Horace bent a stern gaze on the barrister. "I did as you asked. Was this the Lord's will?"

"David Proctor was involved in the deaths of two women."

"He was and I could not allow Cassandra to fall into his bloodstained hands. But I do not like what I have done this night. I go now to pray for the souls of the dead. I will pray for Viola and for the woman known as Katherine. I will also pray for the soul of David Proctor."

Carleton gazed after the old man. "Crazy as a loon!"

"I find him rather magnificent," Forsythe said.

Sir Amyas said heartily, "And I find your work magnificent. You've cleared the Dancer name. We didn't discuss fees but there will be a check in the post. Goodnight, Mr. Forsythe. Miss Sanderson, remember a position will always be waiting for you in my employ. Carleton, would you show our friends out?"

Carleton led the way into the hall. As Forsythe opened the door the young man held out his hand. On the narrow palm rested a large tortoiseshell button. With childlike pride he told them, "I yanked it off Proctor's coat when we were hoisting him up the ladder."

"You're going to add it to your Crime Collection?" Forsythe asked.

"Yes. It will be the star of my collection."

As the Rover turned back toward the village Miss Sanderson said morosely, "That lad's true vocation is as a mortician."

Forsythe shot a look at her tired face. "Going to take Sir Amyas up on his offer?"

"It might be rather interesting to help erect a Roman amphitheater." She squeezed his arm. "But I think I'll stick with you. You may have the makings of a detective."

"I'm a *great* detective."

"Watch it, Robby! In your next life you could be a peacock." She considered for a moment. "Or maybe a weacock."

Chapter Fifteen

The summer storm cleared the air and put an end to the oppressive weather. The morning that Forsythe was loading up the Rover was sunny but the air was pleasantly fresh. He lifted his pigskin case into the trunk and reached for his secretary's traveling bag. Her typewriter case fitted in between the other pieces of luggage. As he slammed the trunk lid down Miss Sanderson, carrying only her outsized handbag, came out of the Harper Arms. She was wearing her green linen suit and Madame Helena's silk scarf was tucked into the vee of the jacket. Her ankle was still bandaged but she had discarded the cane. Behind her paced their innkeeper, cradling in his arms a large wicker basket. Old Bob, his eyes fastened on Miss Sanderson's long shapely legs, hovered behind Mr. Bantam.

"Fine morning," Bantam told Forsythe. "Be a pleasant trip back to London. Mind how you handle this basket. Bit tetchy."

Carefully Forsythe positioned the basket in the middle of the rear seat. Then he held the door for Miss Sanderson but she was busy with Bob. Putting a hand on the old man's frail shoulder she dropped a kiss on his bald dome. He grinned from ear to ear. "He won't be fit to live with now," Mr. Bantam complained. "You've fair turned his head."

As Forsythe started the car their host stuck his head in the window. "Come back anytime, folks. Always be a warm welcome at the Harper Arms."

The car clattered over the cobblestones and Miss Sanderson twisted around to wave. The innkeeper lifted a majestic hand and old Bob was brandishing his cane. "Nice people," she told her companion.

"Salt of the earth. Sad to leave?"

"In a way, but I find I hunger for double-deckers and swarms of cars and breathing noxious petrol fumes. I'm afraid I'm not quite ready for a bucolic life. But I will miss some of the people here. While you were busy with Inspector Fitzgerald I had swarms of visitors."

"Any interesting tidbits?"

She smiled. "Oodles. Carleton is planning on renting a salon in London and showing his collection. Seems he plans to use Katherine's bone skulls and Proctor's tortoiseshell button as a special exhibit. He gave us pressing invitations and told me he expects crowds of people out to view them."

"No doubt he'll get them. Morbid types scenting blood. What about his father?"

"Going ahead full speed with the Roman amphitheater. Sir Amyas has made arrangements for Sir Godfrey's ancient bones to be interred at St. Jude. The vicar is going to have a small service and appropriate music will be provided."

"I wonder what selections will be played."

"Probably 'John Brown's Body.' By the way, Sir Amyas sacked his housekeeper and her brother. Seems he finally had a look around the Priory and decided to get rid of them."

"Have they any plans?"

"Nell tells me she and George will be hitched and her old dad is setting them up in a pub. I suppose Mrs. Larkin will tag along to give the place some class and probably drive the newly-weds mad."

"Did you see Cassandra?"

"Oh, yes. She still has it in for you but doesn't hold anything against me. Figures I'm just the hired help. She told me she intends to 'stand by her man.' Cassandra is arranging for the best legal counsel available. She's also encouraging her David to write a documentary about his little problem with Lady Dancer and Katherine St. Croix. Cassandra feels it will be a bestseller."

Forsythe sighed. "That is probably the truth. And if she feels he'll get off with a light sentence she's right. With that profile, those soulful eyes, and his temporary insanity, Proctor will have the jury firmly on his side."

"Did you believe his story?"

"Let's put it this way—David Proctor has the makings of a fiction writer."

"He killed both women in cold blood, didn't he?"

Forsythe guided the Rover over the humpbacked bridge and swung the hood into a right turn. "In Lady Dancer's case it was probably hot blood, practically on the boil. Proctor's ego had already taken a pounding from Vanessa Linquist and when Viola Dancer tried to discard him I should imagine he broke. I can picture him throwing or shoving the woman out of the boat."

"She didn't go down like a stone."

"My guess is Viola thrashed around while Proctor enjoyed. I can see him fending her off with an oar. For once Katherine wasn't lying when she threatened Proctor. She *did* see him murder Lady Dancer. When she blackmailed Proctor she was a dead woman. All he did was wait for a chance to finish her off."

"Which she gave him."

"He came prepared, Sandy. Gloves. That night, as we learned from George Clark, was warm and balmy and Proctor was wearing gloves."

Miss Sanderson's brow crinkled in thought. "For the life of me I can't understand why he didn't take those packets of money."

"They were rather a mess—covered with blood and bits of brain and bone. Too messy for our sensitive young poet. Anyway, Proctor, with marriage in sight, had no need for a trifling amount of money. Why are you looking so perturbed, Sandy?"

"As soon as he's free Cassandra plans to marry the man. Robby, he killed *twice*. What if he decides he wants the beautiful money and not a homely wife?"

Forsythe shrugged. "That happens to be Cassandra's funeral."

"You're rather callous."

"Fatalistic. She knows all about him. Anyway, Proctor's bright and may not try anything too drastic. He may feel you and I are lurking around, waiting for a suspicious death."

"And he'll be right," Sandy said grimly. "Odd, I can't understand the girl. Of all the Dancers she seems the most sensible."

"Cassandra is still a *Dancer*." He patted her knee. "Now, forget about the whole business and tell me what's in the 'tetchy' basket."

"Gifts. Fresh-baked bread and Cheshire cheese from Mr. Bantam and his missus. A yummy fruit pie and a pot of jellied veal from Miss Bella. A crocheted doily from Prudence Pyne and a heavy tome all about reincarnation from Miss Sybil. Sir Amyas gave me a gift for you but I'm not to say a word about it until we're back in London."

"Say a word about it, Sandy."

She debated and then said, "He insisted you have that jade Buddha. He—"

"Sandy!" Forsythe pulled the car over to the side of the road. "That's ridiculous! The jade is worth a small fortune."

"I know, but there's no way of saying no to Sir Amyas Dancer."

He looked over his shoulder. "And it's rattling around in that basket?"

"Hardly rattling. All swathed in cotton wool and in a metal box. The best course is to accept it gracefully."

"It will look well on my desk. All right, I'll be graceful about it. I also better arrange for insurance. You can come in and admire it occasionally if you share your bread and pie with me."

"Not a chance."

"Don't be greedy. Tell you what, I'll stop and pick up paper plates and cups and we'll picnic on the banks of some meandering stream. I'll even throw in a couple of bottles of wine."

"Make that nut brown ale and you're on," Miss Sanderson said.

"Done," Robert Forsythe told her.

Who killed the Foster family?

DORA CAMPBELL — The proprietress of Dora's Tea Shoppe, where the specialties of the day are bad food and malicious gossip?

SIR DONALD MADDERSLEY — The middle-aged man who never got over Gillian Foster's rejection of him in favor of the doctor?

IRENE MARKHAM — Gillian's ugly-duckling sister, who was once engaged to marry Dr. Foster herself?

MATTHEW JOHNSTON — The Fosters' crippled neighbor, who was ever so devoted to Gillian?

NURSE INES — The woman who single-handedly got Dr. Foster's medical practice off the ground, or so she claims?

This book is for Florence Shannon Fast and Jack J. Fast

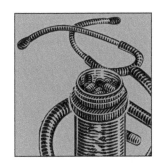

A Death for a Doctor

Chapter One

"No," Robert Forsythe said.

He didn't speak explosively, in fact the monosyllable was uttered mildly but his secretary, who had been watching Chief Inspector Kepesake, transferred her attention to the barrister. To a person who did not know Forsythe well the danger signs wouldn't be apparent. But to Abigail Sanderson, who not only was Forsythe's secretary but also once had been his father's, the signs were there. His normally pale skin was now ashen, his mouth had tightened into a tense line, and, most significantly, all color had drained from his ears. He was in the grip of a tremendous fury and was quite capable of throwing both policemen bodily from his flat.

Miss Sanderson glanced back at Kepesake, wondering whether he was aware of his danger, and found that worthy placidly examining his beautifully kept nails. Everything about Adam Kepesake was beautifully kept, she decided disdainfully. From the perfectly styled hair to the gleaming handmade shoes he was a fashion plate. Not so his sergeant, however. Detective Sergeant Brummell, dubbed with the unfortunate nickname Beau, as usual looked as though he had slept in his clothes and on rising had neglected to shave or run a comb through his shaggy hair. Once again she decided that the brains of that team lay with the sergeant, not the chief inspector. Kepesake was oblivious to her employer's rage but Brummell was staring apprehensively at Forsythe.

Adjusting his silk tie, Kepesake said, "I really can't see how you can speak for Miss Sanderson, old boy."

Forsythe's hands knotted into fists and Sergeant Brummell said hastily, "Been admiring your collection of jade, Mr. Forsythe. Is that Buddha the gift from Sir Amyas Dancer?"

"Of course it is," Kepesake said impatiently. "You know that as well as I do. Sir Amyas was quite impressed with the way Forsythe handled that nasty business for him last year. Nice little job, old boy."

Forsythe disliked being called "old boy" almost as much as he disliked the chief inspector. Again Brummell interceded. "You cleared that Farquson business up pretty fast too, Mr. Forsythe. Don't know what the chief or I would have done without you. That's why we came here tonight. This case in Maddersley-on-Mead has got us baffled."

"Hardly, Beau," Kepesake snapped. Sitting up straighter in his comfortable chair, he gestured. "After all, we're the professionals. Forsythe has simply blundered into a few cases and had incredible luck. I'll admit the newspapers have taken him up and made him sound like Sherlock Holmes but as a private detective—"

"I am *not* a private detective," Forsythe told him crisply. "I'm a barrister. And to be blunt, I've no intention of leaving London and assisting you on another case." Jumping up, he slammed a log on an already roaring fire.

Miss Sanderson inched her chair back from the hearth. Even on this nippy October evening the heat from that blaze was not really necessary. Forsythe's flat had excellent central heating, but perhaps it was better for her employer to slam logs around on the grate rather than use one on the chief inspector.

Kepesake, still blissfully unaware of his host's mood, was busily heaping fuel on Forsythe's inner fire. "It's not as though we're asking anything from *you*. All we want is for Miss Sanderson to go down to Maddersley, talk to the locals, pick up any bits of gossip she can, and—"

"And pretend to be the dead woman's cousin." Forsythe swung around and stood menacingly over the chief inspector. "Stay in a house where mass murder has recently taken place, be a target for some maniac who has killed four people. Let's get one thing clear, Kepesake. Sandy is not a *detective*. She's a legal secretary. Sandy wouldn't know how to take the safety off a revolver let alone engage in unarmed combat. The answer is no. Get one of your policewomen to do it."

Kepesake was finally looking apprehensive but Brummell reached up a placating hand and touched Forsythe's arm. He said slowly, "You haven't given the chief much of a chance to explain, sir. If you'd be kind enough to sit down and...Thank you. Now, sir, we've combed the files of women officers in the Central Bureau. Not one fits the bill. Same with female private inquiry agents. And if you want to blame someone for suggesting Miss Sanderson, blame me, not the chief. When we located the dead woman's cousin in a rest home I figured she was the same age as your secretary and even resembles her."

"And has this cousin agreed to allow another woman to masquerade as her?"

"She certainly has, sir. Her name—again that similarity—is Abigail Sanders. Miss Sanders never met either the dead woman or her other cousin who's living in Maddersley. Some sort of family feud. But Miss Sanders is shocked at her relatives' deaths. The idea of those kids being murdered sickened her. Miss Sanders says we've just got to get the bastard—" Breaking off, Brummell looked contritely at Miss Sanderson. "Sorry about that."

"Don't be," Miss Sanderson told him. "Tell me, sergeant, if my namesake and look-alike feels so strongly about this why doesn't she go to Maddersley and do the detecting herself?"

Turning his long head, Forsythe gazed at his secretary. Some color had returned to his ears and his mouth had relaxed. "Sandy, Beau said Miss Sanders is in a rest home."

"Has a terminal disease," Brummell said. "Doctors figure she won't last much longer. Miss Sanders has a lot of courage. Offered to do anything in her power to help. Says she'll brief you on everything she knows about the family. Even is willing to lend you some jewelry and other family mementos."

Miss Sanderson cocked her neat gray head. "And she looks like me?"

"A superficial resemblance." The chief inspector had decided it was safe to speak again. "Tall, thin, fine bones, blue eyes, gray hair. As Beau mentioned, about the right age too. Perhaps mid-fifties."

It was Miss Sanderson's turn to glare at Kepesake. She resented references to her age. It was one of her few vanities. Under her breath she used Brummell's expression. The bastard! And as usual Kepesake was wrong. Mid-fifties indeed! Forsythe caught her eyes and grinned. At least *he* was feeling some better. "Care for a drink, Sandy? Kepesake, Beau?"

Miss Sanderson's sherry and the chief inspector's whiskey were poured from cut crystal decanters that had been brought up from the barrister's Sussex home. Forsythe had to go to the kitchen for Brummell's beer. When his guests were supplied with drinks Forsythe sank back on his chair and took a sip of his own. "I think we deserve the details, Kepesake. This business about the locals. Haven't they talked to the police?"

"They talked all right. Babbled on about the Fosters. Paul Foster was a wonderful doctor. Gillian Foster was a wonderful wife and mother. The boys were wonderful children. Everyone loved them. Didn't have an enemy in the world let alone in Maddersley-on-Mead." Kepesake's deceptively kind hazel eyes glinted. "Even Mrs. Foster's sister gave us the same story. There's no way they'll open up to the police. We need someone who seems to belong, someone related to the victims. I'm certain the locals will open up to her."

Miss Sanderson gazed down into her sherry. "Perhaps they *are* telling the truth. Couldn't some deranged person have been passing through the village and murdered on impulse? Senseless killings have happened before, you know."

"The famous homicidal maniac? Not a chance. The killer was a person who knew the family, knew the house, someone the Fosters didn't fear."

"And who left one member of the family unharmed," Brummell said. "The youngest child, a baby girl, was untouched." Without warning and despite the waves of heat from the fireplace, Miss Sanderson shivered. Adam Kepesake nodded. "I know how you feel, Miss Sanderson. Beau and I have been involved with many homicides. I thought we were fairly hardened, but this one...We were called in immediately, you see. Maddersley hasn't a constable but the officers from Lambert took one look and rang up the Central Bureau. When Beau and I got there nothing had been touched. It was grisly. No, that's not quite the word. Beau?"

The sergeant's shaggy head shook. "Grisly right enough but more than that. Hard to explain."

"The children?" Forsythe suggested.

"There's that, of course. Got three kiddies of my own and deaths of little ones are awful, but no. I've seen kiddies we've had to scoop into baskets and it wasn't as bad as this." Brummell gazed into the flames. "I think what got the chief and me was that it was all so...so cozy."

Miss Sanderson's pale blue eyes widened and Forsythe cocked his head. "A strange word to describe murder," he told the sergeant.

Kepesake banged his fist on a green tweed knee. "Exactly the right word! *Cozy*. Damnably, unbelievably cozy. An immaculate family home. Not a thing out of place. Mother in the kitchen, seated at the table, a paring knife in one hand, chopped vegetables ready for salad—a pretty young woman wearing a ruffled apron. Father at his desk in his office. In front of him an opened medical textbook, a cigar on a tray at his elbow. Two handsome little boys sitting in child-sized chairs in the living room with the television showing a children's program." Gulping the rest of his whiskey, the chief inspector extended his glass for a refill. "And all of them dead! Mrs. Foster and the boys stabbed in the back, Dr. Foster horribly mangled.

And someone moved around that house after killing them. He propped up the bodies, washed the cups and glasses, switched the television onto another channel with a long children's show that came on at eight, built up the fire..."

Forsythe put down the whiskey decanter and tilted the sherry one over his secretary's glass. Miss Sanderson shook her head. "Whiskey, Robby. My flesh is crawling."

"So did ours," Brummell told her somberly. "There was something in that house to make flesh creep. Something evil. And I'm not talking about ghouls or goblins. I'm talking about something that looks human but isn't. Something that's still in that village."

Handing the sergeant another foaming glass, Forsythe asked, "How can you be sure of the movements of the murderer after his victims were dead? You said the fire had been built up and—"

"Witnesses, sir. The housekeeper, Mrs. Toogood, and the doctor's nurse, Miss Sarah Ines. Both of them knew all about the family habits. Seems Mrs. Foster was a pretty indulgent mother but on one point she was strict. The boys, Arthur and Andrew, had early suppers, were allowed to watch cartoons on the television from to six to seven, and then were sent up to bed.

"Nurse Ines and Mrs. Toogood left within minutes of each other, shortly after five. At that time the boys were in the kitchen being given supper by Mrs. Foster. The parents usually dined around eight but that evening they were dining at seven because the next day was Arthur's fifth birthday and Mrs. Foster planned to do baking and so on for the party. Before Mrs. Toogood left she lit the fire in the living room."

Brummell took a long drink of beer and ran a handkerchief over his lips. "The murders were discovered by Mrs. Foster's sister, Irene Markham, a few minutes past nine. According to the police surgeon the deaths had occurred around six and yet when Miss Markham arrived the fire had been built up and the channel of the television had been switched to one showing an animated fairy tale—a long one, running for three hours."

"And the dishes had been washed?" Forsythe asked.

"By hand. Mrs. Foster had a dishwashing machine but three cups and saucers, three teaspoons, and two glasses had been washed and neatly set to dry on a dishcloth on the drainboard."

Miss Sanderson's fine brows drew together. "Surely Mrs. Foster might have rinsed the dishes herself."

"No," Chief Inspector Kepesake said. "Prior to the stabbings the Foster family were given massive doses of Seconal. According to Nurse Ines the drug was taken from the cupboard in the doctor's office—"

"When?" Forsythe asked.

Kepesake shrugged. "Before the crimes were committed. Indefinite. The drug was in liquid form, kept for patients unable to swallow pills, and was rarely used."

"Surely that narrows the list of suspects down."

"To patients and friends. In other words to everyone in the village. Dr. Foster was somewhat careless with that cupboard. Would leave people in his office alone and never locked it up. Anyway, as I started to say, it looks as though the drug was put in the teacups and glasses of orange juice. The coroner estimated the children had consumed enough to have killed them. After drinking a powerful dose like that I find it hard to believe Mrs. Foster was capable of gathering up the cups and glasses and washing them."

"I take your point," Forsythe agreed. "You say the doctor's body was mangled?"

"Rather gruesomely. If you like I can show you the official photos."

"Not necessary. But the wife and boys were not?"

"One stab wound in each back. Carefully done, as a medical man might. Looks as though the hate was directed at the doctor, doesn't it?"

"Maybe not, chief," Brummell, said. "Could be the other three were stabbed first and by the time the bastard—sorry, Miss Sanderson. By the time the killer got around to the doctor he just had a taste for blood and ripped and tore."

"Then why didn't he kill the baby girl?" Miss Sanderson asked.

Brummell wiped beer foam from his lips again. "Don't know. Maybe something scared him off. Maybe…maybe his lust for blood was satisfied when he mutilated the baby's dad. Hard to say."

She asked another question. "Was the weapon left on the scene?"

"No," Kepesake said. "The police surgeon said the knife blade was long and narrow. Possibly a very sharp butcher knife. The knife didn't come from the Foster's kitchen."

Leaning forward, Forsythe jabbed at the logs with a poker. The fire blazed up and this time Miss Sanderson, feeling strangely chilled, was glad to feel the surge of heat. They sat quietly, Brummell drinking his beer, Kepesake eyeing the glass case containing pink, white, and green jade, Forsythe tapping a long finger against the arm of his chair. Then Kepesake said rather diffidently, "If you agree to cooperate, Miss Sanderson, we'll give you all the assistance we can. You can visit Miss Sanders's rest home and soak up the family history. I'll give you all our files and photos to study and also a list of the names and descriptions of the villagers. I know you have a remarkable memory."

"Sandy has," Forsythe said. "I can appreciate your position, Kepesake. It does look as though help is needed to loosen the tongues of the locals. But I strongly object to Sandy being stalked out like a goat. What about using me? I could pose as a friend of the family—"

"Won't work, old boy. For one thing the newspapers have printed your picture too often. Maddersley-on-Mead may be a bit ingrown and backward but they do get London papers. Besides, how are you going to convince the dead woman's sister, Miss Markham, that you're an old friend?"

"The sister is a suspect?" Miss Sanderson asked.

"A prime suspect. One thing we did discover is that Paul Foster was once Irene Markham's fiancé. Seems she brought him home to meet her pretty young sister and within the month Gillian and Paul were married. Irene was estranged from them until about a year ago. She lived in London and didn't even acknowledge the births of her two nephews. But when Gillian was pregnant with the little girl Irene was persuaded to return to the village. The only person we've located with a motive is Miss Markham."

Without waiting for Forsythe Miss Sanderson reached for the decanter and refreshed her glass. "Who's looking after the baby now?"

"Irene Markham."

"The prime suspect is caring for the only surviving member of the family?"

"I don't like it myself," Kepesake admitted. "But it's only for a short time. The baby's guardian is Dr. Foster's brother. Leonard Foster and his wife are in Saudi Arabia. He's an expert on oil development. They'll be back in England shortly and the child will be given to them. Anyway, if Miss Markham is the murderer I can scarcely see her harming a baby in her care."

"What's the child's name?" Miss Sanderson asked.

"Lucinda," Brummell told her. "Lucinda Gillian Foster, known as little Lucy. A bonny baby, looks like her mother. One thing we haven't mentioned. At the time of her death Mrs. Foster was about three months pregnant."

"Dear God," Miss Sanderson whispered. After a time she glanced up at Forsythe. "Robby, I know you disapprove but I'm going to Maddersley. Mrs. Sutter can take over my work."

"And if I forbid you to go?"

"You'll have my resignation."

Her words dropped like stones into a pool. The silence that followed them rippled out like tiny waves in water. Both Abigail Sanderson and Robert Forsythe were appalled by her threat. More than their professional relationship was at risk. Miss Sanderson was the only mother Forsythe had ever known. He was the boy she'd cherished from childhood. Above all they were friends.

Adam Kepesake looked embarrassed but Brummell wagged his shaggy head. "Surely," he said gently, "it needn't come to that."

Forsythe moved forward. He took one of his secretary's hands in both of his. Her hand was cold. He squeezed it, trying to warm it. "No," he said. "It certainly won't. Sandy, I'll trust your judgment. But why? The children?"

"The child. It's too late for Arthur or Andrew or for the unborn baby. It's not too late for little Lucy. I have a feeling…"

"One of your fey feelings again?"

"Perhaps. But I'm needed. When Lucy's guardian claims her, when she's safe, I'll leave that place like a shot. In the meantime…"

"In the meantime be careful. Be very careful, Sandy."

Chapter Two

Be very careful, Miss Sanderson warned herself as she clambered down from the single-decker bus and took her heavy case from the driver. Remember you're now Abigail Sanders, an affluent but frail and aging lady. After the charming letter to Irene Markham that the dying woman had dictated to Miss Sanderson and the way her delicate health had been stressed, it certainly wouldn't do to hop about athletically. Cousin Irene's reply to that letter, although brief to the point of curtness, had acknowledged the need for Miss Sanders's support. A postscript had been added, caustically pointing out it was indeed odd that it had taken a tragedy to bring the two cousins together.

Allowing the case to drag her arm down, Miss Sanderson gazed around the village of Maddersley-on-Mead. The bus had stopped in front of the Fox and Crow and she turned to scrutinize the inn. It wasn't an authentic relic of a long-passed century but rather was a fairly modern structure tarted up with mullioned windows and a brass-bound door. Completely pseudo, she decided, fake beams, imitation leather, and artistically battered pewter, doubtless imported from Japan.

The brass-bound door creaked open and a man strolled out, bestowed a genial smile on her, and took the case from her hand. "Paddy Rourke," he told her. "Innkeeper. If you're looking for accommodations you've come to the right place. The Fox and Crow is the best in the village. Also the only. Lunch is being served right now."

She smiled back. "Killarney?"

"County Clare. At least my old dad was from that little bit of heaven. Does it show?"

"It sounds. The lilt is there."

More than the lilt was there. His milk-white skin, black curls, and impish blue eyes fairly shrieked Ireland. He was steering her toward the door but she shook her head. "Sorry, I won't be staying at the inn. Could you direct me to the Markham house? I suppose it's called the Foster house now."

"We still call it the Markham house. You'll be Miss Sanders then. Come to keep Irene company in her hour of need. Ah, don't look so surprised. It's a wee place and news travels fast in Maddersley. I hear you've not been well. It's a fairish walk and if you'd like to come in and rest I'll have a delivery van give you a lift to the house."

Miss Sanderson debated. It might be better to walk. Give her a chance to look the village over. "You're kind, Mr. Rourke, but my doctor insists on exercise. I'll walk slowly. But if you could send my case…"

"That I'll do. Rog Austin will be making his rounds about two. Now, as to directions." With his free hand he pointed up the hill. "The Markham place is on Jericho Lane. Can't miss it. Church on one corner and Abercrombie's pasture on the other. House is the last one on the lane. Irene won't be there. Keeps the shop open until five. But Mrs. Toogood will welcome you."

She thanked him and set off up the walk, shortening her normally loping strides and attempting to look frail. It was a dreary day and sullen clouds banked up in a solid overcast hinted of rain or sleet. Probably sleet. The wind was cold enough to make her turn up her collar and burrow into her heavy coat.

The village looked as dreary as the weather. Past the inn was a greengrocer's, a notion shop, and a chemist's. The notion shop was boarded up. On the other side of the street a number of small shops huddled together as though for protection from the chill wind. She checked them mentally against the map Kepesake had showed her. Dora's Tea Shoppe, The Cheese Tease, Marlow's Bakery, Austin's Meat Market, Ferne's General Store. The last shop catered to female clientele. The window was crowded with sweaters, blouses, gloves, and scarves. A gold-lettered sign said merely *Irene's*. Miss Sanderson wondered whether she should cross over and meet her cousin. She decided against it. Few of the villagers seemed to be braving the October weather. An aged couple tottered out of the meat market and a buxom matron was heading for The Cheese Tease. All of them carried umbrellas.

Beyond the chemist shop was a straggle of row houses, narrow and squalid looking. The last one fell behind and was replaced by a hedged pasture where two cows leaned together under the bare branches of a huge maple. The cobblestoned road trailed off into a gravel surface and curved away toward a stone bridge. The road led to Maddersley Hall, home of the local gentry. That way wasn't for her, at least not yet.

A sign at the corner of the hedge told her she was about to turn onto Jericho Lane. She crossed the narrow road and stopped to examine the church. St. Mark's was on a par with the rest of the village. It was built of gray stone and flint, couldn't decide whether to appear Gothic or Elizabethan and managed to look merely grotesque. The manse, set well back among dark pines, looked like an excellent setting for a horror film. This was the lair of the Reverend Doctor Daniel Clay and his aged housekeeper Mrs. Gay.

The banked clouds, weary of retaining their burden of moisture, decided to release it. Icy sleet pelted down and Miss Sanderson yanked her headscarf closer, drew her long neck turtlelike into the fold of her collar, and resisted an impulse to break into a run. Careful, she warned herself sternly, as Mr.

Paddy Rourke had said, this is a wee place and there may be an invisible but avid audience.

Beyond the pine-shrouded manse were three cottages. She gave them an approving look. These were the nicest places she had yet seen. They were identical, neatly fenced, slate-roofed, half-timbered, with small perfectly proportioned windows. They were owned by a gentleman in London and rented to sundry tenants. The first cottage had a bright red door, the next a blue one, and the last a sunshine yellow.

As she neared the first cottage the red door opened and a young woman moved jerkily down two shallow steps. She was modishly dressed in leather—a white coat belted around a narrow waist, black boots reaching high on sparrow legs, and a black leather tam perched jauntily on fair hair that fell lushly to white leather shoulders. In a triangular face huge brown eyes bulged—eyes that didn't need the emphasis of the heavy coating of shadow and black eyeliner that had been painted on.

As Miss Sanderson reached the gate the girl clattered it open and stepped out on the walk. She flashed the older woman a tentative smile and for a moment it looked as though she were about to speak. But the black tam jerked to one side and the girl brushed by. Not as friendly as the innkeeper, Miss Sanderson thought, but then not in a commercial business. Reaching into her splendid memory bank, she brought out the name—Linda Beauchamp, ex-schoolmistress, apprentice writer, ex-patient of Dr. Paul Foster. And, according to Sergeant Brummell, full-time neurotic.

She identified the occupants of the other two cottages. Blue door—Miss Sarah Ines, former hospital nurse and, until recently, devoted aide to the young doctor. The yellow door led onto a shallow wooden ramp. Matthew Johnston—retired carpenter, close friend of the Foster family, a cripple. Taking a deep breath she stopped before the wrought iron gate of the last house on Jericho Lane.

The Markham place was not a cottage but a sprawling two-storied building in plaster and flint. The windows were outlined with dark green shutters, a wide veranda ran the full length of the house and was framed in vines bare now but promising heavenly shade on a hot summer day. A small brass plaque set into the gate announced this was the residence of P. A. Foster, M.D. It was well cared for; the gate didn't creak but swung back silently on well-oiled hinges. Three walks led like spokes in a wheel, one directly to the foot of the veranda, the left one circling around to the back of the house, the right leading along the other side and bearing a white-painted arrow sign lettered *Surgery*.

Sleet stung at her face as she climbed the steps to the shelter of the veranda. On wide boards were bulky objects shrouded in canvas. She pictured wicker furniture awaiting a summons on duty on a drowsy July day. She stepped onto a mat telling her in green letters that she was welcome, and pressed the bell. Within the recesses of the house the first bars of the *William Tell* Overture pealed. She waited…and waited. As her hand reached again for the bell the door opened a couple of inches revealing a heavy chain and one small gray eye.

"Well?" Miss Sanderson said impatiently.

The welcome mat appeared to have been lying. The eye unblinkingly regarded her but no move was made to remove the chain. "Who are you?" a disgruntled voice demanded.

"Abigail Sanders. I'm expected."

"You're late. Thought you'd be here about noon and it's after one. Figured you'd drive faster than that."

"I don't drive," Miss Sanderson told the eye. She certainly did and would have preferred to have brought her own sporty car but her namesake couldn't drive and it was necessary to stay in character. "Are you going to let me in or not?"

"Hold your horses."

The door thudded closed, the chain rattled, and then it opened wide and the woman stepped to one side. Miss Sanderson, chilled, miserable, and now thoroughly annoyed, lunged into the hall. She had time only to note black-and-white tile, a scarlet telephone on a stand, a staircase that only missed

204 E. X. Giroux

being gracious, and double doors opening to the left, before the housekeeper began to speak. "Toogood's the name. Hannah Toogood. You're all wet. Raining?"

"Sleeting and I'm nearly froze."

"Be warm enough here. Got central heating. Wish Bert and me had it. Take off them wet things and get them in that closet. Don't go tracking up the floor. Just got done scrubbing it."

As Miss Sanderson obeyed she slid glacial eyes over the housekeeper. Mrs. Toogood was a blowsy woman of indeterminate age, clad in a gaudy cotton dress, a voluminous apron, and ancient carpet slippers. Her expression was as disgruntled as her voice. Miss Sanderson had a hunch Hannah Toogood was not going to prove to be one of her favorite people but she must attempt to get along. She held out a small olive branch. "Sorry I was later than expected. Did you hold lunch for me?"

"Don't do meals. Have enough on me hands with the baby and this house. Have to get your own." Mrs. Toogood took off her apron and plucked a gray coat with a ratty rabbit collar from the depths of the closet. "That is if'n you can find any food. Miss Irene don't keep enough food for a sparrow. Now, when the missus was alive it was different. Set a good table did the missus." The woman kicked off her carpet slippers and pushed her feet into rubber boots.

"What are you...Mrs. Toogood, are you leaving?"

"My half day. Should have got away sharp at twelve. Gotta take one of the kids—got six little ones, Bert and me—over to the dentist at Lambert. Gonna cost, that dentist acts like he's setting pure gold in them teeth but Edgar, he's our oldest, had me up half the night with the toothache. Not my Bert. Never fear. Swear that man could sleep through anything."

"But you can't leave. The baby. I know *nothing* about babies. The only time I ever see babies are in prams being pushed through parks."

Mrs. Toogood gave her a wide smile. One of her front teeth was missing. "Guess you'll have to learn in a hurry. If'n you'd got here earlier I'd have been able to show you how." At the panic in the other woman's face the housekeeper relented and patted Miss Sanderson's arm. "No need to take on, Miss Sanders. I just put the little one down and she'll be good for about two hours. Some babies are a trial but not little Lucy. Child's an angel like her mother, rest her soul." She tugged a woolen hat down over untidy mouse-colored hair. "Clothes laid out in the nursery. When she stirs, diaper her—"

"Diaper!"

"Nothing to it. These are them disposable nappies. Couldn't afford them for my kids but there's some as can. Bottles made up in the fridge, her food in the cupboard, Miss Irene will be home after five and take over. Best of luck."

"Wait!" Miss Sanderson wailed as the door started to close. A gray eye peered through the crack. "Clean forgot to tell you. Get that chain on this door and keep it on. Don't let no one in 'less you know them."

"I don't know *anyone.*"

"Be awful careful. This is one bad house. Always has been. Someone could come right in and slit your throat!"

Beyond protest Miss Sanderson watched the door thud closed. With a shaking hand she reached for the chain. Nothing, she thought wrathfully, like leaving a person in a strange house where four people had recently been murdered and making an exit line like *that.*

Chapter Three

For moments Miss Sanderson stood glaring at the blank panel of the door. Then she swung around and peered up the shadowy staircase. Somewhere up there little Lucy, blissfully unaware she was now in the hands of a rank amateur, was sleeping. At this point, Miss Sanderson thought, she would rather face that murderous stranger Mrs. Toogood had warned her about than a baby who would have to be diapered and fed.

She gave herself a mental shake. Only minutes into the house and already going to pieces. Perhaps Robby had been right and she should never have come here. At the thought she lifted her chin and squared her thin shoulders. Instead of going into a blue funk she would use the time to look the house over. Again she reached into her memory and drew out the police artist's plan of the house. This wide hall bisected the main floor. Left side devoted to the family's living quarters, right to the doctor's surgery.

Best to get the worst over first. She opened the door into the waiting room. As she stepped onto sand carpeting she noted the door directly opposite. This was the exterior one that opened onto the walk at the side of the house. The patients had been admitted through it. Crossing the room, she examined the white molding around the doorframe. This was the door by which the police thought the murderer had left. Bloodstains no longer marked the pristine surface. She opened the door and looked down a flight of steep steps. The door, like the front one, locked automatically when the latch clicked. She turned and looked around. The waiting room looked like many she had been in—four imitation leather chairs, a matching couch, plastic-topped tables piled with ancient magazines, in one corner a bank of file cabinets with the nurse's desk in front of them. On the shining desk top there were only two objects. A telephone, brown this time, and a nameplate—*Sarah Ines.*

At the end of the room was the door to the doctor's office. Remembering the police photos she was far from eager to enter that room. The worst first, she reminded herself, and swung open the door. It looked as ordinary as the waiting room. Someone had done a good job cleaning it up. A wide desk, a swivel chair in back of it, two armchairs in front of it, a bank of file cabinets, a bookcase filled with heavy medical books, and the drug cupboard. She wandered over and tried the glass door. Locked. Looking at the empty space that once had contained a bottle of liquid Seconal, she thought: nothing like locking the barn door...

As she backed away from the cupboard she glanced at the floor area around the desk. The scrubbing hadn't been a success here. Tan carpeting was marred with ugly dark blotches. She closed her eyes, trying to will away the photo of this room, but there it was in dreadful color. Paul Foster's head had rested against the chair back, his face untouched—a handsome man with thick dark hair, wide-set eyes, a good chin. From the throat down, a horror—shirt, vest, pants sliced with powerful strokes, straining away from a mass of protruding intestines—slit like a filleted fish from collarbone to groin. Blood welling onto the desk, the floor, blood spattering the wall. Most dreadful of all—the arms. Lifted onto the desk, one hand touching the open textbook, the other reaching for the tray where a half-smoked cigar lay. Merciful God, Miss Sanderson thought, I hope that drug was powerful. I hope Paul Foster didn't feel that knife shredding his body.

Her eyes snapped open and she saw only dark marks on carpeting. Swinging the last door open, she took a perfunctory look. An examination table, a linen closet, a sink, one straight-backed chair. She made record time returning to the hall. Where now? The living room, of course. Double doors opened onto a bright cheerful room, salmon and chocolate brown—salmon walls and salmon carpeting, much more luxurious than in the surgery, and brown velour furniture. Two armchairs facing each other across the hearth, gleaming tables, a television set into an expensive rosewood cabinet. On the tabletops the glint of small copper and brass ornaments. Above the mantel was an oil painting of a pastoral scene, not well done but cheerful—white sheep grazing on vivid green turf, lavender hills rising against a cloud-specked sky, a farmhouse perched on a rise, in the foreground two small boys rolling a hoop across improbable green grass.

Small boys. Miss Sanderson looked for and found the children's chairs—a miniature rocking chair with a salmon velour cushion, a small armchair upholstered in chocolate brown. Her mind flashed the scene as it had been that night when Brummell and Adam Kepesake arrived. The younger boy propped up in the rocker...Andrew James Foster, aged three years, eight months. The older boy in the armchair...Arthur Paul Foster, who hadn't reached his fifth birthday. Two small boys, quite dead, facing a television screen on which figures from a fantasy moved and laughed and sang. On the grate a freshly kindled fire beaming heat that could never warm those children.

Tears prickled bitterly at her eyes and Miss Sanderson moved jerkily across the room to the bay window. She pulled aside salmon-and-brown-striped curtains and looked across the veranda at lashing sleet. She glimpsed the gate of the neighboring cottage and leaned forward. A wheelchair was briskly trundling up to the gate. In it crouched a figure swathed in a heavy coat and tweed cap and a tartan muffler. A matching tartan rug was tucked around the man's legs. Matthew Johnston, who once had baby-sat for his younger neighbors, was returning home. She felt slightly comforted. If she came to a desperation point with Lucy she could always run next door for some expert counseling.

She made her way to the dining room. It was rather small but well appointed—a round cherry table centered with a bowl of dried flowers, six matching chairs, a towering breakfront sideboard, a silver wine cooler set in a metal tripod, fine china and glass in the sideboard. She didn't care for the damask wallpaper or the heavy velvet at the window but she admitted blowsy Mrs. Toogood was an excellent housekeeper. Not a speck of dust and the silver was gleaming. A door opened onto a tiled hall and in a few paces she reached the swinging door to the kitchen.

Ah, here was a room to be appreciated by lovers of fine food, and Miss Sanderson, despite her greyhound build, had a robust appetite. This kitchen was, as all kitchens should be, the heart of the home. Modern convenience had been marvelously blended with traditional comfort. The wide window was curtained with a checked material and the sill was crowded with red, pink, and white geraniums. A matching checkered cloth covered a large round table. More red-and-white cushioned four ladder-back chairs. Black-and-white tile floored the room and the snowy white squares were echoed in a combination refrigerator and freezer, a dishwashing machine, the metal cupboard doors, and so many small appliances that Miss Sanderson lost count. She cast an approving glance at a long spice rack, patted the wall oven, touched a countertop stove, and realized breakfast was long passed and she was famished. She headed toward the fridge and then pulled up short. Time for her stomach later. Now, back to business.

She returned to the round table and this time deliberately recalled the kitchen photo. Of the four this had been the easiest to take. Gillian Foster, twenty-seven, was seated at the table. Her head had fallen forward and a mass of red-gold hair mercifully masked her face. The ruffled apron Adam Kepesake had mentioned had been tied around her narrow waist. She had looked peaceful and domestic. In front of her a chopping board had been strewn with carrots, tomatoes, celery. In one delicate hand was a paring knife, her other hand lay across the table, slender, shapely, even in death possessing a sense of grace. This time there were no dark splotches. There had been only a small amount of blood and the tile had been wiped clean. Circling the table, Miss Sanderson pulled out a chair. She'd been wrong. Only three chairs had gay cushions. The one Gillian had died on had been removed.

Between the towering refrigerator and the back door was another door, this one louvered. Behind it was a laundry area containing a clothes-washing machine, a dryer, two deep sinks, and a bank of cupboards above a long counter. The room was bare now but in the police photograph it had been a riot of color. All the party materials had been stored in this room. The dryer had been lost to view under red and blue and yellow balloons, and eight small baskets, heaped with candy, had been lined up near eight party hats. Four were pirate hats for small boys, the rest silver tiaras for equally small girls. On the wall a message cut from red drawing paper and covered with glitter had been tacked. *Happy Birthday, Arthur.*

She found she had been in error when she thought the worst to be faced was in the doctor's office. This room, so festive that night and with no signs of violence, proved to be the hardest to bear. Arthur and Andrew who had been waiting excitedly for the birthday morning, anticipating a party, propped in front of a television and dead, beyond birthdays and parties and life. A wave of rage engulfed her, blurring the contours of the room, knotting her hands into helpless fists. The beast who had wrenched life from those innocent children must be found, must be destroyed.

A bar of the *William Tell* Overture pealed lustily through the house and she jumped. Forgetting Mrs. Toogood's admonitions, she tore off the chain and flung the front door wide. The young man on the veranda looked startled. Behind him, parked half over the curb, was a small gray van lettered in scarlet— *Austin's Meat Market.*

"Rog Austin," he told her. "Paddy from the Fox and Crow asked me to bring this bag up."

She stood aside and he stepped into the hall. For a moment she had thought the innkeeper had decided to bring the case himself. Rog Austin had the Irishman's wiry build and dark curly hair but he was younger, looking barely in his twenties. On closer examination there was little resemblance between the two men. Austin's eyes were that shade of gray that is almost color-less, and he had a fall-away chin, and a full girlish mouth. Miss Sanderson had liked the looks of Rourke but she didn't care at all for Austin's. The colorless eyes were staring avidly around, the full moist lips were parted. He reminded her of the type of person who stops to look at the site of car accidents, hoping to see a mangled body or bloodstains.

His eyes wandered from the closed door to the surgery to the double doors of the lounge. "Miss Markham said as how you aren't well. If you like, Miss Sanders, I can carry your bag up."

"No. The baby is sleeping." Lifting her handbag from the telephone stand she opened it.

He lowered the case and waved the tip away. "Had to make a delivery to Matthew Johnston next door anyway. No problem. Glad to do what I can. Awful thing about those boys, isn't it?"

"To say nothing of their parents."

"Some people ask for what they get, miss. But those kids sure didn't." The restless eyes wandered over her face. "Sure can see you're Miss Markham's cousin. Look something like her. Saw Hannah Toogood getting on the bus with young Edgar and she thought Miss Sanders must be fair nervous 'bout being in this house all alone."

"I fail to see anything to be nervous about, Mr. Austin."

"Rog. Mr. Austin's my dad. Tell you what. No amount of money could keep *me* in this place. Can't figure why Miss Markham didn't stay on in them rooms behind her dress shop."

Miss Sanderson was edging him toward the door. "Kind of you to be concerned and thanks for bringing my case."

"Be careful how you open this door, hear. Make sure you know who's on the other side. Bad place, this house."

"The Fosters, you mean."

"Goes back beyond that, miss. Back to when this house was built."

Rog Austin had titillated her curiosity but before she could ask a question he was through the doorway and loping down the steps. Fine detective, she lectured herself. A golden opportunity to pump that boy and you speed him on his way simply because you don't like his eyes or mouth. She glanced at her watch—after two. She'd better have a look around the first floor before Lucy woke up.

As she mounted the stairs she found she was glad not to have any photographs to recall for these rooms. On the landing she paused to get her bearings. A wide hall led past four closed doors, two to a side, to white painted double doors at the rear. She tried the door to her left—the nursery. Pink walls dotted with blue and silver angels, a white chest and change table, a pink and white crib over which two large ceramic angels hovered protectively. She stepped onto a shaggy white rug and peered down into the crib. Sergeant Brummell had been correct. Lucinda Gillian Foster, aged ten months, was indeed a bonny baby. Red-gold ringlets clustered moistly around a rosy face, coppery lashes rested against plump cheeks, dimpled hands were flung above her head. From one hand a teddy bear dressed in a knit sweater had dropped onto the pillow. A little beauty, Miss Sanderson thought, and tiptoed out, inching the door closed.

Directly across the hall was a large bath with two basins and much tile. She drew her breath in sharply. On the tile counter two china kittens were perched. Jutting from the heads were toothbrushes. Metal tags dangled from their necks. Arthur on the black kitten, Andrew on the white. Why hadn't these things been removed? Without caring about her hostess's reaction she opened a drawer and thrust the kittens in it.

She took only a glance in the room beside the bathroom. Bunk beds, shelves of toys, two small desks, a row of boys' books, toy trucks lined up in a row on the floor. Beside the nursery she found the guest room. Charming, she decided, spacious, with a double bed, a comfortable armchair and reading light, decorated in primrose and ivory. Rather a lot of ruffles on the spread and curtains. She wondered if this room had been intended for Lucy when the next baby arrived.

Behind the double doors at the end of the hall was the master suite—a huge bedroom, a bath, a dressing room. It was lushly and expensively decorated. The furnishings looked like period pieces, white and gilt and graceful. Her eyes narrowed as she looked around. Every surface was covered with photographs. She picked up one in a silver frame from a bed table and gazed down at the wedding picture of Paul and Gillian Foster. His dark good looks and height accentuated the petiteness of his bride. There was amazing resemblance between mother and daughter. Red-gold hair spilled over narrow shoulders, wide eyes smiled, a dimple peeked from a rounded cheek. Putting down the frame, Miss Sanderson looked at the other pictures. On the dressing table was a family group. Paul stood behind his wife's chair, two boys with their father's coloring and wide chin smiled at the camera, Gillian looked fondly down at the baby in her arms, Lucy wore a lacy christening gown.

On the chiffonier was another charming pose of the three children and on the other bed table was a head-and-shoulders shot of the beautiful Gillian. Miss Sanderson blinked. This obviously was the room Irene Markham was using. How could she bear those faces surrounding her? Why hadn't they been put out of sight? On the dressing table was a silver-backed set of comb and brush and hand mirror with entwined initials—*GMF*. On the chiffonier was a set of military hairbrushes. She looked in the shallow door of the dressing table and found a tortoise shell comb and brush with Irene's initials. Had the entire suite been left with the murdered couple's possessions still in place?

She checked the bath. There were a huge marble tub

with a glass enclosure, double sinks in one counter, the other shaped like an antique dressing table with matching chair. She opened one side of the medicine chest. Ranks of cosmetics and perfumes and nail polishes. In the other were masculine toiletries and two electric razors.

"Blimey," she whispered and walked into the dressing room fully expecting to be faced with rows of Gillian and Paul Foster's clothes. But the long rods were virtually empty. Only three women's suits, a trouser suit, several dresses, and a tailored robe huddled at the end of one. On the shoe rack were two pairs of walking shoes, a pair of leather slippers, and one pair of black pumps. She instinctively knew these clothes had not belonged to the lovely Gillian.

At the head of the stairs she paused and considered. Thus far her tour of the house had only disclosed three facts. The Fosters had lived well, surrounded by all modern conveniences and expensive fittings. The couple had doted on their children. Irene Markham, who once had expected to marry Paul Foster, wasn't squeamish about living with their pictures and intimate possessions.

Not an impressive list. Perhaps after she had a good meal her mind would hum along at a better pace.

The good meal, much to Miss Sanderson's dismay, didn't materialize. In the wonderful kitchen with all its promise and appliances the cupboards were close to bare. Aside from bottles for the baby and a plentitude of milk the huge refrigerator contained only a chunk of moldy cheese. A search of the cupboards revealed rows of tins and jars of baby food and a lone tin of peach halves. The bread box yielded half a loaf of stale bread. There didn't appear to be any butter to put on it.

Miss Sanderson decided to console her groaning stomach with a strong cup of tea. It wasn't brewed when a whimper, followed by a lusty bellow, alerted her to the fact she was to be denied even that small solace.

Swearing under her breath, she headed toward little Lucy's room.

Chapter Four

Late afternoon found Miss Sanderson seated at the kitchen table wearily sipping the tea she had promised herself nearly two hours before. In desperation she was dipping baby biscuits and inelegantly gobbling them.

"When Aunt Irene gets here," she promised the baby, "I'm going to give her a large piece of my mind. Fine welcome for a long-lost cousin who supposedly hauls herself from a sickbed to render assistance. No food, an empty house, and a baby!" Lucy hauled herself up the bars of the playpen and gave Miss Sanderson an enchanting smile, displaying two teeth and a deep dimple. Miss Sanderson couldn't help smiling back. "I take that back about the baby. Mrs. Toogood was right, Lucy, you're an angel."

The angel tolerantly had allowed herself to be picked out of bed, stripped down, washed, powdered, and, after trial and error and fumbling, swathed in nappies and fluffy pink coveralls. Before that had been accomplished Miss Sanderson's brow was dewed with perspiration, but Lucy had cooed, smiled, blown bubbles, and gone willingly into a stranger's arms.

In the kitchen Miss Sanderson moved the walnut high chair out from the wall and spread food on the table. She spooned into the baby's eager mouth dreadful looking puréed spinach, banana custard, and then gave her a bottle of formula. The process was a messy one and when Miss Sanderson turned her back the angel, with a crow of delight, added to the mess by dumping a bowl on the floor.

"Don't waste food," Miss Sanderson scolded. "Heavens knows in this house it's a precious commodity."

After the child was deposited in the playpen Miss Sanderson collapsed at the table and proceeded to fill an ashtray with partially smoked cigarettes and ashes. She didn't smoke much but Cousin Abigail Sanders had admitted that during her days of better health she had been a heavy smoker. "Although Gillian and Irene never knew me," the sick woman had warned her stand-in, "some word about me might have filtered back to them. To be on the safe side remember you don't drive, do smoke a great deal, and enjoy an occasional Scotch and soda."

Miss Sanderson told the baby, "Right now I'd enjoy a Scotch and soda and a steak three inches thick." She cocked her head and listened. "Ah, think I hear your aunt, no doubt bearing ingredients for a large and delicious dinner."

A key grated in the lock, the knob turned, and Irene Markham, dressed as though she'd just returned from an expedition to Antarctica, stepped in. A knitted hat was pulled down over her eyes, the collar of a wet anorak was pulled up to her ears, and, to her hungry guest's dismay, she carried only a handbag and an umbrella. Kicking off dripping boots onto Mrs. Toogood's freshly washed tile, she advanced with a mittened hand extended. "Abigail," she said in a high, light voice. "We finally meet. Rather odd, isn't it?"

"Distinctly odd," Miss Sanderson said, touching the wet woolen mitt gingerly. Could that delicious dinner be stuck in the anorak's bulging pockets?

Irene glanced down at her hands and hastily pulled off the mitts. "I feel so awkward, not knowing whether to embrace you or…" She looked around. "Where's Mrs. Toogood?"

"Gone."

"That dratted woman! I asked her to stay until I got home. To keep you company and see you got a good rest after your trip. When did she leave?"

"About one. She bolted as soon as I arrived."

"Oh no," the other woman wailed. "Lucy! How did you manage? Do you know anything about—"

"Hadn't the foggiest but I muddled through."

Pulling off the hat, Irene smoothed down her short brown hair, and zipped down the anorak. "Well, at least you had a decent lunch."

"A bit difficult to make a decent lunch from moldy cheese and stale bread."

Irene marched to the fridge and threw open the door. "She didn't even do *that*. She was told to ring up and have an order delivered. That—" The other woman proceeded to give a detailed opinion of her housekeeper. Miss Sanderson's mouth dropped open. Irene Markham had swearing down to a fine art. She questioned Mrs. Toogood's parentage, the possibility her mother had belonged to the canine race, her lifestyle, and some rather unusual sexual habits. Finally she ran out of curses and sagged back against the white enamel door. "The shops are closed and it's too late to get anything. Well, there just has to be something in the freezer." Opening the other door, she pulled out a frosty package, looked at it, and threw it on the counter. "Fish fingers and chips. Oh, my God!"

She burst into tears and buried her face in her hands. Forgetting her own problems, Miss Sanderson put her arms around the damp anorak and heaving shoulders. "There, there. It's not as bad as all that. We'll manage." She nudged the other woman over to a chair and gently pushed her down on it. "We could both use a drink. Do you have anything?"

"Dining room," Irene sobbed.

"Get that wet coat off."

In the sideboard she found a supply of wines and spirits. Selecting a bottle of single malt, she poured two large drinks with a dribble of soda. When she carried the glasses into the kitchen she found Irene had regained her composure. Her coat was hung on a peg near the door, she'd neatened her hair, and was scrubbing her face off with a damp towel. Taking the drink, she blurted, "I don't know what you think of me, Abigail. Going to pieces like that. I'm at my wit's end. It was only two weeks ago I came in here and found…them. It's been a nightmare. Hellish!"

"I know. That's why I'm here. You relax and I'll get supper on. There's a tin of peaches for dessert and some tomato sauce to go with the chips."

The baby threw a stuffed toy out of the playpen and Miss Sanderson gave her a biscuit. The child cooed and started to gnaw at it. "Good baby."

"And Mrs. Toogood *is* good with her. As she tells one who'll listen, the only reason she stays on here is because of her dead missus' memory and little Lucy. She was devoted to Gillian."

Miss Sanderson turned on the oven and located a shallow pan. "She seems a fine housekeeper, too."

"To have satisfied my sister she would have to be. But now Mrs. Toogood does exactly as she wishes. We don't get along and the only reason I keep *her* on is because I simply can't find anyone else willing to work here."

"She did mention it's a bad house. And Rog Austin, when he brought my case up, said it's been since it was built. Any idea what the boy was talking about?"

"Village rumors and superstition."

"Nothing factual?"

"If you don't mind I'd rather not discuss things like that now. I know you're anxious to hear about Gillian and the boys but perhaps later?"

"No rush," Miss Sanderson told her falsely. There was a rush. Until she got some details she was at sea.

While she got the scanty supper Irene polished off her drink and went to the dining room for the bottle. She held it up invitingly but Miss Sanderson shook her head. "Maybe after supper."

Pouring a hefty amount, Irene told her, "I'm drinking too much. Funny, before this all happened I barely touched the stuff but now I'm reaching for the bottle far too often."

Go right ahead, Miss Sanderson told her silently as she served the fish fingers and chips. Alcohol loosens tongues. While they ate, she shot sidelong looks at her supposed cousin. Irene Markham bore a striking resemblance to the genuine cousin, Abigail Sanders. She had the sick woman's fine features, the same fine texture of hair, the same milky blue eyes. Irene was much the younger. Miss Sanderson couldn't see much resemblance to herself. Chief Inspector Kepesake had been correct. There was only a superficial resemblance. Height, build, coloring. Her own nose was longer, her chin stronger, her eyes larger and a pale clear blue.

Scooping up the last shred of peach, Irene said, "That wasn't bad. I promise you an abundance of food tomorrow. In the morning I'll phone the shops and have Rog Austin bring the other supplies with the meat order. Any preferences?"

"I was wondering. While I'm here would you like me to shop and cook dinner?"

Milky blue eyes fastened on the older woman's face. "I hardly expected you to be able to cook. I mean your parents were so much better off than mine and you probably had servants."

Miss Sanderson opened her mouth to answer and then hesitated. She'd been about to blurt out the truth, that her Aunt Rose had insisted she learn to cook. She'd better watch her tongue. She said carefully, "Mother thought a girl should know her way around the kitchen. I'm rather a good cook."

"Did Aunt Grace teach you?"

Not knowing whether Aunt Grace had been a good cook or not Miss Sanderson decided on the truth. "Our cook Aggie took care of lessons. She's a bit of a tyrant." And was still being a tyrant. She'd inherited Aggie from her aunt and right at present the cook was impatiently awaiting Miss Sanderson's return to the flat Aggie ruled with a mailed fist.

"It must have been nice," Irene told her enviously, "having oodles of money and servants and going to the best schools. My parents had quite a struggle."

Miss Sanderson cast an ironic glance around the dream kitchen. "It doesn't look as though you really suffered much."

"Oh, this." Irene waved a hand. "Gillian and Paul had the entire house done over shortly after their marriage. Converted the drawing room and den into the surgery and had central heating installed and new bathrooms put in. Believe me, during my parents' time it wasn't like this. I've always loved this house. Never forgiven father for willing it to Gillian. Strange how this family runs to trouble between sisters. Gillian and me. Your mother and mine." Her eyes coldly examined Miss Sanderson's borrowed brooch and earrings. "I see you're wearing grandmother's amethysts."

"They're not valuable, Irene. I've always considered a few trinkets were a silly reason for our mothers' estrangement."

"There's such a thing as sentimental value," Irene snapped. "And it was more than the amethysts and that gold locket and the rings. Grandmother left Aunt Grace her china and silver too. Mother never forgave her sister. She thought Aunt Grace should have shared the family heirlooms with her."

Miss Sanderson said mildly, "All this happened before either of us were born."

"It wasn't only the inheritance. There was more to it than that."

Having been filled in on the family history, Miss Sanderson asked, "Husbands, you mean?"

"Your father was my mother's suitor until he met Aunt Grace. Mother had to settle for an estate agent and your mother married a factory owner."

"Somewhat similar to the breach between you and Gillian."

Irene had been becoming quite heated but now she settled back in her chair and took a sip of whiskey. "History does tend to repeat itself. But the trouble between Gillian and me began long before she took Paul away from me. Mother had difficulty bearing children, you know—" She stopped abruptly. "How foolish of me. Of course you don't know. Anyway, there were seven years between Gillian and me. By the time she came along mother was in her forties and had given up hope of having a second child. Mother always called my sister 'her miracle baby' and father called her 'his little princess.' " Irene turned and looked down at her tiny niece who was hugging a stuffed lamb. "Lucy's the picture of my sister at the same age. Neither mother nor father were good-looking people and they were overwhelmed by Gillian's beauty. They doted on the child. From the moment of her birth I was pushed aside. Irene was only Gillian's plain gawky sister."

"It must have been difficult to adjust."

"Impossible. Comparisons were constantly made, not only by my parents but by everyone. Gillian's hair and eyes and dimples. I felt like the ugly stepsister."

"This house was left to your sister?"

"Everything was hers. Every cent my parents could scrimp and save was set aside for her. I was given a business education and as my father told me years ago, I was competent to make my own way in life but Gillian wasn't and had to be looked after." Irene bowed her head. Her neck looked long and incredibly fragile. "And then I was fool enough to bring the only man I'd ever loved here to meet her."

"Why did you do it?"

"A good question." Irene lifted her head and shook fine brown hair away from her thin face. "One that often occurs to me. I suppose I felt sure of him, secure. I was so proud of Paul. His family were quite poor but a godfather had provided funds for his education and he was educated at Rugby and New College at Oxford. When we met he had just finished his training at Guy's Hospital. We were planning on marrying as soon as he set up practice. Paul asked to meet my family and there were only Gillian and you and, of course, you didn't count."

"Thanks," Miss Sanderson said coldly, thinking of the gentle courageous woman she was impersonating.

"Abigail, I am so *sorry*. That was rude, wasn't it? But how could I take my fiancé around to meet a cousin I'd never met? Anyway, Paul and I came here. Gillian and Paul took one look at each other and a month later sneaked off to London and were married."

"You were estranged from them for a time?"

"For nearly five years. I went back to London and buried myself in my work. Gillian sent birth announcements for Andrew and Arthur but I ignored them. Then Paul came to see me. Gillian was pregnant again and not well and he begged me to return to Maddersley for her sake. He wanted me to live with them, to be as he said 'a part of their family.' "

"And you came back."

"Again I wonder why. Perhaps it was to be near Paul. Perhaps it was because I was lonely. I've never made friends easily and in London all I had was my work, a tiny flat, a few acquaintances. So I agreed to come back to the village but I refused to live in this house with them. I had some savings so I rented my shop and started a little business in ladies' apparel." She gave a rueful laugh. "Not terribly profitable but I manage to get by and there are a couple of small rooms at the rear of the building that I fixed up as living quarters." Irene stretched out a hand for the Scotch bottle as the baby threw the lamb out of the playpen and wrinkled up her face as though about to start howling.

"Shouldn't Lucy be in bed?" Miss Sanderson asked.

"Look at the time!" Irene jumped tip. "I'll tuck her in and tidy up the kitchen. You can wait in the living room."

Miss Sanderson scooped the child up. "I'll take care of her."

"Do you think you can? She'll need a bottle and—"

"I'm practically a professional now. Had lots of practice this afternoon and I'm a quick study."

There's really nothing to this baby stuff, Miss Sanderson decided happily as she washed, oiled, powdered, and adjusted nappies neatly. She sang to the baby as she snapped up powder-blue sleepers and Lucy responded by blowing bubbles. Tucking the baby into the crib, she pulled up the comforter, snugged the teddy bear in beside the warm body, and handed a bottle to the little one. Nothing to it, she thought as she jauntily blew a kiss and snapped off the overhead light. Beside the crib a night-light cast a rosy glow over the hovering angels. "Take good care of her," she told them and closed the door.

In the downstairs hall a rectangle of light fell from double doors across the tile. Stepping into the living room, she found Irene Markham had made good use of the time. A fire was burning briskly and a gateleg table had been pulled over between the armchairs flanking the hearth. The Scotch bottle, glasses, an ice bucket, and soda sat on the gleaming tabletop. Irene, she was pleased to note, had filled her glass and, from the liquid's deep amber color, hadn't paid much attention to the soda.

"Do help yourself," Irene said.

Miss Sanderson made a weak drink and scrutinized her companion. The single malt was doing its job. Color mantled Irene's cheeks and her thin lips looked looser. Good, now for some alcoholic confidences. "Irene, I feel so…so at sea. Gillian is only a name to me. What was she like?"

"Oodles of pictures upstairs. She loved having her picture taken. I'll get them and you can see for yourself."

"Don't bother. I don't mean what she looked like. I'm sure she must have been lovely judging by her daughter. But what was she actually *like*?"

"She was an eighteen-carat bitch-on-wheels."

"Do you really mean that?"

"No. That's spite and jealousy talking. What was Gillian like?" Irene leaned her head back against brown velour and for a moment the older woman thought she'd passed out. But then she said softly, "Many people liked her. Some loved her. Gillian was possibly the most dangerous woman I've ever known."

"Was she conceited? A troublemaker? Promiscuous?"

"God, no! She was sweet and rather gentle. She devoted every minute, every bit of strength to her children and her husband and her home. After her marriage she never looked at another man. She tried to be kind to her neighbors and the other villagers."

"And she was dangerous?"

"In a strange way—by trying to be *too* kind and good, by thirsting to be liked and admired."

"Most people want to be liked and admired."

"Not as passionately as my sister did." Irene stretched long legs toward the hearth. "I doubt I can make you understand."

"Try."

"Gillian tried to give everyone what he or she wanted from her. For example, take our parents. She had each of them convinced she loved them best. Mother believed Gillian loved her more than Father and Father was convinced his little princess cared most for him. In a way she drove a wedge between them. It extended far beyond family. Another example is Mrs. Toogood. She worshipped my sister and yet if Gillian had decided she wanted another housekeeper, Mrs. Toogood would have been sent packing. Abigail, it's a dangerous game to toy with people's emotions."

"I take it Gillian's emotions didn't run deep."

"Completely superficial."

On the last word Irene slurred and Miss Sanderson hastened to milk more information from her. "Did these shallow emotions include her children and husband?"

"Not her children. Gillian was devoted to them, considered them extensions of herself. Paul? I don't believe she genuinely loved him. When she saw him she wanted him but perhaps it was because he was handsome and a professional man who would make a wonderful father for her wonderful children."

"Before Paul. Were there men in her life?"

"Any number."

"Did she have them convinced she reciprocated their affection?"

"Absolub...ab-so-lute-ly." Irene chuckled. "Methinks I'm getting a little tiddly."

Methinks you're getting a little sloshed, Miss Sanderson told her silently. Aloud she asked, "Who?"

Irene was looking owlishly at her—one eye closed—and Miss Sanderson thought it was a wink. "See two Abigails. You see two Irenes?"

Well, Miss Sanderson thought resignedly, what can I expect? Irene's put a huge hole in that bottle. "Did these men think your sister loved them?"

"Led them right down the garden pash...path. Shocked...you wouldn't believe when dear little Gillian married." Irene tilted slightly and pushed herself up. She swayed. "Gotta get to bed. Warm bed for Paul and Gillian. Cold for poor gawky Irene. Where in hell's the door gone?"

Even with Miss Sanderson's help the trip to the hall was an erratic one. Loath to give up, she asked, "Why do the villagers think this house is bad? What happened here?"

"Murders."

"You mean the Fosters."

"More'n that." The woman listed slightly to the left and grasped at the newel post. "Not to worry your little head. Doors and windows all locked tight." She hauled herself up the stairs. On the landing she made a laborious about-face and peered down the stairwell. Her face was in shadow but her voice was loud and clear. "Nothing *bad* in this house. Comes from outside. With *knives*."

She lurched out of sight and Miss Sanderson stood as though turned to stone. Mrs. Toogood wasn't the only one with great exit lines. Resisting a strong desire to bolt up the stairs, she forced herself to return to the living room. She banked the fire, carried the bottles back to the sideboard, and took the glasses to the kitchen. Depositing the glasses in the dishwashing machine she stepped over to the windows and hastily yanked the gay curtains over the dark glass.

From outside, she thought, and with knives.

Chapter Five

By the time Miss Sanderson left the Markham house the sun was directly overhead and lemony light streamed down over the village. The wind was still brisk and she was glad of her heavy coat, muffler, and sturdy boots. She strode along Jericho Lane and had reached the church at the corner before she recalled her delicate health. As she shortened her steps she thought of the morning just past. By the time she'd crawled out of bed Irene Markham had left for her shop. The woman had a number of excellent reasons for loathing the Fosters but were her feelings strong enough to kill?

As for Mrs. Toogood, Miss Sanderson found her initial distaste for the woman waning. Granted, the housekeeper's manner hadn't improved from the previous day and she'd appeared delighted to mention there wasn't a "crumb" in the house for lunch. To add to Miss Sanderson's misery she'd pointed out a bulging brown bag containing her own lunch. But at the same time she had been spooning gruel into Lucy's eager mouth with every evidence of a tenderness of which Miss Sanderson, Lucy's ardent admirer, strongly approved.

Hitching her shoulder bag up and swinging a string shopping bag, Miss Sanderson strolled down past Abercrombie's pasture and the decrepit row houses. Mrs. Toogood had confided that she and her Bert and the kids lived in the one beside the chemist's shop. It looked like a suitable home for her. As Miss Sanderson crossed the street toward the row of shops she saw the buxom matron she had noticed the previous afternoon marching down the walk. The woman looked stonily at a point past Miss Sanderson's left shoulder but did jerk her head. Let's hope, the secretary-turned-sleuth thought, the merchants prove friendlier than the pedestrians.

Conscious of her empty stomach she made a beeline for Dora's Tea Shoppe. Dora, despite the fact that it was the lunch hour, wasn't doing a roaring business. An elderly couple hunched over a pot of tea in one corner and they comprised the entire clientele. The decor was no more reassuring. A combination of lavender wallpaper and lilac paint had been used with disastrous results. The tables were covered with lavender linen and the rattan chairs looked hideously uncomfortable. Selecting the window table, Miss Sanderson sank on a chair and found her hunch had been correct. She picked up a menu encased in lilac plastic and winced—creamed peas on toast, creamed tuna on toast, creamed sweetbreads on toast. Ugh!

Swinging doors opened and a woman looking somewhat like a large sheep draped in lilac print bustled out. A grimace that might have been a smile twitched up long lips. She extended a gracious hand. "How nice that you've dropped in, Miss Sanders. I saw you yesterday when you arrived and I thought, Dora, that poor dear looks exhausted. I was glad to see Paddy Rourke take your bag. It looked frightfully heavy." Miss Sanderson accepted the hand and found hers not only wrung vigorously but retained in Dora's moist clasp. "Now, you must call me Dora. We don't stand on formality in this little place. You're…"

"Abigail."

"Of course. Irene Markham mentioned your name. We're all so glad you came to her aid. Such a horrid business and dear Irene has aged since it happened. But we mustn't spoil your nice lunch talking about that. You will be wanting lunch?"

"Yes." Miss Sanderson managed to extricate her hand from the woman's clasp. "I notice you have a special."

"Have a special everyday. Takes work and I don't keep a girl on in the winter—not enough business, you see. Today's is a nice shrimp and veggie plate."

Sounds more promising than creamed toast, Miss Sanderson thought. "I'll have the special."

"Good choice. You'll like it." Small eyes wandered to the window and Dora leaned forward to twitch a lilac curtain aside. The buxom matron was just pushing through the door of the Fox and Crow. "That Nettie Seton! How ladies can stand greasy grill food I can't fathom. Shows too. Nettie's much too heavy and her skin's deplorably oily. I pride myself on no grill and no grease. Well, never mind. Nettie will see the error of her ways. I'll get your luncheon. Only be a jiff. I'll bring you tea."

Miss Sanderson enviously eyed the wide door of the inn. Behind that door was lovely greasy grill food. She pictured crisp bacon, links of sausage, kidneys...In a swirl of lilac print the tea was delivered and it was excellent, hot and dark. The china was also nice, blue-and-white willowware. The lunch, when it arrived, was more deplorable than Nettie Seton's oily skin. Stifling a groan, she stared down at a few unidentifiable pink objects swimming in a white paste—on toast, of course. An anemic slice of tomato and a drooping leaf of lettuce completed that day's special.

Dora told her jovially, "Now that won't expand your waistline, Abigail."

It certainly won't, Miss Sanderson thought. If I was starving I still couldn't eat this goo. How on earth did Dora maintain her own generous figure? Could she be a closet patron of the Fox and Crow?

The elderly couple had drained their teapot and were pulling on coats and adjusting scarves. They passed Miss Sanderson's table and flashed smiles at her. She smiled back and watched them totter out. On the walk they paused to speak to a heavy-set woman dressed in shapeless tweeds and heavy brogues. An equally shapeless felt hat drooped over the matron's face and she clasped a sturdy blackthorn cane. From the way the old people were practically bowing and scraping this woman must be a figure of some importance in the village. She soon proved this. Banging open the door she entered the shop, bringing with her a gust of cold air and an aura of command.

"Dora," she bellowed. "Where in tarnation are you? I'm starved."

That makes two of us, Miss Sanderson thought. Dora bolted from the kitchen. She snatched a menu from a table. "You won't be long. The special—"

"Blast your special. I've been taking a tramp on the moors and I'm hungry. I want *food*. Got any sausage?"

"Alfred didn't make any up this morning."

"What *have* you got?"

"Boiled beef, the way you like it."

"That'll have to do. Fry up a heap of potatoes and make sure the mustard is hot." Without lowering her voice, the newcomer brayed, "Dora, have you forgotten your manners? Introduce us."

Miss Sanderson thought the woman hadn't noticed her but the blackthorn was poking in her direction. Dora, practically simpering, hastened to comply. "This is Miss Mary Maddersley of Maddersley Hall. Her brother is—"

"I'm well aware who my brother is." The cane struck the floor sharply. "For God's sake, Dora, stop babbling and tell me *her* name."

"Abigail Sanders," Miss Sanderson said crisply. "Irene Markham's cousin and—"

"The long-lost cousin, eh? Got the Markham build and height. Don't have their nose or chin or eyes." Without waiting for an invitation she thumped down in a chair, unbuttoned her jacket, and propped the cane against the table. She gave Miss Sanderson's plate a disgusted look. "You're not planning to eat that goop, are you?"

"I don't think I can."

"Dora! Get that garbage out of here and make that two orders of beef. Hop to it."

As the plate was whisked away, Miss Sanderson breathed a sigh of relief. "Thanks. You saved my life, to say nothing of my stomach."

"Got to assert yourself. Dora's a fair cook but she's got the insane notion ladies shouldn't eat anything unless it's dripping with mucilage. Hmm, you look much healthier than I figured you would."

Conscious of the shrewdness of the eyes in the strong-featured face, Miss Sanderson said, "Since I arrived in Maddersley I do feel better. Must be the country air."

"If it works that fast we should bottle it." Her companion fished in a handbag and extracted a package of small cigars. "Care for one?"

Shaking her head, Miss Sanderson produced her cigarettes and they proceeded to smoke in what appeared to be a companionable silence. She decided she liked the other woman. Miss Mary Maddersley, chatelaine of Maddersley Hall and only sister of Sir Donald Maddersley, struck her as her own type of person. And she certainly could handle the overly genteel Dora. She wondered how to edge the conversation in the direction she desired. With this formidable grande dame she had a feeling she would get straight answers. As it worked out there was no necessity to verbally maneuver Miss Maddersley. The other woman puffed but a cloud of aromatic smoke and confided, "Shouldn't be smoking. Shouldn't drink either. Blood pressure. Dr. Foster warned me repeatedly cigars and whiskey could finish me off. Told him at least I would die happy. Good doctor, young Foster, but he certainly had a taste for the lassies—"

"Really, Miss Maddersley!" With trembling hands Dora lowered hot platters in front of them. Lowering her voice, she whispered, "If Ernie hears you've talked about his daughter with Abigail...well, you know how violent he can get."

"Balderdash! Ernie Marlow doesn't scare me. Shouldn't bother you either." Grabbing the knob of her cane, she flourished it. "Now, you get back to your kitchen and no eavesdropping."

Despite her interest in the lassies and Paul Foster, Miss Sanderson was devouring her meal. She had a feeling it wasn't wise to prod Miss Maddersley. The other woman cut up her beef, dabbed mustard on it, and proceeded to talk. "Must admit I didn't tell the police much about the Fosters. Didn't take to the chief inspector who interviewed Donnie and me. Looked like a tailor's dummy." Miss Sanderson bent her head to hide a grin. That was her own favorite description of Adam Kepesake. "But I don't mind talking to you and, to tell you the truth, I want to see whoever did that put away. Can't say I was fond of the Fosters but no one should die that way, particularly children. How's the baby?"

"Flourishing. Lucy's a lovely child."

"Takes after her mother. Though where Gillian got those looks from is anyone's guess. Emma and Roger Markham were people you wouldn't look twice at. Irene's plain too. Always felt sorry for Irene. Must have been harrowing having a little sister who looked like Gillian."

Miss Sanderson steered the conversation back to Paul Foster and his lasses. "I fail to understand how a man could be interested in other women with a beautiful wife like Gillian."

"That isn't hard to figure out." Dabbing mustard from her lips with lavender linen, Miss Maddersley chuckled. "Like caviar and champagne, have them everyday and you get a longing for mince and beer. Now, I'm not saying Paul Foster cheated on his wife and I'm not saying he didn't. But there was Melanie Marlow and that Beauchamp woman. No one can tell me Melanie was hustled out of the village by the Fosters just because her father was giving her a few licks. From what I saw of that miss she *needed* a good belting. No siree, Gillian wanted her out of the house. Melanie was only sixteen, pretty as a picture, and wild as they come. Probably set her cap for the doctor. But I will tell you this. The Fosters not only made enemies of the Marlows but had Nell Austin ready to kill them."

"Austin's Meat Market?"

"Rog's mother. Now, there's a virago. Too bad Ernie and Nell Austin hadn't teamed up. She'd have been a match for him. But people are always drawn toward their opposites and Maybelle Marlow and Alfred Austin are both rabbits."

"But why would Nell Austin care about Melanie Marlow?"

"Rog, that's why. Nell had her heart set on making a match between her son and the baker's daughter. Nell and Ernie Marlow planned on the marriage from the time the young ones were babes in arms."

"Were Rog and Melanie agreeable?"

"Rog couldn't wait to marry the girl but Melanie couldn't see him for dust. Has a lot more spirit than her mother ever did. Maybelle's always has been like Dora's lettuce—wilted." Setting down her cup, Miss Maddersley leaned across the table. "You're drinking this in. I'm glad we met. Had me puzzled why the sudden interest in a group of relatives you had never met. I've a hunch I've the answer now."

Miss Sanderson struggled to look puzzled. This woman's intelligence could well not only unmask her but put an end to her sleuthing. "I think any person would be outraged at having relatives killed the way the Fosters were."

"I agree." Miss Maddersley lowered her voice. "I sense things. Always have. My grandmother was born with a caul and she did too. I sense you are not what you seem. Are you connected with the police?"

"No."

The other woman gnawed her lip thoughtfully. "I don't feel you're lying. Let me put it another way. Are you here to uncover the fiend who killed those children?"

Miss Sanderson debated. Then she threw caution to the winds. "Yes."

"Thought you were. No way the villagers will open up to the police. Inbred bunch and I'm no better. Didn't tell that stuffed shirt Kepesake anything. But I like you and I admire your style. As I said before, the murderer must be unmasked. God only knows what he'll do next."

"Miss Maddersley, do you think Lucy Foster is in danger?"

"Hard to say. My guess is she isn't."

236 E. X. Giroux

"But the rest of her family—"

"True. If the baby was on the murderer's list she would have been killed that night. I think Gillian or Paul or perhaps both of them were targets. The boys were killed simply because they were witnesses and quite old enough to give the name. Lucy wasn't and so she was left unharmed. Make sense?"

"It does."

"You come to the Hall tomorrow. I'll tell you what I know. Mind you it's rumors and conjecture—"

"I'd be grateful."

"Make it around four. We'll have tea. Donnie won't be home then."

She buttoned up her jacket, threw some money on the table, and retrieved her cane. Without a backward glance she strode out of the tearoom. Dora popped out from behind the kitchen door as though she had been stationed there. Miss Sanderson had been wondering how this woman felt about Mary Maddersley, whether she resented the woman's brusque treatment. Dora's words bore out not only her resentment but also the fact she had been eavesdropping. "Fine one she is to talk about the Marlows and Austins! Don't believe a word she said about them, Abigail. If anyone in this village had a grudge against Gillian and the doctor it's that brother of hers!" She added venomously, "And him not right in the head either."

Miss Sanderson had had enough of the tearoom and of Dora. She had no desire to listen to the woman and liked her no better than she had her creamed shrimp. As she paid for her lunch she found it an effort to be civil. Dora charged her double, for the untouched special as well as for the beef. She added a tip and the sheep face beamed. "Didn't hear all she had to say, Abigail. Started to whisper."

And I'm grateful she did, Miss Sanderson thought. She told the woman, "Miss Maddersley invited me to tea tomorrow. Lovely person."

Dora looked thunderstruck. "Oh, she is, she certainly is. A valued patron and a valued friend. I do trust, Abigail, you won't mention what I just said. Nerves, you know, we've all been so nervy since the dear Fosters died."

Miss Sanderson contented herself with a noncommittal smile. Let two-faced Dora simmer in her own foul sauces. But, as she admitted, she couldn't afford to be so selective of informants. She had a tendency to shy away from the ones she didn't like.

She headed toward The Cheese Tease, vowing that even if she loathed the proprietor she would dig for all the gossip she could.

Chapter Six

When Miss Sanderson began the return journey to the Markham house her arm was weighed down by the purchases in the string bag. But except for the time spent in Dora's Tea Shoppe her efforts had been wasted. The Cheese Tease, as its name implied, did specialize in a wide assortment of that delicacy and also featured homemade preserves, small crocks of honey, and exotic blends of tea. It was run by a mother-daughter team. The daughter had bright blue eyes and soft brown hair. The mother had soft brown eyes and bright blue hair. Both women were pleasant and extended Miss Sanderson a warm welcome to the village but weren't given to gossip. All she had acquired in their shop were remarks on the weather, a fine piece of Stilton, and a jar of ginger jam.

Her visits to the butcher shop and the bakery hadn't been any more productive. Alfred Austin proved to be a short man with a narrow chest and a paunch that belled out his stained apron. He had the round pink face of a cherub and a hairless skull. His wife Nell, the virago, was several inches taller than her husband and displayed icy civility to their new customer. There was a marked resemblance between Nell and her son. Both had curly dark hair and colorless eyes. But Nell didn't have loose lips and a fall-away chin. Her mouth was as tight as a rattrap and her chin jutted like a rock. While Alfred and his wife made up the order Rog wandered in from the rear of the shop. He greeted Miss Sanderson like an old friend and promised to bring her order on the first delivery. Rog was evidently the apple of the maternal eye. When Nell looked at him her rattrap mouth softened. Alfred seemed to be busy avoiding looking at either his wife or son. Miss Sanderson thought the little man hardly fulfilled the popular image of a brawny butcher.

In the bakery shop next door she found a man who *did* look like a butcher. Ernie Marlow was huge and reminded her vividly of Boris Karloff. Above gigantic shoulders was a huge head, brutish features, a shock of coarse hair. Yet, as he arranged pastries on a long tray, his enormous hands moved with an odd delicacy. His wife, as Mary Maddersley had remarked, was his direct opposite. Maybelle was short, curvaceous, with a softly pretty face. She was heavily made up but the powder and rouge didn't quite conceal a fading bruise under one eye. She was much younger than her hulking husband. Miss Sanderson tried to entice the couple into conversation but Ernie ignored her and Maybelle said only what was absolutely necessary.

Pausing in front of the dress shop, Miss Sanderson peered in and spotted Irene waiting on Nettie Seton, who was running to avoirdupois and had oily skin. Glancing up, Irene waved and Miss Sanderson waved back.

So much for my detecting, she thought as she climbed the slope toward the church. Perhaps she could spot a neighbor and try a bit more. But not a soul was stirring around the vicarage or the cluster of cottages. She'd reached the gate of the Markham house when she heard her name called. She swung around and saw the same man she had seen the previous day, trundling his wheelchair up the walk. He wore a tweed cap, a heavy jacket, and a matching tartan muffler and rug. Over one arm of his chair a heavy leather satchel hung. She walked back to him. "Tried to catch up with you earlier but couldn't," he panted. "I can beat anyone on a downslope but not on a rise." He stuck out a hand only fractionally smaller than the baker's. "I'm your neighbor, Matthew Johnston."

Miss Sanderson told him truthfully she was delighted to meet him. He swung his gate open. "Care to come in for tea, Miss Sanders?"

Again she told him she would be delighted and followed him along the short walk to the ramp. She put a hand on the back of the chair but he shook his head. "Must let me do it myself."

He wheeled the chair up the ramp and unlocked the yellow door. They went into a small sitting room that managed to look larger because it was so bare. There were only a television set, an end table, and one armchair. The room had lovely proportions and a charming fireplace. She pictured it with chintz, a touch of brass, mellow wood. Her host must have guessed her thoughts. "Shame, isn't it? Could be a nice home. But I have few visitors and don't need much for myself. Come into the kitchen. That's where I spend most of my time."

The kitchen was rather nice. Old oak cupboards lined one wall and in a nook was a table covered with a bright plastic throw and one straight-backed chair. On the windowsill was a red geranium. From one side of the room a bedroom opened, from the other a bath. The room smelled deliciously of spices and baking. "You're lucky," Johnston told her. "Baked this morning and have fresh currant buns. Sometimes I pick up something from the bakery but mainly I do it myself. Helps pass the time." Taking off his cap and jacket, he hung them on low pegs. As he draped the muffler over the jacket he patted it affectionately. "Gillian and Paul gave me this rug last Christmas and had the boys give me the muffler. Laid them away because they're pure wool and figured they were too good to use everyday. But after they...after they were gone I got them out and threw away my old rug and scarf. Wish now I'd worn them sooner so they could..."

"I understand," Miss Sanderson told him gently. "You were close to my cousin's family."

"They made me feel like a member of their family. Hang your duds over there, Miss Sanders. Had a couple of higher hooks left for visitors. You take that chair and I'll get tea on. No, I don't need any help and from what I've heard you can use a rest after shopping. Shouldn't be lugging groceries like that."

"I'm having most of the shopping delivered, Mr. Johnston—"

"Mind calling me Matthew? Gillian always called me that and the boys called me Uncle Matt."

"If you'll call me Abigail."

She watched while he boiled water and measured tea leaves. The fixtures were all normal height but he used only the lower cupboards and the lowest shelf on the fridge. She guessed he used only the front burners on the stove. "Wouldn't it be handier to have those lowered?" she asked.

"Rented house. Can't change much. Owner did let me install metal bars in the bedroom and bath, to swing myself around on. I make out fine. Don't need much space for supplies anyway." He put the teapot, cups, and plates on a tray, deposited it on his lap, and wheeled his chair to the table. Miss Sanderson made no effort to assist. Returning to the counter for a plate of buns and a butter dish, he rolled his chair opposite hers.

"Seems nice to have company, Abigail. It's been lonely lately. Went over to the Markham house a couple of times after Irene moved in to see whether I could help out but Mrs. Toogood didn't need me. When Gillian was alive it was different. Helped out all the time then. Mended furniture and things—once I was a carpenter—and tried to take the boys off her hands. Used to take them down to the shops with me. Arthur and Andrew always coaxed to go to the chemist's for an ice cream." He poured the tea. "All past now. No sense in dwelling on it."

"Have you lived here long?"

"Newcomer to Maddersley and the locals don't let me forget it. Have to have had your family here for generations to be one of them. But Jericho Lane's chock-full of outsiders. I arrived over a year ago, about the time Irene Markham came back and started her shop. The vicar's been here about ten years and Miss Beauchamp—she's the cottage with the red door—came about six months ago." He chuckled. "Even Nurse Ines is considered an outsider and she came with Paul when he set up practice here."

"The young chap at the inn—Paddy Rourke—has he been here long?"

"Born here. When his dad came to Maddersley he tore the old inn down and put up a new building. That would be about thirty years ago. Paddy senior passed away but his wife Kate and his son run the place. Villagers have accepted them. I suppose because they have the only inn and Paddy's a nice young fellow."

"When I arrived yesterday he was kind to me."

"Heard he sent Rog Austin up with your bag," Johnston laughed. "Can see from your expression you never lived in a place this size. Drop a pin in the Fox and Crow and we hear it in Jericho Lane."

Munching a tasty bun, Miss Sanderson ran over the information she had about this man. His home had been in Gloucester, Cheltenham to be exact. Ten years ago he'd lost his only child and not a year later had been crippled in an automobile accident. His wife had died in the same accident. Only good things were said about him in the police report. Honest, hardworking, decent, his word as good as a legal contract. She regarded him sadly. A fine reward for a good life—crippled and quite alone. At one time he must have been a big man. He had powerful sloping shoulders, a massive chest, and thick arms. But his legs, outlined in red and green and yellow plaid, looked like twisted sticks. His hair was snow-white and cropped short. Traces of a ginger color still lingered in his brows and lashes. His brow was noble and his blue eyes still youthful but his face was deeply furrowed and he looked much older than his recorded age. The furrows, she decided, came more from suffering than age.

He regarded her with sympathy. "It must be hard for you to mourn people you never met."

"It is. I feel like a stranger here. I know so little about them and I suppose I feel...guilty."

"There's always that feeling of guilt when it's too late. I still feel guilty about my daughter's death. Ariel died young, only nineteen. Just starting her life."

"Was she in an accident?"

"You mean this?" He touched a knee. "No, this happened afterward. When Ariel got sick she was living in London. Came home to us and I was all for calling the doctor but her mother put her to bed and Ariel seemed some better. Just had a pain on one side. Turned out to be a ruptured appendix and my girl died before we could get her to the hospital. Dr. Brown felt as bad as Julia and I. He'd delivered her and Ariel was his goddaughter. Here, I'll show you her picture." He pulled a framed picture from a drawer. "Ariel and her mother taken about a year before we lost her."

There were two women in the picture, both slender, dark, with misty hair, looking like twins and with a fragile haunting type of beauty. "My family," Johnston said proudly. "Folks were always surprised a rough fellow like me would have a family like that. Julia came from a wealthy background and had a good education. Musical. She played the piano like you wouldn't believe. She passed talent on to Ariel...girl was studying ballet at a school in London when it happened. Teachers told us Ariel would have been a marvelous dancer if she'd lived."

Johnston ran a thick finger over the pictured faces. "Couldn't believe a lovely creature like Julia would want me. Family tried to break us up and when we married they cut Julia right off. I felt bad but Julia always told me, 'Matthew, I'd give up the world to be your wife.'" He sighed. "That's what she did. Gave her world up for me. I earned a good living and took care of both of them. If it'd helped them I would have ripped my skin off. Then...I lost them both."

"Did your wife die in the accident that—"

"Yes. She was driving our car. That guilt you mentioned. My fault she was at the wheel. Should have known better.

Julia never got over Ariel's death. Dr. Brown warned me she was...disturbed, he called it. But I hated driving and Julia loved to. So, I let her get behind the wheel and she wrecked the car deliberately."

Miss Sanderson gasped and he nodded his white head. "On purpose, Abigail. She didn't want to live. Wanted both of us to die. Well, she got part of her wish. Me...often I wish Julia had gotten it all."

Sadness overwhelmed Miss Sanderson. What right, she thought, have I to come into this bare house and pry into this man's life? But Johnston was speaking rapidly, as though welcoming a chance to talk. "I stayed on in our home, coping as best I could. We had friends and they tried to help but even friends drift away in time from a cripple. Finally last year Dr. Brown—funny I've known him all my life and never called him by his first name—anyway, he told me I had to get away from that house, out of that city. Told me it was slowly killing me. Asked where I could go and Dr. Brown tells me anywhere, just go. So I did. Rented this house and moved in next to the Fosters. For this past year I thought the doctor was right. I found myself another family, a second chance at life."

"Matthew, I'm glad my relatives were kind to you."

"*Kind.* They were wonderful. Paul took care of me all the time and wouldn't take a penny in payment. Gillian welcomed me in their house anytime I wanted to go. Had me over to dinner every week. Baked things and ran over with them. Gave me that geranium. They even had a ramp built up to their back porch so I could come and go. And the children—" Breaking off, he covered his face with big carpenter's hands. "Then I lost *them.* In one night they were gone. You've no idea what it's been like."

"No, I don't. I've never lost one family, let alone two." She made a move to rise. "I'm sorry I upset you, Matthew. I'd better go."

"No, please don't. Does me good to talk. Nobody to talk to now." His hands fell away from his face and youthful eyes drilled into hers. "You're going to be told a lot of wild tales in the village. Folks are going to be filling your ears with filthy things about Paul and Gillian. May have started already."

"They have. I heard something about Melanie—"

"Lies, all lies! The Fosters hardly laid to rest and those vultures tearing at them!" With an effort he composed himself. "Paul worshipped his wife. He never put a hand on that girl. Gillian and he were sorry for the child. Ernie Marlow is a brute. Goes to the Fox and Crow and then beats his family. The Fosters took the girl as a live-in maid to help Mrs. Toogood out. Ernie didn't like it but figured it would keep his daughter in the village, where he could get at her. But he beat her once too often and Paul, he took a look at the bruises and tells Gillian we've got to get Melanie away before Ernie kills her. So the Fosters gave the girl some money and sneaked her off to London. Melanie wanted to be a hairdresser, you see."

Johnston scowled. "They did a good turn and what did they get for it? Ernie Marlow and Nell Austin and that good-for-nothing son of hers were after them something fierce. Came right into the house when Paul was out and lit into Gillian. When it happened I was in the kitchen and I was going right into the living room and straighten them out. But I didn't have to. Gillian stood right up to them and told them they couldn't force her to tell them where Melanie was. Ernie threatened to call in the police and Gillian said 'Go ahead; the police will be after you when Paul tells them how badly Melanie was beaten.' Then Ernie and Nell and Rog all started yelling and Gillian ordered them out or she would ring up the police herself." With satisfaction, Johnston added, "They got out fast. Knew she was spunky enough to do it."

This version of the Austin-Marlow-Foster feud sounded much different from the one that Mary Maddersley had told her. Miss Sanderson sent out a feeler. "Another name was mentioned, Matthew. Beauchamp, I believe."

He waved a dismissing hand. "Linda Beauchamp was Paul's patient. High-strung girl with nervous problems. Nothing but back-fence chitchat."

She came in from another angle. "When did this quarrel over Melanie Marlow take place?"

"Let's see." He rubbed his square chin. "Must've been just before the dog poisonings. That's right. Gillian threw them out on Friday and the dogs were poisoned the following Monday. Ugly business. I have a suspicion maybe Ernie Marlow had a hand in that. Hitting back at the Fosters."

Dog poisoning was news to Miss Sanderson. No mention had been made of that in the police report. "The Fosters had a dog poisoned?"

"An Alsatian, big brute called Wolf. Looked like a wolf and acted like one too. He was Gillian's dog. Didn't like Paul or the children. Growled when the boys tried to pat him. I suppose he would have had to have been put down anyway but Gillian was all broken up. She loved that dog and Wolf was crazy about her."

"Were other dogs poisoned?"

"Two more. One of Paddy Rourke's old terriers and Dora Campbell's Peke. Paddy really got his Irish up about his dog. Said if he could prove who did it he would go after the poisoner with a gun."

"How long was this before the Fosters died?"

"About a month. Why? You think there might be a connection?"

"If the Alsatian had been alive that night it would have been difficult for anyone to have harmed the family."

"To harm Gillian, anyway. You know, Abigail, you could be onto something. Maybe I should ring up that Sergeant Brummell and tell him."

"Someone else may have mentioned it to the police," Miss Sanderson suggested, knowing full well no one had.

"I don't think anyone did. But it wasn't just Gillian's dog that was killed. Why kill the other two?"

"What better way to conceal the real target?"

"Hey!" He gave her a wide admiring smile. "Abigail, maybe you missed your calling. Should have been a detective. By the way, what work do you do?"

"Not much." She gave him details on the real cousin's life. "I've never had any financial reason to work. Oh, I'm on various committees and help out with charity drives and that sort of thing. But I do...or did a great deal of travelling when my health was better."

"Irene didn't mention what you suffer from."

A superstitious dread kept her from saying the name of the disease that was slowly wasting Abigail Sanders away. She improvised. "A number of ailments. A wonky heart..." She touched her chest. "Blood pressure, a thyroid condition. As long as I get proper rest and diet I manage to get by fairly well."

"See you look after yourself. Shouldn't think coming down here at this time would be good for you."

Leaning back in her chair, she touched the red bloom on the geranium. "I had to. Irene and little Lucy are my only living relatives."

"I understand." He reached out a hand and patted hers. She noticed again the size of that hand. It must be almost twice the size of her own.

"Would you...would it disturb you to tell me about the last day?"

"Do you really want to know?"

"I feel I must."

He hefted the teapot. "I'll make fresh." As he wheeled around the kitchen he told her his memories about the Fosters' last day. "It was the day before Arthur's birthday but I guess you know that. Gillian was as excited about the party as the boys were. She was in the family way again and hadn't been feeling chipper, so I went over shortly after lunch to see whether I could help. She was tickled to death I came. Showed me a list of things she had to do. She sent the boys up to their room to play so we could get things ready. Paul was in the surgery looking after the patients and Mrs. Toogood was bustling around."

"Nurse Ines was there too?"

"She never missed a day. Even if she was sick she thought Paul couldn't get on without her. That day she *was* sick. Nurse

Ines had a dilly of a cold and had given it to Lucy. I remember
telling Gillian it might be better if the nurse did stay off when
she was ailing and Gillian laughed and said the blasted woman
would drag herself to the office if her leg was broken." His eyes
looked past Miss Sanderson, at something she couldn't see. "We
worked at the table in the kitchen, Gillian and I. Soon's we had
something finished we would put it in the laundry room where
the boys couldn't spot it. I blew up about three dozen balloons
with a little pump while Gillian made up paper and ribbon
baskets for the candy. Then she cut out the letters for the Happy
Birthday streamer and had me put paste and glitter stuff on
them. We made the party hats too. Pirate hats for the boys and
tiny crown things for the girls. Gillian called them…"

"Tiaras."

"That's the word." He smiled, lost in a memory he was
enjoying. "Gillian told me she was making one up for little
Lucy and I said the baby would either try to eat it or rip it up.
She smiled and said when she was a little girl her daddy always
called her a princess and on her birthdays she always had a tiara.
It was a good afternoon."

"Cozy," Miss Sanderson said, hiding a shiver.

"About four, Gillian said I was looking tired and I'd better
get home and rest. I offered to stay on and help but she said she
didn't have much to do, just some baking, and she could do that
after the boys were in bed."

"The cake, I suppose."

"No, Irene was bringing that up. Had it made up special at
the bakery. Arthur was mad about planes and Ernie Marlow was
putting a toy plane on it with clouds and everything. But Gillian
was going to make up some gingerbread men and some pigs in
a blanket. Arthur loved both. I was wheeling out of kitchen to
get my coat when Mrs. Toogood brought the baby down and
put her in the playpen. Mrs. Toogood said she figured the baby
should be bedded down soon, and Gillian picked Lucy up and
hugged her. She said no. Lucy seemed better and she would
keep her up until the boys went to bed. Laughed and said that

way maybe the baby would sleep straight through and let her get some rest. Mrs. Toogood said she hoped so because the next day was going to be tiring with eight kiddies racing around. I wheeled down the hall to the closet and the telephone rang so I answered it. It was Irene. I called Gillian and she started to talk so I got my coat and waved goodbye to her. She waved back...and she blew me a kiss. That was the last I saw of her."

He bowed his head and Miss Sanderson looked sadly at him. After a moment he raised his head and the blue eyes were blurred with tears. "I came back here and wrapped up my present for Arthur. I'd gotten him a kit for a model airplane, a Spitfire. To old for the lad but I was going to help him put it together. Then I went in there—" He pointed toward the sitting room. "—and sat by the window. Thinking about the next day. I was looking forward to the party. Gillian had asked me over to help with the children, and I guess I was feeling a little sad too."

"Why?"

"Because it would be the last birthday party I would go to in that house."

"You had a premonition?"

"Didn't Irene tell you the Fosters were leaving Maddersley?"

Irene hadn't but Miss Sanderson knew all about it. She shook her head. "Didn't say a word about it. Where were they going?"

"To London. Paul had always wanted to set up practice there. Gillian wasn't quite as eager but he persuaded her it would be much better for the children than to be raised in a village. They'd bought a nice home in a good district and were nearly ready to go. They were going to either rent the Markham house or have Irene move in and look after it."

"It takes quite a sum of money to set up a fashionable practice in London. Was it Gillian's?"

"No. She spent most of her inheritance fixing the house up. A few months ago Paul came into a large inheritance—"

"Irene said his family were poor."

"His godfather wasn't and when he died everything went to Paul."

"Then Lucy is an heiress."

He nodded his head and said with a touch of malice, "Which may be why Paul's brother Leonard is so anxious to get back and look after the baby. Be sizable allotments for the guardian of that little girl."

"Does the Markham house go to Lucy too?"

"That's Irene's now. Their father was a fair man and left the house entailed. On Gillian's death it was to be her sister's."

"How did you feel about the Fosters leaving?"

"Terrible at first. Kind of deserted. I'd gotten so used to going over and I was so fond of the boys and everything. But Paul and Gillian cheered me up. Told me I would be welcome to visit in London anytime. Wouldn't have been the same, though."

"No. You would have missed them." Miss Sanderson glanced at her watch. "How time has flown. I must get back and start dinner." She put a hand on his sloping shoulder. "Matthew, you've been wonderful. I feel now as though I had known my cousin and her family. You've brought them to life. They sound like such an ideal family. I can't see why anyone would want them dead."

"Neither can I." He gazed up at her. "But this is a bad world now, Abigail. Maybe there's someone who couldn't bear to see them so happy. I don't know. I don't know much about anything anymore. But I'm going to tell you three things and you better listen."

She stared down at him and he said heavily, "Look after yourself. Let Irene and Mrs. Toogood do the work over there. You're doing your bit by being there to keep Irene company. You've asked a lot of questions. I know you want the person who did that caught as much as I do but let the police handle it. And, Abigail, keep those doors locked."

In a brown study, Miss Sanderson walked the few yards to the Markham house. The same warning. Lock the doors. They come from outside, Irene had said, with knives.

Chapter Seven

Irene kicked off her shoes and curled up like a cat in a brown velour chair. Shaking short hair back from her face, she smiled at Miss Sanderson. "Your cook's lessons must have taken, Abigail. Dinner was tasty. I'd almost forgotten what decent food was like." Miss Sanderson gestured toward the Scotch bottle, and Irene shuddered. "Not for me, I'm a reformed sinner. I was so hung over this morning I could barely stagger to work. Felt rather foolish too. Nothing like you coming here and finding no food and a drunken hostess."

"Probably did you good. You were wound up like a spring."

"It probably did." Irene asked casually, "Did I babble a lot of nonsense last night? I can't remember much about the latter part of the evening."

"I thought you made sense."

"What did I talk about?"

"This and that. Your youth. Gillian. About the men who were disappointed when she married so suddenly."

"They've probably recovered. That was years ago."

"You didn't mention names."

The answer was a shrug. Miss Sanderson decided to do a little probing but Irene had a question to ask her. "Mrs. Toogood tells me you're giving her lunch tomorrow. Is that true?"

"I plan to. Any objections?"

"Nary a one unless she gets the idea she's going to make a habit of eating here. But I can't see how you can possibly have taken a fancy to that woman."

"She hasn't taken my fancy but Lucy has and you must admit Mrs. Toogood takes good care of the baby."

"That's what she's paid for. By the way, Dora Campbell dropped in to pick up a sweater—"

"Lavender, I'll bet."

"Close. Lilac. Dora said you'd had lunch at her tearoom and had met our lady of the manor. How did you like Mary Maddersley?"

"She's a forthright person. Invited me for tea tomorrow."

"My, what an honor."

"On my way home I met Matthew Johnston."

"Who told you what a paragon Gillian was. Abigail, I don't want you encouraging that man to start coming over here again. When I moved in I gave Mrs. Toogood to understand he wasn't welcome."

"Don't you like him?"

"It's not a matter of like or dislike. I don't want him making a nuisance of himself like he did with Paul and my sister."

"They considered Matthew a nuisance?"

"If they didn't they should have. He was in and out all the time. Acted like it was his house. It happens to be mine now and I won't stand for it."

"He seems like a harmless old man. Terribly lonely."

"Most people are."

Miss Sanderson studied the younger woman. A sober Irene was going to be much harder to handle than Irene in her cups. She was cool and controlled and rather wary. The milky eyes looked like small hard marbles. Those eyes snapped to Miss Sanderson. "What on earth are you doing?" Irene asked.

Realizing she was clicking her thumbnail against a front tooth, Miss Sanderson guiltily dropped her hand into her lap. She thought of Robby who had complained for years about that mannerism. "A bad habit. I do it quite unconsciously when I'm thinking."

"You seem to do a lot of thinking, Abigail, and you ask too many questions. Even Dora Campbell commented on that—how curious you are."

"*Curious.*" Time for some well-feigned anger. Jumping to her feet, Miss Sanderson started to stride up and down the salmon carpet. "This attitude of yours and the villagers makes me believe you don't want to think or ask questions. Oh, it's sad but let's forget about it. Sweep it under the carpet. Irene, four people died in this house and no one seems to give a damn!" She paused to catch her breath and found she wasn't acting; she *was* angry. "Those people happen to have been my relatives and I *care.*"

"We all care but the police are handling it."

"How much help are they getting? Did *you* try to help them?"

The marble eyes dropped and a flush crept up the woman's thin cheeks. "I couldn't bring myself to repeat gossip about Gillian. We didn't get along too well but she was my *sister.*"

"Look!" Pulling to a halt, Miss Sanderson glared down at the other woman. "The murderer didn't drop in out of the blue. Gillian and Paul and their sons were killed by someone in this village. The answer to their murders lies in the past, in who hated them enough to kill horribly. That is *not* gossip."

Irene threw up an arm as though warning off a blow. "Please, Abigail, no more. It's so frightening. Every person I see, every person I talk to…I think, Is it you? Are you the one? I'm terrified. I've no one I can trust."

I've got her on the run, Miss Sanderson thought, and dropped back on her chair. She patted Irene's hand. "My dear, you know you can trust me."

"I think I'll have that drink now." She made a move to get up but Miss Sanderson waved her back. She made up a drink, heavy on Scotch, light on soda. As she handed the glass over, Irene asked meekly, "What do you want to know?"

"Names. The men in Gillian's past who you said were 'led down the garden path.' "

"Dr. Clay and—"

"The vicar?"

"Yes. And Sir Donald Maddersley and Paddy Rourke. Gillian worked part-time for all of them and they were mad about her—"

"What kind of work?"

"Typing for Sir Donald and the vicar, books for Paddy. To put in her time, I suppose. Gillian wasn't much good at that type of work but she was so pretty I don't suppose they cared how efficient she was."

"And each of them thought she loved *him?*"

"Gillian had a way about her. She could make anyone think she adored him. Didn't I tell you that last night?"

"Three men," Miss Sanderson mused. "At the same time in a place this size. Gillian must have been a charmer."

"If she'd wanted to I swear she could have charmed birds from trees."

"When did these men find out about her marriage plans?"

"Not until after she and Paul were married."

"Blimey. How did they react?"

"Paddy got drunk and stayed that way for a week. He also hurt his hand. Alfred Austin told me he smashed it through a window in the inn."

"Were you in the village at that time?"

"No, but the villagers have long memories. When I set up shop last year they were willing to tell all. According to Dora Campbell, Sir Donald went right off his head and—"

"Yesterday she hinted he was...She said, 'not right in the head.' "

"Dora has a vicious tongue."

"He isn't mad?"

"Of course not. Sir Donald has nervous problems and must live quietly but he certainly isn't mad. Why, he's written a number of books on gardening and even does a column about it for the newspaper. Does that sound mad?"

Depends on the type of madness, Miss Sanderson thought. "How did the vicar react?"

"For a man of the cloth rather violently." Irene's lips twitched in a smile. "Preached a couple of sermons that were dandies. Rather glad I wasn't in the congregation. Mrs. Toogood said Dr. Clay ranted on about prostitutes—" Her brow crinkled in thought. "No, she said strumpets. She said he kept using a quotation about strumpets and plague. Anyway, although Dr. Clay didn't mention Gillian by name, all the villagers knew who he was raving about."

"Plague. Strumpet," Miss Sanderson muttered. Then she had it. " ' 'Tis the strumpet's plague,' " she quoted slowly, " 'To beguile many and be beguiled by one.' "

Blue marble eyes widened and Irene asked. "The Bible?"

"The Bard. *Othello*, to be exact. I've a friend who quotes Shakespeare continuously." Robby, Miss Sanderson thought longingly, how I wish you were here quoting Shakespeare right now. "I suppose we can cross those three men off the suspect list. The murderer had to have had access to Paul's office to get the drug—"

"How did you know that?"

How did she know it? Miss Sanderson wondered wildly. She grasped at the obvious. "It was reported in the news accounts that the drug came from a cupboard in the surgery."

"So it was. I'd forgotten. But Paddy and Sir Donald and the vicar were Paul's patients and they could easily have taken the drug."

"The way they felt about Gillian and her marriage to Paul...and they were *his* patients?"

"The nearest doctor is in Lambert and he's old and quite doddering and never was much good anyway. As I said, this all happened over six years ago. None of those men would hold a grudge that long."

What about you? Miss Sanderson asked silently. You've held a grudge against your sister since you were a child. Aloud she said, "I want to hear about this house. Why does it have a bad reputation?"

Evidently Irene had decided to cooperate. She answered readily. "Because the villagers are a bunch of ninnies. You can't blame a building for what happens in it. There've been a number of unrelated tragedies here and the superstitious idiots blame this house for it. That's why Father was able to buy it so cheaply. Our family house is on the way to Maddersley Hall but it's huge and needed so many repairs. My parents couldn't afford to keep it on so we moved in here when Gillian was three and I was ten."

"These tragedies..."

"The man who built it received a head wound in the Second World War and he killed his wife. Apparently he was terribly jealous of her and suffered from the delusion she was being unfaithful to him. They found her body in the drawing room—that's the surgery now—and the man confessed. He was put in a mental home." She rubbed her chin. "I can't recall his name. Then a middle-aged couple from Leeds bought the house and one night their maid was killed—at the foot of the staircase. The police thought she'd interrupted a burglary but they never found the killer. The couple, I think their name was Hawes, rented the house to a young woman from London. I remember her vaguely. Quite pretty. She was an artist and ran with a tacky crowd. Another artist, a man, came to visit and they must have quarreled. He killed her. After that the Hawes were glad to sell to my parents."

Miss Sanderson became aware that her thumb was noisily drumming against her teeth again. Folding her hands in her lap, she asked, "How were they killed?"

"Stabbed."

"All of them?"

The brown head bobbed and Miss Sanderson gulped. From outside...with knives. She was tempted to jump up and check the doors. "You do plan to stay on here."

"Of course. It's my home."

"Won't it be lonely after Lucy's guardian comes for her—"

"How do you know that?" Irene snapped. "That fact certainly wasn't reported in the newspapers."

"Mathew told me."

"That busybody! Hears all, sees all, tells all. I suppose he also told you Lucy is inheriting a good-sized estate."

"He did."

It was Irene's turn to jump up and pace up and down. "The whole thing is so unfair. I should have been my niece's guardian. When the solicitor read the will and he said Leonard and Marjorie Foster were to have Lucy I simply couldn't believe it. They have so much now. Leonard has a good job and they travel to so many interesting places. And they have *three* children." She swung on Miss Sanderson. "Do you think it's fair?"

"It's a responsibility raising a child. How could you keep your shop on?"

"I wouldn't have to. Lucy's guardian receives a generous allowance. And I can't possibly keep house like this on the tiny income I make from the shop."

"Perhaps Leonard Foster would be happy to let you care for the child. Why don't you ask him?"

"I have. He rang up after he heard about his brother and Gillian and I suggested just that. He said no, Marjorie and he are better qualified to raise Lucy. He said they're making arrangements to take her off my hands." Irene scowled. "*Qualified.* Their children are spoiled rotten."

"Did you expect to be the children's guardian?"

"I didn't *expect* anything. I didn't expect young healthy people like Gillian and Paul to die before I did. But I have a right to my niece. Wasn't Paul's will unfair?"

"Totally," Miss Sanderson agreed tactfully. "If anything were to happen to Lucy, what about Paul's estate?"

Slumping back in the armchair, Irene said, "Split between the next of kin."

"Leonard Foster and you?"

"Yes." She asked tartly, "Do you suspect *me*?"

"Of course not. I was only—" Miss Sanderson broke off. She'd been about to say curious. "I was only wondering. So…if Lucy had died that night you and Leonard would have inherited."

"But she didn't. When I found her alive I couldn't believe it. I thought she must be dead too."

"Tell me about that night."

"Must I?"

"Yes."

All fight seemed to have gone out of the other woman. "I've told this over again and again. You'd think repetition would blunt the horror. It doesn't." She took a deep breath. "Very well, Abigail, into the breach once more. I rang up a few minutes after four in the afternoon. I'd planned to come directly here after I closed the shop to give my sister a hand with the party preparations. Gillian wasn't having an easy pregnancy this time and she tired so easily. But at the last minute I found I had to do alterations on a suit for Mary Maddersley and I would have to work late.

"Matthew answered the telephone and Gillian came on. I told her I would be delayed until after nine and she said not to worry. Matthew had helped her out that afternoon and all she had left to do was a bit of baking. She asked whether I'd picked up the cake from the bakery and was it nice. I said yes, it was and Ernie had put a toy plane—"

"Matthew told me about the cake decorations."

Irene held out her glass and while Miss Sanderson attended to it she continued, "Then we chatted for a bit—"

"What about?"

"The party. Gillian said she and Paul were giving Arthur a small radio for his bedroom and that Matthew had bought him a model plane kit. I laughed and told her I'd bought Arthur a plane kit too and she said Matthew would help the boy put both of them together. She sounded tired so I advised her not to bother too much with dinner—Gillian and Paul always dined in the dining room and she fussed over meals. She told me she intended to make a simple meal that night, steak and salad, and they'd eat at the kitchen table. I warned her not to get overtired and she laughed and said not to be a mother hen. Said both Matthew and Paul were fussing over her enough. Then we rang off."

Irene paused and applied herself to her drink. Watching her, Miss Sanderson hoped it wouldn't have as rapid and disastrous an effect as the drinks had had the previous evening. "Do you know what time you got here?"

"I should. I went over and over that with the police. I finished the alterations up a few minutes before nine. As I left the shop I looked at my watch and it was nine sharp. It didn't take me long to get here. It had been raining earlier and was raw and cold and I was hurrying. Pockets of ice were forming on the walks. I was tired and chilled and was lugging my gift and the cake. All I wanted to do was deliver them and get back to bed. I didn't notice lights at Miss Beauchamp's cottage or Nurse Ines' but I could see a light on in Matthew's sitting room. I went up to the door here and—"

"Which door?"

"The kitchen door. I expected to find Gillian in the kitchen. I took the walk that runs between Matthew's cottage and this side of the house. I knocked—"

"Surely your sister would have left it unlocked for you."

"Not in this house," Irene said grimly. "Mother and Father drilled it into both of us about locking doors. Anyway, I could see a line of light between the curtains but there was no answer. I did try the door and it was locked—"

"You didn't have a key?"

"The only people who had keys were Gillian and Paul. Another of my parents' rules. And if you're wondering whether I had a key left from when I lived here, the answer no. After his marriage Paul had new locks put on."

"And after you tried the door?"

"I knew Gillian wasn't in the kitchen. Lucy had been sick with a cold so I thought Gillian was upstairs with the baby. I put the packages down on the porch and trotted down the ramp and back the way I had come. Again I noticed the light in Matthew's cottage. I ran up on the veranda and rang the chimes. There was the light in the living room and I could hear music. I thought Paul must be relaxing and watching a television program. Again no one answered."

"Were you worried by this time?"

Irene considered. Then she shook her head and hair spilled away from her face. "Annoyed. After all, I was expected. I wondered whether Paul and Gillian could have dropped over to see Matthew and then I thought, no, they would never leave the children alone. So I decided to try the side door, the one to the surgery…"

Her voice trailed off and Miss Sanderson envisioned that dreadful evening. Irene, muffled in anorak and knitted hat, angered at being kept out in the cold, tired and wanting only her bed, making her way around the house, up the walk to the steps that led to the surgery. Irene said slowly, "I slipped on the bottom step and looked down. There was a glaze of ice on it. These are steep steps and can be treacherous. I grabbed at the door handle and it—the door—swung open. It had been left ajar.

"That was when I got worried. After the last patient left Nurse Ines always locked that door. And Gillian always checked it afterward. That annoyed Paul's nurse. She figured the surgery was *her* territory. I think…I remember calling Paul's name. Then I turned around to close and lock the door and I saw marks on the woodwork around it. They were red and moist and for a moment I thought they were paint. I wiped a finger through them and knew it wasn't paint…it was blood."

No longer did Irene's eyes look like blue marbles. They were filled with terror. Her glass was empty again so Miss Sanderson took it from her hand and went to the gateleg table. This time she splashed a considerable amount of soda on the single malt. Should she force this woman to relive the nightmare? Then she knew she must. Perhaps Irene would remember something, some tiny thing she hadn't told the police. Closing Irene's fingers around the glass, she said, "Go on."

"It's easy for you," Irene said brokenly. "You never knew them. Gillian was my younger sister and Paul—once I'd loved him."

"It's not easy for either of us," Miss Sanderson told her sternly. "But it must be done."

Taking a long swallow, Irene said jerkily, "The door to his office was open and I could see him. There was so much blood and things protruded from his chest. They were his—"

"I can guess what they were."

"I ran into the hall and heard the music from the living room. Before I saw the boys I saw the television screen. Silly little figures dancing. Arthur and Andrew looked like they were asleep. The fire was burning. I ran to the kitchen and I found...Gillian. I remember standing over her, thinking that the murderer might still be in the house. I threw open the back door and tripped over the cake."

"But you didn't run from the house?"

"Lucy! I thought, she's dead too. Run! I couldn't. I went back up the hall. The shadows seemed to move and I was so frightened I could hardly move. Then I heard Lucy cry out." Irene shook her head. "I must have gone upstairs and picked her up. I can't remember doing it. The next thing I knew I was at Matthew's back door and he opened it and took the baby and called the police and a doctor came and gave me a shot and..."

Irene was tearing a paper hankie into bits. Miss Sanderson took the scraps and threw them onto the grate. She put a comforting arm around the younger woman's thin, shaking shoulders. "I'll help you up to bed."

Whether it was the drink or the memories Miss Sanderson had no idea but Irene Markham did need help. She found pajamas, helped Irene into them, eased her into bed, and pulled the duvet to her chin. She rested a hand on Irene's brow. "Sleep," she told the woman. "You're safe. I'm right here."

Lashes drifted down and Miss Sanderson waited until Irene's breathing deepened into a soft snoring sound. Then she walked to the door and put her hand on the switch. Before the lights snapped off she took a long look at the portraits of the Foster family. Their eyes seemed to coldly examine her. Can you find the one? she fancied they were asking. I don't know, Miss Sanderson told them silently, but I'm sure as hell trying.

She went to the nursery and stood over the crib. The rosy nightlight showed a chubby hand gripping a teddy bear in a red sweater. With a tender finger she touched a warm moist cheek.

As she closed the door of the nursery she glanced down the hall at double doors. It would have been simple, she thought, for Irene to have made two trips to the Markham house that night—the first to commit the murders, the second to have discovered the bodies. If Irene had murdered for hate and profit she was an amazing actress.

Miss Sanderson had known murderers before. Some of them had been consummate actors. Keeping this in mind, she went to her bed.

Chapter Eight

Mrs. Toogood, her tiny eyes bright with anticipation, sat at the kitchen table watching Miss Sanderson moving around the stove. "Decent of you, Miss Sanders, and my, haven't you done it up brown! Pork pie and beer and raspberry tart. Takes me back to when the missus, rest her soul, was alive. Always gave me a hot lunch she did. Waited on me too like you're doing. Can't believe her and Miss Irene were sisters. All *that* woman would give is the back of her hand."

Miss Sanderson cut into the greasy pie and put a large slab on one plate and a thinner wedge on another. She poured beer and set the foaming glass and the large piece of pie in front of her guest. "It's a shame you have to have cold lunches now."

"Don't have any choice, do I? First thing Miss Irene told me when she moved in is bring me own food or go hungry." Mrs. Toogood fell on her lunch and proceeded to wolf it down. Sipping beer, Miss Sanderson wondered how to get her companion talking. There was no need. Not only was the housekeeper a self-starter but she could eat and talk simultaneously. Her conversation consisted of remarks about her former mistress, all highly colored and complimentary. "Give me all her boys' clothes, she did, soon's they grew out of then. Some good as new and fit my Percy and Willy fine. Every Christmas the missus give me a check. Always told me to see the kiddies have a good Christmas. Give me stuff of little Lucy too for my Mollie." She buried her mouth in beer suds and her voice became muffled. "Couldn't ask for a finer lady than the missus."

Most commendable, Miss Sanderson thought, but of no help. She threw out some bait. "From what I've learned not everyone in the village agrees with you."

"Ah, that'll be the Austins and the Marlows, miss." She looked longingly at the pie dish and Miss Sanderson lifted the last slice onto her plate. "Thanks. Goes down good with beer." Taking the hint, her companion refilled the glass. "That was a sad day for the missus when she took that Marlow brat under her roof. Told the missus, no good will come of this, but missus wouldn't listen. Always felt sorry for Ernie saddled with that Maybelle as a wife and then getting a daughter like Melanie."

"I heard he abused both of them. Yesterday when I stopped in the bakery I noticed Mrs. Marlow had a bruise under her eye. And he's such a hulking brute."

"His looks is against him, miss. If Ernie looked harmless like Alfred Austin no one would think the worst of him for cuffing his women around. Poor man's only trying to keep them decent. Maybelle's always had a wandering eye, making up to anything in pants. And Melanie was worse than her mum, been after men since she was knee-high."

"But he does strike them?"

" 'Course he does. Gives them a lick now and then. If'n they were mine I'd use a skillet on them. Told the missus that and she spoke real sharp to me. Tried to tell her Melanie was lying about her dad but that girl pulled the wool over both the missus and Dr. Foster's eyes."

Mrs. Toogood had finished her second slice of pie and was eyeing her companion's untouched plate. Miss Sanderson shoved it over. "Oh no, miss, can't eat your lunch."

"I don't care that much for pork pie." Miss Sanderson added casually, "So, you sided with the Austins and Ernie Marlow?"

"Didn't side with no one. Know my place I do. But I speak my mind and the missus and Dr. Foster was dead wrong to take that girl in and then give her money to run away. Melanie's not even seventeen and heavens know what mischief she'll be up to on her own."

"And you told my cousin and her husband all this?"

"Came right out and told them. But Melanie she cried and showed them bruises and took them in. Set them right against Ernie and Nell Austin."

"And Rog Austin too."

"Rog isn't a bad lad, miss. Just says and does what his mum tells him. 'Course he had his heart set on marrying that girl and he was real upset when she left. Could use a chunk of tart now, miss."

Miss Sanderson's eyes widened. Mrs. Toogood certainly had a hearty appetite. Perhaps Irene couldn't afford to feed her if she ate this much habitually. While she cut tart and poured beer she said, "I'm surprised a girl like that could take Gillian in."

"Lot of people thought because the missus was so pretty she weren't too bright but the missus was smart enough. Melanie never took *her* in. Leastways not for long."

"But you said—"

"Said the missus wouldn't listen when she had the girl come live here. Soon's Melanie was in the house missus saw I was right. She wanted that girl outta here and away from her husband." Miss Sanderson turned and found the housekeeper regarding her shrewdly. The effect was somewhat spoiled by a large crumb dangling from her lower lip. "Doctors get a lot of females going gaga about them. 'Specially a young well-set-up one like Dr. Foster. Melanie set her cap for the doctor, always rubbing up against him like. And missus had her hands full with that Miss Beauchamp. Didn't need Melanie after him too."

Mrs. Toogood smiled widely and the crumb trembled and fell into her lap. "Missus handled both of them good."

Miss Sanderson took a sip of beer. It had gone flat. "Surely my cousin could have discharged the girl."

"Wouldn't have looked good, miss. People'd be wondering why. As it was there was enough talk when Melanie left town."

"Did the doctor reciprocate Melanie's affection?"

"Huh?" The housekeeper blinked. "Oh, I see what you're getting at. Wouldn't know. I was only here days. But Melanie's a good-looking girl and it was a fine idea to get rid of her. I just didn't like the way it was done."

This version of the feud sounded more like Miss Maddersley's than Matthew Johnston's. The thought of Johnston spurred Miss Sanderson's next question. "Mr. Johnston told me he was here the day the Austins and Ernie Marlow were trying to find where Melanie had gone. Were you here too?"

"Sure was. Putting dishes in that machine right over there. Mr. Johnston was at this table, busy mending one of Andrew's toy trucks. Missus took them into the living room and didn't bother shutting the doors. They was hollering loud enough we'd heard them even if those doors had been shut. Had my hands full with Mr. Johnston. Set a lot of store by the missus he did and wanted to go in there and set them right. My, they was steamed up. Nell was yelling about the missus taking away her son's bride and Ernie was shouting about standing between a child and her parents and Rog kept yelping he'd bought the girl a ring and all." Mrs. Toogood's eyes glinted with unholy glee. "Had to grab onto Mr. Johnston's chair and hold it back. Kept telling him the missus could look after herself. She sure could too. Got rid of them and I told Mr. Johnston, 'See, missus don't need any help.' The old fellow really gave me a turn. Kinda collapsed in his chair, his shoulders all bowed, and he kept saying, 'That woman, that terrible, terrible woman!' I told him not to take on so, that Nell Austin isn't all that bad. She's got a temper and a bad mouth but she cools down fast."

Not only had Mrs. Toogood finished her lunch but also managed to finish every scrap of tart. Sitting back, she patted her stomach and stifled a belch. "When the missus come into the kitchen she sure looked pretty. Lot of color in her face and she was laughing. She says, 'I certainly told them, didn't I?' And Mr. Johnston he perked up some and didn't look so awful and he pats her hand and says, 'Gillian, you're an amazing lady.'" She shook her frowsy head. "He thought the world of the missus. Broke his heart when her and the doctor and the kiddies—" With a red-knuckled hand, the housekeeper yanked up a corner of her apron and dabbed at damp eyes. "Still can't believe it, miss. How could anyone…"

Miss Sanderson patted a beefy shoulder. "Have you any idea who might have done it?"

"Thought on it a bit. Don't know. Sure, there were some who didn't like them. Lot of people thought the missus was stuck-up and the boys was spoiled but you don't come in and butcher four people just 'cause you don't like them."

"Can you think of anyone who had a strong grudge against either my cousin or her husband?"

"Well, like I told you there was the Austins and Ernie—"

"Besides them."

"Some men who didn't take to the idea of the missus marrying the doctor. But they was married for years. Seems to me any of those men would have hurt them before if they was gonna. Oh, there's Dora Campbell. She still goes on about the missus taking her man away from her."

"Dora Campbell?"

"All the missus did was go out a couple of times with a chap who was courting Dora. He dropped Dora like a hot potato and who could blame him. Her with a face homely as a hedge fence. Missus sure didn't mean to break them up. Men just went wild about her. That was a long time ago too. But Dora raves on about it as though it happened yesterday."

There would have been no contest, Miss Sanderson mused, between beautiful Gillian and Dora with the sheep's face.

So…Dora Campbell had reason to hate Gillian Foster. She was about to mention the mysterious Miss Beauchamp when the housekeeper looked at the kitchen clock and jumped to her feet. "Look at the time! Got to go up and tend to little Lucy. Tell you this, miss, only reason I stay on here is for the missus and little Lucy. Soon's the doctor's brother comes for the baby I'll be gone. Were I you I'd leave things to Miss Irene and get back to London. This house is hard enough on a body who's got her health."

"Kind of you to be concerned, Mrs. Toogood, but until Lucy leaves I'm staying."

"Suit yourself, miss." Plodding over, Mrs. Toogood swung open the door. A few words drifted back. "Nice lunch. I thank you."

Miss Sanderson sighed. All that time and food appeared to have been wasted. The only tidbit she'd gained from the house-keeper was the item about Dora Campbell. Perhaps she would fare better with Mary Maddersley. She had a couple of hours to put in before she had to arrive at the Hall. I think I'll visit the neighbors, she decided, and headed for the hall.

She was taking her coat out of the closet when Mrs. Toogood called down the stairwell, "Going out?"

"Yes, and I may not be back in time to start dinner."

"I'll tell Miss Irene. Mind you put your muffler and boots on."

Miss Sanderson decided perhaps the lunch effort was proving to have a fringe benefit. The housekeeper seemed to be mellowing. Once outside she found Miss Toogood's advice had been sensible. The sky was again overcast and a cold western wind was whistling. She strolled past Johnston's cottage and paused beside his neighbor's fence. A hand was pulling the curtain back in the sitting room window. Ah, Nurse Ines must be home. The blue-painted door sported an old-fashioned bellpull. She rang it lustily and the door opened wide. The woman framed in the doorway was as tall as Miss Sanderson and looked about twice as wide. She had shoulders like a rugby player. She regarded Miss Sanderson silently and with no evidence of pleasure.

"I'm Abigail Sanders, Gillian Foster's cousin."

"I know who you are. I've seen you going back and forth. Do a lot of gadding around for a sick person."

"On my doctor's orders. I've a heart condition."

Pushing the wire-rimmed glasses up on a sharp nose, the nurse said, "Reasonable exercise is a good idea. So, you're the cousin who finally came to Miss Markham's aid. I always say better late than never. Don't stand there, get in. Cooling the house down. No central heating here."

No invitation was proffered to remove her coat but Miss Sanderson did it anyway. As she did she glanced around. The room was identical in shape to Johnston's but here were the chintz, mellow wood, and brass she had envisioned in his sitting room. On the grate a brisk fire radiated heat. "This is perfectly charming," she told the other woman. "What a lovely job you've done."

"Always try to make a place homey. I've had years to work on this one." Nurse Ines pointed an imperious finger. "Sit over there. Won't be in my way as I work." She strode over and continued packing books in a crate.

"Are you leaving Maddersley?"

"As soon as I finish packing and hire a van."

"But the police investigation—"

"If the police want to keep me they'll have to charge me. They've no grounds for that. I've no choice anyway. Gave my notice on this cottage for the end of this month."

"Then you must have planned to leave before the Fosters' deaths."

"When a body gets their notice they leave, don't they?"

"You weren't going to London with Dr. Foster?"

"Wasn't young enough or pretty enough for his fine new surgery. At least that's the excuse he gave." She plucked another book from the white-painted shelf, looked at it, and set it on the floor. "That's one he lent me. Have to take it back to the surgery."

Nurse Ines certainly was neither young nor pretty. She looked over fifty. She wore a baggy maroon skirt and a matching jacket. Large feet were shod in sensible black brogues and salt-and-pepper hair was strained back into a bun. In starched whites and a cap she would be impressive. Deciding on a meek approach, Miss Sanderson murmured, "What a shame. And the wonderful home you've made here, too."

"He didn't care." Apparently Miss Sanderson had hit the right note. In an aggrieved voice the nurse continued, "Doctor didn't quite put it that way. He said he would need a younger woman to handle the extra work. I'll tell you this, Miss Sanders, the doctor didn't think I was too old when he was training at Guy's. Took all the help he could get from me and when he qualified and set up practice here he begged me to come down. I left everything I'd worked for—a good job with a promotion coming along, a nice comfortable flat, friends and colleagues— to come down to this dreary hole."

"Why did you do it?"

"My entire life has been devoted to medicine." Nurse Ines swung around to face her visitor. "My father was a surgeon and my mother a matron. Dr. Foster was a fine doctor. From the time he came to Guy's I knew I'd never seen better. He was a *healer.* Down here he was absolutely wasted. Should have been in London years ago. When I heard of his plans for moving his practice I was overjoyed. Finally we were coming into our own. I had such plans for us. If I do say so myself, we were a good team."

"I imagine you were."

The last book slid into the crate and the big woman bent, lifted it without effort, and set it against the wall. Picking up a brass bowl, she wrapped it in tissue and tucked it in a cardboard box. "When the doctor told me I wouldn't be going with him I couldn't believe my ears. Then I thought, ah, this is your wife's doing. I'm a frank woman, Miss Sanders, and I speak my mind. I didn't like your cousin and she made it quite clear she couldn't stand me. Jealous because her husband depended on me so much."

"I never knew Gillian, but Mrs. Toogood tells me she was kind."

"On the surface. If it didn't cost her anything and it pleased her. She poisoned the doctor's mind against me. The moment I met her I knew she wasn't right for a doctor's wife. Took no interest in his work. All Mrs. Foster cared about was her house and gadgets for it and her children. And those children! They were little hellions."

"Not little Lucy," Miss Sanderson defended staunchly.

"Too young yet. In time she would have been like her brothers—spoiled and sassy and whining. That wasn't the doctor's fault. He had no say in raising them."

"Were you in close contact with Gillian and the children?"

"Stayed as far away from them as I could get. The surgery was my area and I made certain to keep those children *and* Mrs. Foster out of it." Nurse Ines neglected her packing and straightened, her hands planted firmly on her hips. A formidable woman, Miss Sanderson thought. The nurse continued, "Didn't even let the housekeeper in there. Told Mrs. Toogood no messing around. I did the cleaning there and kept everything in order. If I do say so myself it was always spotless."

A thought struck Miss Sanderson. "Did you clean up after..."

"Of course. As soon as they took the doctor's body away I went right in and started scrubbing. Couldn't do much with the rug in the office. That will have to be discarded. Blood is hard to get out of carpeting."

"Didn't you find it terrible?"

"Why should I? I'm a nurse. Cleaned up worse things than blood."

"But you knew this man; you'd worked with him for years. Surely you were fond of him."

Nurse Ines, for the first time since Miss Sanderson had been admitted to her house, smiled. At least her lips pulled back from large white teeth. "I respected the doctor's ability, not him. And I lost even that respect when he dismissed me. Threw me aside like a…"

"An old shoe?"

"Like a piece of rubbish. Devoted the best years of my life to that man and that was my reward. He didn't *care* about me. I was no more use to him and he didn't even care if I could find a decent job."

Miss Sanderson was struck with the horrible thought that there was a possibility that Nurse Ines had *enjoyed* scrubbing up Paul Foster's blood. "But you said you blamed Gillian for that, not Paul."

"I said I started out blaming her. I ended up blaming him. If he could be that ungrateful, that easily swayed by his wife, well…good riddance to bad rubbish."

Nurse Ines hadn't been exaggerating. She *was* frank. Watching the woman's powerful hands wrapping up a slender glass vase, Miss Sanderson asked, "Did you tell the police all this?"

"I told them only what was necessary. That was none of their business."

"Did anyone else know about your dismissal?"

"The only ones who knew were the doctor and Mrs. Foster. No reason for them to talk about it. The doctor's patients may not have loved me but I'll tell you straight, they respected me."

And so do I, Miss Sanderson told her silently. You're strong and possibly ruthless. According to Beau Brummell the wounds in Gillian's back and her sons' had been done as a medical man might, or, perhaps, as a nurse would. Despite the heat from the fireplace she shivered and the nurse noticed. "Miss Sanders, I do hope you're not coming down with a chill."

"No, I'm just tired. I haven't been sleeping well. Strange bed, you know."

"You're in no shape to be here. I'm surprised your physician allowed it."

Miss Sanderson said simply, "I had to come."

Rugby shoulders shrugged and Nurse Ines reached for a handsome ormolu clock. "Well, you know what they say good intentions lead to." She held the clock up and regarded it fondly. "Pretty, isn't it? It belonged to my mother. If the movers break it I swear I'll butcher them."

Blimey, Miss Sanderson thought dismally, that's all I need. Well, on with the detecting. "Could you tell me what you remember about that day?"

"*That* day." Setting aside the clock, Nurse Ines took a chair near her visitor. "Rather divides one's life. Certain things happened before, other things after. Well, Miss Sanders, there was nothing outstanding about that day. As usual I went to work even though I was quite ill. I had a bad chest cold but I'm not a shirker and I work no matter how I feel. Mrs. Foster complained I'd given the cold to her baby but I certainly was not near the little thing." She paused and then asked, "Do you want the day in detail?"

"Please."

"I fail to see what bearing this has on anything but here goes." She took a deep breath. "I always arrived at nine sharp and I did that morning. Mrs. Foster wouldn't trust me with a key to the surgery door and so I was required to go to the front door. Mrs. Toogood admitted me and told me her 'missus' was sleeping in because the older boy's birthday was the next day and Mrs. Foster wasn't feeling well. Pregnant again. That woman was like a rabbit, one baby after the other. So I went directly to my desk and took some appointments by the telephone and brought records up to date. Oh, yes, I made up some billing notices. People ask help freely but don't pay very promptly at times. From eight until eleven the doctor made rounds at Lambert General. He was usually back around twelve and had lunch with his family. I had my lunch and as was my custom ate it at my desk."

"You didn't take luncheon with the family?"

"I told you I stayed as clear of them as I could. I always brought my own. I wouldn't eat food from *her* table, anyway.

Surgery hours were from one until five. Will you want the names of the patients?"

Miss Sanderson had no doubt Nurse Ines could recite those names. "No, that's not necessary."

"Mrs. Rourke was the doctor's last patient and she didn't leave until three minutes after five. I saw her out and then I locked the door. Miss Sanders, I *know* my job and locking that door was part of it. But that cousin of yours always checked it. She didn't trust me."

"Did she check it that day?"

"She did. I didn't speak to her and she ignored me. Swept in like a duchess, rattled the knob, and swept out again. *Silly.* All the doors in the house lock automatically when they're firmly closed. Then the doctor came out of his office and told me I'd better get home and look after my cold. He said he would clean up. I always tidied the waiting room and examination room before I left. Checked the supply cabinet and cleaned the sink and bathroom and emptied the ashtrays. I never was able to understand why the doctor tolerated patients smoking in the surgery. Filthy habit and so dangerous to the health."

Miss Sanderson had been taking her cigarette package from her purse. She hastily pushed it back but Nurse Ines said tartly, "Now, *you* should know better than that. Smoking leads to heart problems."

"I don't believe that has been conclusively proven," Miss Sanderson said weakly.

"You take *my* word for it, it does. You're digging your own grave with those disgusting things."

"I thought one dug one's grave with a fork and knife."

The nurse ran icily professional eyes up and down Miss Sanderson. "I must admit, you're not overweight. Quit that filthy habit and you may have a few good years yet."

Thanks a heap, Miss Sanderson thought. Aloud she said meekly, "You were telling me about Paul advising you to go home."

"I didn't argue. I really was feeling dreadful. I cleared my desk and went out to the hall. Mrs. Toogood had been lighting the fire in the living room and she came to the doorway and told me if I waited a few minutes she would walk me home. So I hurried to get my cape and boots on before she did—"

"Don't you like Mrs. Toogood?"

Nurse Ines considered briefly. "I don't care for her grooming. She could certainly comb her hair and have a dentist fix that missing tooth but she is a good housekeeper. I have nothing against her but her conversation tired me. Her only topic was her 'missus' and how wonderful that woman was. So I hurried out of the house and down the lane. It had been raining earlier and was turning quite cold. I made a mental note to sprinkle some ashes on the side steps to the surgery the next morning. I warned the doctor countless times about those steps. In frosty weather they ice up and a patient might have had a bad fall. As I reached my gate I saw Mrs. Toogood stepping out on the veranda. When I came in here it was cold and I built the fire up. I couldn't bear to think of food, so I ran a hot tub and made up some lemon and honey. Then I went to bed and fell almost immediately into a deep sleep. At five minutes after twelve the next morning the police came battering at my door to tell me about the murders." She spread blunt-fingered hands. "That is all I can tell you, Miss Sanders."

Miss Sanderson's hand had been creeping toward her mouth. She jerked it down. If Nurse Ines caught her drumming her nail against her teeth she would doubtless get a lecture on dental hygiene. "Did Paul clean up the surgery as he promised?"

"The next morning when the police took me in to check the drug cupboard the rooms had been neatened. Not the job I would have done but the ashtrays had been washed, the sink scrubbed out, fresh linen put on the examination table. Yes, the doctor must have done it before he settled down at his desk to have a look over a new medical textbook that had arrived in the post that morning."

"Was Paul in the habit of remaining in his office after surgery hours?"

"I wouldn't say he made a habit of it but yes, he frequently did stay at his desk reading. It's my opinion he was seeking refuge from those sons of his. Waiting until they were ready for bed before returning to the living quarters." Removing the wire-rimmed glasses, she polished already shining lenses. "Odd, that's the same question one of the officers from London asked me. The nice one—Chief Inspector Kepesake. Clean as a whistle and well groomed. The only fault I could find with that man was his deplorable smoking habit."

"Did you speak to him about it?" Miss Sanderson asked hopefully.

"I most certainly did. Very sensible man. Put his jade holder in his pocket and promised that was the last time he would ever use it." Miss Sanderson was fighting to keep from smiling. When Adam Kepesake had visited Robby's flat on his return from Maddersley he had been making good use of his elaborate cigarette holder. Nurse Ines's look of beaming approval vanished and her mouth quirked with distaste. "The detective sergeant with him was disgusting! The most slovenly creature I ever saw. Brummell was his name. A positive disgrace to a uniform!"

"Detective sergeants don't wear uniforms."

"You know full well what I mean. Now, do you have further questions?"

"Only one. Your neighbor—"

"Mr. Johnston? Sad case. In constant pain."

"I was thinking of Miss Beauchamp."

Nurse Ines's pointed nose wrinkled as though she'd suddenly caught a whiff of cigarette smoke. "I know nothing about Miss Beauchamp. She was the doctor's patient but he made house calls on her."

"She never came to the surgery?"

"Once, only. If you have any questions I suggest you ask *her.*" Coming majestically to her feet, the nurse resumed packing.

"You didn't mention your dismissal to the chief inspector?"

"I told you I didn't. It has no bearing on the case."

"Why did you tell me?"

Nurse Ines turned her head and light reflected from her glasses. "Because I thought you should know. Don't bother grieving for your relatives. They weren't worth it. You're fortunate you never knew them. Both Dr. and Mrs. Foster were selfish and callous and cruel."

Scooping up the carton, she strode from the room.

Chapter Nine

"Now you make yourself comfy and I'll get some coffee," Linda Beauchamp said and scurried into the kitchen.

Miss Sanderson eyed the two available chairs, passed the one made of chrome and what looked like burlap sacking, and took the one with a high back and brocade covering. It was an odd sitting room, nearly as stark as Matthew Johnston's. The floor boards were bare and besides the two mismatched chairs there were only a bookcase and a table bearing a portable typewriter and sheafs of paper. But the window was hung with thin cotton curtains and spaced along the mantel were an array of ornaments. These consisted of an ivory elephant, a water glass holding a few dried flowers, and a fine set of Georgian candlesticks. However, as in Nurse Ines's cottage, a fire burned brightly on the grate and sitting before it was a large Siamese cat. It was washing one rich brown ear and it paused with crossed turquoise eyes to stare balefully at the visitor.

Miss Sanderson stared balefully back. She disliked Siamese cats. Generally she disliked people who owned Siamese cats. She wondered whether she would dislike Linda Beauchamp. It was hard to tell. The young woman seemed as odd as her sitting room.

Hardly before Miss Sanderson had crossed the threshold Linda had told her rapidly that she was so sorry that she hadn't stopped to speak the day Miss Sanderson had arrived in the village. She said the reason she hadn't spoken was that she had a morbid fear of strangers and that this fear had been diagnosed by Dr. Paul as a lack of confidence because she'd failed at every single thing she'd ever tried. If she failed to complete the book he'd encouraged her to write she knew she would do something dreadful to herself.

Much more of this prattle, Miss Sanderson thought morbidly, and I may do something dreadful myself. She hadn't been allowed to say a word, had merely been plucked from the stoop and deposited in this chair. The only consoling thought was that it wasn't going to be necessary to prod Linda Beauchamp into talking.

The girl returned bearing a tray and unleashing a flood of words. "I see you've met my Mitzi. Isn't she a pretty girl? I do so love cats, don't you? So aloof, you have to work for their affection. Not like dogs. Nasty beasts. They either nip at you or jump up with great muddy paws." She handed her guest a cup of muddy fluid. "Powdered coffee and it won't be good. I'm not a good cook. But Dr. Paul told me I have the soul of an artist and artists aren't expected to cook properly. Do have a cake. They're from Marlow's Bakery and are *very* good. I talk too much, don't I? But that's simply because I'm nervous."

"No need to be nervous of me," Miss Sanderson said as rapidly as her hostess. Contagious, she thought, and slowed her voice to a soothing drawl. "You were Paul's patient."

"Not really his patient. There's nothing *wrong* with me. He acted as my mentor. He simply dropped in and talked. Almost every day. On his way home after his hospital rounds. Always sat in that chair you're using. I think of it as Paul's chair. Sometimes he had only a few moments, sometimes he could stay longer. But he always came. He saved me, you know."

"No, I didn't know. Saved you from what?"

The deluge of words slowed. "From...something awful. Perhaps I was going mad...perhaps I was...well, going to take my life. When I came to Maddersley I was a perfect wreck. I'd tried teaching in a school for girls but I failed at that too. The headmistress tried to be kind and told me I was too sensitive for the profession but the truth is I *loathe* children. I'm terrified of them. They're such cruel beastly creatures. Even Dr. Paul's sons were cruel. Do you know what they used to call me?" Leaning forward, she whispered, "Miss Linda Top-heavy."

Miss Sanderson had to fight to control her expression. When she'd seen Linda Beauchamp before, the leather coat had disguised her figure. But in tight jeans and an equally tight sweater the woman was grotesque. She had a sticklike build, sparrow legs, no hips, scrawny arms. Her shoulders were frail and appeared to strain forward under the weight of the largest breasts Miss Sanderson had ever seen. Even on a woman with the sturdy build of Nurse Ines those breasts would have been astounding but on this delicate creature... She managed to say, "That certainly was unkind, Miss Beauchamp."

"Please. I'm Linda and I'll call you Abigail. That way you won't seem so much of a stranger." One clawlike hand gingerly touched the bulging pink sweater. "I begged Dr. Paul to arrange an operation. It can be done, you know. He told me I must accept them first. But he did promise in time I could have it done. First he wanted me to accept my mother's death and how I felt about her."

"Your mother died?"

"About eight months ago. After I lost my position at the school I went home to her. Mother had a nice house in Kent and she was delighted to have me back. Then, she died."

"And Paul helped you come to grips with the grief?"

"With the joy! The wonderful freedom. And the *guilt*. One should not be happy about a mother's death. But she was a monster! An invalid and she simply *devoured* me. As soon as she was buried I sold the house and looked around for a place to rent." The triangular face lit up and the bulging brown eyes glowed. "Abigail, you aren't drinking your coffee."

One sip of the coffee had been enough. Linda definitely must be an artist. She certainly couldn't make coffee. "Was Paul acting as a psychiatrist to you, Linda?"

"He wanted to send me to a specialist in London but I refused to go. I told him, 'Dr. Paul, you're my salvation. Heal me!' And he was doing it. We talked and gradually I realized I had nothing to feel guilty about. Mother had made me an emotional *cripple*. She'd convinced me I could do nothing *right*. Dr. Paul told me he was certain that I have the makings of a great writer. He said I should write a book about my life, share my experiences with people who may need help." She swept long fair hair from her face and pointed at the typewriter. "My book was coming along so *well*. I would read it to him and he would make suggestions. Then *she* ruined it. She ruined *me*."

Miss Sanderson carefully set her cup down. I've a terrible feeling, she thought, who *she* is. "Gillian?"

"I refuse to say her *name*." Jumping to her feet, Linda started walking around the bare room. Sparrow legs and thin hips jiggled immense breasts. "Abigail, how can a lovely person like you ever have had a cousin like her?"

"What did she do?"

"Ruined my life!" The girl pulled to a halt on the hearth. She braced an arm on the mantle and rested her chin against it. Her voice was muffled. "Dr. Paul died on a Thursday night. The Monday before, he dropped in here as usual in the morning. I was so happy to see him. I gave him coffee and we sat here by the fire and I had my notes on my lap to discuss with him and then...Then he told me that that was the last visit he would be making. At first I thought he was joking. He told me I had two choices, either to go to that specialist or go to his surgery once a week until he left for London, of course. Then he tried to explain. He said his wife had said people were *talking*, they were saying there was something *going on* between us. I told him he couldn't desert me. I *needed* him. He became quite cold and curt. He ordered me to make an appointment with Nurse Ines. Then he walked out."

"Did you go to his surgery?"

"Once. I went the day he was…the day they all died. He was still cold and aloof. I looked across the desk at him and I started to cry. I told him it was no good; I couldn't sit in the waiting room with all those people staring and whispering about me. I begged him, Abigail; I got down on my knees and begged him for *help*. He told me not to be silly. *Silly*." As though exhausted she collapsed in the chrome chair. "Why did she do it? She had so much. A wonderful home, children, Dr. Paul. She was so pretty. I have nothing. Why did she *do* it?"

Why had Gillian Foster done it? Miss Sanderson wondered. Taken from this poor wretch the only comfort she'd had. But Linda's question must have been rhetorical because she was racing on. "I came back to this house and I got down on my knees again. I begged God to punish the Fosters, to strike them *down*. To make them *suffer*." The thin shoulders heaved and it looked as though the girl was sobbing. That black stuff around her eyes will run, Miss Sanderson thought; it will streak all over her face. But the girl raised bright dry eyes. "And He did it! He killed them all. Her and Dr. Paul and those awful boys. All *dead*. And I don't feel guilty because it makes me *happy*. I don't feel guilty because of Mother *or* the Fosters."

It wasn't easy to frame the question but Miss Sanderson managed. "Did you tell the police this?"

"Of course not," Linda said calmly. "They would have thought me mad. Abigail, do you think me mad?"

"I think," the older woman said carefully, "that you're a sensitive person who's had an unfortunate life. In time I'm sure you'll find what you're looking for. Tell me, Linda, will you finish your book?"

"Yes. For Dr. Paul."

"To please him?"

"To *spite* him. To prove I can do something right. If he's beyond knowing, I can prove it to the world, can't I?"

"Yes," Miss Sanderson told her. "You can prove it to the world."

That world looked cold and depressing as Miss Sanderson crossed the stone bridge and trudged along the road leading to Maddersley Hall. It had started to drizzle and moisture clung to her head scarf and woolen coat. She passed two houses. The first was set well back from the road and its windows were shuttered. This had to be the ancestral home of Gillian and Irene Markham. The second was smaller, modern, and the lawn was cluttered with gnomes. Some of the tacky little figures held fishing rods over yellowing grass, others clasped tiny gardening tools. She wasn't surprised to spot a sign with ornate letters telling the passerby that this was the residence of Nettie and Oscar Seton. Having seen Nettie, she conjured up a mental picture of a stout, florid-faced man as her mate.

She had no high hopes about the Hall. If it followed the rest of the village it would be either a small shabby manor or an architectural atrocity. It proved to be a pleasant surprise. The Hall was set in grounds that did full justice to its owner's literary reputation in the gardening field. Even in this bleak season the grounds promised spring and summer beauty. Turf swept down from the house like a rich carpet, flowing around the roots of ancient oaks and chestnuts. Masses of hawthorn and rhododendron followed the curve of the driveway and on the east side of the house a formal rose garden had been planted. It was centered by a charming piece of statuary, three small children clutching marble baskets of fruit and flowers.

The house matched its estate. The main portion looked Elizabethan and the two wings were later additions, possibly Georgian. Ivy clung to rose brick and long windows looked out over the valley. It was huge. How many servants would it take to staff a house this size, Miss Sanderson wondered.

She steered a course toward the gracious entrance and then detoured to inspect a maze that wound along the west wing. She loved mazes and edged along between it and the house. One of the long windows opened and a clear voice called, "How thoughtful of you to come around here instead of forcing me to walk practically miles of hall to the front door. How on earth did you guess I was here?"

"I had no idea. I was taking a look at the maze."

"And a fine specimen it is. In my parents' lifetimes it became badly overgrown but Donnie has put it back in marvelous shape. There's a small garden with a fountain at the center that's worth seeing. If the weather weren't so nasty I'd take you through to it. But do come in, Miss Sanders. You look blue with cold, and how did you get so wet?"

Stepping over the sill, Miss Sanderson told the other woman, "I walked out from the village."

"Really? Why didn't you drive?"

"I don't drive."

"You should have told me that yesterday. I would have come in and gotten you. I most certainly will drive you back. Do give me those wet things."

While her hostess attended to her outer garments Miss Sanderson gazed around. She liked the room. It was high and white and had hunting prints dispersed at wide intervals on the walls. The furniture matched the room—old, graceful, highly polished. She selected a chair near the hearth. An electric fire was glowing, the coils cunningly simulating coals.

Against this background Mary Maddersley looked much at home. This was a different woman from the one in baggy tweeds in the tearoom. In a silk shirtwaist dress and high heels she looked taller and slimmer. The shapeless felt hat had concealed a fine head of silvering hair sweeping back in soft wings from a high brow. Her voice was lower but her eyes were still shrewd. "I fear," she said, "I was a bit abrupt yesterday. Dora always seems to bring out my worst side. I had no business prying into your reason for coming to the village."

"It was as well you did. It makes it easier for me to ask for assistance. You still are willing to help?"

"In any way I can." Miss Maddersley tugged at a velvet pull. "We'll chat over tea. Have you made any progress since we met?"

"It would appear any number of villagers had no affection for my cousin or her family. As you mentioned, there were bad feelings between Gillian and the Austins and Marlows. Then there is the vicar. To say nothing of Paddy Rourke and Dora Campbell."

"You're trying to be tactful. You also must have heard about Donnie—" She broke off as a stout woman in a blue uniform wheeled a tea wagon in. "Just leave it, Hester. Thank you."

Watching her hostess lifting dishes from the wagon to a low table, Miss Sanderson said, "As I came up the driveway I was wondering how many servants are necessary to keep a house this size running."

"Far too many. We get by with a cook and a housekeeper. Of course, we only use this wing. The rest of the place is closed off. Now, don't be embarrassed. Tell me what you heard about Donnie."

"I understand your brother is an author and also writes a gardening column."

"True."

"That Gillian once worked for him doing typing and—"

"False. She *tried* to do typing for Donnie. I only use two fingers to type and I'm faster and more accurate than she was. What else?"

Miss Sanderson found she *was* embarrassed. How do you tell this woman that people say her only brother is not right in the head? She accepted a Spode cup and reached for a dainty sandwich. Miss Maddersley chuckled. "Let me put it this way. After I left the tearoom yesterday what did Dora tell you?"

"That your brother isn't right in the head," Miss Sanderson said bluntly.

"A typical Doraism. The woman is much like a dog she once had. I'm happy to say someone had the good sense to poison it. As long as the creature was facing you it fawned and licked at your hand. When your back was turned it proceeded to bite at your ankles."

"Why do you patronize her shop?"

"Certainly not for the cuisine. Kate Rourke at the inn is a splendid cook. But Dora's grandmother was my grandmother's parlor maid. One tends to feel a sense of responsibility. Dora's tearoom is a financial disaster. In the summer she does manage to snare the unwary passing through but in the winter she makes barely enough to pay her rent. Do have another sandwich. I sense, like myself, you enjoy the creature comforts. I suppose with women like us they replace other things we've missed."

"Husbands and children?"

"I was thinking mainly of careers. At one time I was a most ambitious person. I—But I'm getting away from the subject. In all fairness I feel I should briefly tell you about my brother. No, don't object. Since the Fosters' deaths I've had to face the fact that of all the people who had motives my brother had the strongest." She put down her cup and muttered, "Until the killer is found I'll have to live with suspicion."

"What if the killer *is* your brother?"

"Haven't you ever noticed that it's uncertainty that is the hardest to deal with? Once one knows the truth…well, that can be faced and handled. First I must tell you Donnie is *not* insane. He's highly nervous and can't stand the slightest stress. Older generations would call his condition melancholia. I call it depression and acute anxiety. The reason for this condition goes back to his childhood."

Miss Maddersley waved a hand. "In this room you will notice there are no family pictures. I couldn't bear my parents' smug faces. Mother and Father had what is now known as an 'open' marriage. Years ago a union of this type was considered novel and disgusting. Mother, as a liberated woman far in advance of her time, paid as scant attention to her children as she did to her husband. And Father was the same. They went separate ways. Mother flitted from Paris to the Riviera to New York. Father buried himself in African jungles and other primitive places. Their children were left to the mercies of servants.

"I was a tough independent child and it did me little harm. In time I went up to Oxford to take a medical degree." She held up her hands and studied them. "I wanted to be a surgeon and I feel I would have been a skilled one. But it wasn't to be. Donnie was a late child, much younger than I. Because of my parents' behavior I always felt responsible for him. He was high strung and delicate. While I was at Oxford my father made a flying trip home, decided Donnie was too frail to be sent away from home to school, and hired a tutor. He didn't take time to check the man out, to examine the validity of his credentials. The references had been forged and Donnie, at the age of eight, was placed in the hands of a sadist and a pervert."

"Dear God," Miss Sanderson murmured.

"Even He proved to be no help to the boy," Miss Maddersley said grimly. "It was weeks before the other servants summoned up enough courage to alert me. By the time I got here the tutor had fled. It was as well for him he did. If I'd gotten my hands on him I'd have used one of those." She pointed toward the wall over the mantel. A number of antique swords sent sparkles of light back from sharp blades and polished hilts.

"Did you call in the police?"

"No. Oh, don't bother saying it. I know full well I should have. But there was the scandal and Donnie. He simply couldn't have stood up under questioning. I called for the family physician and he arranged for a psychiatrist. Donnie was like a little...like a wounded animal, hiding under beds and in closets. He'd been badly abused."

"Sexually molested?"

"Among other things. I immediately sent for my parents. True to form they didn't bother coming directly home. They decided to break their trip by dropping into a Latin American country, one that was having what they called 'civil disturbances.' Both Mother and Father were intensely curious people and quite fearless. They decided to go out and watch the disturbances. They were promptly set upon and killed." Miss Maddersley smiled. "Funny."

"That your parents were killed?"

"That they died together. Except for conceiving Donnie and me they avoided each other. Anyway, with their deaths my career was finished. I left Oxford and came back to act as guardian, surrogate mother, and keeper for a disturbed child." Picking up the teapot, Miss Maddersley asked, "More tea or brandy?"

"Brandy."

"Excellent choice." She opened a bow-fronted cabinet and took out a decanter and matching glasses. They looked like Waterford.

Miss Sanderson took a sip. In quality the brandy matched its exquisite container. She lifted the glass, smiled at her companion, and said, "To creature comforts."

"And to my parents who I fervently hope are roasting in hell. Back to Donnie. He improved. In time he came close to what is called normal although I have always failed to see what that word signifies. He showed an interest in and a talent for gardening. I encouraged him. Our lives fell into a pattern. We spent the spring, summer, and early fall here and in winter months went to a villa in Corfu purchased by our mother shortly before her untimely end.

"Many times I've tried to persuade Donnie to rent or sell this huge place and find a smaller one elsewhere. But he regards this house as a refuge. After what happened to him in it I fail to see why but we've kept it on. When... if this Foster business is cleared up I'm determined we'll leave. Do some traveling, find another garden for Donnie."

Whether it was the thought or the brandy, there was a change in Miss Maddersley. She was smiling and there was no bitterness in that smile. She splashed more brandy in her glass and held the decanter out. Miss Sanderson shook her head. "Tell me about Gillian."

"Ah, yes, the enchanting Gillian. I blame my father for criminal negligence in selecting a tutor and yet I was responsible for bringing Gillian Markham, as she was then, into Donnie's life. And, in her way, the girl did just as good a job on my brother as that perverted monster did." Squaring her shoulders, the woman said crisply, "Donnie was working on a book. I'd been doing his typing and found it tedious. I couldn't work up any interest in mulching and organic fertilizer and pruning. So I looked around for a typist. I'd heard that Gillian Markham was doing some work for the vicar and keeping books at the Fox and Crow. I'd known of Gillian since she was a baby. I'd seen her around the village and she was pretty and bright and had the reputation of being a kindhearted girl—"

"How old was she at this time?"

"Let me see." Miss Maddersley stroked her blunt chin. "That was about six months before her marriage. About twenty-one."

"And your brother?"

"Forty-two. I know what you're thinking. April and December. But Donnie is—or was—young for his age. Completely unworldly. He'd never had a date with a girl and he was still much of a boy." Miss Maddersley reached for a metal box and extracted one of her small black cigars. She took her time lighting it. "Gillian came here three afternoons each week. When I saw a sample of her work I was tempted to let her go but there was a change in Donnie. For the first time in my memory he was truly *happy.* Simply glowed. Gillian seemed so good for him. She never talked a great deal but she listened to him by the hour. To be truthful, Miss Sanders, I began to have selfish hopes. The girl seemed genuinely fond of Donnie and I thought there was a good chance for marriage. There would have been advantages for her—"

"The title?"

"More than being Lady Maddersley. Our family managed to hold on to a good share of its wealth and she would have been able to entertain, to travel, to enjoy what I believe they call the 'good life.' And I'd finally be able to make a life for myself, a bit late but one never knows."

"But it didn't work out?"

"My dream turned into a nightmare." Getting up abruptly, she said, "Come with me." She led the way to a door at the end of the room and flung it open. "My brother's study."

The study was as large and gracious as the sitting room. The walls were lined with bookcases and the books didn't look merely decorative; they looked well handled. There were mullioned windows and directly in front of one was a handsome desk. Near it was a smaller desk with an electric typewriter on its polished top. Clamped on a work table was a small flytier's vise and heaped around it was a litter of feathers and silk. Over the mantel was a Constable.

The room, Miss Sanderson mused, of a solitary man, one depending on books for company, on gardening and fishing for occupations. Miss Maddersley made an imperious gesture and her companion walked around the room. On the large desk, the small one, the mantel, were framed snapshots. In all of them were the same two people—a tall gangly man and a petite, very pretty girl. Despite the backgrounds the poses were the same. The girl smiled an enchanting, dimpled smile at the camera; the man gazed down at her with adoration and wonderment.

"They say," Miss Maddersley said in a husky voice, "a picture is worth a thousand words. What do you see?"

"He was infatuated with Gillian."

"Donnie was obsessed with the girl. She always came out here faithfully, never missed an afternoon. Then one day she didn't arrive. Donnie waited, getting more and more upset. I was going to ring her up and then I decided against it. I thought it was time for Donnie to take a little responsibility. He sat over there—" A shaking finger pointed at the larger desk. "He said a few words, he shook his head, the receiver dropped from his hand, and then he got up and crept over there—" The finger moved and pointed at a corner behind a high-backed chair. "He crouched over there like an...like an injured animal.

"I immediately rang through to the Markham house. Gillian answered. I said, 'What did you say to my brother, Miss Markham?' and she said, very brightly, 'Not Miss Markham. I'm Mrs. Foster. I was married this morning.' I couldn't utter a word and she laughed and said, 'Aren't you going to congratulate me?' " Naked hate twisted Miss Maddersley's face. "I asked her why she had done that to my brother, why she had pretended to love him. She said, so innocently, 'I'm sorry that Donnie got the wrong idea. I do like him but I certainly don't love him.' I told her…I said I hoped she would one day suffer as she was making my brother suffer. Then I rang off."

"Yet I understand your brother was Paul Foster's patient and so were you."

Turning her back, the other woman strode from the room and Miss Sanderson followed her. "How to make you understand. Dr. Foster was in practice almost two years before we used his services. Donnie doesn't just direct gardeners; he works with them. He gets cuts and scratches and once had blood poisoning. In the winter he frequently has bouts of bronchitis. Dr. Foster was in the village and he knew his business. And…Donnie seemed to want to go to him. Whether he was hoping to catch a glimpse of Gillian I don't know."

"Was he home the night of the murders?"

"No." The older woman sagged back in her chair. "I don't know where Donnie was that evening. It had been a foul day with steady rain. Shortly after tea, around five, the rain stopped and it turned cold. Donnie had been restless all afternoon and he said he was going out for a walk. He said not to wait dinner for him. When I went to bed he still wasn't home."

"What time was that?"

"Around ten. The following morning when I heard about the murders I went out to a shed he has fixed up at the back. His oilskins were hanging on a peg above his rubber boots. They were damp. I wondered whether he had washed them."

Blood, Miss Sanderson thought, blood sprayed from Paul Foster's wounds. Not from Gillian's or Arthur's or Andrew's; from those bodies there had been little blood.

"Later in the day," Miss Maddersley said dully, "I went up to his room. The jacket he'd been wearing the previous evening had stains on the cuff. They looked like blood. When I asked about it Donnie told me he'd slipped on the ice, grasped at a branch, and gotten a gash on his wrist. He showed it to me."

Compassionately Miss Sanderson regarded the other woman. What a hell she had lived in, still was living in. She said gently, "And you wonder…"

"Yes, I wonder. On one hand I can't believe a timid man like my brother could kill four human beings. But thinking of what he's gone through, the way Gillian treated him...Miss Sanders, I simply don't know."

"Tell me, why didn't anyone in the village try to help the police? Why didn't *you* tell them about Melanie Marlow and Dora Campbell?"

"Because we all have something to hide. People who live in glass houses simply must not throw stones. If I had mentioned anyone else there's a good chance that person might have hit back—told the police about Gillian and Donnie. So, we all told the same story—how wonderful the Fosters were."

"A conspiracy of silence?"

"An unspoken agreement. Rather cowardly. Will you tell the police?"

"Yes."

"And they'll come back and root out all our tawdry little secrets."

"Among those secrets is the identity of a mass murderer. When you offered to help, you must have known this is what I would do."

"I did. And I want this finished but...I don't want my brother hurt." Miss Maddersley pulled herself from her chair as though she'd suddenly aged. She opened a drawer, burrowed into it, and handed Miss Sanderson an enlarged snapshot. "Donnie. Taken shortly before Gillian came to this house."

Sir Donald stood in his sunbathed rose garden. Behind him were the marble children holding baskets of flowers and fruit. He was wearing a shabby green jacket and wrinkled twill trousers. His face was boyish and painfully sensitive. One hand tenderly touched a yellow rose bud.

"Does he look like a mass murderer?" his sister demanded.

"What does a mass murderer look like?"

Miss Maddersley's shoulders sagged. "I'll drive you home, Miss Sanders."

Miss Sanderson followed the other woman down a series of lofty halls. Shadowy rooms opened from the halls. They were high and stately and the furnishings were shrouded in ghostly dustcovers. The walls were lined with oil paintings. In one a young man in jerkin and feathered cap was brandishing a rapier. He had Sir Donald's slender build and sensitive mouth. In another an elaborate ruff framed the face of a woman who looked much like Mary Maddersley. Her chin was lifted and she looked haughty and imperious.

Miss Sanderson found she was eager to leave the beautiful but deathly quiet home of the Maddersleys.

Chapter Ten

When Miss Sanderson stepped into the kitchen she was greeted by a gap-toothed smile from the housekeeper, a gurgle from the direction of the playpen, and the tempting odor of sizzling bacon. "Sit right down, miss," Mrs. Toogood ordered. "Breakfast's nearly ready."

"This is awfully good of you."

"No problem. I was making up little Lucy's and heard you stirring around. Thought I'd cook something up for you. Sure could use some flesh on them bones of yours. Thin as a picked chicken." Swinging around, she inspected Miss Sanderson's trim suit and high-necked blouse. "All dressed up and no place to go."

"I thought I'd take a walk around the village this morning."

"That won't take long."

"Perhaps drop into the Fox and Crow for lunch."

Smacking her lips, the housekeeper cracked eggs into sputtering bacon fat. "Kate Rourke does a nice grill. Should try it."

Mrs. Toogood did a nice breakfast herself. Miss Sanderson's was bacon and eggs and fried bread. Lucy ate her thin gruel with every evidence of delight. She managed to knock the spoon out of Mrs. Toogood's hand and smear gruel over herself and the high chair. Mrs. Toogood good-naturedly mopped the baby off and set her back in the playpen. As Miss Sanderson left the room the housekeeper was spreading rashers of bacon in the skillet. Forbidden fruit, and Irene Markham would be most upset if she knew her housekeeper was devouring her food. She won't find out from me, Miss Sanderson thought as she stepped out on the veranda. She looked out on a cold, rain-drenched morning. Hellish weather.

She loped down the steps and along the walk. By the time she reached the gate, she remembered the supposed state of her health and slowed. This being a semi-invalid was becoming a bore. She was approaching the vicarage when she spotted a brightly colored blob in the distance. The blob approached rapidly and became a tall man in a scarlet exercise suit bounding through the pelting rain. One arm rose in salute, and he drew to a panting stop.

"Miss Sanders, I presume. Daniel Clay. I've been hoping to catch you for a moment. Are you planning to attend services this Sunday?"

"I've no idea whether I'll be here on Sunday, Dr. Clay."

"In that case perhaps you'll have coffee with me." Taking her arm, he escorted her through massed pines to the manse. "Dreary looking house, isn't it? Built in the days when the vicar usually had a good-sized brood."

Miss Sanderson, whose father had been a vicar, remembered those days. Her parents had had such a large family that when her childless aunt offered to raise a tiny Abigail, that offer had been accepted eagerly. But her family home, although as sprawling and shabby as this one, had been cheerful.

In a gloomy hall her companion paused and bellowed, "Mrs. Gay, we have a guest." He lowered his voice. "Sorry if I startled you, Miss Sanders, but my housekeeper is, as the villagers put it, 'as deef as a post.'" From the shadowy recesses an ancient woman, clad in a floor-length dress of black bombazine, shuffled. The vicar shouted, "Coffee, Mrs. Gay. Please show Miss Sanders to the library."

The crone beckoned and Miss Sanderson followed her down the hall. A finger silently pointed and Miss Sanderson stepped into a room fully as gloomy as the hall. Shadows crouched in corners and it smelled of old leather, smoke, and the cold ashes heaped on the grate. It was chill and damp. Feeling sympathy for anyone forced to use this room, she wandered around.

This room, like Sir Donald's study, contained two desks but both were large and unpolished. There were no snapshots of Gillian Foster. The only pictures were of a religious nature. Above the mantel was a large oil of the crucifixion. It was garish and rather ghastly.

A voice spoke tiredly behind her. "This is one house where the interior does full justice to the exterior." Dr. Clay had changed into a tweed suit with leather patches at the elbows and a stem of a pipe protruded from a breast pocket. "I shan't invite you to remove your coat, Miss Sanders. Mrs. Gay hasn't gotten around to lighting a fire and this room feels like Siberia. Sometimes I think I run each morning simply to keep the old blood circulating. But I can offer a chair. Do sit down."

He took his place behind one of the desks and Miss Sanderson dropped into a chair in front of it. Rather like one of his flock, she thought, here to pour out her woes. What did she know about the man facing her? Actually not much. Daniel Clay, widower, forty-four, an early marriage and the death of his young wife through pneumonia. For slightly over ten years the spiritual leader of Maddersley-on-Mead. Also formerly an employer of Gillian Foster. Rather a good-looking man—tall and athletic, a frank open face, thinning corn-colored hair, large glasses like an aviator. She didn't care as much for his voice. It was rich and fruity.

The door creaked open and the crone deposited a tray on the corner of the desk. The vicar shook a rueful head. On the tray were a battered enamel pot, a creamer and a sugar bowl, two mismatched cups, one cracked. He sighed. "At least the coffee is fair. I must admit Mrs. Gay is…hem…a bit beyond housework or cooking. I do most of it myself. And don't ask, Miss Sanders, why I keep her on. I ask myself that question often enough. I suppose the answer is that I inherited Mrs. Gay when I inherited the vicarage and the poor woman has no other place to go."

He handed her the uncracked cup and she took a cautious sip. The coffee proved to be excellent. Daniel Clay was kindly regarding her. "So your visit is only a brief one?"

"I plan to stay until Lucy's guardian comes for her. It's a trying time."

"For all of us, dear lady. It might be easier for you if you had known your cousins. But past is past and we can only strive to make amends. I suppose you've heard Gillian was once close to me. Yes, I can see from your expression the villagers have been talking."

"I was told that she helped you with office work."

"She tried but actually she was about as good at that as Mrs. Gay is at housekeeping. But I didn't mind her inexperience. Gillian was amazingly lovely and she lighted up this house and my life. I was deeply in love with her."

Amazed at his frankness, Miss Sanderson merely stared. After a moment he continued. "Her marriage to Dr. Foster came as a devastating shock. It took me quite a time to recover from it."

"Gillian didn't tell you about her plans?"

"Not a word. I knew, of course, that she'd met the young man. The entire village knew Miss Markham had brought her fiancé to meet her sister. But Gillian kept on coming in to work in this very room and never gave a hint of what she planned. Why, a couple of days before they went to London and were married I jokingly told her when she became mistress here we would have to make changes. She smiled—Gillian had a wonderful smile—and said yes, the trees around the house would have to be cut and new furniture bought." Behind the aviator glasses his eyes were bleak. "Mrs. Gay told me about Gillian's marriage at breakfast time. I didn't believe it. I went directly down to the shops and the villagers were buzzing like a hive of bees about the news. I still thought some ghastly mistake had been made. Later that day I went to the Markham house. Gillian answered the door and right behind her was Paul Foster. She tried to introduce him—"

"Tried?"

"I fear I reacted like an idiot, Miss Sanders. A jealous fool. I spun on my heels and walked away from them." He ran a hand over his thin hair. "It took some time before I came to my senses."

In that time, she mused, this man of God had preached a couple of blistering sermons about strumpets. The vicar wrenched his pipe from his pocket and taking a penknife, cleaned the bowl. His movements were savage and the tiny blade jabbed into he bowl as though trying to cut through it. "You did reconcile with my cousin," she prompted.

"The Lord lent me strength and I accepted my loss. I went to Gillian and her husband and humbled myself. They were most gracious. Gillian again attended church and in time Arthur and Andrew came with her. I baptized all three of her children and fully expected to baptize the child she was carrying."

"Did Paul not attend church?"

"Not regularly, but as a medical man his time was limited. The boys went to Sunday school classes. I'd expected Gillian to be a fine mother but she disappointed me. She doted on her children and indulged them too much. Now, if I'd been the father of those boys they would have been disciplined. I received several complaints from their teacher, Mrs. Seton, on their conduct during her classes."

"Did you handle the funeral services for the family?"

"I did. It was my painful duty." He waved a hand toward a velvet shrouded window. "The Fosters are resting in the Markham plot. I wondered whether Dr. Foster's brother would prefer to have his body interred with his own family but I was instructed to bury him with his wife and children. A wise choice."

"You were Paul's patient?"

"Indeed I was. In fact I was in his surgery the day of the deaths. As is my habit I'd been running that morning and had slipped and twisted an ankle. Luckily no serious damage was done, simply some muscles pulled. Dr. Foster put an elastic bandage on my ankle and gave me some painkillers. Mrs. Gay was also his patient and I took her with me as she had a stomach upset that was worrying."

Miss Sanderson watched the man closely. His face was composed and his voice unctuous but his hands gave lie to both tone and expression. He was cramming tobacco into the carved bowl as savagely as he'd scraped it. Under that calm exterior, she thought, this man positively seethes with emotion. "What did you think of Paul?"

"He was a skilled physician, by far the best I've ever had. I wasn't surprised to learn he was taking a practice in London. A village like this could hardly expect to keep a doctor like he."

"What was your opinion of him as a man?"

"I barely knew him." The vicar lit his pipe and smoke spiraled in blue clouds through the chilly air. "Oh, I heard various rumors about him but I pay no heed to gossip. In a place this small it's wise not to bother with that sort of thing."

"Did you hear about Melanie Marlow?"

"Among other matters, yes."

"What other matters?"

"Surely, dear lady, you know it is unkind to speak ill of the dead."

"If we speak only good I'm afraid we'll never find my cousins' murderer."

"That must be left in the hands of the police."

Miss Sanderson caught the eyes behind the outsize lenses and held them. "I insist you tell me."

"Very well. I understand the doctor was most…hem…interested in a young lady who works at Lambert General Hospital. She's not a nurse but works in the office there, I believe."

"Interested? Do you mean they were having an affair?"

"That is what I heard. You must keep in mind that gossip can be deceptive. But I believe this...hem...association was common knowledge in the village."

Like hell it was, Miss Sanderson thought inelegantly. If the villagers had known about it one of them would have told me. She had a suspicion the good vicar had been only too pleased to have had this fact elicited. Her mouth set. "Were you interviewed by the police?"

"By a Detective Sergeant Brummell, yes."

"And did you tell him what you've told me?"

"About the girl at the hospital?"

"And your...hem...association with Gillian Foster."

Ugly color flooded into his face and his jaw jutted. "I don't care for your tone. My friendship with your cousin was quite innocent and long in the past. You must remember I am a man of God."

"You are also a man."

His hand clenched the pipe stem until his knuckles whitened. But the outburst she'd been trying for successfully was fought down. He said gently, "Dear lady, this whole affair must be terribly upsetting. And with the state of your health I'm certain you're completely unnerved."

"You haven't answered my question," she said doggedly.

"No, I did not tell Sergeant Brummell what I've told you. I didn't lie. I merely answered his questions. Those questions didn't touch on our conversation."

Goading him wasn't going to work, she thought, time for a softer approach. She rubbed her brow and sighed. "I'm sorry if I've been rude, Dr. Clay. You're right and this is all a terrible strain."

He refilled her cup and murmured, "I understand completely. Perhaps it would be best for you to return to your home."

"As soon as I possibly can. Did the sergeant ask about your movements on the evening of the murders?"

"Indeed he did. As I told the good man, only the guilty prepare alibis and flee where none pursueth. I spent the evening in this room, quite alone. As soon as I brought Mrs. Gay back from the surgery I sent her to bed. I cooked dinner and then I worked on notes for a sermon until after ten. My ankle was aching abominably and I swallowed a painkiller and went to bed. I heard or saw nothing that could help the officers."

And that seems to be that, Miss Sanderson thought. She found she was as anxious to leave this dark unkempt house as she had been Maddersley Hall. The vicar didn't press her to stay. He walked her to the front door and stepped out on the porch. With the hand clutching the pipe, he made a wide gesture. "A dying village, dear lady."

"Really?"

"Ah, yes. As soon as they can the young people leave for other places—the cities, I suppose. At one time I conducted weddings and christenings. Now, mainly, my work runs to funerals. I look out over my congregation and each year find it smaller. I see middle-aged faces and those of the elderly."

"Perhaps it would be better for you in another church."

"I have requested that. In the new year I have hopes, God willing, I will be sent to minister to a larger flock. But enough of me. May God go with you, Miss Sanders, and give you strength."

She straightened her shoulders and lifted her chin. "I'm sure we'll all feel better when my cousins' murderer is behind bars."

Light glinted from his glasses as he looked down at her. "Vengeance is mine; I will repay, saith the Lord."

"I'm not looking for vengeance," she told him tartly. "I'm looking for safety."

"Safety from what?"

"A person who killed four times could kill again."

"I hardly think so. The violence is directed against one family."

"Lucy is still alive."

"Ah, but soon she'll be gone with her guardian to a new home. Rest easy, dear lady."

The dear lady, fuming inwardly, made her way past the church and crossed the road. She thought of Daniel Clay's hand as he savagely wielded the penknife and wondered whether that hand had once clasped a knife with a long bloody blade. Her thoughts veered to Lucy and she devotedly hoped the child would soon be taken from that house, from this village. Well, on to the inn and the man with dancing Irish eyes who for frustrated passion had plunged his own hand through a pane of glass.

The saloon bar of the Fox and Crow proved to be a welcome change from the vicar's library and the wet, windswept street. It was warm and smoky and smelled deliciously of beer and food. Granted there was little of ye olde English pub about it but the plastic-covered seats looked comfortable and a battered brass rod that looked like it had been salvaged from the original inn ran along the foot of the bar. Two middle-aged men in farming clothes were playing darts and in a corner Nettie Seton bent over a heaped platter.

Paddy Rourke, in shirt sleeves and a knitted vest, presided behind the gleaming expanse of bar. He smiled expansively as she entered. "Beer or something more substantial, Miss Sanders?"

"Both."

He worked the handle and handed her a stein with a flourish. Artistically battered pewter, she noted with a smile. "Japan?"

"Taiwan. If you're looking for antiques you won't find them here. You also won't find roaches and mildew and leaky plumbing."

"Touché. What's on the lunch menu?"

"Nothing creamed." He leaned over the bar. "Nice greasy grilled food. Kate does a mixed grill to a turn."

"So be it," she told him and carried her beer to a table near one of the fake mullioned windows. Across the street she noticed a lilac curtain fluttering at the tearoom window. Dora Campbell was probably counting the clientele of her rival.

306 E. X. Giroux

Wonder what she will say about me? Miss Sanderson thought. Probably call me that nasty, nosy cousin. Ah, well.

The darts players had finished their game, drained their steins, and thumped them on the bar. Paddy reached for them but one of the men shook a grizzled head. "Nowt more, lad."

"Wife after you again, is she, Tom?"

"Tongue never rests, lad. Thinks a pint leads down the path to damnation." The farmer winked. "Be back before closing time."

As they left Miss Sanderson glanced at Mrs. Seton. The matron's knife and fork were fairly flying. She lifted her head, wiped grease from a puffy chin, and inclined her head a fraction of an inch. Miss Sanderson nodded back and wondered whether it was worthwhile to strike up a conversation. She decided against it.

Paddy delivered a heavy china platter and cutlery wrapped in a paper napkin. "We may not be fancy," he told her, "but we're good."

She tools a look at the mixed grill. "You're heavenly."

As she cut into a kidney she thought, so who needs genuine beams and sloping floors and leather? So engrossed was she that it took moments to realize someone was hovering over her table. She looked up into Nettie Seton's fleshy face.

"Terrible weather," the woman informed her.

"Dreadful. Unseasonable."

Mrs. Seton grasped eagerly at this. "Just what I told my husband only this morning. 'Oscar,' I told him, 'this is unseasonal weather. Why, we may well have snow.' Oscar agreed."

Miss Sanderson had a hunch Oscar possibly agreed with anything his wife said. Having exhausted this topic, the woman leaned closer and breathed, "I want to extend our condolences on your recent bereavement."

"Thank you." Miss Sanderson willed her eyes away from the delectable but cooling food.

"I assure you, Miss Sanders, we did all we could to render assistance in that tragic hour. The night it happened Mr.

Johnston rang us up and Oscar and me got out of bed and went to his cottage. Irene Markham was in awful shape."

"I can well imagine."

"Having hysterics, she was. The police doctor was trying to give her a shot to calm her and she was fighting him. I had to hold her down. Mr. Johnston, poor man, couldn't help. He was holding the baby and she was squalling her head off. I said maybe she's cold and Mr. Johnston, he put a fold of that tartan rug around her. Then Oscar and me took the poor mite and Irene right home with us." Mrs. Seton paused to catch her breath and then raced on. "Kept them for two days we did. Then Irene tells us she's taking the baby home. Oscar and me begged her to stay on with us or take the wee one to her rooms behind the dress shop but Irene said, 'No, the child is going home.' Took Lucy back to *that* house. Miss Sanders, what do *you* think of that house?"

Hiding her distaste, Miss Sanderson gazed back into the brightly avid eyes. "It seems extremely comfortable."

"It's cursed, you know. Should be burnt to the ground and then sprinkled with salt," Mrs. Seton hissed. She straightened and said in a lofty tone, "If Oscar or I can render any assistance to you and Irene you need only ring us up."

She swept out of the bar and Miss Sanderson sighed with relief. Paddy, smiling broadly, circled the bar and picked up her empty stein. "After that I think you could use a refill." He raised his voice. "Kate, safe to come out now. Nettie's gone."

The door behind the bar opened and a plump woman in a pink dress and flowered apron bustled in. "Draw one for me, me boy." She came directly to Miss Sanderson's table and sat down. "That woman! Talk the ears off a brass monkey." She looked down at Miss Sanderson's platter. "And your lunch all cold. I'll cook more up for you."

"No, thank you, Mrs. Rourke—"

"Kate. Even me boy calls me that."

"I managed to eat a good part of it before she descended on me. What's her Oscar like?"

"Big red-faced buffoon who wouldn't say boo to his wife."

The women exchanged smiles. Kate Rourke may have gained weight with the years but she still had a fresh, blue-eyed prettiness. Paddy came back with three steins and sat down beside his mother,."Cheers."

"Surely," Kate told him, "an Irish lad can make a better toast than that."

"Too long-winded, Kate. By the time the toast is made me beer is flat."

They drank deeply and then Kate Rourke asked, "You'll be staying much longer?"

"Only until Dr. Foster's brother arrives."

"Glad am I that the child is to be his. Irene's a well-meaning woman but knows little of children. Your health is poorly?"

Miss Sanderson touched the lapel of her jacket. "Not too robust."

"And you coming down at a time like this. For the baby's sake it's a kind idea. For your cousin and her husband...they were gobshites."

"*Kate*," her son chided.

"Only truth passes my lips."

"And your tongue outraces your brain."

Irish eyes locked and Kate tossed her glossy dark curls. "Miss Sanders, will you be telling this boy the truth? Four days since you've come and I know you've heard worse than I just said."

"Gillian and Paul certainly didn't seem popular, Kate."

"See. She knows," Kate told her son. "Almost ruined my lad's life did that cousin of yours. With her lying tongue and her false pretty smiles. And me, taken in as surely as my Paddy was. Starting to count my grandchildren I was and then that Jezebel married her fine doctor. Then to find she'd led astray not only us but Sir Donald and the vicar."

"You didn't have any idea about the other two men? Surely in a place this size..."

Kate held up her stein and Paddy took it and his own to the bar. His mother ranted, "Gillian Markham had the face of an angel. She smiled and dimpled and led us astray. I could have sworn on the Good Book she loved my boy. And all the time Sir Donald and the vicar thought the same. I well remember the morning Alfred Austin came in for his pint and told us the hussy was wed. My Paddy reached right across the bar and picked the little man up and shook him like a rat. He thought Alfred was lying about his girl. But it was the truth. When we finally believed, Paddy walked over there and drove his fist through that window. See, these scars on his hand." Paddy was putting down the steins and his mother grabbed one of his hands and held it up. On the back of it was a network of fine white scars. "The good Lord was merciful and the cuts were shallow. Soon's I bound them up he took a bottle of whiskey and went to his room and drank himself senseless."

While his mother applied herself to her beer, her son said gravely, "I seldom touch spirits, Miss Sanders. Content myself with a pint now and again. But how I loved that girl…"

"And yet you were Paul Foster's patient."

"I was. Kate and me both. He was a good doctor and handy. And Gillian was no longer my girl. She was his wife and she had babies—"

"Who should have been my grandchildren," his mother said brokenly.

"Hush, you'll get your grandchildren." He looked earnestly at Miss Sanderson. "Maybe love wears out. Gillian was another man's wife. She bore his children. Can you understand?"

Miss Sanderson nodded but she asked herself, does hate wear out? "When did you last see Gillian?" she asked the innkeeper.

"I remember well the day. I'd fallen bringing up a keg from the cellar and my chest was paining. Rog Austin took me up to the Markham house in his van. Gillian was on the veranda with her sons. She said, 'Paddy, you're hurt!' She was wearing a coat the blue of her eyes and a white fur hat. Her face was so rosy and pretty framed in white fur."

"Only skin deep was that beauty," his mother rasped. "My Paddy had cracked two ribs."

"How long was that before…"

"A week," Paddy said. "But Kate was in the surgery the day they were killed."

"Change of life," Kate said. "Hot and cold flashes. Dr. Foster gave me a prescription for hormones. Helped some."

Miss Sanderson turned to the man. "The evening of the murders, I suppose you were here in the bar."

A smile with no mirth displayed fine white teeth. "No alibi for that evening, Miss Sanders. As I told the chief inspector who questioned us, I was up in bed. Kate was handling the bar. Slow night anyway."

"Your ribs?"

"They weren't troubling me. I had taken a chill and Kate told me to get to bed. I went upstairs about four in the afternoon. And to get out of the inn I had only to drop out of my window onto the roof of a shed and no one the wiser." He touched his chest. "Number one suspect. The motive and the opportunity."

"Don't joke about it, Paddy," his mother muttered. She lifted a defiant chin. "My Paddy could never harm a woman or children."

"What about a man?" her son asked.

His mother's mouth snapped open but at that moment the door opened, bringing in a gust of cold moist air and the elderly couple Miss Sanderson had seen in the lilac-and-lavender tearoom.

Paddy was on his feet. "You'll be wanting a toddy to warm you."

"And a meat pie," the man said.

"Beef," the old lady told Kate.

Nodding cheerfully at Miss Sanderson, Kate headed toward her kitchen.

❉ ❉ ❉

As Miss Sanderson trudged through the rain up the slope to the pasture she mulled over the days she had spent in this village. Chief Inspector Kepesake had been correct about the villagers talking to a relative of the Fosters. I'm fairly adept at digging up information, she told herself, but no damn good at putting it together. That has always been Robby's work, not mine. And it's a job at which he's extremely talented. I've gone as far as I can go, she admitted, time to call the experts in.

When Mrs. Toogood admitted her to the Markham house, Miss Sanderson glanced at her watch and sat down on the telephone chair. Lifting the scarlet phone, she dialed a familiar number. The housekeeper made no move to leave the hall but Miss Sanderson didn't mind. Arrangements had been made to cover eavesdroppers. Regular cloak and dagger, she thought wryly.

In Robby's chambers at the Temple the receiver was lifted and Mrs. Sutter's crisp voice repeated the number just dialed. "Abigail Sanders, nurse. I'd like an appointment with Dr. Forbes."

"One moment, Miss Sanders, and I'll check with the doctor."

As she waited, she glanced in the mirror opposite. She admitted she looked as though she could use the services of a physician. Her austere face was thinner, there were indentations under her cheekbones, faint hollows in her temples, and the clear blue eyes were circled by dark smudges that resembled the eye makeup Linda Beauchamp used with such a lavish hand. Nothing like a few days in a quiet village…

Mrs. Sutter's voice crackled in her ear. "Doctor is able to work you in early tomorrow, Miss Sanders. Shall we say nine A.M. Will that be convenient?"

"That will be fine."

"Doctor suggests you come to the city today if possible. He'll want tests and you know how tiring they can be. He suggests you have a good rest tonight so you'll be fresh in the morning."

"One moment." Miss Sanderson looked up at the house-keeper. "Are there any buses to London this afternoon?"

"One at two." Mrs. Toogood consulted her watch. "If you hurry you can make it. I'll help."

Miss Sanderson told Mrs. Sutter she would be leaving the village at two. As she put down the telephone, she said, "I'm going to have to rush."

"I'll get your bag packed." Mrs. Toogood was on her way up the stairs. "You sit and rest. Poor lamb, you do look peaky. You won't have to lug that big case. I'll stick a few things in the missus' overnight bag."

"I'll need—"

"I know what you need."

In a remarkably short time Mrs. Toogood was back and handed the other woman a small leather case. "Now, don't you run, hear? Time enough to get to the bus. Stops right in front of the inn. I'll tell Miss Irene." Removing the chain, she opened the door. "You'll be coming back, miss?"

"I'll be back," Miss Sanderson promised.

She forced herself not to break into a run. She passed the houses on Jericho Lane and trotted down the hill. The bus was already drawn up in front of the Fox and Crow. Near it Paddy Rourke was talking to Alfred Austin. As Miss Sanderson drew level with the chemist's the doors of the bus closed and she broke into a run, waving frantically. Paddy grinned and thumped on the bus door. It swished open and Paddy grasped her arm and helped her up the steps. "Where are you off to in such a rush?"

"To see my physician."

"Keep moving at that pace and you'll need the man." He stepped back and called, "Walk softly, Miss Sanders."

She paid the fare and sank on a seat. This acting the role of an invalid was debilitating. She actually *was* short of breath. Glancing around at the other passengers, she saw no familiar face. She opened her handbag, took out a small journal and a pen, and proceeded to bring her notes up-to-date. Each evening, upon retiring in the guest room in the Markham house, she'd filled out the events and conversations of the day. Too bad she hadn't dared use the large handbag fitted with a miniature tape recorder that she had on other cases. But it would have been too risky.

When her notes on Dr. Clay, Nettie Seton, and the Rourkes had been faithfully recorded she tucked the journal away and rested her head against the seat back. I'll close my eyes for a moment, she thought.

She slept all the way to London.

Chapter Eleven

Robert Forsythe unlocked the door of his flat and Miss Sanderson, with a sense of homecoming, stepped into the foyer. This place as well as his family home in Sussex were as familiar to her as her own flat. She took off her coat and muffler and hung them on the brass knobs of an old-fashioned clothes tree. This and many of the other furnishings had been brought up from Sussex. They fitted in well with the high ceilings and spacious rooms of his London home. While he carried her case into the guest room where she had spent countless nights she wandered into the sitting room and switched on table lamps.

When he joined her she handed him the journal. "The product of four hellish days and three nights that were worse. Adam Kepesake had better be grateful. There're enough suspects in there to satisfy even him. Would you like to read it?"

"We'll discuss it later, Sandy. Right now we're going to dine in high style. You rest—"

"Robby! That word makes me furious. I've heard it ad nauseam."

"From the looks of you I'm not surprised. You've lost pounds. Never mind, this dinner will put weight back on."

"Not if you cooked it."

He held up a hand and smiled. "Hardly back and insulting me already. And I didn't cook it. I rang up Raoul—"

"*Lionne d'Or?*"

"Yes. And I told Raoul I was entertaining a special lady, so he sent dinner around."

"What's on the menu?"

"Haven't the foggiest. Everything's in hot boxes or cold ones. And a basket of wines." He walked across the Bokhara carpet toward the hall. "We'll soon know."

While she waited she wandered around the room. She touched the corner of a Queen Anne table that once had graced the drawing room of the Sussex house and paused beside the glass case. Sir Amyas's Buddha was the largest figure and the one that had spurred Robby into this hobby. She lifted the glass and fingered a tiny Fu dog carved from pink jade. She'd given this to Robby on his birthday and still winced at the price.

"Madame, dinner is served," Forsythe called from the doorway.

She regarded him affectionately. Even in his pose as maître d' with his long head humbly bent and a linen napkin draped over one wrist he looked elegant. She ruffled his fine hair and brushed a kiss across his cheek. "What's this all about?" he asked. "You generally aren't demonstrative."

"I may be getting senile but I find I've missed you and even those cramped ancient chambers."

"Damp spots and smoking hearths and all?"

"Even those. Let's eat!"

They dined by candlelight at a table with fine linen, china, sparkling silver, and a centerpiece of pink roses. After a time Miss Sanderson looked up from her smoked trout, took a sip of superb Chablis, and said, "My compliments to the chef. As Mrs. Toogood would say, Robby, you've done this up brown."

"No shop talk. Enjoy."

She enjoyed course after delicious course. As she scooped up the last fragment of Tournedos Rossini, she moaned. "Blimey, I'm stuffed! I can't eat another bite."

"Not even mousse?"

"Chocolate?"

"Blueberry."

She was tempted but shook her head. "Perhaps as a bedtime snack. I think you're right and I just put weight back on."

"Good. Amuse yourself while I haul this stuff into the kitchen."

"I'll help."

"Not necessary, Sandy. One advantage of a service flat is a good fairy called Mrs. Tupper who will put all in order in the morning."

Returning to the sitting room she gazed indecisively at the hearth. All was prepared for the touch of a match. The room was pleasantly warm and there was no necessity for a fire but she snapped her lighter and watched the kindling catch. Then she stooped and laid a chunk of wood on the small blaze. Forsythe touched her shoulder and she jumped. "Nervy, aren't you? And also using up the logs Meeks faithfully brings up from Sussex."

She perched on an armchair, the one Adam Kepesake had used the last time she'd been in this room. "There's something about an open fire that central heating can't compete with."

"Touches a memory of remote ancestors crouching around a blaze. Appeals to something primal in all of us."

"Warding off an evil that lurks just beyond the ring of firelight."

Forsythe gave her an intent look. "Methinks I have a quotation that sums up your frame of mind. It goes—"

"Please, Robby!" She lifted a protesting hand. "Don't spoil Raoul's masterpiece with *Macbeth*."

"In this case I think Coleridge said it better."

Like one that on a lonesome road
Doth walk in fear and dread,
And having once turned round walks on,
And turns no more his head;

Because he knows a frightful fiend
Doth close behind him tread.

Miss Sanderson repeated, " 'Doth close behind him tread.' That does sum it up. That's exactly my reaction to the little village of Maddersley-on-Mead."

"And you haven't been sleeping well."

"Understatement. I've hardly been sleeping at all. By evening I was exhausted and yet when I was in bed I merely dozed. You know the creaks and groans in a house. I'd swear every time a timber creaked I'd sit bolt upright. And I went into the nursery any number of times every night to stand over Lucy's crib and make sure she was safe." She gave a shaky laugh. "I think I'm losing my grip."

"Not much wonder, Sandy. But there's an answer." He tapped the journal with a long finger. "You've done your job. Ring Miss Markham in the morning and inform her your physician refuses to allow you to return."

"Not to return would be cowardly. And don't give me that quotation about living to fight another day. I am *not* leaving that child in that cursed house."

He lifted his brows. "Cursed? More of your fey feelings?"

"Recorded fact. Three previous murders in the Markham house. All using a knife." She pointed at the journal. "Read it."

"I'd rather you tell me about it. And about everything else you've seen and heard."

She glanced at the mantel clock. "It will take hours."

"Not as long as you may think. Beau Brummell gave me duplicates of the material you had. I've studied the layout of the village and the plan of the house as well as the names and data on the residents. That should help. But you'd better start talking. On the stroke of midnight, finished or not, you're off to bed."

Settling back against the cushions, she started to talk. She began her account when she'd stepped down from the bus in front of the Fox and Crow. Robert Forsythe sat as quietly as she did, his eyes on her face.

❀❀❀

"—and so I got on the bus and left Maddersley this afternoon." She took a deep breath and rubbed her throat. "Half past eleven. Not bad, Robby."

"Excellent! Sandy, you've a mind like a computer."

"At times I wish I had the emotions of one." He busied himself at the liquor cabinet and handed her a glass. She had no need to wonder whether this one was Waterford. It was. She took a sip and beamed. "Your best and oldest brandy. Now, have you any sparkling ideas?"

"Not as yet. This will take some mental digesting." He shook his head. "But this explodes the idea of Happy Family, doesn't it? It appears the Fosters were not wonderful people beloved by all."

"Hardly. You can practically cut the hate with a knife—" She laughed. "I wish I hadn't used *that* word."

"Have you any favorite candidates for murderer?"

"Practically any person mentioned in the journal. And not an alibi among them."

"The exceptions?"

"Mary Maddersley."

"Why?"

"From the moment we met in the tearoom she knew I wasn't there solely to support Irene. Miss Maddersley was aware I was searching for the killer and yet she volunteered all that information about her brother and told about others who had reason to hate the Fosters."

"She sounds intelligent."

"She is."

"Have you considered Mary Maddersley could be using a clever ploy? Throwing you off her own scent by dragging red herrings along before your quivering nose. She had as good a motive as Donald Maddersley and the opportunity to commit the murders."

"I still don't think—"

"Anyone else?"

"Matthew Johnston. No motive. And he had everything to lose by his neighbors' deaths."

"Hmm." Forsythe templed his fingers and gazed down at them. "Gillian Foster was famous or perhaps infamous for toying with people's emotions. Suppose she'd tired of playing wonderful neighbor to the old chap and had tried to discard him? She had played that dangerous game with many others."

"True. The job she did on Melanie and her parents was heartless and cruel, to say nothing about Linda Beauchamp and Nurse Ines and—"

"How about the three men she led down the garden path?"

"Right. But Matthew was in the house the afternoon of the murders. Not only did Gillian welcome his help but she welcomed *him*. When the Fosters moved to London they planned to have him visit. And, Robby, Matthew adored Gillian."

Forsythe shrugged. "Not one of my better suggestions. And now, Cinderella, off to the guest room."

"I still have ten minutes before midnight."

"Which will be put to good use by showing you your props."

"Don't tell me you're sending me back in a false mustache."

"Come along and see." He led the way down the hall to a comfortable guest room. Opening the wardrobe, he pulled out a shopping bag. "*Voilà!*"

"Blimey. Harrods, no less."

"If a well-to-do lady like Miss Abigail Sanders has time to put in in London town, where does she head? To Harrods, of course. Incidently, Mrs. Sutter took this chore on. Let's see what we have." He emptied the bag on the bedspread. "A pattern book of sweaters for tots and knitting needles and wool. You can knit, can't you?"

"Of course." Miss Sanderson fingered pale green wool and white angora. "This would look sweet on little Lucy." She picked up a jar. "I've excellent taste in caviar. Beluga!"

"And in whiskey." He handed her a squat brown bottle.

"What's this thing?"

"Obviously a book. Quite a tome."

"All about the Tudor dynasty. Robby, I never read history."

"But Mrs. Sutter is a history buff. No doubt hoping you'll pass it along to her."

Handing him the book, she repacked the bag. "You can pass it on. I'm not lugging that heavy thing around. What's that? More props?"

He handed her a folded paper. "Prescriptions from old Dr. Forbes."

Her eyes widened. "Does he really exist?"

"He's a police surgeon. We decided on some heart medicine and something for blood pressure—"

"Exactly the ailments I dreamed up, Robby. What about my thyroid condition?"

He chuckled. "Sandy, your power of invention exceeds ours. You're to have the chemist in Maddersley fill these prescriptions and then you are to promptly flush them down the loo." He paused and cocked his head. The mantel clock was booming out Westminster chimes. "The witching hour. Into bed." Putting his hand on her shoulders, he dropped a light kiss on her brow. "Tonight you will sleep soundly, Sandy."

"Is that an order?"

"It is."

"Then clear out so I can obey."

Miss Sanderson was barely under the eiderdown before she obeyed. Sleep came down in soft, comforting waves and, happily, was dreamless.

Chapter Twelve

Forsythe had been in the office at New Scotland Yard long enough for the watery morning sunlight, which had merely touched the window pane when he had arrived, to be streaming into the room and settling in a pool on the carpet at his feet.

Behind a desk that was graced by a handsome silver and ebony desk set Chief Inspector Kepesake bent his head over Miss Sanderson's journal. To his right his sergeant, looking like something the cleaners had neglected to remove, lounged in an armchair. Brummell did look out of place in the luxurious surroundings provided by Kepesake but Forsythe noted the man had worked through the journal at twice the speed of his superior. I must stop having these niggling thoughts about Kepesake, Forsythe told himself sternly. Despite his foppishness he really is quite a competent officer.

Kepesake grimaced and muttered, "Miss Sanderson certainly put every detail in. Even Nurse Ines' remarks about my smoking."

The barrister looked pointedly at the cigarette smoldering in the jade holder and Kepesake said quickly, "I am contemplating giving up smoking. Nurse Ines is right; it's a filthy habit. Why only last week I burnt a hole in my favorite vest."

Forsythe grinned and Brummell winked at him. Closing the journal's cover, Kepesake sat back in his chair. "I don't think there's any argument about our wisdom in sending Miss Sanderson to Maddersley-on-Mead. In a short time she's managed to ferret out information from the villagers that we didn't get in two weeks."

"At a price," Forsythe told him curtly. "Sandy's face looks like a death's head and she's so jumpy it's distressing."

Brummell tapped on his own notebook. "She's given us a number of leads."

"Which we will follow up immediately," Kepesake told him. "Directly after lunch we'll go back to the village and this time those people are going to think they're perched on that grill at the Fox and Crow that Miss Sanderson keeps mentioning."

"You most definitely will *not*," Forsythe rasped. "You'll wait until Sandy is out of there. You owe her that much."

Brummell said quickly, "Chief, those folks will guess where our tips came from."

"So? I don't imagine Miss Sanderson will mind a little displeasure from the locals."

Forsythe came half out of his chair but Brummell waved him back. "The chief hasn't thought it out, Mr. Forsythe. It could be dangerous for the lady, Chief."

"In what way?"

"The killer might figure she knows more than she does. Might get the wind up and go after her."

"I'll admit that hadn't occurred to me. No, we can't endanger her. Very well, Beau, we'll leave it until Monday. By that time she'll be out—"

"What do you mean?" Forsythe demanded.

Fitting a fresh cigarette into his holder, Kepesake said, "Shortly before you arrived we heard from Leonard Foster. His wife and he will be back in London on Sunday—"

"The day after tomorrow."

"That's right, old boy. So you can rest easy. I told Mr. Foster about Miss Sanderson and he was most gratified she's been watching over his little niece. He promised he'd bring Miss Sanderson back with them when they pick up Lucy Foster."

"Only two more days," Forsythe muttered.

The chief inspector flicked an ebony and silver lighter and exhaled a cloud of smoke. "I still don't understand why your secretary insisted on going back to that place. Her work was finished."

"Not quite. There's the baby. Anyway, Sandy is like a bulldog. Once she gets her teeth in it's impossible to make her let go." Forsythe glared across the desk. "And you're the one who got her into this mess."

"Not the chief," Brummell said soothingly. "As I told you, it was all my idea."

"And an excellent one, Beau." Kepesake pointed at his sergeant's notebook. "Do you have the names of all the suspects jotted down?"

"Every last one. Makes quite a list."

"We'll tackle the likely one first."

"Who's that, Chief?"

"That Maddersley chap. It's obvious he's dreadfully unstable."

Pulling out his pipe, Forsythe tamped fragrant tobacco into its carved bowl. "That applies to Linda Beauchamp as well."

Kepesake waved smoke and the suggestion away. "Old boy, stabbing is traditionally the crime of a male."

"No more than poisoning is a woman's crime," the barrister said drily.

"I still like Maddersley." Kepesake turned to his sergeant. "We'll leave Doctor Clay until last."

"Why, Chief?"

"You interviewed him. Can you picture that man murdering four members of his congregation?"

Rumpling his shaggy hair, his sergeant said mildly, "He's a powerful chap, Chief, and has strong motive and no alibi."

"Nonsense! Daniel Clay is a *minister*."

"So was the man who killed two of his choirboys and dismembered their bodies in Essex last fall."

"Nonetheless at present I happen to like Maddersley. What a headline that would make! *Baronet Butchers Doctor's Family.*"

It's no use, Forsythe thought, I really can't *stand* this ass. Aloud he said, "I'd keep Miss Markham in mind too."

"We'll do a thorough job, Forsythe. None of them will be neglected. Not even that dowdy woman who has the tearoom. Lavender and lilac!" Kepesake gave a delicate shudder.

Glancing from his superior to Forsythe's set face, the sergeant said quickly, " 'Bout this list you gave us to run down, sir—"

"Yes, that list," Kepesake said testily. "Forsythe, so you think we simply sit on our hands and let private detectives like you do our—"

"I am *not* a private detective."

Again Brummell interceded. "What the chief is getting at, sir, is we've already checked out both matters. When we found Melanie Marlow had been the Fosters' servant and had left the village recently we ran her down. Didn't know then about her father going after the Fosters but we figured maybe she could tell us something."

"Is she taking a hairdressing course?"

Brummell grinned. "Not so's you would notice. Melanie's an attractive girl in a flashy way but as cheap and hard as they come. Located her in one of those places making porno films for clubs and rundown cinemas in the East end. When I interviewed her she was wearing high heels and a string of beads and that's about all. Didn't seem to bother her a bit."

"Good Lord! She's only a child. Not seventeen yet."

"Know that, sir. We've taken steps and Melanie's gone into early retirement. At least from the film business. Slimy character who was kind of the director swore she'd claimed to be over twenty. Looks that old too."

"I've known many girls like her," Kepesake said philosophically. "Generally end up as prostitutes."

Ignoring him, Forsythe asked Brummell, "Could she tell you anything?"

"Not much. Didn't let on about her parents not knowing her whereabouts but she did gabble on about the Fosters. Boasted the doctor was wild about her and had his hands on her all the time. Said he'd promised to come up and see her in London." Brummell's wide jaw set. "If she were my daughter I would take a belt to her and then buy a chastity belt."

"If she were your daughter, Beau, there would be no problem," the chief inspector told him expansively. "Bad blood, I've seen many girls like—"

"And that's all she said?" Forsythe asked the sergeant.

"That's about it. Oh, she carped about the boys, said they were brats. Made a lot of snide remarks about Mrs. Foster. Called her a jealous bitch and claimed Mrs. Foster paid her off to get her out of the house." Brummell looked down at the short list Forsythe had made. "This item about Miss Beauchamp, sir. No, she's never been in a mental institution. I rang up the headmistress of the school where she'd worked and the woman told me Miss Beauchamp simply couldn't handle the girls. She was afraid of them and they knew it and made her life hell."

"And Miss Beauchamp's mother?"

"Mrs. Beauchamp had arthritis, the crippling kind. But she died from an embolism. Died in the hospital and there's no way her daughter could have had a hand in her death."

Kepesake waved his jade holder. "Which ruins your idea, old boy, of the young woman being involved with a previous murder."

The barrister continued to ignore him. He sat quietly, his neglected pipe in hand, his eyes fixed on a point beyond Brummell's shoulder. The sergeant watched him with bright hopeful eyes. "You thought of something, sir?"

"A few words," Forsythe said slowly. "Words that don't fit. As you know Sandy has a remarkable memory. She can repeat entire conversations word for word. Last night I didn't catch this but after I put her on the bus this morning I checked it in her journal. It may be nothing…"

"Tell us about it sir," Brummell urged.

Forsythe told him. The chief inspector listened as intently as his sergeant. When Forsythe was through, Kepesake ran a hand over his perfectly styled hair and said dubiously, "That's going to present some difficulty. Beau?"

"Well, I don't know, Chief…"

"We'll give it our best," Kepesake said decisively. "That's a remarkable secretary you have, old boy."

Getting to his feet, Forsythe looked down at the other man with hard eyes. "I'm well aware of that and I want her back. I want Sandy back soon and unharmed. If anything should happen to her, *old boy*, you will answer to me."

As Forsythe was leaving New Scotland Yard his secretary climbed down from the bus in front of the Fox and Crow. She shifted the shopping bag to her left hand and picked up the overnight case with her right.

She was struck with a sensation of *déjà vu*. When she'd left London the sun had been shining but the sky over Maddersley-on-Mead was as sullen and gray as it had been the day of her arrival in the village. Behind her the shops huddled drearily and directly in front was the façade of the inn. To complete her feeling the brass-bound door swung open and Paddy Rourke, wearing a wide smile, strolled toward her. At his heels a small terrier trotted stiffly. Its muzzle was white with age.

"Back again, are you?" Paddy said jovially. "And you've been spending your money in the fancy shops."

"I did a bit of shopping. Nice dog." She bent to stroke the animal. "What's his name?"

"Sammy." Scooping up the terrier, he nuzzled his chin against its grizzled head. "And I fear he's not much longer for this world. Gone downhill since we lost Sally. Litter mates they were and Sammy took it hard."

"Sally died?"

"Poisoned! Some cowardly gobshite—" He broke off and his Irish eyes shone with tears. "What kind of fiend would poison a harmless old beastie like Sally?"

The same fiend Coleridge had written about in his poem, Miss Sanderson thought as she shook her head. The innkeeper blinked his tears away. "But I'm forgetting, Miss Sanders. Irene Markham's inside having a bite of lunch and asked me to step out and tell you to join her. Your bag—"

"No. It's light, Paddy."

He held the door for her and she stepped into the warmth of the saloon bar. The Fox and Crow was doing a rushing business. Only two tables were unoccupied and a drone of voices competed with the blare of the television turned to a soccer game. She made her way to the bar and Paddy drew a pint for her. "Market day," he told her, "and the lads are wetting their whistles before driving to Lambert. Will you be wanting a bite?"

"I think not. I had rather a large breakfast."

"There's your cousin, then, waving to you."

She circled a table surrounded by men clad in rough clothes and smelling pungently of their barns. Irene sat alone by a window. On the table was a pewter stein and a plate containing half a ham roll. Setting her case and the bag on one chair, Miss Sanderson sank down into another. "Sorry to run off like that, Irene. I didn't have time to write a note."

"Are you all right? What did your doctor—"

"The tests aren't completed as yet," Miss Sanderson lied. "But not to worry. Simply a precaution."

Her reassurance wasn't really necessary. Irene didn't seem all that concerned. Her color was high and there was a sparkle in the milky blue eyes. Flinging back short hair, she blurted, "I heard from him. This morning. He rang up and—"

"Who?"

"Leonard Foster, that's who. Marjorie and he will be back this Sunday. Told me, just like that, they'll expect Lucy to be ready. Even asked me to drive to Heathrow and pick them up. The nerve!"

Miss Sanderson sagged with relief. Sunday! Only another forty-eight hours and she would be free to leave. Fervently she hoped never to see this village again. Irene was staring at her and she managed to ask, "Are you going?"

Nibbling at the roll, Irene said, "I was tempted to tell Leonard to get here any way he damn well could. Then I reconsidered. I haven't been out of this village for months. I feel...oh, I don't know."

"Stifled?"

"Yes. As though I should see something beside The Cheese Tease and Ferne's Market." She regarded the Harrods bag with envy. "Do some shopping, perhaps go to the theater and have dinner with one of the women I once worked with. Do you understand?"

"Completely."

"Good. I want to request a favor, rather a large one. That is, if you feel well enough to—"

"I'm fine. What is it, Irene?"

"I'd like to drive to London tomorrow and have the day there. I've spoken to Mrs. Toogood and she's willing to stay with you tomorrow and remain the night. She'll be in the house until the Fosters and I arrive on Sunday. I know it's an imposition but—"

"I'd be happy to." Reaching over, Miss Sanderson patted Irene's hand. "A change will do you good."

The younger woman beamed. "I knew I could count on you. Perhaps I haven't told you but I do so appreciate all you've done. It's so comforting to have a cousin to rely on. And we'll keep in touch from now on, won't we?"

Feeling incredibly false, Miss Sanderson nodded. She took a sip of bitters and asked, "You're serious about keeping that house on?"

"I am. I don't know quite how yet but it's my home and I'm staying on in it."

"Mrs. Toogood won't be with you, you know."

"I won't be able to afford her anyway. And with the baby gone there shouldn't be much to do. Well, I must get back to the shop." She rose and so did her companion. "Are you going directly home?"

"After I stop at the chemist's and have a couple of prescriptions filled."

As they left the inn Irene asked, "Would you like me to take your case? I'll bring it home with me." She exclaimed, "Why, this is Gillian's."

"Mrs. Toogood lent it so I wouldn't have to lug that big one of mine around. Do you mind?"

"Why should I? See you this evening." Irene stopped and called, "What are you doing this afternoon?"

"Having a nap," Miss Sanderson told her with great satisfaction.

That is exactly what she did. She paused and hugged Lucy and then fished in her shopping bag. Taking the pattern book and wool, she handed them to the housekeeper. "I was going to make up a sweater for Lucy but there won't be time. Can you use these?"

"Sure can, miss. What a pretty green. Be just right for my youngest. Mollie's got kinda reddish hair." She added regretfully, "But Mollie's not as pretty as little Lucy."

"No one," Miss Sanderson told the baby, "is as pretty as you."

Then she went to her room and curled up under a down comforter. If I can't sleep at night, she told herself drowsily, I'll do it in the daytime while the staunch Mrs. Toogood is here to ward off fiends. Anyway, two more days and that fiend would trouble her slumbers no more.

That night Forsythe was as restless as his secretary. While Miss Sanderson started up and slipped out of bed to pad barefooted into the nursery, her employer twisted in a tangle of sheets, staring at the shadowy ceiling.

About the time that Irene Markham turned the hood of her shabby little car toward London the following morning,

Forsythe, in robe and slippers, was disturbing Sergeant Brummell's sleep.

"Awful early, sir," the sergeant mumbled. "Hardly daybreak."

"Any progress, Beau?"

"Not yesterday, sir. Maybe we'll have better luck today."

"I've a feeling this is important and time is of the essence."

Brummell's voice was more alert. "Think you're on to something?"

"I've this feeling..."

"Like Miss Sanderson's fey feeling?"

"Similar. Beau, get back to me the moment you have something. I'll be here in my flat waiting."

There was a pause and then the other man asked, "Care to give me a hint, sir?"

"Lucy Foster is leaving Maddersley tomorrow."

"Ah, I see what you're getting at. I'll do my best, Mr. Forsythe."

The barrister rang off. He felt a bit reassured. Sergeant Brummell's best was generally very good indeed.

Chapter Thirteen

It was after nine when Miss Sanderson got out of her rumpled bed and showered. She pulled on a robe and slippers and padded down to the kitchen to find the housekeeper hovering over the stove and the baby perched on her high chair. She chucked Lucy under the chin and asked, "Miss Markham away?"

"At the crack of dawn, miss. Had me come early and left soon's I stuck my nose in the door. Making up waffles and sausage for breakfast. That all right with you?"

"Fine." Bending, Miss Sanderson picked up Lucy's stuffed lamb. "You're staying the night with us?"

"Promised Miss Irene I would. Brought a little bag with me. Miss Irene said I could sleep in one of the boys' bunk beds."

"It's awfully decent of you."

The housekeeper slid a steaming platter on the table and beamed. "Tell the truth, miss, it's gonna be a treat for me. Having six kiddies in that poky house can be a trial. Bert's taking care of them and Mrs. Rugg—she's right next door to us—promised to look in on them." She attacked her breakfast with gusto. "Figure I'll cook us a good lunch and there's lamb chops for supper. There's a couple of dandy shows on the telly tonight or we could play a game of rummy. You play rummy, miss?"

"I haven't played it in years."

"Like bicycling, never forget how. You'll do fine."

As soon as breakfast was finished Mrs. Toogood shooed Miss Sanderson out of the kitchen. Lucy held up imploring arms and Miss Sanderson scooped her up and carried her to the living room. She deposited the baby on thick salmon carpeting and rummaged in the toy box for blocks. As soon as the block house was finished the baby, with a triumphant crow, knocked it flying. Patiently Miss Sanderson built another one.

The morning passed peacefully and after a hearty lunch Miss Sanderson put Lucy down for her nap. While she was upstairs she slipped off her robe and pulled on a heavy tweed skirt and a woolen pullover. Then she returned to the living room and picked up a magazine. While she leafed through it she could hear the hum of a vacuum cleaner. The machine shut off and a tousled head craned around the door. "Any plans for this afternoon, miss? Got the work just about finished."

Wary of being inveigled into a game of rummy Miss Sanderson said, "When Lucy wakes up I'll take her out for a walk. We could both use a breath of air. Where's her pram kept?"

"On the veranda. Got a piece of canvas over it. Be sure to cover it up when you get back. Pram could get horrible damp." Wandering over, the housekeeper peered between striped curtains. "Hope the fog holds off till you get back."

Miss Sanderson joined her and looked over the heavy shoulder. "Why, it's quite clear."

"Right now. But the wind's changing and fog is coming. Can smell it. Get a powerful lot of fog this time of year." The phone rang and she nudged Miss Sanderson. "Bet you that'll be Miss Irene, asking how you're making out. You better get it."

It wasn't Irene Markham's light high voice. This voice was male and rather gruff. She called, "Mrs. Toogood, it's for you."

"Bert...when?...how high? Well, you get over to the chemist's and get one. And you ring back soon's you take them." Slamming down the receiver, the housekeeper turned a wrathful face to her companion. "If that don't beat all! That Bert is the clumsiest man ever born. Broke the thermometer, he did. Now we gotta buy a new one."

"What's wrong?"

"The twins. Percy and Willy. Bert says when he got them up they was all flushed and fretting. He waited a while and they got worse." She snapped her fingers. "Bet I know what it is! Let them play with Joey Rugg when he was coming down with the chicken pox. Didn't know the boy was ailing and that Mrs. Rugg didn't say a word. Didn't care if my kids got sick!"

Conscious of a sinking feeling in the pit of her stomach Miss Sanderson prowled up and down the hall waiting for Bert Toogood to report back. It took some time. When the phone rang she jumped. This conversation was as brief as the first and when Mrs. Toogood rang off she looked worried. "Temperatures of both little chaps is way over a hundred. Percy and Willy are both pretty sick though Bert says he thinks Willy is the worst." She was twisting her apron in both hands. "Give Miss Irene my word I wouldn't budge outta this house till she gets back tomorrow. Don't want to leave you alone here. What's a body to do?"

"What you must." Miss Sanderson patted her arm. "Your place is with your children."

"Know that, miss. Not even a doctor here now. Have to take them over to Lambert. Well, better get my duds together." She headed up the stairs. When she came down she was carrying a shabby carpetbag. While Miss Sanderson helped her on with her coat Mrs. Toogood rattled off instructions at high speed. "Supper in the fridge. All you gotta do is stick them chops under the broiler. If'n you want to keep the baby down here for a time this evening get her basket outta the laundry room. Missus used that basket a lot. Mr. Johnston made it up for her." She buttoned the coat and pulled her woolen hat down over her ears. "Bottles for Lucy all made up. Give her some of that minced beef and peas for supper. If'n you get nervous ring up Mr. Johnston. He's a nice old fellow and tell you straight I never did agree with Miss Irene keeping him outta this house after the missus passed on."

Tucking her plastic purse under an arm, she bent for her bag. Miss Sanderson unchained the door and held it open. The housekeeper's prediction was coming true. Threads of mist spiraled along the walk. At the edge of the veranda the housekeeper paused. "If'n you take little Lucy out for an airing don't go far. Fog's gonna get thick. And Miss Sanders…"

"Yes?"

"When you get back you get that chain on the door. Other two are locked but you check them anyway. Stay right in the house and don't let no one in."

"I won't."

Miss Sanderson watched the muffled figure waddling down the walk to the gate. She watched until Mrs. Toogood was out of sight. How, she asked herself, could she ever have felt distaste for that woman? Right now she'd give anything to have the woman with her. Frowsy hair and missing tooth and all. The housekeeper had given sound advice. Perhaps she'd better skip the walk. Then she turned and looked down the shadowy hall. No, she must get out of this house for a time.

Silence pressed down and then, from the nursery, came the tentative wail of the baby. Miss Sanderson took the steps two at a time.

It took all Miss Sanderson's strength to get the high-wheeled pram down the flight of steep steps. When she returned to the house for Lucy she was breathless. Before she shut the door she shifted the baby from one arm to the other while she checked her pockets for the key Irene had left for her. Her fingers touched metal and she closed the door and then tried it.

Tucking the baby under a blanket, she told her, "In that outfit you could take first prize at a baby show."

The comment was justified. A white fur bonnet framed the vivid little face, and hands waved matching mittens. A fur-trimmed coat and leggings completed the picture. Lucy bounced and cooed and Miss Sanderson steered the unwieldy pram down the walk. Ground mist swirled around the wheels and her feet. As she passed the row of cottages she noticed mist was creeping over the shrubs in the yards. Among dark pines the vicarage was almost obscured. They reached the church and in the graveyard behind it fog swirled around grave markers pointing pallid fingers toward a pewter-colored sky. Miss Sanderson wondered which of those marble fingers stood guard over the graves of Lucy's family.

At the corner she stood indecisively and then turned the pram down toward Abercrombie's pasture. She'd have liked to have walked over the stone bridge toward Maddersley Hall but she wasn't going to jolt the baby on the gravel road. At the base of the hill the fog was thicker. In the chemist's window ruby and emerald globes glowed with eerie light. Across the street yellow lights could be discerned in all the shops but one. Irene's shop was dark.

The door of the inn opened and someone came out. Miss Sanderson couldn't tell who it was or even if it were a man or a woman. For a moment light poured across the walk and she wistfully regarded it. In a bit people would be playing darts or watching the television, people would be drinking pints and clouding the air with cigarette smoke. Paddy would be leaning across the bar and Kate poking her dark head around her kitchen door. She longed to join them but she could hardly take Lucy into a bar.

"Better get back," she told the baby and her own voice sounded hollow and remote.

Hidden in the fog she no longer had to play the part of invalid. She sped up the hill and the baby waved a fur mitten and crowed with pleasure. When they reached the crossing she found she couldn't see more than a few feet in either direction. Stopping, she strained her ears. No sound of a car. She rushed across the lane and jolted the pram roughly up on the curb. The baby gave a protesting wail. "Hush, Lucy, consider yourself fortunate. It's easier to ride than pilot this monster."

The church, graveyard, and vicarage had disappeared behind a wall of yellowish fog. So had the cottages. Miss Sanderson's loping stride covered ground rapidly but she had to slow down to locate the gate of the Markham house. As she did she heard the thud of running footsteps behind her. She spun around and a figure in a white leather coat with long hair streaming from under a black tam lunged out of the fog.

"Abigail." Linda Beauchamp panted. "I've been trying to catch you all the way up the hill." She waved a brown bag. "Stopped in at the butcher shop to pick up a meat pie and I thought I saw you farther up the hill. My, but you can move *fast.*"

"I was rushing to get Lucy home. This dampness may not be good for her."

The younger woman bent over the pram. "She's sweet!"

"I thought you didn't like children?"

"I don't mind babies. They're so *harmless.* Too bad they have to grow up." Bulging brown eyes brushed over Miss Sanderson's face. "I heard about the Toogood twins—how sick they are. And I thought of *you,* all alone in that dreadful house."

"In Maddersley news travels with the speed of light."

"Doesn't it though? Kate Rourke was in the chemist's when Bert Toogood came in to buy a thermometer. He told Kate his wife was going to have to go home and look after the twins. And everyone knows Irene Markham drove to London this morning."

"I'd hate to try to keep a secret in this place."

"Oh, there are *secrets,*" the young woman said darkly. "I've been thinking how I can help. You were so *decent* to me the

A DEATH FOR A DOCTOR 339

other day. I couldn't bear to spend the night in that house but perhaps you would like to bring the baby to my cottage. I've only a camp bed but I could sleep on the floor and you can have the cot."

"I wouldn't dream of putting you out of your bed."

"And that was a silly idea, Miss Beauchamp," a voice snapped in Miss Sanderson's ear. Whirling, she faced a tall bulky figure draped in a dark cape with a hood pulled low over the face. Under the hood wire-rimmed glasses glinted. "Sleep on a cold floor and you'll be a sick girl. Miss Sanders and the baby will be better off in the Markham house. I must admit it is comfortable and warm."

"Nurse Ines, the villagers say that house is *cursed*," Linda wailed.

"Balderdash, Miss Beauchamp! You're an educated woman. Surely you don't believe that sort of rubbish."

"They say many people have died violently in it." The girl lowered her voice to a whisper. "They say blood calls for *blood*."

"And I say the villagers are still back in the dark ages. If they could find a witch they would burn her. Now you get right along home, my girl, and make up a pot of strong tea. That'll settle you down."

It was an order and the girl didn't argue. She turned away and fog swallowed her up. Nurse Ines chuckled. "Bundle of nerves. No business living alone. Miss Sanders, you get that baby right in the house. You're right; she shouldn't be out in this damp. Need help getting the pram up?"

"No," Miss Sanderson said firmly.

She fumbled at the gate and the nurse stepped forward and opened it. As she humped the pram up the steps she wondered how long the woman had been standing silently in the fog. Long enough to have heard her remark about damp.

She unlocked the door, lifted the baby from the nest of blankets, and threw the canvas cover over the pram. Stepping into the hall, she clicked a switch. Light streamed down on black-and-white tile. She was conscious her heart was thudding.

Could those women have frightened her? She used Nurse Ines's word. Balderdash. But one thing was definite. By this time the entire population of the village knew she was alone. That thought was far from comforting.·

She put the baby down in the lounge and took off her coat. By the time it was hung in the hall closet Lucy had managed to crawl over to a table and pull herself up, and she was now reaching for a vase.

"You are an imp," Miss Sanderson scolded. "And the way it looks you're soon going to be a walking imp."

She took off the baby's bonnet and coat and was working at the leggings when the telephone rang. "Better come with me, imp," she said and hoisted Lucy from the floor. Holding the baby balanced on one hip, she lifted the receiver. The voice was fruity and rich and was one she recognized immediately. "It has been brought to my attention," the vicar said, "that you've been…hem…deserted by Mrs. Toogood."

"Two of her children are ill."

"Yes, the twins. Chicken pox, I believe. It occurred to me that with the fog you may be somewhat uneasy. Mrs. Gay could make up a room for you and the child. We do have many unoccupied rooms but I must warn you they're unaired and may be quite damp."

Miss Sanderson had a flash of Lucy and her crouching in a clammy room in that cold dark house. She would take her chances here. Cursed or not the beds weren't damp. "Very kind of you, Dr. Clay, but we'll be fine here."

"I hope so, dear lady." He didn't sound overly optimistic. "Should you change your mind you need only ring me up."

"Fat chance of that," she told the wriggling baby. She pulled off the leggings and felt the round bottom. Now you're *damp*. Blimey, how many nappies do you go through in a day?"

Her foot was on the bottom step of the staircase when the phone pealed again. Still clasping the wet bottom she retraced her steps. This voice she recognized too. The decisive tones of Nurse Ines.

"After I left you I had second thoughts," the nurse announced. "Do you have the wind up over there?"

"Why do you ask?"

"The villagers have probably been filling your ears with dire tales. And then, Miss Beauchamp and her wild imagination. I wondered..."

"As you said, it's balderdash."

"Of course. But you're welcome to stay with me. I'm in the middle of packing, of course, and everything's frightfully muddled. I've only one bed so we'd have to share. Lucy could sleep in her pram."

Miss Sanderson shuddered at the thought of sharing a bed with Nurse Ines. After all, this woman was a prime candidate for mass murder. She politely declined the offer and rang off.

She shifted the baby. "You're not only damp but you weigh a ton."

Another sound blasted the silence. This time it was the *William Tell* Overture. Exasperated, she was about to tear off the chain when she, like Nurse Ines, had second thoughts. Leaving the chain in place, she inched the door open a crack and applied one eye to it. All she could see was a form looming out of the fog. A dark object was thrust at her and she jumped back. "Your meat order," the dark form said.

She discerned Rog Austin holding out a small carton. "I didn't put in an order."

"Maybe Miss Markham did."

"If she had she would have told me."

He moved and light from the hall fell over his face, colorless eyes and moist girlish mouth and fall-away chin. "All right if I come in and ring up my dad? Musta got the wrong name on this here box."

Her hand was reaching for the chain. It stopped abruptly. She wasn't letting Rog Austin or anyone else into this house. "No," she said.

Avid eyes wandered over the portion of her face he could see. "Scairt, aren't you?" There was a note of relish in his voice.

"Can't say I blame you, not after what's happened in there. But you could turn on some light. Maybe I can figure it out."

No harm in that. She switched on the veranda light. The baby had had enough and was wailing. "Hurry up," she ordered.

He lifted the carton and peered at it. "Blast Dad's scrawl! Got Matthew down here. Could have sworn it was Markham. This is for the next door. Sorry to bother you."

She banged the door shut. I'll leave the veranda light on, she decided. This time she not only got upstairs but managed to change Lucy's nappies and slip her into coveralls. The baby was still fretting. Hungry, Miss Sanderson thought, which makes two of us. "An army," she said aloud, "marches on its stomachs. We'll fill ours."

Lucy had the priority. She ate the noxious-looking mince and peas in her usual carefree manner. Part of it went on her tray, part smudged her face and hands, some of it went on Miss Sanderson when she smiled charmingly and blew a mouthful directly into her nursemaid's face.

Miss Sanderson mopped at her face. "I've an inspired idea how to feed you, imp. Both of us strip and get in the bathtub. When you've finished chucking your meal around I turn on the shower. Think I'll write a how-to book on babies. Put your picture on the cover and it should be a bestseller." The baby gurgled and she added, "And you're a great conversationalist. How about some applesauce?"

After the baby was fed, washed, and put in the playpen with a bottle clutched in her plump hands, Miss Sanderson opened the fridge door. Ah, dinner was indeed ready. Mrs. Toogood had made a salad, laid out six plump lamb chops, a plate of cheese rolls, and a jar of mint sauce. There was also apple tart. Too bad the housekeeper was missing this bounteous repast. Miss Sanderson took out the salad, one roll, and hesitated over the chops. Finally she decided on two. When the broiler had been switched on she lighted a cigarette and waited for the stove to come up to heat.

The telephone sent a strident summons and she swore and trotted down the hall. "Mary Maddersley," a crisp voice told her. "I understand you were in London yesterday. Did you see your physician?"

"No."

"I thought not. I felt you had gone to…to report." The line hummed and then she said, "Did you lie to me about not being connected with the police?"

Time to put some cards on the table, Miss Sanderson decided. "I'm not a member of the police force, Miss Maddersley, but in the past I have been involved with police officers. I'm also no relation to the Markhams."

"I didn't think you were." There was another pause and when Miss Maddersley spoke her voice wasn't as crisp. "Now the police will be back. Miss Sanders, or whoever you really are, my brother can't stand up under an interrogation. Do you know Chief Inspector Kepesake?"

"Yes. He's competent and fair. I hardly think he'll be brutal with your brother."

"Perhaps I misjudged the man. I want you to know I hold nothing against you. I'm aware you're doing what is necessary, And I haven't breathed a word about you to anyone else."

"Not even to your brother?"

"Particularly not to Donnie." The voice again became crisp. "One thing I shan't worry about. You'll be safe in that house. I should imagine you know how to handle yourself."

As Miss Sanderson returned to the kitchen she made a wry grimace. Miss Maddersley probably imagined she held the black belt in jujitsu or excelled in a similar form of martial art. Robby had been accurate when he'd told Adam Kepesake she had absolutely no training. Even if she did have a revolver she wouldn't know how to use it.

Pausing by the playpen, she smiled down at Lucy. The milk in the bottle was fast disappearing. She pulled the curtains over the big window and closed the shorter ones on the glassed section set in the back door. She noticed fog had crept right up against the panes.

When the chops were broiled they looked delectable but she found her appetite had vanished. She ate part of one and nibbled at a roll. Pushing the plate away, she considered having a large drink of the whiskey purchased by Mrs. Sutter. Better not. "This house," she informed the baby, "is enough to drive one to drink."

As she was stacking the dishes in the dishwashing machine the door chimes pealed lustily. She moved slowly down the hall. Despite lights blazing in the hall and the lounge, shadows seemed to crouch in doorways and huddle under the staircase. As she passed the darkened dining room she paused to flip on the chandelier. This time she made no move to detach the chain. She inched the door open and peered out. The overhead light on the veranda illuminated a tall figure dressed in loose oilskins and high rubber boots. Both hands were thrust in slash pockets. He stood well back near the steps. She'd never seen him before.

"Miss Sanders?" he said hesitantly. "We haven't met. I'm Donald Maddersley."

"I have met your sister."

"Mary sent me around. She...we both feel it a poor idea for you to be here alone. We thought you might consider coming to the Hall for the night."

"Your sister rang up a short time ago." Her nails were biting painfully into the palms of her hands. "She didn't mention anything about this."

He moved a step closer. His hands were still jammed in his pockets. Was there anything else in those pockets, she wondered. They were deep enough to hold a long sharp knife. "This house, Miss Sanders, has a bad history. Horrible things have happened here. A woman and child are not safe in it. I urge you to bring the baby and come with me. Open the door and I'll wait while you get ready."

"No!"

"Don't be frightened. I'll admit this wasn't Mary's idea but—"

"Go *away!*"

She banged the door shut and jumped back. Her heart was racing and she was breathing heavily. Then she moved the few feet and pressed an ear against the panel. Was he moving across the veranda, down the steps? She could hear nothing. Was he circling the house, looking for a way in? God! She hadn't checked the surgery door. She wrenched open the door to the waiting room, turned on the switch, ran over to the exterior door. It was locked.

She glanced around. Light from the waiting room spilled through the doorway to the office. The office where Paul Foster's mutilated body had slumped back in his chair, where blood had spattered the walls and...

She fled from the surgery, down the hall, pushing the swinging door open. Running across the tile floor, she yanked at the door handle. Locked. She slumped down at the table and buried her face in her hands. Nothing here but the tick of the wall clock, the soft purr of Lucy's breathing, the comforting odor of broiled lamb.

She glanced up at the clock. Only a little past six. Hours until this night was over and daylight and Irene Markham and Leonard Foster arrived. Long dark hours in this fog-shrouded house. From outside...with knives. Was Maddersley still out there? Was Nurse Ines in her long dark cape or Paddy Rourke, his Irish eyes no longer merry, moving stealthily through the fog? Had Irene Markham's trip to London been feigned? Was she even now circling back to the village to destroy the last member of her sister's family?

With no compunction Miss Sanderson opened a cupboard and took down the squat brown bottle. Pouring out a couple of inches, she downed it like a dose of medicine.

"There comes a time," she told the baby shakily, "for demon drink. There comes a time for all good cowards to come to the aid of their sanity. It's my Scottish grandmother who's to blame for my present state. Granny MacPherson was a firm believer in ghosties and curses and things that go bong in the night. She carried a rabbit's foot and possibly strung garlic around her neck. But tomorrow your aunt and uncle will be here and they'll take you to a nice safe home where you'll have cousins to grow up with. I must be very pleasant to them and perhaps they'll extend visiting privileges to me. I'll go to see you at Christmas and take a present. Maybe a big doll with ringlets like yours...And if you think I'm talking too much you're right. I'm babbling away like Linda Beauchamp and for the same reason. I'm nervous. What the hell! I'm terrified. Shaking in my boots."

The baby didn't even gurgle. The bottle had fallen from her hand and coppery lashes were drifting down against her cheeks. Her chin was decorated with a drop of milk. And I'm not taking you up to the nursery, Miss Sanderson told the child silently. I want you right where I can see you. That basket Mrs. Toogood had mentioned...I'll tuck you up, take you to the living room, light a fire to ward off evil, and there we'll spend the night.

She found the basket in a corner of the laundry room. It was fashioned ingeniously of a wicker basket suspended on a metal stand. It had small wheels and a leather strap with which to rock the basket. The mattress was covered with a sheet patterned with ducks, and a matching blanket was folded across the bottom. Lucy didn't rouse when she was lifted into the basket and the blanket was drawn over her. She slept soundly as the basket trundled along black-and-white tile into the living room. Mrs. Toogood had laid the fire and in moments paper and kindling were blazing. Sitting back on her heels, Miss Sanderson positioned a log. Her head jerked up. A noise. But where?

She was on her feet, standing over the basket, her knuckles whitening as she grasped the poker. Another sound—at the back of the house. She looked down at the baby and then moved slowly to the hall. Her breath catching in her throat, she forced herself to the kitchen door and swung it open. Someone was knocking at the door. Clutching the poker, she crossed the floor and stood at the door. She eased a curtain to one side and looked out. She could see nothing but fog. She reached for the switch and turned on the porch light. Still nothing. Then there was movement. A hand was flung up, a big capable hand with a calloused palm—a carpenter's hand. Standing on tiptoes, she pressed her nose against the glass and peered down. A tweed cap and a wide furrowed face. With no hesitation she threw the door open.

"Matthew! Thank God!"

Chapter Fourteen

Matthew Johnston looked from the poker in her hand to her ashen face. "Spooked, eh? Thought you might be. That's why I came over. To remind you I'm right next door and if anything bothers you you've only to ring up and I'll be right over."

Lowering the poker, she stepped aside. "Come in."

The tweed cap moved from side to side. "Can't, Abigail. Don't go any place I'm not welcome. And Irene made it plain I'm not welcome in her house."

He started to turn the chair toward the ramp and she reached out and grabbed an arm of it. "*Please.* For God's sake, Matthew, I'm nearly out of my mind."

"If Irene hears about it you'll be in for it."

"Irene can go straight to hell!"

He chuckled. "Nothing wrong with your spirit. All right, get out of the way so's I can get this chair in."

He wheeled in and she retreated to a chair. Her knees felt as though they'd turned to jelly. Johnston flipped his cap onto one of the pegs with a single dextrous movement and straightened the folds of his rug. "What got you in this state, Abigail?"

"People." She realized she was still clinging to the poker. She propped it up against the chair leg. "People coming to the door, ringing up."

"Tell me about it."

She told him. He listened and then said, "Villagers may be nosy and gossipy and kind of standoffish but they're good people. Maybe you should have gone to the vicarage or to Nurse Ines or—"

"How could I? Someone in this village killed Lucy's family."

He rubbed his chin. "Tell you what. I could stay the night. Sit in the living room. Don't sleep much anyway so it wouldn't be a hardship." He looked around. "Where's the wee one? Tucked up in bed?"

"Lucy's in the living room. I couldn't bear her out of my sight. She's sound asleep in that basket you made for her."

"Well, must admit that's as comfortable as anything can be. Took a lot of pains making it."

Reaching for the bottle, she spilled Scotch in her glass. "Would you like a drink, Matthew?"

"Don't touch spirits. Only have a pint now and then. And you leave that stuff alone. Strong tea's better for you. I'll brew a pot."

She smiled. "You sound exactly like Nurse Ines."

"Nice woman. Some people don't care for her but she's been kind to me. Since Paul died she's been dropping in every day to see how I'm making out. Even massages my legs for me. Hurt something fierce at times. Now, I'll make that tea. No, sit where you are. Not sensible for you with that heart condition to get so upset. And I know my way around this kitchen as well as I do my own." He took a canister off the counter and reached for the kettle. "Doctor have some news for you yesterday?"

"The results of all tests aren't in yet." Miss Sanderson found she was relaxing. She watched him fill the kettle, take down a tray, reach under the counter for cups.

"Won't bother with milk or sugar. Noticed the other day you take yours clear too." He rinsed out the teapot with hot water, measured in tea leaves, and poured boiling water. "You know, Abigail, people with good health don't know how lucky they are. Like me before the accident. No money can buy back health. But I guess you know that."

Miss Sanderson was tempted to tell the truth, that her health was excellent. She changed her mind. Matthew might consider she'd lied to him, which she had, and desert her. And I need you, she told the man silently, I really need you. Instead she said, "Shall we have our tea in the living room? I would like to be near Lucy."

"You go along and I'll bring the tray." His eyes twinkled. "And use that poker for what it's meant for, stirring up the fire."

She'd forgotten both the poker and the fire. She carried it with her and built up the fire. In moments she heard the wheels of his chair rumbling over the floor of the hall. He steered the chair in on the other side of the basket and deposited the tray on a low table. "Shall I be mother?"

She nodded and he picked up the pot. Then his head jerked up. "What is it, Matthew?"

"Thought I heard something." He shrugged. "Must be a board creaking. Houses are full of noises."

"Don't I know *that*." She turned her head toward the hall, listening. The telephone pealed and she jumped. "Damn! Another well-wisher."

"If it's Irene better not tell her I'm in her precious house."

"You can count on me."

It wasn't Irene. It was Robby's voice. "Sandy. Are you alone?"

"No."

"In that case mention Dr. Forbes."

"You're ringing up rather late, Dr. Forbes."

"Now listen. Brummell says Miss Markham is in London."

"Yes, doctor."

His voice was edged with strain. "Don't mention who's with you. We have the name of the murderer. Sandy, for God's sake say something!"

"You have the results of the tests," she babbled. "Can you give them to me?"

He told her the name of the murderer. She reached out to the telephone stand and clutched at it for support. "Sandy," he whispered.

"I think," she said clearly, "I agree with you. The situation does seem extremely serious."

"Hold on! We'll be there!"

With a shaking hand, as though handling something fragile, she kept receiver in place and spoke to a humming line. "It was good of you to let me know...No, I won't panic...Yes, I'll go to your office as soon as I get to London tomorrow. Goodnight, Dr. Forbes."

Still clinging to the telephone stand, she thought, it's all right that I'm trembling, that is only natural. Now...

Matthew Johnston had already poured the tea and steam spiraled up from the cups. The fire was crackling cheerily and in the basket Lucy peacefully slept. Miss Sanderson stood behind her chair, her hands reaching for its back for support. It all looked so...so *cozy.*

Matthew raised his head and youthful eyes in his wrinkled face met her own. "Couldn't help overhearing. Bad news, Abigail?"

"Disturbing. The results of the tests."

"Your heart?" She nodded and he said reassuringly, "Don't go thinking the worst. Tests can be wrong. Should know. Spent a lot of time in hospitals. Dr. Brown used to joke that I was there more than he was."

She lifted her head. "Matthew! Now *I* hear something. At the back of the house. Can you remember whether I shut the door properly after you came in?"

"Didn't notice. Where are you going?"

"I'd better have a look."

"No." He swung his chair around. "You sit down. I'll have a look."

It didn't take long. The chair wheeled back and he pulled it up by the basket. "Door's locked. Spooking yourself again. Glad to see you're drinking tea. That'll settle your nerves." He lifted his cup and took a gulp. "Little bitter. Too strong do you think?"

"Just right."

"Want me to stay down here while you and Lucy sleep?"

She drained her cup. "I would appreciate it. You say you don't sleep soundly?"

"Hardly sleep at all. Haven't since the accident. Pain seems worse at night. Told Paul about it and he really had at me. Said I should have mentioned if before. I told him the truth. Hate drugs and never've been able to swallow pills or capsules properly. Paul said he could fix that. Took a bottle of liquid out of his cupboard and poured out some in a smaller bottle. I told him I didn't like to think what folks would say if they heard I was taking that stuff, and he winked and said even Nurse Ines would never know. Said it would be our little secret."

Miss Sanderson extended her cup and he tilted the teapot over it. She noticed her hand was now steady. She thought with dreadful clarity, I see the fiend that close behind me had been treading. Her voice was as steady as her hand. "Did the drug help you sleep?"

"Wouldn't know. Never used it. Saved it. Came in handy too." His hand, holding a knife, came out from under the tartan rug. An ordinary butcher knife with a long thin blade, she thought dully. "Sit steady, Abigail. Moved that poker where you can't reach it. Know you have use of your legs but you can't move that fast. Been watching you. Don't try to run for it or—" He shifted the knife and poised it over the sleeping baby. "You move and she's dead."

"*Don't.*"

He put the blade back in his lap. "Just remember there's nothing wrong with my arms. Fact is, my shoulders and arms are stronger than most folks'—from wheeling this chair and swinging myself in and out of it." He picked up his cup and emptied it.

"Why?" she whispered.

"Sit back and listen. You won't be upset much longer. Put the rest of that drug in your tea. Wasn't much left and may not work too fast but in a while you'll be getting drowsy." With his left hand he emptied the teapot into his cup. "All my life I've prided myself on being an honest man. Ask anyone in Cheltenham. Matthew Johnston, they'll tell you, is honest and never tells a lie. But I've been lying a lot this last year. The day we met, Abigail, I told you lies.

"Lied about my daughter's death. Ariel didn't die from a ruptured appendix. She died because some man had gotten her pregnant and she'd been aborted. Bungled job and by the time Ariel got home to Julia and me she was hemorrhaging. I was all for taking our girl to the hospital but Julia wouldn't hear of it. 'Matthew,' Julia said, 'I can't bear to have our daughter's name besmirched. Get Dr. Brown. He'll save Ariel.' I got him but he couldn't save her. Ariel died in my arms." His fingers closed around the handle of the knife. "Begged my girl to tell me who did it. All she would say was her lover had done the abortion. Then, at the end, she whispered a name. Paul!"

"*Paul.*"

"That's all she said." He turned his head and firelight glinted ruddily across his face. "Julia never got over Ariel's death. Something broke inside her. She killed herself in that car and nearly killed me. Julia drove off the road into a gully and it was nearly two hours before someone noticed and they came for us. I was trapped, couldn't move, and I lay there, looking into her dead face. How I *loved* her. Swore I would find the man who'd killed her and our daughter. Took years to trace him down. I was in and out of hospitals, operation after operation. Pain all the time. Pain in my legs and my heart. Then I got his name."

"How?"

"After we buried our daughter I went to London to try and find Paul. Ariel didn't have any close friends but I questioned the students at her ballet school. One of the girls told me she'd seen a man pick Ariel up several times from school. Said he was young and dark and nice looking. But she didn't know his name. Then I went to the house where Ariel had boarded. Her landlady was real fond of my girl but she didn't know anything about Paul.

"The landlady took me up to Ariel's room and helped me pack her clothes and things. I thought there might be letters or a diary to show me the way but there wasn't anything. Seemed queer because Ariel, from the time she was about eight, always kept a diary."

"There were no leads to Paul?"

"None. After Julia died I kept wondering how to find him. Thought of him walking around on two legs while I was a cripple. Thought of him taking my lovely daughter to some run-down hotel and butchering her in a filthy room. He killed not only my daughter but my unborn grandchild. He killed Julia. He took my family away from me. He took my *legs*. Promised myself and God I would find him and take everything away from him."

Miss Sanderson sagged in her chair, resolutely keeping her eyes away from Lucy's sleeping face. How long will it take Robby, she wondered. Fog will slow him. Oh God, Robby, hurry! Johnston's big head tilted toward the baby. Must keep him talking. "How did you find Paul Foster?"

Hectically brilliant eyes jerked back to her. "Fourteen months ago my prayers were answered. Got a package in the post from Ariel's landlady. She'd been having renovations done on her house and when the carpenter pulled out the wardrobe in the girl's room he found Ariel's diary. It'd slipped down between warped boards. From her grave my little girl was pointing the way for her daddy.

"Ariel wrote about meeting this medical student and she raved on about how they loved each other. Said how she went to her Paul when she found she was with child. She figured he would marry her but he told her he couldn't. He was starting his career and he couldn't afford a family. Paul talked Ariel into letting him abort the baby. She gave his last name and where he'd gone to school and the hospital he was at and—"

"But Paul Foster was a *good* doctor. How could he have bungled the abortion?"

"No practical experience then. Didn't know what he was doing but did it anyway." Johnston smiled happily. "From then on it was easy. I wrote right off to the medical association and got his address. Then I sold our home and went to an estate agent. Found two rental houses here—the cottage Linda Beauchamp has and the one next door to here. Took that. God was helping me. So I came to Maddersley to kill Paul Foster."

She rubbed her brow. "And now you'll kill Lucy and me."

"Last chance I'll get. She's leaving tomorrow. And I'll have to kill you too, Abigail. Don't want to but can't help it. With that heart condition you wouldn't last much longer anyway. You won't feel a thing. Be asleep and I'll slide this knife in like I did with Gillian and Arthur and Andrew."

He glanced down at Lucy again and Miss Sanderson said quickly, "Why did you wait so long? You were here over a year."

"Gillian. I wasn't lying when I told you how much I liked her. She was sweet and kind to me and I knew to get at Paul what I would have to do to her and couldn't bring myself to do it. But then something happened—"

"Melanie Marlow."

"You're a bright lady, Abigail. Yes, Melanie. Must admit I didn't take to the girl. She was a saucy little baggage but she was young and her dad would have handled her same as he did her mother. But Gillian hired the girl as a maid and took her into this house and then when she found Paul was interested in Melanie she got rid of her. Didn't bother sending Melanie back to her folks. Oh no, Gillian gave Melanie some money and didn't care where the child went or what happened to her."

"That woman," Miss Sanderson said. "*That terrible, terrible woman.* You weren't talking about Nell Austin."

"I was talking about Gillian Foster." His eyes blazed. "The scales fell from my eyes and I saw Gillian as she really was. Ernie Marlow may have been shouting but it was a cry from a father's heart. And Gillian *laughed* at him and threatened to have her fine doctor husband tell the police Ernie had abused his daughter. After she threw Ernie and the Austins out she came back to the kitchen and bragged to Mrs. Toogood and me."

"So you poisoned the dogs."

"Hated to do that but to get to Gillian I had to get rid of Wolf. He would have torn me to ribbons. Used some rat poison I found in my gardening shed and made up balls of mince and threw them to Wolfe and Dora Campbell's dog and Paddy's terrier."

He ran a lingering finger along the knife blade. Talk, Miss Sanderson thought, keep him talking. "Had you made plans to kill the Foster family on the eve of the birthday party?"

"Knew it had to be soon. They were leaving and it would have been hard to get at them in London. But the afternoon I helped Gillian with the party stuff she said Irene was coming along right after work to help out. Mrs. Toogood and Nurse Ines would be here until Irene arrived. So I figured I wouldn't be able to do it that evening. Then, just as I was getting ready to go home, Irene phoned. Gillian said, 'You have to work late tonight? Oh, that's all right. Matthew's been helping me and all I have to do now is some baking. Oh, you'll bring the cake after nine.' "

He smiled and Miss Sanderson shuddered. Mad, completely mad. Driven mad by grief and revenge and unrelenting pain. He stretched thick arms and the hand holding the knife lingered over the basket. "I did tell you the truth about what I did when I went home. I wrapped Arthur's model kit up real nice and then I went and sat by the window in the sitting room. I saw Nurse Ines come out of here and go into her cottage. Saw Mrs. Toogood on her way home. Knew it was then or never.

"When I knocked at the kitchen door Gillian was sure surprised to see me back. I showed her the present and said I wanted to put it in the laundry room with the rest of the birthday stuff. She was getting vegetables out of the fridge and she said to go right ahead. When I wheeled back into the kitchen she was sitting at the table. I told her she looked awful tired and did she want me to brew tea for her and Paul. Gillian was all for that and told me to give the boys a drink of orange juice."

He looked at Miss Sanderson as though waiting to be complimented. Her head lolled back against the chair and she watched him through slitted eyes. "Won't be long now, Abigail. Soon you'll be asleep and..." He stretched his giant torso. "Haven't felt so peaceful and relaxed for years. My work's just about finished. Feels good to tell someone about it. And there's no danger of you talking. Where was I?"

"Putting the drug in the cups and glasses."

"Took them in to Paul and the boys and then went back to the kitchen and waited. Didn't take long. Gillian's head fell forward and I just folded her forward and—" The knife rose and slashed down in a gleaming arc. "Did the same with the boys. Fast and painless. When I got to Paul's office I kind of went wild. Ripped him right open. Had sense enough to get my chair back fast when the blood started to spout out of him. But I got blood all over my hands and some spatters on my rug. For a time I sat there and watched him. Thought about Ariel and Julia. Then I went into the waiting room and opened the door a crack and smeared his blood all over the woodwork around it so—"

"Why didn't you leave fingerprints?"

"Forgot to mention before I started that I got a pair of Paul's surgical gloves out of the supply cupboard. When I finished I pulled them off inside out and stuck them right in here." He patted the leather satchel dangling from the arm of his chair. "Pretty smart, eh? Knew the police would figure the killer left through that door and no way a cripple in a wheelchair could have gotten down those steps. All I had to do then was fix things up nice and peaceful, pick up my present, and get along home."

"You took time to position the bodies, build up the fire, switch the television program. Why?"

Rage flared redly in the youthful eyes. "Paul and Gillian prided themselves on their grand home. I wanted to remember all of them sitting in it, surrounded by those comforts they could no longer enjoy. I wanted to remember what I'd taken away from my daughter's butcher."

Robby, she thought, hurry! I can't hold him much longer. She mumbled, "How did you conceal the cause of your daughter's death?"

"Easy. I told you Dr. Brown was Ariel's godfather. Julia begged him not to put down the cause of our daughter's death on the certificate. So he didn't. The only ones who knew how Ariel really died were Julia and I and Dr. Brown."

"How could you bear to kill Andrew and Arthur?"

"Didn't bother me a bit. Lied to you about liking those boys. They were mean little demons. When we were alone those boys called me Uncle Gimpy, and Arthur kicked me right here"—he rubbed a twisted leg—"when I wouldn't buy them an ice cream. Killing those dogs bothered me more." He drew his wrist across his eyes. "I'm going to sleep tonight. From now on I'm going to sleep better than I have in years."

"Lucy has never hurt you," Miss Sanderson pleaded. "She's never hurt anyone. Matthew, for the love of God, spare her! Her aunt and uncle will raise her. She won't be like her parents or her brothers."

"Wasting your time, Abigail. Wouldn't make sense to leave her alive. Promised my dead family and God I would take the lives of Paul and *all* his family." He glared down at Lucy's rosy face. The child stirred and flung an arm over her head. "She looks just like Gillian. Got Paul Foster and Gillian in her. Grow up like them, hurting people just for the fun of it." He looked across the basket at Miss Sanderson. Her chin was resting on her chest. "Taking hold now. Soon…"

With a visible effort she lifted her chin. "Can I have a last drink and a cigarette?"

"No drink." He chuckled. "You would have to get up to go for the bottle. Where are your cigarettes?"

"In my handbag. Down here beside my chair."

He placed the knife blade across Lucy's throat. "Hand that bag over careful like."

She lifted the bag and held it out. Taking it with his free hand, he rummaged through the contents. "Matthew, I don't carry a weapon."

"Didn't figure you did. Pays to be careful though. Like a few more years so's I can remember the Fosters. Here, have your cigarette."

With exaggerated care she took back the handbag. Her lighter flickered and the cigarette was lit. Slowly, she put the bag on the floor and reached for a glass ashtray. Setting it on her lap, she slumped back, gray smoke wreathing around her face.

"Instead of smoking that thing you should be making a last prayer, Abigail."

"You've killed four people and are going to kill an innocent baby and you tell *me* to pray."

"I'm a God-fearing man," he told her earnestly. "Already told you God answered my prayers and led me here. Wouldn't hurt for you to ask mercy from Him."

Both his big hands and the knife were resting against the tartan rug on his lap. She ground the cigarette out in the ashtray. "Matthew," she said firmly. "God helps them who help themselves."

With all her strength she threw the heavy ashtray directly into his face. She came out of the chair with a lunge, grabbed the baby, and ran like a deer. She didn't head toward the door. She ran directly to the staircase. She bounded up the steps and stopped breathless on the top step. The baby was shrieking with outrage. Those howls were the sweetest sounds Miss Sanderson had ever heard.

She watched the wheelchair swiftly rumble to the foot of the stairs. Johnston peered up at her. A welt was raising across his brow. He rubbed at it. "You tricked me!"

She clutched the warm little body to her breast. "I tricked you about a number of things. I'm not ill and I'm not Gillian's cousin. I came to this village to find *you*. And the reason you're feeling so peaceful is because I switched the cups when I decoyed you out of the room."

"How—" He smashed his fist against the chair arm. "That phone call!"

"Right. I was given the name of the murderer who at that moment was waiting for me with drugged tea and a knife. As you said, your tea tasted bitter."

"But the Fosters went under so fast."

"You said there wasn't much drug left. You used massive doses on them." She nuzzled her chin against the baby's curls. "And now I know why Lucy wasn't killed that night. You couldn't get at her in the nursery."

"That lying Gillian! Told Mrs. Toogood she was keeping the baby downstairs and then put her to bed early." His sloping shoulders slumped. "All over now. Got to get out of here."

"Matthew, where can you go? The police will soon be here. They won't hurt you. They'll take you to someone who can help you. Wait!"

"You think I'm insane."

"You're sick. You need help. The grief for your wife and daughter...the constant pain..."

His shoulders straightened. "Matthew Johnston will never be put in an insane asylum."

Weak with exhaustion, Miss Sanderson sank down on the step. Lucy had dozed off again and she hugged the child to her. "There's no escape," she whispered.

"God will help me again. He's calling me home. Telling me to come to Julia and Ariel. Maybe...maybe I should have gone long since." His eyes lifted and met hers. "You've won, Abigail, and maybe I'm glad about that too. I would've hated to kill you. You never did me any harm. Pray for me."

He lifted the knife in big capable carpenter's hands and turned the blade so the tip was cutting into his chest. He threw his big torso forward. He flew out of the chair and it clattered back and hit the front door. Johnston sprawled in a tangle of tartan rug. He moaned, twisted his head, and then sighed. Blood trickled across black-and-white tile.

Miss Sanderson didn't move.

Sergeant Brummell and a uniformed constable broke the door down. The panel crashed forward, rammed the wheelchair, and sent it skittering down the hall. Chief Inspector Kepesake knelt beside Matthew Johnston's body.

With one leap Forsythe hurdled the body and ran up the steps. He gathered Miss Sanderson and the baby in his arms. His secretary pushed him away and held out the baby. She looked into his eyes. "Robby," she moaned. "This house *is* cursed. It happened again. From outside, with a knife."

Then she fainted.

Chapter Fifteen

Despite Forsythe's protests Miss Sanderson was at her desk on the following Friday morning. Although she worked with her customary speed and accuracy the other staff members eyed her warily. Young Peters, known to some as Nervous Nellie, approached the other junior.

"Can't say I think it a good idea for the old girl to be back so soon, Vincent. Have you noticed her eyes? They make cold shivers run up and down my spine."

Vincent, slightly older than Peters, gazed at his colleague. Under Peters's left eye a nerve jumped erratically. "If you'd been through what that old girl has," Vincent said drily, "you'd be under sedation."

Shortly after luncheon Mrs. Sutter, a brief grasped in one capable hand, entered the secretary's room. She came out faster than she'd gone in and headed straight for Forsythe's chamber.

"Wonder what's up," Peters muttered and strolled toward the coffee machine positioned to the left of Miss Sanderson's door. After a moment Vincent joined him. The clerk glanced up, rose from his desk, and sauntered over. Forsythe, with Mrs. Sutter at his heels, walked swiftly past the three men. "Back to work," he told them brusquely and shut the door on their curious faces.

Miss Sanderson sat behind her desk. A brief was spread out in front of her but she was staring directly at the barrister. Her eyes were wide and expressionless and didn't appear to see him. Her teeth were digging into her lower lip and blood trickled down her chin. From empty eyes tears traced paths down her cheeks.

"Sandy," Forsythe said tentatively. There was no response and he slapped the desk with an open hand.

"*Sandy.*"

"Go away. I've work to do."

Pulling a handkerchief from his pocket, he pushed it at her. "Wipe your face."

"Why? I'm perfectly all right."

He circled the desk and pulled her up. Turning her around so she faced the oval mirror, he asked harshly, "Does that look perfectly all right?"

Her eyes focused and she gazed at a white, wet, blood-streaked face. "My God!" The tears came faster. "Robby," she wailed, "what's *wrong* with me?"

He put an arm around her shoulders and eased her back in the chair. "You may have a mind like a computer but you're not a machine. You're a sensitive, compassionate woman." He took the handkerchief and dabbed at her face. "Sandy, you've been in shock and you're beginning to come out of it."

"I've felt so...so numb."

He slid open the bottom drawer of her desk and pulled out a bottle and two cups. "Brandy and this time it's medicinal."

"At least you're not pushing good strong tea." She sobbed and hiccupped and swabbed at her face.

"Down the hatch." He waited for her to drain the cup and then refilled it. Taking his own cup, he slumped in the visitor's chair. "About Maddersley—"

"*No.* I don't want to talk about it."

"Not even to hear how little Lucy is?"

"Well..."

"She's with her foster parents. Foster. I made a pun, Sandy. Lucy's very happy and her Uncle Leonard has decided to take a position with an oil firm in London so Lucy and his three children can have a proper home. Leonard and Marjorie Foster know what you did, how you saved the child's life. They're most grateful. They want you to come and see Lucy whenever you wish."

Miss Sanderson managed a weak, tearful smile. She shoved her cup out and he tipped the bottle over it. "Setting a bad example for the staff, Robby. I may get tiddly."

"Blast the staff and I hope you get sloshed. Right now it's the best thing in the world for you." He added carefully, "Want to hear more?"

"About what?"

"The Maddersleys. Mary Maddersley plans to rent the Hall and take her brother to Corfu for a time—"

"I thought he'd come to *kill* Lucy and me."

"No. Sir Donald was genuinely worried about you. His sister is very grateful and says when they return to England you must visit them—"

"I will *never* go near that village again."

"You won't have to. The Maddersleys plan to take a smaller house with extensive grounds so Sir Donald can continue his gardening. More good news, this time about the Rourke family. It's come out that Paddy has secretly been courting a buxom barmaid from Lambert and they'll be married soon. We both have pressing invitations to a genuine Irish wedding."

"Kate will be pleased. She'll have her grandchildren. Any more good news?"

He grinned. "I'm not certain whether this qualifies as good news but Beau Brummell tells me Melanie Marlow will soon be returned to the bosom of her family. As Beau said, it's doubtful whether Ernie will be able to control the girl but at least he'll have a chance. The vicar has received another church, this one in the Midlands. Reverend Clay is planning on taking his ancient housekeeper with him."

"That man *must* be a Christian. Mrs. Gay is stone deaf and seems utterly useless."

"Nonetheless whither the vicar goes there also goes Mrs. Gay." Miss Sanderson's cup was again extended and he refreshed it liberally. He was pleased to see her pale blue eyes were again alert and a tinge of color had crept into her face. "The Toogood twins are on the mend and their mother is going to be housekeeper for Nettie and Oscar Seton. Irene Markham is overjoyed. Seems the genuine Cousin Abigail is settling an annuity on Irene that will enable her to keep the Markham house on." Miss Sanderson shuddered but her companion pretended not to notice. "Miss Sanders has also given Irene the family trinkets and the china that caused all the uproar between their respective mothers. How's that for good news?"

"How Irene can bear to stay on in that house...Robby, the baby must *not* go back to that house."

"Never fear. Leonard Foster tells me little Lucy will never see the village or that house again. If Irene wants to visit her niece she'll have to come to London." Taking a deep breath, Forsythe asked, "Aren't you curious about how we got onto Johnston?"

"I don't want to talk about him."

He shrugged and dug for his pipe and leather pouch. Taking his time, he tamped tobacco, struck three matches unsuccessfully, and waited. He knew his secretary as well as she did him. An appearance of indifference always aroused her considerable curiosity. As usual, it worked. She blew her nose and coughed. "If I'd had time to think about it I suppose I would have decided Dr. Brown talked."

He struck his fourth match, held it well down in the pipe bowl, and was rewarded with a mouthful of smoke. He sputtered and his eyes watered. "Eventually he did. But you were the one who gave me the killer's name."

"Me? How could I have? I didn't know myself."

"That was obvious."

"Well...tell me."

"Three words, Sandy. And you're the one who wrote them." She shook a baffled head and he continued, "Cast your mind back. You're meeting Matthew Johnston for the first time. You're in his kitchen and he's making tea."

Leaning her head back, she closed her eyes. "Yes?"

"He was telling you about his rug and muffler."

"Tartan. Christmas gifts from the Fosters."

"And?"

Her brow wrinkled and then her eyes snapped open. "He didn't use them until after the murders. They were pure wool and he thought them too good to use for everyday."

"Very well. Now, the day you came to London to see me you had lunch in the Fox and Crow. Mrs. Nettie Seton was there too. She came over to your table and—"

"Babbled and babbled. A detestable woman. Has a yard full of plaster gnomes."

He shook his head reproachfully. "Plaster gnomes and all, Mrs. Seton managed to save your life and Lucy Foster's. Now think back. Mrs. Seton was telling you about the night of the murders. Her husband and she went to Johnston's cottage." He paused. Miss Sanderson was helping herself to brandy. "Tell me about it."

She shrugged. "She babbled on to show what a Good Samaritan she'd been. She helped the police doctor give Irene a shot to calm her and then the Setons took Irene and Lucy to their home."

"What did she say about Johnston?"

"That he couldn't help because he was holding the baby." Miss Sanderson's fine brows drew together in thought. "Lucy was crying. Mrs. Seton suggested the baby might be cold and he put a fold of—" She stopped abruptly.

"The exact words were, 'a fold of *that tartan rug*.'" Forsythe waved his pipe. "So who was lying—Nettie Seton or Matthew Johnston? Mrs. Seton had no earthly reason to lie. That left Matthew Johnston, and he must have known the Fosters were dead before Irene Markham ran over to his cottage. Incidently, Sandy, his old rug, covered with spatters of dried blood, and the surgical gloves have been found in the gardening shed behind his cottage. When I caught those words I knew I'd better check over his background again. It all seemed completely aboveboard. A fine, honorable chap with his life marred by tragedy. Johnston had lost both his wife and his daughter. Julia Johnston's death was a matter of record, just as he described it to you."

"So you concentrated on Ariel Johnston."

"The doctor who signed the death certificate was her godfather. What if he'd falsified the document and Ariel Johnston hadn't died from a ruptured appendix? I checked the time sequence. Ariel had died shortly after Paul Foster had come down from Oxford and started to qualify at Guy's. Paul Foster was definitely a womanizer. Ergo, the good Dr. Brown had to be interrogated."

"Did Adam Kepesake go along with you?"

"He certainly agreed. As usual it was Brummell who did the actual work."

"At that point, Robby, did you suspect an abortion?"

"At that point I hadn't a clue. Brummell had his hands full with Dr. Brown. He insisted it was a matter of professional ethics, that his friend Matthew was a fine chap and wouldn't hurt a fly. It wasn't until Brummell showed the doctor the photos of the four bodies that he broke and told the truth. A few moments before I rang up to warn you that night, Beau Brummell and Kepesake came around to my flat. As soon as I spoke to you we headed for Maddersley at top speed." He added ruefully, "Which because of fog conditions was terribly slow. Sandy...I died a thousand deaths."

She bent her head and her voice was muffled. "So did I."

Putting out a hand, he covered her twitching one. "Why, after keeping everyone else at bay, did you let that man into the house?"

"I liked him and I wasn't...I felt no fear of him. There seemed no reason."

"After I gave you his name and you decoyed him to the kitchen, why didn't you grab the baby and make a run for it?"

"I wasn't thinking that clearly. I couldn't believe my ears. All I could think of was to switch the cups just in case. For moments I thought you had made a mistake. Robby, I was a blind fool to trust him!"

"No," he told her gently. "At one time Johnston was a man worthy of trust. But he'd lived too long with loneliness, with hate, with pain for his only company. He had become twisted and obsessed. Remember this, Sandy. If Gillian Foster had been the way she appeared to him all this would never have happened. Johnston would never have harmed any of the Foster family. But Gillian, like so many idols, showed him feet of clay. Johnston went right over the brink."

They sat silently and then Miss Sanderson reached for the bottle. She knocked it over. As she righted it she giggled. "Good thing it's empty. Blimey, I've drained it and I'm feeling a little tiddly." She struggled to her feet. "Think I'd better go home. Aggie will be scandalized to see me in this condition."

He took her arm and steadied her. "She won't. We're leaving—"

"Chambers?"

"London. We're driving down to Sussex to the old family home for a few days. Wander out for long walks in good bracing air, eat Mrs. Meeks' delicious meals, and talk."

"But the work—"

"If young Peters and Vincent can't handle it they can shut up shop." He gave her a gentle push. "Into your washroom and scrub your face and tidy your hair. Then we're away."

She swayed and peered owlishly up at him. "Must remind, Robby, got to buy a doll for little Lucy. For Christmas. Big, with ringlets and a ruffled petticoat. Will you help me?" Miss Sanderson asked.

"A doll like that must have a ruffled bonnet too. I'll help you, Sandy," Robert Forsythe promised.